Jane Hennigan

MOTHS

ANGRY ROBOT

ANGRY ROBOT
An imprint of Watkins Media Ltd

Unit 11, Shepperton House
89 Shepperton Road
London N1 3DF
UK

angryrobotbooks.com
twitter.com/angryrobotbooks
Can Time Heal All Wounds?

An Angry Robot paperback original, 2023

Cover by Kieryn Tyler
Edited by Eleanor Teasdale and Alice Abrams
Set in Meridien

ISBN 978 1 91520 269 7
Ebook ISBN 978 1 91520 270 3

Printed and bound in the United Kingdom by TJ Books Limited

9 8 7 6 5 4 3 2 1

To Mum, who showed me the way.

PROLOGUE

Where were you when it started? The question women of a certain age ask each other on long evenings when the younger women are not around to roll their eyes and look away. Or perhaps, where were you when it ended? Depending on your point of view. And the other question that might follow, the one whispered, heads close together in that soft echo chamber of friendship – what do you miss?

But there are far fewer women of that age left now.

Where were you when the stories started coming out of Venezuela, and then Mexico? When did you first hear the news reports outlining pockets of unexplained deaths, violent attacks, and confused stories of mass psychosis?

The moths, so the story goes, came from deep within the Amazon. Silent, undisturbed, contained for millennia. Whether it was a warmer global climate or whether they were driven out by loggers or forest fires isn't clear. Whatever happened, out they came, away from natural predators, nesting in damp corners and in the tops of trees, crossbreeding with common cousins and laying thousands upon thousands of eggs.

Then, forty-three years ago, as any schoolgirl can tell you, the eggs hatched, and an army of hungry caterpillars spread their tiny toxic threads on every breath of wind.

This was the waking of the new world.

Where were you? They ask, those who are left – at the death, the birth, the beginning, the end.

Mary

Tuesdays and Thursdays, if I'm on duty, I oversee the residents as they wash their own bedding, along with their daywear. Their attire is a plain, grey, ankle-length shift and canvas sandals. Decades ago, there were complaints that the shift was too much like a dress, that it made the men seem effeminate. But trousers have too many seams and creases in which a tiny, poisoned thread could hide, so it was decided that a shift would have to do. Everyone got used to it after a while; the men said that they enjoyed the freedom a skirt provided. Now few men alive might remember a word like *effeminate* – or the word *freedom* for that matter.

At my age, I don't have to work nights. In fact, if I'd wanted to, I could've retired years ago – gone to live in one of the villages beyond the facility. My young colleges all in their twenties and thirties, would prefer it if I did, if I just scuttled off. It would save them the effort of deferring to me, then rolling their eyes when I left the room. But I like the rhythm here. I like the men – especially the new arrivals – they make me think of my son.

What would I do if I retired, anyway? Grow vegetables? Help out in the schools? I've been to the schools as a special visitor. I stared down at the girls, all of them cross-legged on the floor, a garden of bobbing little faces staring up at me. Those are the times when I felt really out of place. I couldn't even answer their questions about the time before. They lacked words like "cinema", "takeaway", or "boyfriend".

I don't have to do the night watch but last week I did it anyway just to prove to myself that I still could. Also, I knew that there was a transfer on the rota: Olivia. She was not as old as me but old enough, I thought, when I caught a glimpse of her at breakfast.

It's long, the night shift – nine hours – and with the men sleeping, there's little to occupy your time. Olivia and I sat in the dimly lit carers' station, just outside the dormitories, and talked about Coventry, her old facility – the food, the men and how the filtration system had failed, infecting three of the dorms.

She was a sturdy woman, not fat exactly, but heavy – curvy, as it used to be known. Her hair was brown and cropped, and she moved slowly, pausing before she spoke. As we talked, she had a habit of nodding, just slightly, along with my words. It was like a tacit agreement, softly nudging along the conversation.

She talked of her wife, Lucie, and of their two daughters, both grown, one working in agriculture and the other in marine conservation. I didn't ask about sons, of course; it would have been inappropriate. She asked me about myself. Safe questions, curious rather than probing. Did I commute from one of the villages? Had I visited the shrine at Waterloo Station? Was I married? All of which I answered in the negative and followed up with a polite question of my own. But I was listening for something in particular: for a signal, an offering that might lead to a more interesting conversation. It came late in the shift, past midnight. I'd nearly given up waiting. And when it arrived, it was a *peach*.

We'd been talking about the dogs in the local woodlands: whether the animals still had a sense of their domestic origins or whether they were fully wild now. Not an incendiary topic but at least we'd graduated from pleasantries. She paused, this time for a beat longer, then said quietly, "In Coventry, there was a ward sister who was keeping a man in her apartment."

I stared at her for a moment, confused, trying to work out what she meant. "Like a servant?" I asked, finally.

She shook her head slowly and her eyes slid to mine, "Like a husband."

I couldn't help myself – my mouth hung open. Hearing the word spoken aloud felt odd, like an attack of déjà vu. *Husband.* Her voice had quietly lingered on the S – a conspiratorial and deliberate inflection.

"How did you…? Did you see him?"

I thought that she wasn't going to answer, that she was going to change the subject – I half wanted her to.

But she carried on. "She kept it a secret, but I delivered food to her living quarters. She always asked for a large serving and kept the door to her suite half-closed when I arrived. But one time I looked through the doorjamb. He was sitting at the table, just sitting there, holding a drink. He was dressed in clothes from before." Her breath came quickly and her eyes shone in the low light of the carers' station.

I felt a fierce sense of outrage towards this unknown ward sister: how dare she be so irresponsible, after all the suffering, the sacrifices? What gave her the right to endanger herself *and* him – what if he'd become infected? The filtration systems are weaker in the staff quarters, the surfaces less often scrubbed. I felt something bitter beneath my anger, fanning it: a man sitting at a table, nursing a glass of wine or whisky, beer perhaps, stretching his long legs, music playing in the background or the sound of the TV, the smell of cooked chicken – just a man, relaxing, glad to be home after a long day.

Husband.

Suddenly, I was aware of Olivia watching me. She'd stopped nodding and was sitting completely still. She was weighing up my reaction.

I chose my words carefully, "But she must have known how dangerous that is."

No reply. She wanted more from me. She'd opened the door, but I had to walk through. I leaned in closer. "What happened when the filtration failed? Was he infected?"

Olivia shifted her heavy frame towards me and her voice was barely above a whisper. "I don't know. But the next time I went there, after it was repaired, she was the only one in the room."

A man living in a sister's quarters. This sort of thing hadn't happened for decades. There was a time, just after everything changed, when we thought it would go back to the way it was. We believed that we just had to wait it out and we could carry on, drag everything we knew with us. But then more waves of moths came, more heartbreak, more violence. Eventually, we had to come to terms with what we had and what we would never again have.

And now this. Were there secret affairs happening everywhere or had this been a one-off? What could they even find to talk about together? It's not like before. They don't go out to work or read books and there's no TV, no internet. The men just pass their time doing chores and crafts or gossiping in the rec-room. Every now and then there's a campaign to improve the men's education, laminated reading materials, more advanced teaching for those who show aptitude. But the MWA comes back with the same arguments, again and again, lack of resources, higher priorities.

Olivia leaned back, her round cheeks flushed. It was on the tip of my tongue: *Did you report her?* But of course she hadn't. This was her offering – the trust she sought to barter.

I nodded and offered a tentative smile. She smiled back.

After that, those quiet hours wrapped us up together. We were protected, complicit. Our soft voices spread out into the night.

"Where were you when it started?" she asked. "Tell me everything."

CHAPTER 1
Mary – then

Memory is guesswork, guided by desire. It happens in general terms with only the briefest flashes of clarity. But there are some things, some images, that I can remember in complete detail. It is around these pockets of clarity that I have arranged everything else, what happened next, who said what and when.

The dead crow is one of these images.

I remember walking the dog before work in the copse of trees that backed onto our house. I was rehearsing a difficult conversation in my head with my husband, Adrian. I was trying to explain how a person can usually be so careful but it's possible, let's say, if you've been out to your favourite restaurant, and you've both had a lot of wine, and it's your thirty-third birthday, and you've had a great night, and you fall asleep exhausted and sated, that it's possible you might forget to take a pill.

Birth control – another thing that the women of today wouldn't understand.

It was light even under the canopy of oaks and beeches – a thing I loved about the summer months. I walked that route every morning – my place for unknotting. I was so caught up in dates and weeks and monthly calculations that the subtle difference didn't register right away. It wasn't until our old spaniel, Doc, pressed himself into my legs and whined that I paused a moment. It was too quiet. Not completely silent, the breeze still brushed the leaves, trees creaked, but there was no birdsong.

Doc growled and strained on his lead towards home. "C'mon boy, just a little farther." I tugged him onwards.

The copse widened out into a large clearing, about the size of a football pitch, with trees and brambles around the edge. We'd had a few weeks of hot weather and the grass was coarse and patchy yellow. Doc would usually bolt forwards in the fervent hope of flushing out a rabbit but today he stood by me, mute.

There was something black lying amidst the grass a few metres away from us. I approached the small lump, but Doc remained behind. I nudged it with the tip of my boot: a dead crow. I squatted down to take a closer look. Its beak and wings were closed, which made it look solemn, dignified somehow. I leaned in closer and I could see a fat drop of blood resting just below its eye – like a teardrop. That crow is the first really clear image I have of those days. Doc's whining, the noise of the trees, it's all approximation, but the image of that dead crow is as vivid in my mind now as it was when I was staring right at it forty-four years ago.

"It's all of them," a man's voice came from my left. Surprised, I stood and stepped back, clenching my fist to my chest.

"Sorry," he said, frowning. "I didn't mean to creep up on you."

I recognised him. A widower with a chocolate Labrador. She was sniffing another small black body a few metres away.

I scanned the field and realised that it was littered with neat little corpses. Most were black but some were black and white – magpies, I guessed – and a few grey pigeons. There were no smaller birds. "How many are there?" I asked.

He shrugged. "I've walked around the whole field and it looks like there're hundreds of 'em," he said, rubbing his bristly chin and scanning the field.

"What could do this?" I looked up at some electricity pylons overhead. But *really* – this many? Doc was whining again now, soft and high. I wanted to get away from this field too. I felt an itch on the back of my neck – some buried instinct twitching my nerves.

The man whistled softly and his dog came to him. He clicked the lead onto her collar. "Could be some new pesticide or another bout of bird flu."

"Should we keep the dogs away?"

Just then a large, solitary moth fluttered down and landed on the dead crow. Its body was dark brown, fat, hairy and four or so centimetres long. Each wing was brown, oily looking and about the size of a playing card. The way the light caught the moth's wings made it hard to see, even against the black of the crow. It called to mind the negatives of old-fashioned photographs – a kind of inverse iridescence. As I watched, it dipped its proboscis into the corner of the crow's eye and remained still.

"I think I'll walk her over to the park next time," the man said, backing up a few steps from the feeding moth. "Just to be on the safe side."

Then he sneezed hard, twice.

"Bless you," I said absentmindedly, still staring at the crow.

Did I think back to those sneezes later on that day when I was watching the reports on TV? Did I think about him the next day when the BBC website uploaded that map of Europe, the one dotted with expanding red circles over Hamburg, Berlin and Paris? When they closed the borders, thinking it was spread person-to-person? By then we were all under house arrest anyway, hunkered down, preparing to wait it out. If I'd thought about him at any of those points, I might have realised that it had already been there, back then– on that summer wind, in the water, on the ground. Amongst Doc's fur.

"Hope *I* haven't got bird flu," he'd said.

It looked as if the moth was threading its long proboscis deeper and deeper into the eye of the crow, and was still feeding. I tore my gaze away and looked up as the man blew his nose on a big red hanky, then stuffed it into his anorak pocket. He smiled at me.

I smiled back. "I think as long as you don't actually *eat* the crow, you'll be fine."

"I'll bear that in mind," he said. Then he led his dog away, back into the woods.

I bent over the dead crow for a moment. The moth, seemingly having finished its grim meal, was now cleaning itself, repeatedly rubbing its long forelegs along its straight antenna. The movement was deliberate, almost languorous.

I straightened and attached Doc's lead, although he hadn't left my side the entire time we'd been there, and gave him a reassuring pat on his soft flank.

"Good boy," I said.

Then I led him home – home to my husband, home to my son.

On the news later that morning, they were saying that the French authorities were stopping people from crossing the border from Luxembourg. I was half watching a panel of experts talking about plausible explanations for the "virus". An specialist in infectious diseases was describing how a virus could affect the central nervous system; how it could trigger a psychotic state. The doctor gave rabies as an example. There were various terms by which the phenomena was being identified – H7N1 lepidopterous andro-psychosis etc. – but the one that the media stuck with was SANS: Severe Acute Neurological Syndrome. Did I think about the dog walker sneezing then? His joke about bird flu?

Ryan was up, but not yet down for breakfast. I could hear him padding around. We needed to leave in twenty minutes. It had been a long term, full of mock exams, and he was feeling it.

"Ry! Come and have breakfast," I called up the stairs.

"Mary, where's my phone!" Adrian was late for work.

"Have you looked in the bathroom?"

"It's not there... of all mornings to be late!"

"Try by the door. Here. It was by the door." I handed it to him.

"Thanks. Love you." He leaned down to kiss me. He smelled good – of toothpaste and sandalwood soap. His cheek was soft and slightly damp from shaving.

"Love you too." I said it automatically; however, if I'd considered it, my words would still have been true. We'd been married thirteen years and we were happy – most of the time.

He had to give a software presentation that afternoon and he'd been awake into the small hours tweaking it and fretting. When he'd come to bed, he'd kissed the back of my neck and run his fingers up and down my spine. It was a warm night, so the sex had been close, viscid. I'd stretched out in the plane between dreams and sex, binding the familiar and the strange.

As I stood by the door, I'd wanted to snake my arms around his neck and recapture some of the feeling of the previous night but he was rushed and flustered, so I let him be. *I'll text him later*, I thought. *I'll make a nice meal later. I can tell him then.*

Ryan appeared at the foot of the stairs, his school tie squint and his shirtsleeves rolled up past his elbows.

He didn't speak, just poured himself a heap of cereal and sat at the breakfast bar. He'd inherited Adrian's curly brown hair rather than being blonde like me. Ryan liked to wear his fringe longer than his father's. He was always scooping his fringe to the right so he could see. He had my mother's hazel green eyes and the most ridiculously long eyelashes.

As he bent over his bowl, his fringe flopped forward, hiding him from my view. He was scrolling on his phone as he ate.

"What do you have first thing?"

Shrug.

"Have you got your PE kit?"

One nod.

I turned away.

"Some of my friends aren't going in today, 'cos of SANS."

"That's silly," I replied, packing a sandwich into Ryan's lunch bag and then throwing a banana in on top. "It's happening hundreds of miles away, in a different country. No one even knows if it's an actual disease."

"Fine. I'm just telling you. Christ."

I stuffed the lunch bag into Ryan's bag and handed it to him. He snatched it. "Look mum, it's all over the internet." He waved his phone at me. "They say it's pretty bad. And they say it's only happening to men."

Would it have made a difference if I'd kept him home? Probably not. But I might have listened to him, instead of thinking about the lesson on modal verbs I had planned for period one. "Ryan, they're not even sure if it is something contagious or just a rise in crime rates."

"I don't see why I have to go in if Josh isn't going in."

"Perhaps Josh's mother doesn't work," I said with a little more bitterness than I'd intended.

"His big sister's at home. I could go round to his, maybe? She wouldn't mind." He said this a little too keenly.

"No. This is just some media circus and it will have died down by lunchtime. Until the government says otherwise, you're going to school."

He scowled and carried on eating his cereal.

The TV was showing a young man being taken away by three policemen somewhere in Germany. He was struggling and it was taking all three officers to control him. The news ticker ran on a loop: *Fifth man arrested in connection with Marriott massacre. Eighty-seven confirmed dead. Suspects may have been under the influence of unknown pathogen. Early Reports coming in from Manhattan, US: Mass shooting…*

Did I waver then – consider staying home with Ryan? If I did, it was only for a second. The kids of teachers everywhere know that you have to be at death's door for your parent to stay home. I switched off the TV. "Come on, then."

Ryan was just finishing drinking down the milk in the bowl. He wiped his mouth on the back of his hand.

"Where's your blazer?"

He rolled his eyes. "We don't have to wear it when it's this hot."

There was still a smear of milk on his top lip. I wanted to wipe it off with my thumb. Instead, I pointed to it. "You've got a bit of milk, just there."

Ryan wiped his face and tutted. He put on his headphones as soon as we were in the car and he didn't even look back when I dropped him off. Not a word. *It's not personal*, I thought to myself. But it still hurt.

I arrived at work fifteen minutes early. Claire was already sat at her desk. In one perfectly manicured hand she clutched a mug of earthy smelling black tea and in the other she was holding a small mirror, checking her make-up. She'd made me a coffee – it was sitting on my desk, catching the light in its steam.

"I think I love you," I said as I sat down and gripped the mug.

"You're welcome," she replied. "Although, you know you're not my type – I prefer brunettes."

I did know. We'd discussed it at length over many glasses of expensive champagne. She would only drink the best, on those Friday nights after work. Just like I knew that Claire didn't talk to her dad; that she'd lost her mum to cancer when she was eleven; that she'd attended Harrow and hated every moment; and that she used to be called Mark.

"No sign of Karen or Dan yet?"

Claire put down the mirror and blew on her tea. "Half the staff and most of the kids aren't in. I'm surprised you are." She looked to the door and then, in a quiet voice asked, "Have you told him yet?"

I shook my head. "I'll do it tonight, when we've got some time to talk it through."

She picked up her phone and began scrolling. "He'll be fine. I know that people say they don't want more kids, but when it happens, they come around."

"I hope you're right."

We were quiet for a minute, then Claire asked, "What do you make of these attacks?" She flipped the screen of her phone so I could see the headline. *SANS – Fears Grow Over Mystery Man-Flu!*

I shrugged. "The one in Germany? It's horrible – they say they could have been on magic mushrooms. Or that they had some kind of rabies. But I wouldn't worry. The other reports are probably just fake news on social media."

"There's been loads more reports in the last hour or so. An armed group has stormed the United Nations. They're not sure whether they took guns in there... some reports say that it was the UN guards that were shooting the delegates. They're saying France is issuing a state of emergency and closing the airports. They think whatever it is... is contagious."

It wasn't the first time that a disease had run rampant. There'd been Covid, of course, and its various variants. We'd done it all before. But Covid had killed one in a hundred and it took its time, relatively speaking. Also, what we didn't know at the time was that SANS wasn't spread from person to person – it was airborne. That made all the difference.

I flicked on my laptop and opened up the BBC news website. I was greeted with a large, red *Breaking News* icon. *Prime Minister to address the nation at 9.30am regarding SANS.*

"Is it still just men affected?" I asked.

This time when Claire looked up, her face was pale and drawn, which scared me far more than the news reports. "So far, they say that those infected have all been men and that they don't seem to respond to reason when they are in that... whatever it's called... that state. They showed one guy from the hotel massacre, sobbing uncontrollably. Apparently, his wife and two daughters had been in the hotel when it had been set alight. All three tied to a bedframe in one of the rooms. One of the German police officers said that the CCTV footage was the worst thing he'd ever seen." Her attention returned to her phone, and she kept scrolling with her thumb. "Twitter, KanWo, Mayday, they're all going nuts – conspiracy theories saying Russia is behind it all, people are claiming that water supplies have been poisoned. One female medic in Afghanistan posted a video on YouTube. She walks from bunk to bunk and the Marines, they're all just lying there in their beds, stone-cold dead, their faces a weird blue colour. She just keeps saying 'Oh God, oh God', over and over again."

I frowned. "Is that even related? So, did they go crazy first – or did they just die in their beds, the Marines?"

Claire shrugged, "It doesn't say."

I suddenly had a desperate urge to go back and get Ryan from school – to ring Adrian and talk to him about what to do. I looked at my phone on the desk.

"You should go," said Claire. "Get Ryan and take him home. This is not going to go away. The country will be on lockdown before the end of the day – trust me." Her face was as serious as I'd ever seen it.

"I might just text Ryan," I said as I picked up my phone. "To be on the safe side." Ryan had already texted me – s*chool's closing! need pickup!* But there was a second text, this time from Adrian – *Cancelled meeting. I'm on my way to pick up Ry. See you at home X*

On the BBC website was a map with pulsing red dots in areas that had reported an upsurge in unexplained deaths and violent incidents. The more reports, the bigger the dots. Germany, Canada, USA, Brazil, China – every single one was covered in a red rash of expanding dots and as I refreshed the page, more appeared. A number of the large, red circles covering South America and mainland Europe were beginning to merge. Only Poland, Australia and most of Greenland were clear. The dots had reached Calais but the UK was unmarked – for now. There was a caveat at the bottom of the map – the figures had been adjusted to exclude average levels of criminal activity, which I guess meant that the usual everyday stabbings, beatings, and rapes were still going on. As I refreshed the page again, a solitary red dot appeared above Cardiff. I sat staring at it, fixed to my seat. "Claire."

"I've seen them," she replied, "one in Cardiff and one in Grimsby."

She was right. I refreshed and there they were now – two tiny dots, not yet pulsing outwards, but appalling nonetheless.

About a year ago, I'd found a lump in my breast: a firm little stranger under my skin. It turned out to be nothing – just a harmless fibroadenoma – but the thudding fear that gripped me as I stood at a weird angle to the mirror, worrying that pea with my finger, was like what I was feeling at that moment while staring at those two... no, three, dots. One had appeared on the north coast of Cornwall.

I jumped as the bell sounded for the first class. I looked at Claire. "They can't be expecting lessons to go on as usual?"

Mike, a biology teacher, leaned in the doorway to the office. "Where are Karen and Dan?"

I shook my head in reply.

Mike ran a hand over his jaw. "The college is closing. Apparently, the government is shutting down all the schools as a precaution. The Principal is gathering the students in the main auditorium," he said.

Claire stood up. "Go get Ryan," she said. "I'll stay with the kids."

"Adrian's picking him up," I said. "I'll stay for a bit. They won't be back home yet. Anyway, I want to listen to what the Prime Minister has to say."

I closed my laptop. Just as I did, I noticed the UK had gained a few more dots, Blackpool, Manchester... Central London.

CHAPTER 2
Mary – present

I looked up to find Olivia staring at me. When I failed to continue, she nodded and gave my hand a quick pat. "It's getting light," she said. "The others will be about soon."

She was right – a pearlescence clung to the edges of the skylights, casting shapes onto the walls of the corridor. There were quiet mumbles from the dormitories.

A team of cleaners were inching their way down the corridor, wiping every bit of the ceiling, floor, walls and doors at a well-practised pace. As they passed by, they didn't stop, didn't break their concentration. Other cleaning teams would be doing the same in every part of the compound every morning and every evening. I'd been on a cleaning crew many years ago. It's backbreaking work, but necessary for the continuing safety of the men.

Daisy, one of the ward sisters, appeared for a morning walk-round. Of the four sisters at this facility, she was my least favourite.

"Morning girls," she said brightly, although *girls* was a bit of a stretch, especially as she was half my age.

"Morning," replied Olivia.

"Was it a busy night for our newest recruit?" asked Daisy, smiling. There was something unappealing about her smile – it was just a bit too stiff, too moist.

Olivia answered, "Not really. I heard someone crying out in block C but when I checked it out, everyone was asleep. Probably just a bad dream."

Daisy leaned in and rolled her eyes in a conspiratorial manner. "A few weeks ago, there was such a rumpus in C. One of the residents had been excluded by the others from the dorm drama project. The resident in question tried to hang himself from a light fitting with a rope made of torn-up strips of bedsheet. Melody was the ward sister on duty and she managed to get him to the infirmary. But what a commotion! I mean, what would these men do if they had real problems to worry about, hey?"

I knew about the incident. Tony, a flamboyant character in his mid-twenties who'd been through a lot over the past couple of years, had really wanted to play Romeo. He'd spent weeks rehearsing the lines, trying out different intonations, and practicing different actions and expressions in front of the dorm mirror. I entered the dorm one evening to find out why he hadn't appeared at supper to find him holding up a home-made paper flower to the window as if gazing up to an imaginary balcony.

See how he leans his cheek upon his hand!

O, that I were a glove upon that hand,

That I might touch that cheek!

He put a hand on his cheek and then flung himself heavily to the floor.

"What do you think, Mary?" he asked as he gathered himself up.

"A resounding performance Tony," I replied, "but you've nearly missed supper."

"Romeo needs no food – he lives on love!" replied Tony, although he'd said it whilst hurrying in the direction of the canteen.

For two whole weeks he didn't break from character, asking people to pass the salt in a mock Tudor accent or shouting out as he entered a room – *IS THE DAY SO YOUNG?*

On the day of the auditions, he'd even tucked his shift in a way that made it look like pantaloons, which was completely against the rules, of course, and he was ordered to standardise his attire before he could start, but you couldn't deny the passion he had for the role. Despite his best endeavours, the others decided that Luca would be best for the part. Tony had been completely crushed. Later, after his suicide attempt, I'd sat with him for a few hours in the infirmary. Usually gregarious, he'd hardly spoken. However, when I'd asked if he'd wanted me to go away, he'd murmured that he didn't mind having the company, so I'd hung on for a while and read to him from a rare, laminated copy of *The Owl and the Pussycat*.

"Was he okay?" asked Olivia, "The resident who tried to kill himself?"

"Yes, yes," replied Daisy. "Melody was thinking on her feet. She's a good woman and saved his life, no question. I just wish the men would think a bit more about the consequences of their actions before they pulled something like that. I mean, there was paperwork and psych assessments to arrange, along with counselling sessions. And the thing is, I don't think he wanted to die at all, I think he was just sore about the part going to someone a bit, you know, more handsome than him." She rested her elbows on the carers' station. "I'm quite looking forward to seeing the project." As she leaned in closer, I caught a whiff of her breath – heavily minty – and I suspected that her pale blonde fringe, which was jiggling as she spoke, was slightly longer than the mandated three-centimetre limit. "That boy, Luca, is the lead and he's a very good-looking resident – very watchable. I'm hoping for a visitation with him at some point, if he's amenable to the idea, of course." She laughed several nasally snorts.

Neither Olivia nor I answered. The silence lengthened as I kept my eyes fixed on the floor.

Daisy suddenly straightened herself up and took a step back. "Well, anyway, don't expect every night shift to be that easy, Olivia," she said tightly. "Both of you, make sure you write up the crying incident in C before going to breakfast. And wash down the carers' station; it'll be the eclipse soon." With those words echoing round the pale walls, she marched off down the corridor.

Olivia turned to me and raised her eyebrows. "Wow."

I wearily shook my head, "I know."

"I enjoyed last night," she said, tearing the wrapper from a pre-packaged cleaning wipe.

And so had I. It had been years since I'd felt the intimacy of being understood. I usually guarded my words, my past, not because I was forbidden to talk about it, but because my old life was considered inappropriate. Women like Daisy paid homage on remembrance days, acted with respectful tolerance, but quietly and in derisive tones I was referred to as a *dolly* – a woman from before.

But this morning I felt affirmed and fortified. Despite the fact that I'd been awake for twenty hours, despite the usual niggling aches that came with my age, I felt clean and after-the-rain fresh. "Are you on nights all week?" I asked, trying to keep my voice from rising in pitch.

"Yes," she answered without turning my way. "You?"

"Yeah, I mean I think so." I wasn't. But perhaps I could get someone to swap with me.

"Great, see you later." She cast her used wipes into bio-bags and placed them in the sealed containers.

I did the same and then set the containers for collection. "Cool," I said as she moved off to the carers' shower block. *Cool*, I thought to myself, who do I think I am, Bart Simpson? "See you tonight," I shouted, trying to make my voice sound normal, but she'd already gone.

The men were filing out of their dorms, pushing and jostling each other as usual. Their long-sleeved shifts go right to the floor and the fabric is light grey – grey helps any tiny black threads show up better. The soft cotton slippers on their feet and their shaved heads gave them a kind of monkish look. They don't act like monks, however, they clown and jostle and play-fight with each other like bear cubs.

"Calm down, calm down," I said, loudly and firmly, but their hustle towards the showers was good-natured enough. One of the men sauntered up to the carers' station just as I was about to go and shower before breakfast.

"Good morning, Mary," he said, flashing me a movie-star smile.

"Good morning, Luca." Luca had joined us from a preparatory house about two years ago. Men usually come to us at eighteen, but Luca had been invited to stay on at the prep for an extra two years to help raise and guide the younger boys. I can imagine he was a very good mentor. He was friendly and popular with the other residents. He had a strong singing voice and last midwinter he'd taken the lead in the lamentations. At twenty-two, he seemed like a child to me, but he was already a keen participant in the visitation programme. Very popular too, so I'd gathered.

"I was just wondering if you heard how Tony was?"

I stopped cleaning and returned his smile. "I think he's okay. I spoke to him yesterday and he was feeling a little better."

His soft brown eyes regarded me with seriousness, despite his ready smile. "I had a chat with the rest of the drama guys. We all decided that it would be better to make me Julian Capulet instead, so… perhaps he could be Romeo, you know, after all? If he still wants to, that is."

A tiny flame kindled in my chest at the prospect of how Tony would react to such news. "I think that would be great," I replied. "Perhaps you can go and get permission from one of the ward sisters before breakfast? Then tell him yourself after lunch."

"I'll ask. Thanks." He turned to go.

"Oh, and Luca? That's a really nice thing to do."

Luca shrugged and grinned again, showing off an impressive set of dimples. "No problem," he said and sauntered off towards the showers.

* * *

Breakfast was the usual: porridge, eggs, salad, and toast. No meat, of course. The three carers sitting with me were discussing a new tech project run by the Engineering Authority. Apparently, we would soon be able to use computers to access the information databases of all the facilities across the country instead of faxing through data when a resident was being transferred or downloading his history to a USB. Now we'd be able to send it, via a network of servers, wherever and whenever we wanted.

"It will be amazing, Mary," said one of the carers to me, her eyes bright with enthusiasm. "It will help organise supply lines. Share research. There are so many applications."

I nodded and carried on eating my eggs. I missed aspects of the internet, of course. I missed being able to look up things by tapping a few keys, rather than plodding down to the town library. I missed streaming films and knowing what was going on in the world. But did I miss the feeling of being always contactable, of being monitored? Did I miss the trolls, or the fake news, or the weird porn in which people choked and spat at each other?

What was more important to me was that we now had reliable electricity. For the first few months, after everything changed, it was touch and go as to whether any of us would make it. We couldn't bury the dead fast enough. We had no clean running water nor heating in the compound, and it was a brutally cold winter that first year. Sometimes women just gave up rather than face those bitter days of labour and loss. We tried to protect each other, to look out for each other, but no one argued with you if you really wanted out. We hoped that the intense cold might at least kill off the moths. But they'd laid their eggs deep underground, in sewers and caves, tube tunnels and basements, and they returned the next year and every year after that. The Eclipse, as it became known. That time in July when the moths burst from their chrysalides to breed and feed and lay their eggs for the following year. The air would become thick with them and everyone would have to stay indoors.

I spent some time in those early years finding generators and learning how to fix them up. I enjoyed it, that first thumping pull of the engine, the grinding hum, the heady smell of diesel that stays in your hair despite scrubbing yourself in a tepid shower. None of these girls were around then. They were born into a world of wind farms and plant-based protein, in which a female engineer is not considered an oddity. I finished up my eggs and looked down at my plate. What do I miss? If I was really honest, I missed bacon.

The girls went on to gossip about the residents. This time of year was often tricky. The men were nervous about the coming season of confinement and the prospect of spending most of July cooped up in the private rooms with no access to the courtyard nor even to the canteen. It was done for their own safety. The Eclipse, the time when the moths bred and filled the skies, marked a much higher risk of infection. Understandably the men were jumpy and a little more emotional than usual. There were more fights, more arguments, more affairs, jealousies, tantrums and accusations, of course. Who was stronger? Better looking? Funnier? The old economies of love lived on, not for all the residents, but for most.

"Did you hear that Luca is playing Romeo in the talent show?" asked Matilda, another one of the carers.

A spiky-haired girl replied, "I know! I was going to give it a miss, but I might go now."

"Is he the really cute one from dorm C?" asked another. "Oh, I would love to see him play Romeo."

I interrupted, feeling slightly smug, "Sorry to disappoint you all, but Luca's giving his part over to Tony. The men decided yesterday that it was the right thing to do."

There was an awkward silence and some pained looks passed around the table. "No, sorry, Mary, that isn't the case," replied Matilda, obviously anxious to be contradicting her elder.

"But," I said, my smugness giving way to confusion, "that's what Luca said was going to happen. They voted on it."

Matilda blushed. "I was with ward sister Daisy when Luca asked about half an hour ago, and she flatly refused. She told him that he shouldn't be blackmailed into giving up his part and that he should be proud that the others had voted for him in the first place and that everyone was looking forward to his performance."

I felt a thick disappointment settle in my gut. I clenched my hands beneath the table and tried to make my voice light. "Oh, my mistake, Matilda. I didn't know."

"That's okay. We all make mistakes," said Matilda and she smiled indulgently – the sort of smile reserved for children.

The girls started talking about preparations for the upcoming confinement. I slouched in my seat, arms crossed, hardly listening.

Daisy was in the ward sisters' office, alone, when I caught up with her after breakfast. It was in the same block as the Warden's suite and the sisters' living quarters, so the anti-thread regime was a little bit laxer. She waved me in. "Shut the door, Mary," she said, giving me her tight, plastic smile. "Are you okay?"

I had to play this right – my age only carried so much weight.

I grimaced as if in pain. "Is it all right if I sit down for a moment, Daisy? My old legs are giving me some trouble today."

"Of course!" She jumped to her feet and started clearing stacks of paperwork from one of the chairs. The office was awash with notepads, three-ring binders, and piles of correspondence. There were four desks, one for each ward sister, placed island-style in the centre of the room with various cabinets and shelving units scattered along the edges, each one stuffed to bursting with documents and files. At the far end stood a large, reclaimed fax machine, which looked as if it had been patched with bits of an old microwave. Next to the fax stood a door leading to the Warden's office.

I had to pick my way over piles of printouts to the chair Daisy was offering.

"It's ward sister Danika's chair. I'm sure she won't mind." And then when I'd settled, she added, "I don't know how you do it, Mary, at your age. It must take its toll. Still, the month of confinement is nearly upon us, so a few weeks of rest for us all, eh?"

"Yes, indeed," I replied, choosing not to point out how far from excited the residents felt about July.

"So, what can I do for you, Mary?" She rubbed her hands together and gave a small anticipatory clap.

"I'm sorry to bother you," I began, "but I hear that you persuaded Luca not to offer his role as Romeo to Tony."

"That's right. I thought it would be a pity if Luca missed out due to some misplaced loyalty to one of his co-residents. Don't you agree, Mary?"

I proceeded cautiously. "I can see the sense in that, of course, and I know that you have a lot of experience with these situations. I just wondered if perhaps it might be good for Tony to take the part. I don't know if you are aware, but a couple of years ago his friend and partner was infected and had to be moved to a sanatorium, which was, of course, a painful time. I thought that perhaps this play might really help Tony's mental health."

"Hmmm. It was before my time here, but I heard something about it." She frowned, suggesting she was trying to remember. "Logan, was it?"

"Yes," I replied, "that's right." I was annoyed by her pretence. Of course she knew of Logan – the man who'd started a riot. The year before last, he'd petitioned the Warden for more autonomy, self-governance and a comprehensive education programme. When he'd been refused due to lack of funding, he'd organised a protest in the courtyard.

The protest had started out peacefully. The men had painted slogans on their bedding and then held them up as they gathered in the quad.

Voices and choices! Less Rules, More Tools! – that sort of thing.

Logan had spoken with measured passion on the rights that men could – *should* – expect and the importance of solidarity. His voice carried weight, a deep baritone that demanded your attention.

"But what can we do?" asked one young resident when Logan had finished speaking.

"We can argue! We can strike! We can withhold visitation rights," he replied and was met with murmured consideration.

We carers stood back in the hope that they'd get bored and return to their dorms. The ward sisters stood by too, a little more nervously than us, hands resting on the batons at their sides. A few of them traded concerned glances at Logan's suggestions.

However, after about half an hour, the energy bled from the room and the men began fidgeting. Tony pointed out that it was nearly dinnertime and perhaps they could continue this tomorrow. Everyone began inching towards the canteen, the heavy aroma of mushroom pie calling them like a siren's song. But then one man, an older resident named Owen, turned to the crowd and said in a booming tone, "My friends, the government has been lying to us. I know for a fact that the toxins are a myth, a lie to keep us inside, to keep us quiet." There was a shocked silence in the quad. He went on to describe in increasingly passionate and detailed terms how there were men living outside in communes all around the world.

The idea gained traction and the men began to chatter angrily. It was not the first time this particular conspiracy theory had surfaced, but it was the first time it'd been spoken about openly and in front of all the men.

Logan turned to the agitated crowd and waved his hands to get their attention. "It's not true," he said. "I've seen men get infected. Don't lose focus. They're not lying to us but they are denying us. They deny us our rights. They deny us useful occupations. They..." But he'd lost the crowd and some of the men were turning to face the ward sisters, mutiny on their faces.

The ward sisters' nervousness tipped over into panic and the men, seeing the sisters unsheathing their batons, erupted into a full-scale riot. I was pushed and shoved in the ensuing chaos; not hurt but shaken. A group of four men, Owen amongst them, overpowered a couple of carers and a ward sister and forced their way outside. Logan followed them out, trying to reason with them, begging for them to come inside before it was too late.

It was only April, and they were not out for more than ten minutes before they were persuaded to return, but within a few hours, four of the five showed symptoms of infection. I was informed by the Warden at the time that Logan became manic six hours after his exposure. He and two others who survived the infection were sedated and sent to a specialist monitoring and treatment facility. I assume that from there they were passed to a sanatorium – a home for the infected.

Tony and Logan had been together for many years and Tony was distraught. He'd requested an isolation room and spent months alone in bed, not wanting to speak to anyone. I'd sat with him when I had a chance and read to him, insisting he not stay alone for so long. He gradually came around. It wasn't until a few months ago, when I'd mooted the idea of a production of Romeo and Julian, that he started to seem like his old self – only to become broken-hearted once more when the part of Romeo went to Luca.

Daisy nodded slowly and leaned back in her chair. "Yes, I heard about the trouble. Nasty business." There was a pause and then a sigh. "Mary, I really value the way that you care so deeply for the residents – I do. But we can't have the residents feigning suicide to get what they want, can we? We can't have them throwing themselves around and demanding things. Where would it end?" She gave me a wide-eyed look and an open-handed shrug. I wanted to grab her and shake her and shout: *He was trying to die! He did it during morning showers, so no one would be there.* But what would be the point? Whatever I threw at this woman would come bouncing back to me. *Return to sender.* I stood to leave.

"Mary, Mary, sit, please." She licked her lips again in that feral way. "I can see this means a lot to you. I do think that sometimes you become too close to these residents – all that sneaking off to sit with Tony – you push the guidelines of professionalism a little too much. But I understand. We all need to do what we believe is the right thing." Her manner had changed. She seemed to have arranged her face into a facsimile of concern. "Perhaps, you're right in this circumstance. I feel that I may have been too hasty in telling Luca to hold off."

I couldn't quite believe what I was hearing. In the months I'd worked with Daisy, I'd never heard her come close to admitting she was wrong. "Well, there are arguments on both sides," I mumbled, "but I think the pros outweigh the cons this time."

"Yes, pragmatism is what's in order for situations like these. I think that, on this occasion, Luca could give up his part, although it will be a pity. He seemed to me to be a perfect fit."

Maybe I'd misjudged her. Whatever the reason for her change of heart, I wasn't about to question providence. "I appreciate this Daisy, I really do," I said, rising to leave. "I'll let Luca know, and then–"

"No, don't hurry off. Sit, Mary, sit, sit." She was still smiling and flapping her hands. I sunk back into my seat and waited.

"I've been here for nearly a year and we've hardly had time to have a proper conversation."

"Don't worry. You've been busy, no doubt." I was perching on the very edge of the seat and I realized that this was because I was desperate to make a run for it. *Here we go*, I thought, *retirement plans, time for myself, relax, stand down.*

"Tell me, Mary, what do you think of our new recruit?"

"Olivia?" The question took me by surprise.

"Mmm. I can't quite get a read on her."

This was not the line of questioning I was prepared for, and my instinct was telling me to tread carefully. "In what way?" I kept my voice breezy.

"You worked the night shift with her, didn't you? Did she seem friendly? Did she have any... uncommon opinions? Honestly, Mary, you'd be doing the MWA a service if you were able to offer any information." The MWA stood for The Men's Welfare Authority – although in this case *welfare* was a little vague.

"What kind of opinions? I mean, on what topic?" My mind flitted back to the evening: *like a husband*. Did Daisy know about the ward sister in Coventry? The one keeping a man in her quarters? Olivia could be in trouble with the MWA for keeping it to herself and me too by association. On the other hand, if Daisy knew, why hadn't she just confronted Olivia? Why bring me into it at all?

I looked at the ward sister blankly and her smile disappeared. "Oh, well," she replied with a new coolness in her voice, "I didn't mean that there would be anything in particular, Mary. I just wanted to reiterate the dangers of people bringing in insurgent ideas." She regarded me for a moment, and then her face slipped into an expression of distaste. "For example, some people think that your visits to, to..." her small pink lips puckered up as she said the name, "*Elmwood*, are inappropriate and give the wrong impression to the younger carers."

My skin flushed, a rash of warmth from my neck up to my crown. This was not a petition, it was a negotiation, and the stakes were far higher than I'd realised.

I clenched my hands in my lap to stop them trembling and made my voice as warm and conspiratorial as I could. "I really am very grateful to the MWA for making an exception and allowing me to visit Elmwood. Of course I'll keep my eye on

Olivia for you, Daisy. I could let you know what she says to me and tell you if she discusses anything that is… ill advised."

"Would you, Mary?" The smile was back and on full beam. "Perhaps I could fix it so that you are on night shifts with her this week. That way you can get to know her, make sure she is, you know, professional in her attitude."

I nodded and made sure to meet the ward sister's gaze. This woman held everything dear to me in the palm of her hand.

"The Men's Welfare Authority's number one priority, Mary, is the safety of this facility and those it protects. You understand?"

"Yes. I understand." I stood and began making my way to the door, trying to get out of there as fast as possible.

"Good. And Mary…" A small pink tongue darted out to moisten her bottom lip. "Give my regards to Luca when you see him."

CHAPTER 3
Mary – present

I've worked in many facilities over the last thirty years, mostly adapted warehouses from before the infestation – windowless, cavernous and cold. The perennial drone of three domestic washing machines shared between two hundred men and the constant rumble of an outdated filtration system haunted us day and night. We carers lived in constant fear of a filtration breach, of the men becoming infected, turning on us – outnumbered ten to one, we wouldn't have stood a chance.

So, five years ago, when a high-ranking official in the British Union asked to be shown round the first purpose-built facility, it was I who was chosen to give the tour. I presume the governors were hoping that a woman in her sixties, as I was at the time, would suggest a level of solemnity when representing one of the most expensive projects in our new country's short history.

This modern facility, with its well-lit rooms and its silent air conditioning, represented the future and I was proud to show it off. Also, it made me feel special to be asked. So it was, with childish expectation and a touch of pride, that one damp autumn morning, I stood outside my new place of work, bobbing on the balls of my feet and waiting for the special dignitary to arrive.

A car eventually pulled up. It was one of those pebble-shaped electric models – manufactured rather than reclaimed; it was pale grey and smooth as an otter. Out slid a woman in her late thirties, short, lean and neatly dressed with a mane of black hair held in check by a red scarf.

I smiled and rushed down the steps to meet her. "Hello! Under-Secretary! Welcome. *Welcome*." I offered my hand, but she'd just ducked back into the car to collect her bag, so I hovered, uncertain, leaving it outstretched. She turned, straightened, and then took my hand, shaking it warmly.

"Mary, is it? Mary Langham?"

I nodded and beamed. "Yes, and it's such a pleasure to meet you, Ms Philips, I mean, Under-Secretary Philips," I stumbled over my words.

"Oh, please call me Jade." She grinned, which gave her round face an air of openness. Her dark eyes held mine for a moment and I felt myself relax.

"And this is Skylar."

Unseen by me, another woman had exited the car from the other side, pale and slender with short dark hair, stylishly cut. She looked to be in her mid-forties, perhaps a little older. "Hi," she said before turning to the large building and looking up. "Well, it's certainly big enough."

"Skylar is one of the MWA's top advisors and she was desperate to see what we've done here. I hope you don't mind her tagging along."

"It's fine, of course," I said, although there was something about Skylar's presence that annoyed me. Perhaps it was that she dealt with the MWA, the authority that had left the facility programme under-funded for decades. "It's great to have both of you here. Follow me."

I led them through security and then we spent nearly an hour in decontamination. "Sorry about all that," I said, as we reached the other side, scrubbed and wearing the standard silk shifts required of staff members.

"Don't worry. We were expecting it," replied Jade, although her tone was more muted than before and she kept fiddling with the plastic hat that was struggling to contain her unruly hair.

One rogue lock escaped at her temple. "Excuse me, Under-Secretary, I mean... Jade, may I?" I didn't wait for a reply. I took the hair and gently tucked it back under the cap. "We have to be really careful."

"Yes. Absolutely!" she replied, patting her head to check for any other escapees.

Skylar said nothing, just scraped her short damp hair under her cap band checked her watch.

We passed by the carers' quarters but didn't go in. "Where do the Warden and the ward sisters stay?" asked Jade.

"There's a covered walkway off the east wing. It leads to a separate block." I pointed in its general direction.

After a few more steps, Skylar asked, "Why aren't you a ward sister, Mary? Surely you have the experience."

I kept my face neutral, my voice light. "Oh, I don't really like all the extra paperwork. I prefer the front line." The fact was that I wasn't very good at office politics. I unnerve other women – younger women – or I get on their nerves: one of the two. Or maybe it was something else. My trips to Elmwood, perhaps? Skylar cast me a look and I changed the subject. "It can be a little overwhelming, being near so many men if you're not used to it. But don't worry, you're perfectly safe." Jade and Skylar glanced at each other and I detected a spark of apprehension pass between them. No doubt they'd been told about men by their mothers. The older of the two, Skylar, might even remember the infestation although she would have been young at the time. The lessons on men at school, reports of violence and murder, may well give them pause.

I shouldn't have worried. As we left the corridor and walked out into a Perspex-covered courtyard about fifty metres square, Jade looked about the bright vast space, eyes wide. "Goodness me," she said over the clamour of male voices. "How marvellous!" Skylar kept silent but I noticed a flash of disapproval mark her pale features.

Set around the edges of the large space lay sets of long

trestle tables with benches. Some of the men were sprawled over them in groups chatting or drawing, a few were crowded round a pair playing cards. One must have laid the winning card, as a cheer rose from the onlookers.

We walked around the quad and Jade commented excitedly on the amount of light the roof offered. The men had been forewarned that there might be a visitor but that didn't curb their bubbling excitement that lifted a few metres before us, before falling to a hush as the three of us passed by.

"Am I allowed to talk to them?" asked Jade in a breathless whisper.

"Of course," I replied, surprised she felt she needed my permission to do anything.

She stopped and addressed a resident by the name of Archer. "Excuse me, young man, what do you think of your new courtyard?"

Archer, who was kneeling and potting bulbs at the time, looked up into Jade's face, blushing, and stammered, "It's… it's… er… good. I think I'm really lucky."

Jade smiled and turned away. "That's just marvellous," she muttered to nobody in particular. Then to me, "I will be reporting back to the Council everything you tell me, Mary. There is a lot of interest at the moment in how the men are faring in places like these."

"The Council?" I said, my voice squeaking a little.

She turned and smiled. "It's fine, Mary. They just want to know that their resources are being allocated wisely."

That I might be mentioned to the Council – the seven heads of authorities who governed the entire Union – caused a small thrill to travel up my spine. These were the women who'd built our tiny bastion of humanity – this small sliver of survival in an otherwise decimated world. How exciting that my words, my opinions, even, might make their way to such hallowed ears.

I led the women up a flight of stairs to the men's dormitories on the second floor. The rooms were long and thin, with twelve beds along one wall. Along the other wall stood twelve plastic shelf units, each with two shelves. The men's belongings, those that were not deemed susceptible to harbouring the toxic setae, were arranged on the shelves: hand-drawn pictures in colourful frames, lumpy clay figures, lint rollers and wipes. There were no changes of clothes – that process was done in the showering area – and the whole room was lit by a series of downlighters high up on the ceiling.

"Can they have books?" asked Jade, picking up a lint roller from a bedside table and rolling it over her hand.

"No. Unfortunately, the threads can wedge themselves down in between the pages too easily. All reading material has to be laminated and single sheaf. As I said, we have to be very careful."

"That's a pity about the books. I guess that's also why you have to shave their heads."

"And their arms," I replied. "In fact, every part of their bodies. But we use warm wax rather than razors. Otherwise, we'd have to shave them every day."

"Wax?" Jade looked at me, aghast. "I mean, how?"

I paused the tour for a moment. "You smear it on, then you place a sterile cloth on the top and then you, well, rip it all off." As I spoke, I demonstrated the motion on my own arm.

She shook her head in disbelief. "All over... I mean, their genitals as well? But that must be excruciating!"

Skylar spoke for the first time, catching me off guard. "Women used to do it all the time before the change," she said in a clipped voice. She looked at me as she spoke and I caught her meaning, even though she didn't say it: *women like you.*

Unperturbed, I showed them the carers' station, an alcove with a double desk and two chairs from which you could observe down the corridor.

"This is where we sit when we're on the night shift," I said, gesturing to the desk. "We always work nights in pairs. And further down is a small staff kitchenette and bathroom."

"They don't ask you to do it, do they, the night shift?" said Jade in mild surprise. "I mean, at your age."

"No," I said. "Not anymore." Although I was a little annoyed at the implication of her question.

"Well, that's a relief," and she laughed. "I wouldn't like to think that we were running some kind of gulag for the elderly."

I forced a smile.

Skylar loomed behind us, keeping pace.

I led them to the upper south side, to a viewing room with a huge window looking out over the nearby downs.

"Wow. Incredible!" said Jade, staring out over the vista. "I mean, look at that view. *Look at that view*!" It was nearing ten in the morning, and the autumn fields were just shedding their mist. The downs stretched into the distance, amber and sapid in the thin light. A little way off you could just see a yoga class practising in one of the fields bordering the village, the women stretching and bowing in the morning air.

"Impressive," replied Skylar. "Better than my view of a cheese factory, that's for sure."

"Is this the only viewing room in the facility? It's so nice that the men get to experience the outdoors," said Jade, tapping it gently with her knuckles.

Skylar cut in. "Goodness, Jade. The facility cost more than enough, don't you think. What next? Velvet on the walls? Roasted chicken on a Sunday?"

I led the two women out of the room before Jade had a chance to answer. She chittered away as we went back downstairs, keeping up a steady stream of questions.

"How old is your oldest resident?"

"Forty-one."

"Wow, the same age as me, born two years after the change. They come to you at eighteen, from the prep houses, is that right?"

"Usually. Although we also get transfers from other facilities."

"Do they fight much?"

"Not really. We monitor their hormone levels."

"Do they form attachments? I mean, to each other?"

"Sometimes," I smiled. "Occasionally my job does involve dealing with broken hearts and wounded egos."

She rolled her eyes and laughed. "I bet it does! And what about sex?"

We were entering the kitchens and a group of men were there on catering duty. The novelty of our arrival unnerved them. They stopped chopping, peeling, stirring and cleaning and stood staring at us, unsure what to do.

"Come on, come on," I said in a matronly tone. "There'll be trouble if the others turn up for first-sitting and there isn't any lunch." Then I turned back to Jade. "They can get permission to use one of the isolation rooms but any petting in the dorms or common rooms is forbidden."

"What happens if they break the rules?" asked Skylar.

I led them both round the kitchen, past the new stainless-steel equipment and surfaces, and the watchful faces of the men on duty, then back out to the corridor. "They have to go into isolation for a while, alone, of course. That or their medication gets adjusted."

Skylar nodded. "What about castration? I mean, that's what they used to do in the sanatoriums, isn't it? When the men got older and they required a permanent way to calm them down."

The other two women carried on a few steps, not realising I'd stopped dead in my tracks, unable to keep the shock from my face. "No. We don't *ever* do that."

"I'm sure Skylar wasn't making a recommendation," said Jade quickly. "Forgive us, Mary, if we seem a little ignorant. It's one thing to manage the process from afar, quite another to be here in the thick of it. The truth is that most people know so little about men."

I unclenched my jaw with effort. "I understand. I've been

working here so long that I forget that most women have never even seen a facility. Some have never even seen a man." I turned and walked in front of the other two women for a while, giving the flush in my face a chance to pass.

We came back out into the courtyard and Jade again marvelled at the space, at how the men could choose to bring their meals here to eat. "It's almost like they're eating outside," she exclaimed, smiling and nodding at the residents we passed.

I was pleased at Jade's enthusiasm, encouraged at how invested she seemed in the men's welfare. I felt I'd found an ally, and a powerful one. The men needed all the support they could get from the council. Skylar, on the other hand, followed mutely in our wake, barely supressing a scowl.

It wasn't until we reached the lower north side of the building, the isolation wing, that Skylar spoke again. "Are these the rooms that are also used for hetero-recreation visits?" She seemed a little more enthusiastic than before, her eyes darting around the long corridor with its many doors off either side.

"We just use the term *visitation* rather than *hetero-recreation*."

"How many women can you facilitate during one visit?" she replied, slowing her pace.

"So long as they have the right paperwork, about one hundred and thirty."

Skylar stopped and peered into one of the rooms through a small window in the door. "That's interesting. It's purely recreational now that we have the insemination system, of course. One hundred and thirty, you say? Is that once per month?"

I nodded. "We don't have the staffing to run them any more regularly. I believe the waiting list is very long. It's proving to be a popular pastime."

Skylar opened the door without asking if she could and poked her head inside. "But the men could do it more often, couldn't they? I mean, there's no physical reason they can't?" She was speaking into the room, as if speaking to herself. "I bet loads of women would love to try it at least once, just to say they've done it. The MWA could really make this work."

It was a plain, pale green room with a double bed, a shower and a laundry chute in one corner. On the wall at the head of the bed was a big, red button. "What's the button for?" she asked.

"If a resident feels uncomfortable, if he's asked to do anything he is not one-hundred-percent okay with, then he needs only push the button and a carer will be on hand to mediate the situation."

She turned and looked at me properly for the first time, her sharp features alert. "You've got to admit, it's a far preferable option than the sire houses."

I didn't meet her eye, only shrugged. "Of course."

Jade frowned. "Skylar, I'm surprised at you bringing up such things. The Council has stated it is keen to move on from that particularly difficult part of its history."

Turning away, I led both women towards the exit.

When I told Olivia this story, on our second night on shift, I may have exaggerated how impressed Jade Philips – the woman who had gone on to become Head of the Health and Welfare Association and who was now one of the seven voting members on the Council of the Union – had been with my tour. I may have embellished certain parts of the story, suggesting perhaps that she and I had left on far friendlier terms than was strictly the case. I might have dropped into my conversation with Olivia that Jade had said something along the lines of: *Mary, if you need anything to help these men, anything at all. You just call me. I suspect you know more about this than all of the Council's advisors put together!*

When I told Olivia this story, I might have said something like that.

Sleeping in the late afternoon is dangerous; dreams are more vivid and they linger and bleed into the dying day. I woke just after six in the evening and my dream clung to me, not as an image, but as a collection of feelings, passions without reasons. Adrian was chasing me along a stony beach. The wind was cool and great waves yawned at us from the sea. I was laughing into the briny air. He caught me and turned me to him, his curly hair clinging straight and slick to his face and his hazel eyes bright and alive. For a few moments, I was young and loved and the world had a place for me. Then my husband's eyes changed. They become a misty grey, the colour of old stone, and he looked away from me, up into a cold, bleak sky. I followed his gaze upwards and the sky was alive with dancing moths.

My eyes opened and my joints began to ache.

Age has afforded me my own room, at least. Not fancy, some plastic furniture, a chair, a cupboard, a small desk, a pedal bin and high up, near the ceiling, a squat window, which never opens. The amber light fell in a wide shaft about halfway down the opposite wall, suggesting late afternoon.

The white walls offset the bright colours of the furniture: purple and jade. The whole effect reminded me of a holiday village that Adrian and I had taken Ryan to for his fourth birthday. It was on the coast and we'd booked for a long weekend. Ryan had had the "restaurant birthday package", which meant that Bob the Builder had turned up at our table waving and singing and holding a cake. But it was too much for Ryan, who'd already consumed large amounts of ice-cream before whizzing, like a pinball, from bouncy castle to big wheel to swings. He'd taken an instant dislike to Bob and burrowed his hot little face into my shoulder. Then he'd lifted his head and howled at the poor guy, who'd finally left, still waving and repeating in an increasingly desperate tone: *Can we fix it? Yes, we can!*

By the time I'd carried my son back to the room, he was fast asleep. Adrian went out and got chicken burgers and fries whilst I put Ryan to bed. Later that evening, as Ryan and I were cuddled up watching a black and white film on BBC2, Adrian told me that he preferred this bright, Swedish-style furniture to our shabby, mismatched pine. I replied that that was a pity, as the holiday represented our expendable income for the next six months. He sighed and looked towards the room of our sleeping child. I remembered wondering for the millionth time if he was content with the choice we'd made when we were barely out of our teens.

I lay in my single cot, waiting for the strength to rise and listening to the chatter from the carers' dorm next door. They were discussing the upcoming visitations.

I'm with Declan. I've heard good things about him. He's older and that sometimes means more experienced and more confident.

Yes. I visited him last time and it was a very nice evening. How about you, Janet?

Actually, yes. I finally got Nancy to agree.

Really! Will Nancy be joining you on the visit?

No. I tried to convince her, but she's adamantly not into "sex with men". She offered to be there for my sake, but I said it was fine. There's nothing worse than really getting into it and having someone in the corner rolling their eyes and looking at their watch.

There was a chorus of laughter.

Daisy's visiting Luca.

I petitioned Luca!

So did I!

That's hardly fair. She's the one that signs off on the paperwork.

I sat up.

The trick with getting out of bed these days was momentum. I shifted myself to the edge of the bed and then swung out and upright in one painful movement. I had to stand still and hunched for a while and wait for my limbs to catch up to my will. The time it took for my body to acquiesce was getting longer and longer. One day, I will fling myself upwards and lack the strength to control the momentum. I'll crash forward like a falling tombstone onto the linoleum floor.

I shuffled to the wardrobe and groaned as my knees and ankles loosened up. My uniform, a knee-length cream dress, hung neatly alongside a bathrobe. Despite the fact that they were both made of high-grade satin, I still spent time running a lint roller over the fabric. When done, I carefully checked the roller: only a couple of my own short grey hairs, which I picked off and placed in the bin. I wrapped myself in my robe and made for the shower.

Olivia was already at the carers' station when I got there. She wiped down the surfaces, as I checked the incident form, noting with relief that she'd already filled in the tedious pre-shift report section, then I grabbed a cloth and helped her finish off the cleaning.

"How are you finding it here?" I asked.

"Fine. Good, in fact," she replied, nodding as she worked. "This is much nicer than my last facility, especially the courtyard, of course. Very impressive."

"Are you visiting any of the men this week?"

She stopped wiping, and smiled. "No. I never really was one for that sort of thing, even before things changed. You?"

"I'm a bit old now, don't you think?" I laughed.

"I don't expect the men would mind." She dropped her plastic gloves into the bin. "It's not like before."

"I guess, but it seems a bit… artificial."

"The girls would call you a 'dolly' for saying something like that."

I nodded. "I'm sure they would." I came round the front of the station and stretched out my arms, easing out the worst of the stiffness. "You check A and B; I'll do C and D."

"Okay, see you back here in ten."

We parted and I picked up a stack of laminated picture scrolls before walking the twenty or so metres to the first dorm on the left.

Most of the men were in their beds, except a pair who were finishing up their grooming. One sat with his back to the other and allowed him to gently swipe the lint roller over his head and shoulders. Every now and then, he would pause and check the barrel for anything small, black and suspicious, and then go back to softly brushing the tool in downward strokes over the other man's arms. An evening ritual the men had been taught in the preps.

"Are you nearly done?" I asked.

"Just finishing," the groomer with the roller replied.

I held up the plastic scrolls to the dorm. "Any takers?"

"What is it?" asked Archer.

"It's a new short story, written by a resident from Swindon."

"What's it about?"

"It's about birds. The illustrations are excellent." I unrolled one and held up a laminated watercolour depicting a kingfisher diving onto a dragonfly.

Archer rolled his eyes. "Sure. If it's the only one you have, birds it will have to be."

"I like it better when you tell us a story, Mary," this was from Luca, and the men pounced on the idea, immediately offering up a cacophony of appeals.

"Go on, Mary…"

"Just one story…"

"A short one, please…"

I sighed and shook my head, although their appreciation gladdened me. "Not tonight. I've got things to do. Sorry boys."

My words were met with grumbles and groans, but they accepted my refusal. Next time, maybe when I wasn't required to probe Olivia for… for what? Inflammatory ideas? Seditious opinions? I wasn't planning on reporting anything back to Daisy, of course, but it might prove useful to have some information in my back pocket, so to speak, just in case.

There were one or two other takers for the bird book. The rest turned away and prepared for sleep. I was just heading back to the door when a commotion sounded from another dorm. The men all sat up and looked at each other, murmuring. I left the room quickly, throwing "stay in bed, please", over my shoulder as I went. I clicked the lock on the dorm door, then raced to B from where the noise was coming. There was a scream and the crash of a cabinet being pushed over. I swung open the door.

Olivia was already there, and all of the men were cowering down at the far end of the dorm. All of them, that is, except one.

"It came from Carl! It came from Carl!" spluttered a voice from the knot of the men, who were all pointing and backing away. On the floor lay a lint roller towards which Olivia was striding. She picked it up and brought it back to this end of the room to examine it. I walked over to her and she showed me the roll. "What do you think?" she whispered.

I took it gently in my hands, so as not to allow anything to fall away. The article in question was a short dark hair about half a centimetre long. "It's curved and shiny, not dull. And it's a bit too light, brown rather than black."

She nodded, "It's too thick… eyelash." She was confirming rather than asking. "We'd better take him to solitary, just to be safe. Carl, was it?"

"I'll take him," I said. Poor guy. He'd be in isolation for a minimum of two weeks to see if he showed any symptoms and by that time the confinement would already have begun. It was an overly cautious protocol – the infected show symptoms in twenty-four hours, usually less – but there was nothing we could do. Rules were rules.

Olivia turned to the group of men who were still pressing themselves into the far wall, as far away from Carl as possible. "It is certainly an eyelash," she said in a tone of absolute confidence. "Carl will accompany Mary to solitary only as a precaution. The rest of you need to get into bed right now. We will forego reading time this evening, as we've had enough disruption."

The men responded by shuffling forwards to their beds, giving Carl a wide berth.

Carl came to stand by me. His eyes were downcast, his shoulders hunched. "Am I going to miss the visitations?"

"I'm afraid so," I replied, leading him out and down the corridor to isolation.

After a few steps, he said, "It's okay. I don't mind."

I was surprised. The monthly visits were usually met with fevered enthusiasm by the men. I would have thought Carl would be devastated. "Did you have a visit booked this time?"

"Yeah, but…"

I set the pace a little slower, making sure we had some more time before arriving at his temporary new room. "But what?" I said gently.

"But I wasn't really looking forward to it. I dunno, recently they just feel a bit weird."

"Who was it with?"

He looked sideways at me and shrugged.

"It's okay, you won't get in trouble, Carl, tell me."

"Rosie. She asked for me specifically. She said she liked the shape of my arms." He held out his left arm in front of him as if to illustrate her point. It was a fine arm, muscular and olive, but hairless of course, just a faint pinprick stubble showing despite the hormone inhibitors.

Rosie was one of the four ward sisters, but she dealt with the dorms on the other side of the building, so I didn't have much contact with her day-to-day. She seemed nice enough, calm, professional, good with her team of carers and with the residents. "Have you met with Rosie before? Wasn't she nice to you?"

"Once, yes. Look, it's not her fault," he said quickly, "she was great. It's me, I just felt that it was kind of, I don't know, it was fun and everything, but…"

I didn't speak, just waited for him to continue.

"I wasn't really into it. I felt like I was just acting, like when we do a drama project, and that made me feel weird about the whole thing. I mean, I know it's my duty and everything, and the facilities need the funding. But, Mary, it just feels odd."

I nodded, replying, "That's understandable."

Carl shrugged and crossed his arms over his chest as we walked. "And it's not just me. Some of the others are not sure about the whole thing either, although don't tell anyone I mentioned it. We agreed to keep it quiet. Just in case it upsets the visiting women."

We reached his new room with its shower in the corner, a fresh plastic-wrapped shift on the double bed and the laundry chute in the wall.

"Is that why you agreed to the visit this time, even though you were feeling weird about it?"

He turned and slipped off his shift, stuffing it into the chute, closing the hatch and pressing the extraction button on the wall. I'd seen the naked male form so often, waxed it, groomed it, that I hardly registered it. I tried to see him as the visiting women probably did, as a reprieve, a distraction.

Without looking at me, he went to the shower and started the water running. "Yes, but she's a staff member." He tested the water with the palm of his hand and adjusted the taps. "They sometimes bring, you know, stuff: art supplies, extra scrolls, that kind of thing. A few weeks ago, she brought lemon cake – made with real lemons. Some of the ward sisters can even get you out of chores if they really like you."

He looked back at me from the shower stall, naked and with soapy rivulets now running over his bronze skin. "Don't tell Rosie what I said. I don't want her feeling bad about it."

"I promise I won't say anything. It's fine."

He smiled.

"You know what to do, Carl. Ten minutes scrubbing minimum, use the timer in the stall."

"I know, Mary," he said, picking up the soap again and rubbing it between his hands.

I left him working the suds into his shaved head and returned to the carers' station. On my way back I thought about what he said. The visitation programme had been running for the past twenty years or so, one way or another, since there were men old enough to participate. Before the insemination programme was well established, it was the method some women used to get pregnant, although not a popular way, as the women in question were unable to choose the sex of their child. Nobody wants a boy, of course, having to give him to the arms of the state the moment he is born. The MWA still has to offer huge incentives – education passports, land allocations, extra ration tokens – to women who *Contributed* a male child to the state. To *Contribute* was how the government referred to the process: a contribution to society. Before the Artificial Insemination programme, women would use sperm donated by the sanatoriums or visit them – hence the name *sire houses*. But that is seen as shameful now, and not talked about.

For the last few years, at least, visitations were really just for fun: a kind of sexual novelty. I'd be very naive if I believed that the staff here didn't grow extra fond of their lovers, even though there are strict guidelines in the MWA handbook about such things, and I'd suspected gifts and favours came from carers and ward sisters. But what did concern me was Carl's reluctance and the suggestion that other men felt the same. I reached the carers' station, still pondering Carl's admission.

"Was he okay, about it?" Olivia was already at the station, filling in an incident form.

"Yeah, I guess." I thought about telling her what Carl had said but decided not to. My chat with Daisy earlier had made me a bit wary of my new friend. I didn't want to be Daisy's mole. In fact, I was fairly sure I could claim I was too old and doddery to notice anything. But if pushed, I'd choose my trips to Elmwood over Olivia. I sat and waited as she finished with the form. She handed it over for me to read through and sign off. "How were the men? Did they settle down?" I asked.

"They were okay. I checked in all the dorms. B drove a hard bargain – I'm afraid I've had to sign you up for story time tomorrow afternoon in the viewing area." She grimaced apologetically.

"That's fine," I replied. "I try to get in a couple of story sessions a month. It does them good to have something different to look forward to."

"What type of stories do you tell them? I mean, there's so much they don't know about."

"They like adventure stories, fantasy worlds, anything with outrageous machines or wizards or ghosts. Last week I told them the story of Tarzan, swinging through the trees, talking to the animals. They loved it. I had to draw Shere Khan on a piece of paper, as they'd never seen a tiger before. Sadly, they're all going around thinking a tiger is like a lumpy turtle with whiskers. My drawing skills aren't great."

She laughed, "What about Jane?"

"Jane was turned into John."

"Ahh, good thinking. The notion that a man might rescue a woman might blow their minds." There was a sharp edge to her words, subtle, but there.

We were quiet for a while and then she spoke again. This time, her voice was more serious. "Do you think it's, I don't know, a bit cruel?" she asked. "I mean, telling the men about the outside, getting them to imagine *being* outside, when they're always going to be stuck in here?"

I paused. I hadn't really thought about it. "I think they wanted to hear the stories, even though they can never do any of the things I talk about. The men have so little in their lives, I can at least fire up their imaginations a bit. If they don't like it, they don't have to attend the session." I found this line of questioning a bit annoying and I was irritated at Olivia for suggesting it.

Olivia nodded, but her mouth was in a tight line. I wasn't sure whether she approved or not.

"And how do the ward sisters feel about the stories?" she said.

I shrugged. I really didn't feel like answering, but it would seem churlish to stay silent. "I don't really know. Some are fine with it. Some, I suspect, aren't keen, but as long as there's no 'trouble' they let it pass. They never come to the sessions, so it's not really an issue."

Olivia was quiet for quite a long time and it occurred to me that I might have offended her – that she thought of me as a monster for filling the men's heads up with wonders they could never really experience. Well, fine. She could keep her opinions to herself.

But then she said quietly, "I think it's wonderful, that you take them on these journeys, show them there's more than..." she held up her palms and gestured to the corridor, "... just this."

It had been a long time since a woman had offered me such unguarded praise, and I felt a warmth rise within me.

"Could I come along to the next one?" she asked.

I paused, just for a moment.

"Oh, don't worry. I mean, if you'd rather I didn't..."

"No," I said flustered, "it's okay. Of course you can come."

She looked at me and smiled. "Okay."

In any other circumstance, I would have been pleased. Pleased to have recruited a comrade into my small campaign, and even more pleased that the men had given me such glowing reviews. But I felt like a traitor. I might have to tell Daisy about Olivia's confession, her story about Coventry, and that might mean Olivia would be reprimanded, even moved on.

I made mint tea in the small kitchen area behind the carers' station and handed Olivia a steaming mug. Olivia opened the desk drawer and took out a bundle wrapped in paper. She unwrapped what looked like a flat, brown stone and snapped off a piece. "Here," she said, offering it to me.

I put down my tea. Holding the chunk in my palm, I turned to Olivia, my face sagging with astonishment. "Is this what I think it is?"

"It might be," she said with a grin. "Why don't you taste it and find out?"

I hardly dared to. I took a small nibble and, I'm not exaggerating, tears filled my eyes. "How? I mean, where did you...?" I took another small bite, "The cocoa beans alone would have to have come from..." I stopped babbling and just let the rich, sweet taste sit on my tongue. I sniffed the remaining lump and memories enveloped me: Christmas morning gold coins; crackling bags of Maltesers in cinemas; Ryan, smeared and sticky, waving a claggy spoon from his highchair.

"A recent shipment from Australia," said Olivia. "And don't ask me how they got from that ship to this drawer. I could tell you, but then I'd have to kill you."

I laughed despite myself.

We sat warming ourselves with tea and nibbling on the chocolate. I leaned back and let the sugar seep into my old bones, thinking about the shift ahead.

"Was it the dog?" Olivia asked, after a few minutes of silence.

"What?"

"Your dog? Had he picked up some of the threads?"

The tea I was clutching was hot, so I gently blew on it, making ripples on the surface. The steam warmed my cheeks and nose. This part of the story was clearest in my mind, but hardest to say. I thought of Doc, his wet eyes and his velvet-tipped ears; he was always scratching at the door to be let in, I remembered, as I sipped. I would sit down with a bowl of crisps in front of the TV and, a minute later, scratch, scratch, scratch.

"I expect it was," I said. "But we didn't know what we were dealing with at the time, so it could have just been a draught from under a door, or through an air vent. But, looking back, it was probably the dog."

Olivia was waiting for me to continue, silent, polite, nodding. But I didn't. I couldn't.

She could tell, I'm sure. Suddenly, she changed the subject, "It's not just you who has been keeping exalted company."

A blush threatened to engulf me as I remembered telling Olivia that I'd impressed Jade Philips. "Well, it's not like we call each other up and chat or anything." I mumbled into my tea.

"Have you heard of Jen Harting?" she asked.

"The Council Member and the head of the Men's Welfare Association?" I replied, my guard rising a little. "Of course, I mean, I know that she runs all this." I waved my hand around. Like I knew she set the budgets for all of the facilities in the Union – nowhere near high enough, of course.

Olivia nodded but I noted the briefest of cold flashes in her gaze. "That's right. We were… we knew each other once."

I turned to her, eyes wide. "When? How?"

"Right at the beginning."

I've heard many stories over the years, confessions of grief and violence and bravery. But nothing prepared me for what Olivia told me that night, as I sipped tea and made that small square of chocolate last as long as I could.

"I was only twenty," she began, "when the world changed."

CHAPTER 4
Olivia – then

I was only twenty when the world changed. At the time, I was not convinced I was gay. That is to say: I would rather not have been gay. At seventeen, I'd tried sex with my boyfriend, and it had been awkward. But I'd put that down to my own lack of experience. Also, everyone else said he was good looking and wasn't I the lucky one! So, I went along with it. I remember thinking that I needed to make it work and reminding myself of the hassle that being part of a same-sex couple would bring – all those weird looks from strangers on buses, how my parents would be shocked but would try hard to seem fine with it. In the small town I grew up in, it would have been such a big thing. It seems strange now, of course, that we even needed a word for it, that then I was somehow *queer*.

My first year at university had been tough. I regretted choosing politics and wanted to change to psychology. I drank too much. I fancied my roommate, Emily, and had to watch her get off with boys. I got off with some boys too and, whilst fumbling about with their weirdly-shaped flesh, I thought about other things, usually Emily.

So, when she decided to stay near the university that first summer, I stayed with her. We got a tiny ground-floor apartment behind a charity shop. I worked in a nearby café. I knew she didn't like me *in that way*, and I guess she suspected I felt more for her than I let on, but we never talked about it.

I regret not going back to Oxford that summer to see my

mum and dad. They were happily married for twenty-nine years, disgustingly affectionate and inseparable. They were always one of the first couples to get up and dance at weddings, pressing their stout bodies too close, whispering and giggling to each other as they swayed to some corny song. My preteen ego cringed, accusing them of making a spectacle of themselves and, by association, of me! *Why can't they just be normal,* I'd think, whilst hunching down low in my seat. *Why must they always be so embarrassing? Why do they have to be touching each other all the time?* They didn't make it through the infestation. He beat her and my younger sister to death. Then, in a moment's lucidity, he hung himself. The report I later tracked down was mercifully light in detail.

That summer I spent with Emily was the best time I ever had. Even though most of it was spent with me mooning after a girl I couldn't have and hating myself for being such a sap. We were young – we went out a lot, we drank and we got invited to parties where we stretched ourselves out on warm evenings in pub gardens, drinking cider and smoking weed.

We didn't have a TV, just our laptops, but we were both on social media. I mean, what nineteen year-olds weren't? I remember Emily was worse than me. I checked it every hour or so but for her, the online world was rapacious, a needy infant. She'd wake up in the morning and reach for her phone, start scrolling. Instas, selfies, memes: *what he said; what she wore; what we'd done last night; who was there; who wasn't there and why.* She drew all of those twittering voices into our apartment through a five-inch, glowing window and framed them with her own gasps and snorts and outrage: *watch this, it's so funny, Liv,* or *this is unbelievable! They've gotta impeach him now – what a dick!*

I played along for her sake.

But those many times she'd lost her phone, those moments she felt separated, getting out of the shower, for example, or coming in from work and not remembering where she left it, she'd panic. I mean really panic, heavy breathing, manic rummaging through piles of laundry, shaking. *Help me!* She would scream. *Don't just sit there – help me find it! I know I left it here, Liv!* And she would jab her finger to the sofa, or the table, or the kitchen, and stare at me as if challenging me – as if I'd taken it and was hiding it as part of some vastly inappropriate joke.

So, up I'd get to help, ignoring her twitching and snapping, and we'd find it between the sofa cushions, or in the pocket of a recently discarded pair of jeans, and the world would settle down once more. A few minutes later, she'd be snorting at a video of a dog playing the cello with its nose.

Given this, it was hardly surprising that it was Emily who first noticed something wasn't right. The afternoon before the first infestation hit the UK, I came in from work and she was lying on the sofa, wearing denim shorts and a crop top, one hand wedged in a bag of toffee popcorn, the other tip-tapping frantically on her phone. "You are not going to believe this, Liv."

I dumped my bag onto the kitchen table, which was also the living room table, and sighed. Had Taylor Swift and Beyoncé had a falling out? Was the US Vice President running a child sex ring?

"Hit me with it," I said, flopping onto the sofa. She curled her legs up to give me some space. Then she wriggled her brightly painted toes behind me, into the space between my back and the sofa.

"This pandemic thing in South America, the one that's just affecting men, it's reached Europe. People say that it's bioterrorism, like anthrax or something."

"Oh?" I replied, hyper-aware of how close she was to me. I didn't know where to put my arm – the natural place would have been to rest it on her bare calf, which was pressed against my thigh, but instead I held it in front of me, like a broken wing. I leaned back and tried to look casual.

"They say it's turning them crazy, like it's actually melting the men's brains." Her tone suggested morbid excitement rather than fear.

"I don't think a disease can melt you brain, Em. What site are you on?"

She dragged her gaze away from the screen and towards me. "Fine, but when men's brains start melting all over the place, don't say I didn't warn you." Then she caught sight of my bag. "Did you bring food? I'm starving."

"I did," I replied. "A cheese bap, a sausage roll and some not-quite-stale muffins."

"Nice!" She unfurled herself from the sofa and rummaged around in my backpack, pulling out packets of unsold food from the café I worked at. I relaxed my arm and spread out a bit. My boss had called in sick that day, so the cook and I had been beyond busy.

"Are you working tonight?" I asked Emily. She tended bar in a bar on the High Street, usually getting home at about 3am.

"Yeah," she said through a mouthful of sausage roll. "It's three-for-two on shots. You should come."

"Hard pass. I'm ready for an early night."

"*Liv!*" She screwed up her face, and a large flake of sausage roll dropped onto her t-shirt. "You sleep too much." She grabbed a muffin and started chomping on it. "Don't worry, grandma. I'll be quiet when I come in."

"Thanks," I said, even though I knew she wouldn't be.

That night, I streamed a really bad sci-fi series whilst I soaked in the bath, and then went to bed. I can't remember if I checked the news on my phone, probably not. I checked Instagram, which was full of images of people enjoying themselves. Emily was glassy-eyed and making a peace sign, draped over some beefy bouncer, and I felt like the saddest, loneliest dyke in the world, but that was nothing new.

She came home at some point. There was giggling and a few clinking sounds, possibly of mugs being filled from a glass bottle. And then later moans and rhythmic gasping. Early the next morning I left for work, ignoring the oversized puffer jacket on the sofa and the pair of size eleven boots on the floor.

The morning rush was relatively quiet, which was a good thing, as neither my boss nor the cook was there. I had to open up, set up and prep all on my own. I texted my boss and then, when I hadn't heard anything by eight-fifteen, I called him. No reply. In the end, I had to close off the seated section and cancel cooked breakfasts. The customers who did come in for their coffees and pastries were distracted and more annoyed at me than usual. *I'm working as fast as I can!* I thought, as I manned the coffee machine, the snacks counter and the till all at the same time, whilst repeatedly apologising for the fact that the pastry delivery hadn't arrived. *I don't get paid for this shit. I'm quitting as soon as I can get hold of the manager, and I'm gonna tell him what I think of this minimum wage, zero-hour bullshit.* I never got the chance, of course.

Then, at about eleven-ish, people stopped coming in altogether. I hadn't seen a customer in ten minutes, at what would usually be a busy time for the student crowd and mums with pushchairs. I went out and looked up and down the High Street but there were just two or three people moving hastily, as if they needed to get somewhere fast. As the keening wail of sirens rose in the distance, I tried my boss again. Nothing.

Then my phone rang. It was Emily, which was, in itself, odd, as she never, ever rang. Her MO was exclusively texting.

I answered with, "What's going on?"

"You need to come home. I dunno what it is. Just come home now!" Her voice was throaty and raw. No doubt, I thought, due to her hangover. Or maybe it was all the groaning last night. Whatever it was, I didn't have time for her shit today. I didn't want a bit part in whatever drama she had in mind.

"I can't," I replied sharply. "There's no one else to look after the café, everyone is AWOL and I'm on my own. And it's really busy." I added, looking over the empty shop and to the deserted street beyond.

"I need you. Liv, I really need you. He's got it!"

It was fear, I realised, that was making her voice crackle. Extreme fear.

"I'm in the bathroom. I'll explain, just come home." And then the line went dead.

I pelted home. Those size eleven boots probably didn't belong to someone small. I burst into the apartment, amped up like fury. But there was no one in the sitting room. The jacket was still on the back of the chair, the boots still lying by the sofa. "Emily!" I called, as I ran to the bathroom and banged on the door. "Emily! What's going on?"

The door opened and there she stood, in Wonder Woman pyjamas, pale, shaking, with swollen red blotches under her wide eyes. "I don't know what to do," she whispered.

"Where is he?"

She nodded to her room. "He won't wake up, and his mouth… God, his mouth."

"Did you call an ambulance?"

"There's no answer, just a recording telling me to stay on the line. It's been over ten minutes." She held up the phone, which was playing tinny classical music.

"Keep on holding. Fuck!" Fear gave way to annoyance. "What drugs has he had?"

"Just some coke," she said in a small voice as she held her phone to her ear. I could hear the automated message on the other end of the line kick in. *Please hold the line for the next available operator…*

I started towards her room but she grabbed me. "No, don't look."

Releasing her hand from my t-shirt, I said in a quiet voice, "I won't be a minute, but he might need help."

She let go, and I noticed her hands were trembling.

"Go and put on my red hoodie. You're cold."

Whilst she looked for my jumper, I took a deep breath and opened her bedroom door.

A man lay on his side, facing away from the door. Naked and very tall, his feet poked out from the bottom of the duvet. Next to him was a small Emily-sized imprint in the sheet and pillow. His clothes, black combats and a grey t-shirt, were strewn across the floor. A phone lay next to him on the bedside table, quietly humming as "MUM" flashed on the screen.

"Hello," I said, tapping him on the shoulder. He didn't move.

I pulled him back towards me, noting the warm flush of his skin as his back came to rest on the mattress.

I took a step back and held the back of my hand to my mouth. His lips were blue, like when kids eat a raspberry slushie, and a rash of darker inky veins snaked out from his mouth, down his neck and up over his face. He was breathing, but in shallow, wheezing gasps. His eyes were closed.

Overcoming my instinct to just turn tail and leave, I leaned in and gave him a firm shake. "Wake up!" I spoke loudly, almost a shout, "Can you hear me? I said *WAKE UP!*" But nothing, just the same light, in-and-out panting.

"I got through!" There was a call from the hall. Emily came in, waving her phone. "I called 999 and they said an ambulance is on its way. They said to wait... Oh my God!" She backed away from the man in the bed. "It's all over his face?"

"It's okay, Em. Listen, it's okay."

She looked like she was going to be sick. "I was with him all night. We, I mean, shit, do I have it?" She rubbed her fingers across her mouth.

"No. If it's this thing on the news, didn't you say it was only men getting it?"

"Yeah, but no one really knows?"

His phone hummed and shivered again.

MUM... MUM... MUM...

"What do you want to do about that?"

Emily shrugged. "What would we say?"

I should have answered it. Telling you this now, it feels like it was the least I could have done. I haven't thought about it, to be honest, since then. It seemed such a tiny tragedy compared to what was to come, a detail. *MUM... MUM... MUM...* Forever unanswered.

The paramedics, when they arrived, looked knackered. They wore face masks, plastic aprons and surgical gloves. They wearily hoisted the man onto a gurney. As they trundled him to the waiting ambulance, one turned to Emily and me.

"How d'you know him?" He spoke with a strong Scottish accent, and on top of this, his voice was raw and raspy.

Emily answered, "He's a bouncer at the bar I work in."

"Has he been abroad recently, anywhere in Europe, or South America?"

"I don't think so."

The paramedic nodded. "Are you coming to the hospital with him?"

Emily squirmed. "I, err, I don't think. I mean, I don't know him that well."

The paramedic shrugged. Emily turned to me, eyes wide and rimmed in red. "Should I go?"

I felt the man's phone vibrate in my hand. *MUM... MUM... MUM...* "We'll both go," I said with more conviction than I felt. "We can call his mum from the hospital."

But of course, we never did.

It was nearly all women in the waiting area of the hospital – some had wounds: one was clutching a blood-soaked tea towel to her right arm. A few were holding onto children or trying to keep them busy. There was one dishevelled receptionist attending to everyone and everything and when we arrived, I asked her what was going on. She'd just looked at me narrow-eyed with a *don't-be-a pain-in-my-ass* look and shoved a form over the desk towards us. "Just fill it in."

I looked at the paperwork and realised I couldn't fill it in, as I didn't know jack shit about the guy. He was being taken through the double doors into the treatment area.

"This way," said the paramedic to Emily.

"Where are we going?" she asked in a trembling voice.

"C Wing, intensive care unit. No, just you, she needs to stay here." He nodded at me to stay.

"I'll be right here," I said as she was swept along. She didn't have a chance to reply. As she left, I glimpsed a line of covered bodies on beds lining the corridor just beyond the double doors. I sat down and checked my phone. It must have been about one in the afternoon.

That was when I discovered that the Prime Minister had died, and that the UK was now under martial law.

Masked medics ran in and out of the waiting area, barking instructions. *Will the relatives of Dominic King please report to reception?* Every time a medic entered the waiting room, a small gaggle of relatives would mob them. *Where is my brother?... I need to know if my father is okay... Please help me, I can't find my son, his name is John Cahill...* and the medic would back away. *Go talk to reception. I'm sorry, I don't have any more information for you.*

It was not chaos, but there was a cloud of fear and confusion, and everyone seemed unsure as to how to act, whether now was the time for restraint or rebellion.

I tried Dad's number, but it just rang. The woman next to me was holding a young boy of about four years old on her lap. His face was red, hot looking, and his nose was streaming. He sneezed sharply as she rocked him. I tried to inch away a little. Who knew what this was and whether some women might get it? I was annoyed that this woman had a sneezing kid here. She could at least get him to wear a mask or use a tissue.

Then he kicked me, the little boy on my neighbour's lap – he just kicked out as hard as he could, a vicious stabbing strike into my side. I jumped to my feet in shock.

"Ow! What the...?"

The mother turned the boy around on her lap to face her and was about to speak, to tell him off, I guess, when he started to scream and claw at her face. There were no words, just guttural bestial noises drawn from deep within his small belly. The mother tried to calm him, to hold him tight, but he just kept screaming and flailing. When he wasn't screaming into her face, he was snapping at her with his nubby milk teeth, biting into the air. Those nearest started to back away, me included. She cried out to me, as I was still the closest, "Help me with him, please!"

Another woman, one with a swollen wrist and a purple bruise under her eye, cried out in terror, "It's just like my husband! It's *SANS*. He's got it! He's got it!" She was pointing at the mother and son and looking around at the rest of us.

"Shut up!" shouted the boy's mother, as she struggled to keep him under control, although I was unsure whether she was speaking to the scared woman or the screaming boy.

There was a moment of quiet paralysis in the waiting room, as we all looked at each other. The kid struggling and the mother trying to control him were the only movement. At that moment, a medic came into the waiting room. I suspect the receptionist had gone and found her.

"Come with me, both of you," she said, but she didn't take the child from the mother. As the woman was bundling him out, I saw him sink his little teeth into her arm; she made a noise, a cross between a cry and a gasp, but she didn't let him go.

The waiting room quietened down and from then on, we didn't look each other in the eye. I checked the news online. *People should go home and remain in lockdown... flu-like symptoms... if someone is showing aggressive symptoms, do not approach... armed forces mobilising female personnel.* Twitter was even worse, just panicked stories and clips of violence, but I worked out the basics then, you know, that some men were dying and some were going insane. Just in time, really. When the screams started from behind the double doors, I had a vague idea of what might be about to happen. Loads of doctors were men, as were many nurses, a lot of orderlies, most of security. Whatever this was, it was spreading fast, and I was betting that those medical workers were not immune.

My instinct was to cut and run, go back to the apartment and hunker down, maybe stop by the café for supplies. I had the key, after all.

But Emily. Stupid, thoughtless, gorgeous Emily.

More screams. Others in the waiting room started to stand up. I expect that some of those women, those who had experienced the effects of SANS that very morning, knew what was coming. A few started to hurry towards the exit. Then the double doors burst open and out sprinted a group of terrified women. There was a surge for the exit, everyone climbing over the benches and each other. Some women just stood and watched. I hid behind a drinks machine as the stream of women bolted past, quickly followed by a group of men, yelling and whooping. I thought I recognised our ambulance driver among them – now without his mask, his pale and freckled face twisted into a snarl.

If I'd run home then, so much in my life might have been different.

But I was young. I was in love. So, I can't see any other way it could have gone. I waited until the room was clear and slipped through the double doors and into the madness beyond.

Olivia stopped speaking and gave me a look that said, *let's finish this later*. I understood. These stories, the ones that those who weren't there don't understand, we hold them; we hoard them; we allow ourselves to look at them only a piece at a time. Olivia looked pale in the morning light, her soft face slack with tan smudges under her eyes. You never manage to get enough sleep the first two days to see you through, like your body just refuses to believe you need that much sleep in the afternoon. It always gets better by night four. I tried to picture Olivia younger, thinner maybe, mooning over a girl who didn't love her back.

Light filtered through the high windows and onto the desk of the carers' station. Men began to come out of their dorms and head for the showers. First a bleary-eyed trickle and then a bubbling flood. We had finished our tea and it was nearly morning.

"I stripped the batteries from abandoned cars," I said, after we'd sat there in silence for a while. "In the beginning, I mean. We worked out a way to charge them with wind turbines. It kept everything going for a few years until a grid was established. As a reward for my part in rewiring batteries, spending hours testing and retesting the charges, I was allowed to charge my mobile phone. Not to call anyone, of course – the towers were long dead – but for the photos."

I paused as the memory rolled back through my mind, sitting on my army cot, staring through that little window to the past, the image of two faces squashed together. Adrian's and mine. He'd held the phone at an angle, so my nose was cut off below the frame. And then one of Ryan, his eyes hidden by his fringe, turning away, half smiling, half angry, palm towards me.

"I thought I'd be braver," I said, as I pictured myself casting the smooth, black phone away as if it'd bitten me. "It's too painful to look at them, even now."

Olivia stared at me. "Do you still have it?" she asked. Her voice was even enough, but she was leaning in and there was a flush to her rounded cheeks.

I shrugged. "Yes. I mean, I've never thrown it away."

"And the charger?"

I nodded.

She leaned back in her chair and took a breath, as if to calm herself. Then, in a tone that didn't quite reach nonchalance,

"They'd be worth a fortune on the black market, you know."

"Really?" I replied. "I had no idea."

"Yeah. Clothing allowance, contraband... you could get a ton of chocolate. I probably know someone–"

"Tempting, but I'll keep it for now. I like to have the photos there, even if I find it hard to look at them." As it happens, I hadn't thought about the phone for years. It was still in a box at the back of the wardrobe, yet to be unpacked from when I'd first arrived at this facility. Now, I thought, I might try to look at the photos again, if it still works, that is.

Olivia turned away, but there was a stiffness to her shoulders. "Well, if you change your mind," she said, "let me know."

CHAPTER 5

I love telling stories. When I was a teacher, it was always the best part of my day.

About thirty men were already in the large viewing hall when I arrived. A few stood at the long window and gazed out onto the impressive view of rolling hills, fields and trees. On the horizon, backed by the setting sun, stood a proud line of wind turbines waving back at us, carving at the sunlight with their sweeping blades.

A few years back, we'd secured an industry speaker who came in to talk about the eco-energy network. She explained how the translation of aerodynamic force into the rotation of a generator created our electricity, how this was then stored, and how it was budgeted. The men lost interest after a short time. They lacked a grounding in physics that would've made the discussion meaningful and the speaker, I believe, pitched her talk too high.

When I suggested this afterwards, she replied, a little defensively, "It's the same speech I give to year-nine schoolgirls". I suspect she also resented the men – many do. The facility is by far the biggest draw on energy in the area, dwarfing the needs of the farmers. In fact, due to the proximity of the facility, this whole district has been designated a controlled energy consumption zone – heating, lighting and EV travel are all rationed so that our air filtration systems can run constantly and our water can be properly filtered. We are a bastion of unsustainability – the disposable gloves, the silk for shifts and uniforms, the chemicals for cleaning and the lamination for reading material are all an anathema to a generation raised to sustain, reuse and mend. We are relics in a recovering world.

More men filed in and sat on the seamless plastic sofas. Some lounged, others sat straight and expectant. A few rested their arms on another's shoulder or thigh. Luca sauntered in and there was a rising twitter among those seated. After pausing for a moment and scanning the room, he moved over to Tony, who made a big fuss of shooing away those seated around him by flapping his hands, making room. Luca sat down next to a beaming Tony and shot me his movie star smile. I gave a slight nod. My heart ached for Tony. Luca was friendly and polite with all of his co-residents but I'd never seen him court intimacy. I watched as Tony's hand wandered towards Luca's knee. Luca caught it, laughing, and started a spirited game of thumb war. My mind flicked back to Olivia's story about Emily.

Finally, the room was full. Olivia came in and leaned against the far wall next to the window. She smiled at me and I felt a warm glow. I was glad she was here as I walked to the middle of the room and into a hush. I wanted to impress her.

"Thank you for coming," I said, grinning at the men, catching as many eyes as I could. The art of being a teacher never really leaves you. "Apparently, Olivia has volunteered my storytelling services." They nodded and chattered excitedly, and I basked a little in their keen attention. I then readied myself. I hadn't had much time to think of what I wanted to say, but I'd been saving a story I thought might work – with some adaptations. I took a deep breath. "There once was a boy made of wood." I looked around to see if this would fly. Nobody looked confused or incredulous, so I continued, "His name was Pinocchio." This elicited a few chuckles. The name, it seemed, was ludicrous – but not his being made of wood. "And every time Pinocchio told a lie, his nose grew longer and longer." I did the arm movements for this and was greeted with laughter and applause.

"Who made him?" someone asked.

"A man called Geppetto," I replied. The men always met my stories with a barrage of questions.

"Did he like being made of wood?" asked another.

I thought briefly about this one. "Not really, but he decided to make the best of it – now hush and let me tell you the story." I could see Olivia smiling as she caught my eye. I was glad she was enjoying herself. I felt myself relax into my performance.

My recollection of this classic was sketchy, so I improvised. Pinocchio and his friend, a spider called Jimmy – a cricket would be too hard to describe and they already knew about spiders – went on many adventures for the next thirty minutes or so. Some were scary. Most were funny. He was swallowed by a whale. *What! A fish as big as this room? No way!* He was encouraged to break the rules by a naughty cat – like a tiger, but smaller. No, they don't talk in real life, only in the story. But every time he lied, everyone would know because...? I paused and let them answer me. *His nose would grow, Mary! His nose would grow!*

The men were often told stories such as this in their preps. Stories about loving your fellow man, about respecting authority and playing by the rules. So, they were used to this kind of didactic tale. And although the growing nose elicited the biggest laughs, I felt myself veering away from the preachy nature of the original and exploring its absurdity instead. He said that the grass was blue – more laughter – he said that water was dry. *Dry water, Mary! But that's ridiculous!* I continued when there was a pause in the laughter. "His nose became so long that his spidery friend could climb up almost as high as the moon." I was riffing at this point; what did happen in the actual story? Was there a donkey? A fox, maybe? "Pinocchio, being unable to move due to the weight of his nose, and not enjoying the tickling of the birds and the squirrels who'd made a home in his long nose, saw the error of his ways and started telling the truth." I was running out of ideas, so I decided to bring it to a quick close. "When his nose was eventually the right size once more, he came home and went to sleep."

"What happened next? Tell us a bit more, Mary?" cried Tony in a voice that reflected the feeling of the rest of the group.

"That's the end, I'm afraid." I was getting tired. Despite the men's excitement, this whole affair had turned into a bit of a shambles – a good-natured spot of anarchy – but even so, I was now a little embarrassed that Olivia had been listening and I was wishing I'd done a bit more preparation.

A long groan greeted my admission

"He could fight a tiger if he's made of wood – he can't get hurt!" suggested one of the older men. Many replies of *Yes! A tiger! Cool! Great!*

"He could live on the moon," shouted another. "He wouldn't need air."

This was met by a wave of eagerness. *Yes! Can he go to the moon, Mary? The moon!*

Then Luca piped up, and of course, everyone listened. "I know! I know! When he woke up, he wasn't made of wood anymore – he was real."

I felt a shiver suddenly run down my spine. It was the use of the word "real" that made me pause, so close to the story I remembered. "Have you read this story, Luca?" I asked. "Or been told it before?"

He shook his head. "It just seemed like a sensible ending. Like, he didn't want to be made of wood, and then he learned not to lie, and then his reward would be that he could be real. If that's what he really wanted."

There was some mumbling in the room as the men considered Luca's comment.

"Why would he want to be real?" asked the older man who'd spoken before. "Then he wouldn't be able to fight a tiger *or* go to the moon – in fact, he might be stuck in here with us. If he's made of wood, he could at least go *outside*."

He pointed towards the viewing area and the last few rays of sunshine dipping below the horizon.

It was meant as a joke, but the laughter in the room drained away.

"If I was wooden, could I go outside?" This from one of the youngest residents, a redhead named Curtis. I don't think I'd ever heard him speak before, and definitely not in front of so many.

I caught Olivia's eye again, and her gaze was blank. She turned to face the room, raising her voice. "I think we all owe Mary a big round of applause for such an exciting story," she said, beginning to clap. The men joined in, but it was a hesitant and sporadic attempt.

"Mary," said Luca in a quiet but firm tone when the clapping stopped, "would you tell us a story about..." he swallowed, his Adam's apple bobbing on his neck, "about what it was like before the caterpillars?"

There was an audible gasp. It went against their education at the prep houses to even ask me this. Yet no one challenged Luca's request. The men murmured to each other for a moment, then all eyes were on me. I felt their interest like sharp beams of light. "I'm sorry, Luca, you know I can't."

There was a soft groan from the men, petering out into silence.

I looked to Olivia for support, but she was staring at the floor, her face stony, angry even.

"Both Olivia and I could get into trouble, and it wouldn't be fair to you. That's why it's so important, what they teach you at the prep houses; it's your duty to live in the world as it is, not the world as you wish it to be. If ward sister Daisy heard that I'd−"

"I'll tell you." Olivia's voice cut through my flustered excuses and I fell silent. I didn't know what to do. Her expression was cool and determined, her full lips drawn into a grim line. "Sylvan, stand by the door. Cough loudly if anyone comes."

Her voice was that of a woman used to giving orders. A blonde man, slim, about thirty, got to his feet, positioning himself by the door of the hall with a view of the corridor from both directions.

She turned to the men. The lighting, which had come on sometime in the last few minutes, illuminated the soft sagging in her face. I noticed a light sheen of sweat on her brow, despite the coolness of the air.

I remembered what Daisy had said, that Olivia was trouble. I was tempted to leave, quietly disperse the men, claiming it was nearly grooming time, perhaps speak to Olivia alone about the risks she was taking, with the men's peace of mind and with her own employment. This had gone too far. "Olivia, perhaps if we just–" I began.

"What would you like to know?" she asked a sea of upturned faces, ignoring my mumbled aside.

Silence: no one dared to speak and for a moment, I thought we'd gotten away with it. But then Luca slid up his hand. "What... what did men do before? How did they spend their time?"

Olivia nodded and drew a deep breath. "They did everything that women did. They farmed, they built things, they healed people and they kept the peace."

Another voice called out, "What does it mean to keep the peace?"

The questions came thick and fast after that.

Two hours later, when we had finally got the men to bed, mumbling and whispering between themselves, I finally got Olivia on her own. We walked back to the carers' station together, and I found myself fizzing with anger. "They'll never keep it between themselves. What were you thinking? If this gets back to Daisy, we'll be in for it. She'll accuse us of soliciting – take away our licence. We could be sent away."

"Fuck Daisy," Olivia replied in a flat tone. "You know it's wrong, keeping them ignorant of the past. It's old-fashioned *tyranny.*"

"What do you suggest? We tell them how they used to be masters of their universe, run everything, control the world – would that help them, stuck in here? Would that help any of us?"

She looked like she wanted to argue some more but instead she took a deep breath and said, "Look. You're not working Saturday, right?"

I paused, confused by the change in tack. "No," I replied cautiously, "but I don't see what that has to do with this mess."

"If you meet me at the car depot at seven, I'll show you something that might change your point of view."

I stared at her. "Where? And why do you think I'd risk my job? If you just tell me, then I can–"

"Please, just trust me. I know you think I'm crazy but I swear, if, after Saturday, you want nothing more to do with me, I'll understand." Her soft hand reached for my wrist and gave it a small squeeze. "I'll have you back by eleven, I promise." She was smiling, but there was a grave urgency in her eyes, almost desperation.

We'd reached the carers' station by then and I sat down at the white plastic desk. "I'll think about it," I said sullenly.

She looked relieved, like I'd agreed, which annoyed me.

"Okay. Let me know," she replied. Then she added, "I've got to go and sort out some paperwork. I won't be long", before leaving in the direction of the Warden's offices.

Alone at the carers' station, I sat and pondered the events of the afternoon. I heard low talking from the dorms but when I went to investigate, the men pretended to be asleep. Olivia returned eventually but would not be drawn on the mystery outing. She just kept telling me that if I came as agreed, then everything would be clearer. In the end, I stopped asking and our shift settled into an uneasy quiet.

I was hoping she'd finish her story. That she'd tell me what happened to her and Emily at the hospital. But she was cool with me. I'd almost given up hope and had consigned myself to a slow and claustrophobic six hours, staring at the wall before Olivia finally spoke. "When did you first see one, Mary? Up close?"

I turned to face her and her expression was blank, unreadable.

"What do you mean?"

"A manic: when did you first see a man turn?"

I closed my eyes and didn't speak for a long time.

CHAPTER 6
Mary – then

The Prime Minister was dead by this point, although we didn't know it then. When Claire and I got to the auditorium, only a handful of teenagers remained. Most of the teachers had gone. The Principal was on the phone trying to contact parents.

A sixth-form student, Eliza Bradshaw, called out, "It's starting!"

We all huddled around her phone. The Secretary for Health, Laura Gilmartin, took to the podium. The lighting was odd, harsher than usual, and the picture was shaky as if it were being filmed on a handheld device rather than with TV cameras. The secretary was holding a piece of paper from which she read without looking up.

"Firstly, apologies. The Prime Minister is unable to give this address. He is currently undergoing medical treatment. I'm sure you will join me in wishing him a quick recovery." She paused and looked to her side, at someone who was currently out of view. Whoever it was said something, and the Health Secretary closed her eyes for a moment, then looked back to her notes and carried on speaking; "The UK and, indeed, the world, is facing a biological threat today and this government has made a request to the King that the UK enter into a state of emergency, to which he has acceded. We have convened an emergency committee, to deal with the threat and we are keeping in constant contact with the emergency committee at the World Health Organisation regarding putting in place a cohesive and unified response. All military leave has been cancelled and police and medical staff have received instructions on where and how they should assemble." She paused and took a sip of water from a glass on the podium, then continued to read. "We cannot rule out the involvement of terrorist organisations; however, at this time, it does not seem likely that this is an act of aggression, despite a number of dissident groups claiming responsibility. The infrastructure required to develop and coordinate such an attack, and the sophistication of the toxins involved suggest that, if this were a hostile undertaking, it would need to be from a force with substantial resources." She looked up from the page and spoke directly into the camera, "If any new information suggests that this was an act of aggression by a foreign power, rest assured that our response will be swift and proportional. This biological event may prove a significant hazard in the short term, but be confident that, with the continuing support of our excellent public services and of you, the people of Great Britain and Northern Ireland, we will contain it."

Did I believe her? I wanted to, and at that moment, despite her trembling hands and the way her eyes kept flitting sideways, her words were enough to make me feel a tiny bit better. There was a plan, a response. Things would go back to normal; it might be inconvenient for a while, but we would get through it – we had before.

"I am going to hand over to Professor Sangeeta Desai, a virologist and a member of the environmental hazards committee, who will explain what we know so far and give advice on how to stay safe in the coming days."

The Health Secretary took her notes and climbed down from the podium. From her left rose a woman in her early thirties with bobbed black hair and large, square glasses. She tucked her hair behind her ears before she began, "Thank you, Health Secretary." Her voice was firmer than that of the previous speaker and she did not seem to be using notes. She paused for a moment. Again, her eyes flicked to the side and the camera seemed to flinch slightly, unsure whether to track to the side or remain on the speaker. She took a deep breath before beginning to speak, "Infection by the toxin includes allergy or flu-like symptoms, especially sneezing, followed some hours later by behavioural changes, including violence towards those in contact with the infected. To date, those who have reported symptoms have all been male – biologically speaking."

Claire slid her hand through the crook of my arm. I linked fingers with her.

"Initial figures suggest that approximately fifty per cent of cases do not result in SANS, but instead..." She paused again, this time for longer, and she could not seem to look directly into the camera. She hooked her hair behind her ears again and stared down at the podium. "... instead, about fifty percent of the cases result in unexplained acute heart and respiratory failure. So far, cases that have followed this prognosis have all proved fatal." Her voice faltered on the last word. Claire squeezed my hand.

"Fifty per cent," I whispered. "Half."

Eliza was being shouted at and beckoned by her father. He came over. I'd spoken to Mr Bradshaw at parent's evening, as well as one time when Eliza had received a D on her English essay. He was a belligerent man, hostile. "For god's sake, Eliza, come on, don't you dare keep me waiting. I had to leave work for this." His face was red, his voice thick and phlegmy.

"Sorry, Dad," Eliza stuttered and dropped her phone into her bag. "Bye, guys."

He held her arm and led her out of the hall.

The world started to shift and nausea washed over me. "I need to sit down."

Claire led me across the dusty auditorium to a couple of chairs at the end of the room. "Are you going to be sick?"

"I don't think so," I replied. It had been like this for months when I'd been pregnant with Ryan. I tried not to think about how it would feel to be with child throughout a pandemic, or whatever this was. I took a gulp of air and sat down. "We should carry on watching the broadcast, they might say something important."

Claire fumbled with her phone, eventually bringing up the BBC website, and we carried on listening. It was a different person now, a man from the defence department. In any case, his words kept darting around like startled fish. *Keep out of densely populated areas... violence inflicted on women a particular threat... woodland and damp spaces...* But it was the doctor's words, *fifty per cent*, that thumped around in my head like trainers in a tumble dryer: fifty-per-cent, one-in-two, one-in-two, one-in-two.

"Come home with me," I said to Claire as we were walking to the car park.

"No, but thanks, sweetheart. I'm going to go to my dad's house."

I was surprised. I guess sometimes you just want to be with family, even if that family hasn't spoken to you in four years. Even if he considers you an affront to nature. "What if... what if he's infected?" I asked.

The look on her face was my own fear reflected back at me. "I don't know, I just... What about Adrian? And Ryan? What about me? I don't expect the toxin gives a shit about how I identify."

I didn't know what to say. What was the use of being safe from a disease that could rip away everything I cared about? We hugged goodbye. She held me tightly, and I could feel her shaking as she promised to call later. I wiped the tears from my face as I got into my car. *Just get home,* I thought to myself. *Regroup, make a plan, keep them safe.*

The roads were busy. There was a huge queue at the petrol station – twenty or more cars tailing up onto the pavement.

Looking at my fuel gauge, I was half full. Well, it would have to do, whatever happened.

The supermarket was also manic – crowds of people wandering the car parks laden with bottles of water, teetering towers of packets and tins. Instead, I drove past and pulled up onto the grassy verge of our local shop, planning to get a few essentials, just until it all blew over. I nearly got out of the car but as I was easing myself from the driver's side, some kind of commotion started just outside the shop door and I sat back down.

A couple of younger men snatched bags from a middle-aged woman's trolley and started running away. An older man in his sixties, her husband perhaps, grabbed hold of one of the young men and began shaking him with surprising savagery. However, it wasn't so much the violence with which he was gripping the boy, it was his gaze. There was a confusion in his eyes, even as he continued to shake him. The boy held on to the man's arms, trying to gain purchase, but the man was heavyset and would not ease up.

The woman was crying and trying to pull her husband off, but the older man pushed the boy to the floor. He smashed the teenager's head against the stone walkway.

There was a knot of people just inside the store, unable to leave, bobbing about, unsure of what to do. The boy begged for his life. He clawed at the man's face in desperation. As the man dragged the kid upright and held him against the shop door, I noticed with a kind of detached horror that the boy was losing consciousness and his defensive blows had weakened. The people inside backed away as a tide of blood ran in rivulets down the glass from the wound in the boy's head, enveloping a faded advert of a blonde girl holding an ice cream. The boy hung limp, but that didn't stop the man from hefting a barrage of meaty punches into his stomach.

Finally, he let go and the boy fell to the street like a stringless puppet.

The man turned, panting, scanning. He caught my eyes watching him through the window screen and stilled. I thought for a moment that he said something to me, not that I could hear, but actually it seemed that he was talking to himself. He shook his head as if to clear it and stared right at me again. I scrambled for the button to lock the car, finding it and pressing it twice accidentally. I had to pressed it a third time as he strode over to me, teeth bared, shirt covered in the teenager's blood.

His wife followed, "Jack – what's happening?"

A look of shock was stamped on her powdered features. His eyes broke with mine as he turned to her and, with both hands, grabbed her throat and began choking the life out of her. Her brightly painted nails clawed at him to stop but he squeezed her neck and looked directly into her eyes.

"You bitch, you fucking bitch!" he bellowed, still squeezing her neck as spittle ran down his chin. "Always on my case, always whining," he screamed into her purpling face.

I fumbled for my phone in my bag, fighting against the shock that held me frozen, but when I dialled 999 I was greeted with the quick-fire beeping of the engaged tone. From within the shop came a terrified shrieking and out of the blood-stained door rushed a group of people; men and women, some still clutching their shopping to their chests.

They streamed around the man strangling his wife without even giving him a glance. I started the engine and began to pull forwards but immediately hit the brakes. A tattooed young woman in a yellow vest and jean shorts stood, arms spread, in front of my car. The large carton of milk she'd been carrying slipped from her hand and thumped onto the bonnet, breaking open and glugging out its contents in a thick pool. She stared at me through the milk splattered windshield – a white rolling-eyed gaze of fear – then mouthed the words, "Help me!"

I paused, my finger hovering over the lock button, but she was already looking back over her shoulder.

She sprang off the car and ran out onto the road, into the

beeping traffic. Two men, coming from the direction of the shop, ran past: one in a white shirt, the other in the bright orange t-shirt of a shop worker.

They bore down on her and dragged her into an overgrown verge.

Confused, my mind told me that she'd stolen something – the milk perhaps – and that the men were going to bring her back to the store to wait for the police. But nobody reappeared. *Why haven't they come back?* I thought. And then another, darker voice pierced my thoughts. *This is real. Move!*

I didn't. Instead, I tried 999 again, my fingers shaking, making it hard to hit the numbers. This time I got through to an automated message. *Unavailable… high demand… only the highest priority emergencies… stay on the line…* I hung up.

Should I have done something more? Left my car? Beeped the horn? Screamed "rape"? Or was it "fire" I was supposed to scream to get attention? The *me* of two hours ago might have done all those things. But we all know now that there was nothing I could have done, that I would have been attacked too, and killed. We've all shared our private disquisitions and wept in therapy for each other and for ourselves. But in the months and years that followed, despite the many moments of horror, it's that rolling-eyed look of fear in the young woman's eyes to which my mind returns, that and the dead crow.

I pulled away. Flicking on the wipers only succeeded in smearing the white splashes of milk into pale arcs, but three squirts of screen wash cleared it enough to see. I checked my wing mirrors and adjusted my priorities. We would make do with what we had at home.

The journey home was just stop-start traffic. I sat in the driver's seat and checked the locks every few minutes, wondering when the hammering panic in my chest would cease. Every beeped horn or slammed car door made me jump, turn, gasp. There was still milk on the bonnet and when the car was moving, the air pushed thin tendrils of it back towards the cab.

She probably got away.

About two miles from home, when the traffic was stationary, a woman suddenly bolted from the rear passenger side of a taxicab up ahead and started running. No one got out and followed her. The driver she'd been with sat hunched at the wheel. As the traffic eventually lurched on, crawling its way in an agonisingly slow procession along the main bypass, we had to go up onto the verge to get around that taxi and its motionless driver. Passing it, I kept my eyes fixed in front of me.

After two hours, I eventually pulled up in our driveway alongside Adrian's car. I'd spent the last half hour wondering what would greet me when I got there. I wanted to hold my son and check he was whole. I wanted to tell him, with conviction, that this would be over soon. I wanted my husband to wrap me in his arms and tell me that he had a plan.

Instead, I sat in the driveway staring at the patches of drying milk on the bonnet and I considered the bellboy who massacred his family and the old man at the store with his hands around his wife's neck.

I considered driving away.

Then the door opened and there stood Adrian. At least, the figure in the doorway was about Adrian's size and build, but it was draped in at least four layers of clothes – it was wearing a balaclava, a face mask and a pair of my sunglasses and it was beckoning to me frantically. Doc was barking from the porch.

I ran to the door, which was slammed shut behind me, and I was ushered straight upstairs to the bathroom. The figure, who I was fairly sure was my husband, pointed to the shower and then to a bottle of bleach and a pile of rags on the floor.

I nodded. "Ryan?" I asked.

The covered figure made a gloved thumbs-up sign and then pointed downstairs.

"Okay, shall I see you down there in a minute?"

Adrian paused as if he were considering something and then shook his head. Then he took off the mask, balaclava, and glasses. "I need to shower too, and we both need to change our clothes."

My eyes glazed with tears and a tight knot fixed itself in my throat. "Oh god, baby, it's so good to see you."

On instinct I started to go to him, like I had most days for over a decade, but he backed up and smiled. "I know I'm irresistible," he said, "but you need to shower first."

I got in and the water felt amazing. I scrubbed every part of myself and washed my hair twice. Then Adrian joined me, and we just stood there, holding each other for a while, letting the water stream over us. I told him about the journey home, about the man strangling his wife, about the girl and the milk.

When we got out, Adrian dug into the back of the airing cupboard for some clean towels.

Looking at him in just a towel, shuffling past the pile of discarded clothes on the floor and being so careful not to touch them, I felt a hard weight of responsibility. I knew that I might have to go back out there at some point, to get supplies or help or information. Was he considering what would happen if he became infected with whatever this was? He must have been.

We dressed in fresh clothes and headed downstairs. Ryan was in the living room, sprawled on the sofa. He had on jeans and a long-sleeved top, despite the heat.

I sat down next to him and drew him into a hug. For a moment, he let me, before he pulled away. "Don't. It's too hot," he said, reaching for his phone and scrolling with his thumb. "Have you seen the video on YouTube? The one of Waterloo Station?"

I shook my head. "Why? What's happening?"

Ryan flicked on the TV. The newsreader was speaking as fragments of phone footage were being shown and a warning was displayed at the bottom of the screen:

Caution: unedited footage – contains extremely distressing scenes…

The newsreader was telling us that a crowd of women, thought to number in the hundreds, had barricaded themselves into the Marks and Spencer's at Waterloo as wide-scale violence had been reported in the station.

These days, of course, everyone knows what happened at Waterloo. We sing songs, list names, we teach the children the story of what those shaking mobile phones captured. Women, fighting with bottles or bits of broken shelving or with their teeth, packed in together as wave after wave of the infected tore at them, dragging them down. How a group of older women pushed six girls into a tiny back room and barricaded the door, turning to face down hordes of the infected. The Waterloo Six, as they became known when they finally escaped – the closest thing the new world had to celebrities.

But there, watching it for the first time, we couldn't believe what we were seeing. I felt like I should switch it off to protect Ryan, but I couldn't tear my eyes away. It was Adrian who reached over and flicked it off. I looked at Ryan and then at Adrian.

"It's going to be okay," I said.

Ryan shrugged, picked up his phone and started scrolling again. I could see that he was trying to pretend he hadn't been affected by what he'd just seen. Then suddenly, he flung his phone onto the floor as if it had bitten him.

"What happened?" said Adrian, moving to pick up the phone. He looked at it and paled. "Jesus!" He slammed it face down on the coffee table.

"What is it?"

Adrian was pacing up and down. "It was a… a girl, with her… she'd been cut. No! Don't look at it, Mary!"

But it was too late. I'd flipped over the phone and there, on Instagram, was a girl, seventeen or so, lying on a pale flagged kitchen floor. Her throat had been cut. The knife, a bread knife, was in the frame, lying beside her neck, its jagged tip pointing at the yawning gash as if to say *look what I did!* Blood surrounded her torso, in darkly lewd contrast to the stone floor. Her eyes were open, the eyes of a doll, and around her curly brown hair was a scramble of bloody trainer-prints.

Ryan stood up; he held a shaking hand to his mouth. "It's Josh's sister," he mumbled through his fingers.

Doc was barking and running from room to room. I jumped up and this time Ryan did let me hold him – tightly and for a long time. As we stood there, he spoke into my shoulder. "I was just talking to him an hour ago. He seemed fine. I thought he was fine."

"It's okay," I whispered back. "It's okay. Maybe it wasn't him."

But how could this be fine? I'd known Josh for years; he'd been over for sleepovers, for God's sake, what if it really had been him!

And then Ryan sneezed. He looked at me with terror in his eyes. "Mum?"

I held him by his upper arms and looked straight into his eyes. My voice was firm, the one I normally used for reprimanding a student. "It's just a sneeze." I needed it to be true. I couldn't face the notion that it was anything other than an ordinary reaction to dust. "We all sneeze, every day." I was convincing because at that moment, I was convinced. Adrian came over and held us both, his strong, safe arms gripping us and telling us things were going to be okay, kissing the tops of our heads in turn. Then he left the room.

When he returned, Ryan was sitting at the breakfast bar, face pale, head low; the dog was curled up at his feet. By unspoken agreement, we'd left his phone face down in the other room. The TV was still on but muted. I was checking out what we had in the fridge, mentally ordering it by use-by date. Adrian slapped down one length of cord and some cable ties onto the table.

"What are you planning to do?" I asked, although I had a

fairly good idea. I was horrified by the idea of tying up my family, but the image of that poor girl, slaughtered in her own home – I wasn't going to argue.

"It's the only thing I can think of."

"Does that mean me too?" asked Ryan, eyeing the cable ties.

"I think so. If Josh... I mean, yeah. It's just a precaution."

Ryan nodded. "Okay," he said in a small voice. "I don't mind."

He was a good kid.

CHAPTER 7

I jumped when Olivia touched my arm. I was still right there, in my old house with my husband and my son, thinking it was going to be fine, thinking I just had to play by the rules and everyone would survive.

"It's okay," she said when I turned to her. She must have seen the pain in my face. "Here." She offered me a silk hankie.

I hadn't even realised I was crying. I dabbed my face and the salty tears bled into the cloth.

"We all carry them," she continued, "these stories – those who were there. Sometimes I see the memories like the moths' toxic threads, hiding in seams and between the pages of books or floating in the air. You're okay until you come across one and then it infects everything."

I nodded. "I should try to forget."

Olivia squeezed my hand. "No. We keep them alive, women like us."

We sat there quietly for a few moments and watched the sun creeping in through the high windows.

"Will you come with me on Saturday?"

I clutched the silk hankie and didn't speak.

"I swear, what I have to show you – it's important. You're one of the few women left who might understand."

I swallowed and noticed my throat was raw from the talking and the crying. But beneath the weariness, I felt a warmth I hadn't felt in years. The comfort of sharing pain. "I'll come," I said and handed the hankie back to Olivia.

She didn't respond directly to my decision; instead, she just patted my hand and nodded. "I'll go get us some tea," she said and walked off in the direction of the kitchenette.

I was left on my own in the carers' station to wonder what Saturday would bring.

CHAPTER 8

I miss cars. Imagine just getting up and going where you want to go – three miles or three hundred. I miss singing along to Queen or Katy Perry and thinking about what to cook for tea or rehearsing my lessons for the day.

Cars themselves were not the issue, not at first, at least. There were plenty of them lying around after the first wave – too many, in fact, as they had to be laboriously pushed from the roads. The cars were usually packed: suitcases, holdalls, small *Hello Kitty* backpacks stuffed with toys. Things that were left behind, one assumes, when a husband, father or brother in the car abandoned all reason.

I couldn't do physical work at that point, not in my condition, so I was given an "inside" job. I sorted through the items that were brought back. Later, as I'd told Olivia, I stripped and rewired batteries, but through that first bleak autumn, I was waist-deep in a jumble of other people's possessions in a massive, draughty Amazon warehouse that became one of the five major store hubs facilitating the southern counties. I catalogued everything from sweatpants to sandwich makers. They even brought me a canoe once. I entered everything into an A4 lined notepad before the other women trundled off, deep into the dark, cavernous building, to shelve their cargo under designated sections named "clothing", "household" or "sporting equipment". It was a good job, orderly and soothing, as long as I didn't start wondering about who owned the little *Hello Kitty* backpacks.

So no, it wasn't the lack of cars that was the problem.

Nor was it our lack of mechanical know-how. We still had women who'd been engineers before – not many, nowhere near enough – and those that survived the infestation travelled the Union, teaching others as best they could. And we had books. No, it was petrol – drilling for it, refining it – and then, later, the issue of resurfacing the crumbling roads themselves. We couldn't mine anything. No oil, metals, minerals, salts, clay. Instead, we became a hive of menders and patchers. Recycling wasn't just a lifestyle choice for when it suited, it was our way of survival. Everything was repurposed, stripped and stored. Even now, in schools all across the country, girls begin and end their day by standing in unison to recite the three pillars of society: sorority, maternity and *thrift*.

Unsurprisingly, a lowly carer such as I was not entitled to a private car.

I could have booked out a community car from the depot, but instead I preferred the electrobus. It was a warm June afternoon and as I stood in the shade of the little wooden bus shelter, the gentle scent of wild garlic blended deliciously with the tang of cut grass. There was very little traffic on the road, so I was able to enjoy the sounds of the hedgerows – whistling finches, robins chirping, the caw of a jay... Nothing bigger than a jay, though, as the moths had poisoned all predators generations ago.

Two fat, brown moths fluttered into view and danced around each other in the breezeless air just outside the shelter.

"It'll be the Eclipse soon." Standing in the shelter with me was a young woman, richly tanned with waist-length chestnut-coloured hair, holding a sleeping baby in her arms. I could just see its head – her head – poking out from the woman's arms and sporting a round, purple cap. When the moths came a little too near, the young woman flapped at them to keep them away. I smiled, as you do, at mothers with young babies. She smiled back, jigging side to side as her long skirt brushed her brown calves.

"Are you getting much sleep?" I asked, inclining my head to the baby.

She rolled her eyes and smiled. "Two hours at a time, three on a good night."

I clucked in sympathy. "Hang in there. Have you tried putting a handful of dried catnip into her bath?" I'd heard some of the carers talk about catnip for their own children. I, of course, had used great globs of Calpol with Ryan. My mother, Polish to her bones, had pacified me with shots of vodka, so she'd said.

I nearly added that my son started to sleep through at about five months – but I stopped myself. This young woman, glowing with new life, chattering to me like a blackbird, would not know how to react to the bizarre notion of raising a son. It would have been the conversational equivalent of grabbing her baby from her and giving it a quick shake. I could've lied, altered the pronouns, but it would feel like a betrayal. And for what? I kept quiet and let her talk about the advantages of lavender over catnip; how butter rations were finally being increased, which was helping her milk supply; and how she was taking her daughter to town to visit her aunt who was an agricultural consultant because they, the young mother and her wife, had permission to expand their freeholding.

At her last comment, her voice lowered slightly, and she looked away towards some distant fields. The change was subtle, almost imperceptible but suddenly a thought occurred to me that when the government encouraged women to *Contribute*, that is to say, to bear a son, one of the things on offer was more land. With the advancement of the Assisted Insemination Programme, Contributors could now opt to be implanted with twins – a boy and a girl – one to keep and one to offer up to the state. A buy-one-get-one-free arrangement, if you will. Women usually never even acknowledged the boy twin they had to leave at the hospital, tucked up in his hermetically sealed incubator and off to a motherless life of confinement.

The woman was off again, her voice normal, talking about the different growing cycles of asparagus and beans. As she hitched the baby higher onto her chest, her shirt rode up revealing a softly deflated belly and I found myself wondering, with some bitterness, how many children that belly had been home to this past year.

She gave a small sad smile as she saw me looking, misunderstanding my gaze, and cupped the soft flesh with her free hand. "I really miss... her being here," she said.

I noted the catch in her voice. Did she nearly say *them*?

She hitched the child to her other arm. "I think it's the most important job in the world, don't you? Growing life? Carrying the changes in your body with you forever? It's such a gift."

I remember trying to lose my baby weight. Cutting carbs and attending boot camp fitness sessions in the local park, pushing Ryan's buggy on long walks up and down hills. I remembered the growing dismay when I realised that my flat teenage stomach was never going to come back completely, that there would be a fleshy flap there forever, something to hide or work around, dictating which dresses I could buy and which bikinis I could get away with. Even now, as my old skin hangs in rolls like soft dough off my limbs, I mourn my youthful midriff.

The woman was looking at me expectantly, and I realised that she'd asked me a question.

"What was that?" I asked.

"I'm sorry. I asked you where you were heading?"

"Oh, Elmwood House," I said, absentmindedly. I was still thinking about Ryan. What I should have said in answer to the woman's question was that I was going to the local government office to collect a permit, or shop for art supplies, or attend a talk at the library. I should have allowed her to go about her day, having collected a nice little story about the sweet old lady she'd met at the bus stop.

She frowned whilst she was rummaging through her large tote bag. "I thought that was a sire house." She pulled out a cloth and dabbed at some dribble on the baby's chin. "Are you a doctor?"

Sire house. I sighed and looked up and down the road before muttering, "No. I'm visiting someone."

She stilled for a moment, the cloth still clutched in one hand, the chubby baby squinting up at her, clutching its little fists. I watched my words sink in, watched her blush and clutch her child tighter as she started to squirm. To give her credit, I think she spent a few moments searching for the right thing to say, digging around in her mind like she had done in her tote a minute earlier, but after a fat pause, it became clear that her life to this point had not equipped her with any appropriate response.

"I need to feed her," she said, finally. She unbuttoned her shirt with one slightly shaking hand and awkwardly shucked it off whilst keeping hold of the baby, then pressed the infant to her breast, keeping her eyes averted from mine. As the child latched, I was dismayed to feel my own breasts ache. I looked away from the half-naked, breastfeeding woman out of habit.

The child continued to suck greedily at the woman, who swayed in the warm June air. She avoided looking in my direction and threw frequent, pensive glances down the road in the direction from which the bus would appear. When the adapted EV bus did arrive, a reclaimed single decker, patched up with rusted panels and fitted with off-road wheels, I got on first and sat near the front. The woman alighted and glided down the central aisle of the bus, still feeding, as those on board nodded and smiled warmly.

She made sure to sit as far away from me as the confines of the bus would allow.

Elmwood House is similar in appearance to the older style of the facilities, just without the need for filtered air and sterile surfaces. The patients are housed in a repurposed hotel, four stories high and painted industrial grey. Close to the main road, its shape and location suggest that it was once a *Travelodge*. Every time I'm there, I fancy that I can still see a faint trace of the budget chain's logo beneath the paint on the balustrade above the entrance. The men here, however, are not allowed the freedoms of the men in the facilities.

One of the employees at Elmwood, April, once told me that there were about one hundred and sixty patients here and that there were another two hundred such sanatoriums across the country. There used to be more, nearly six hundred, but most of the men from before are dead now. I estimate that if you add together the sanatoriums, the preps and the facilities, that there must be about thirty thousand men in England – out of a population of roughly twenty-four million. Other countries are not doing so well. We've heard little from the US or China for decades. In the beginning, there were rumours that the American Government, including the President, had survived and were holed up in a network of underground bunkers with their families. But as the months and years went by, and no one heard from them, it was assumed that they perished somehow too. That, or they're still down there, living off army rations and filtered water, and waiting for the air to clear and the moths to move aside.

In the first few weeks, in a desperate attempt to rid themselves of the moths, the President of France, presumably from his own underground bunker, ordered that all fields, forests and heathland in France be burned to the ground. It was a particularly dry, hot summer and the raging fires quickly consumed the agricultural heart of the country and, as there was no way of controlling the fires once they started, many of the villages and towns as well. Here in England, there were rumours that the smell of smoke could be detected as far away as Canterbury.

It didn't work, of course, it just made large parts of France an uninhabitable wasteland. French women huddled in cities

– Paris, Toulouse, Marseille – but dysentery, typhus, attacks from infected men and, eventually, starvation decimated the population. The men died too, those not cared for. Those infected men who didn't die immediately, who became manics all around the world, soon succumbed to dehydration, starvation or acts of self-inflicted violence. Very few other countries managed to set up facilities to care for the manics, as they became known, or to adequately protect their newborn sons. These days, we sometimes hear reports from the trickle of refugees making it to our shore – small tribes of women scavenging, hunting or working smallholdings as their numbers dwindle. It's a story of prolonged global contraction.

Australia did better than most, so I hear anyway. It seems they used the infected men as sires, as we did. Their early investment in solar power and agriculture paid dividends. Their male population could be as big as ours, even bigger perhaps. I've even heard that some uninfected men are able to work in purpose-built factories and farms over there.

The strip of garden around the hotel showed some evidence of being tended. A few climbing roses bobbed from their walled bindings and a scrappy buddleia bowed its purple blooms near the entrance. There were some men working on a flowerbed a little further down. They barely noticed me. One kneeling man, possibly in his mid-forties, although it's hard to tell, as they generally look much older than they are, turned from the hibiscus he was working on and fixed me with a bovine stare, suggesting heavy sedation. I tried for a moment to see what he might have been, in a world where the air had been safe for him to breathe. Groomed and good-looking, in a well-cut suit for work, perhaps, or in a white polo shirt and shorts ready to play squash on a Sunday. Somebody's husband and father. An uncle taking his nephews for a kick-about in the park.

The young carer standing over him, uniformed in a cream jumpsuit, gave me a quick nod of welcome. Her hand never left the plastic gun-shaped device at her side.

Inside the small hallway, which smelled of vegetable soup, I was greeted by another nurse, tall, all elbows and cheekbones, dressed in a cream jumpsuit, plastic gun on her hip too. "Hi Mary, Gale," she said by way of an introduction, holding out her hand.

"Where's April?" I asked as I emptied my pocket onto a nearby Formica desk. "She usually works on Thursdays."

"Yes," she motioned me to step forward onto a square secured in gaffer tape to the grubby blue carpet. "Yes, she did, but April was redeployed a week ago to a sanatorium in Winchester." She was older than April, this new Gale person, in her late twenties. She had a soft, low voice, was lean and stood a whole head taller than me, I noticed as we stood facing each other for my pat-down.

"I thought she wasn't due to move on until December," I said, raising my arms out to my sides.

"Was she?" she said, running her hands along my arms and looking straight into my eyes. "She'd left by the time I got the posting. A promotion, I think."

I found it hard to look directly into her gaze. Her pat-down was a lot firmer than April's had been. I looked upwards, towards the ceiling, as she ran her palms over my torso and chest. "How has he been?"

"Great, great, we're getting on famously. I'll take you to him in a sec." Then she bent down on one knee and rubbed down the inside of my left thigh through the skirt. "I'm sorry about all this, Mary, but I have to do it. I don't want to get into trouble on my third day."

"It's fine Gale, I know the drill." I looked down at her dark, curly hair as she felt down the other leg. My tone had been a little sharper than I intended, annoyed that I hadn't been forewarned that they'd be sending April away. I'd learned over many years that the right carer – calm, patient, gentle – could vastly improve a man's quality of life: fewer episodes, reduced need for medication. April had been one of the good ones.

Gale stood and picked up my facility key card and my identity card from the desk. "Is this all you have with you?"

I nodded.

"Would you sign in here?" She gave me a clipboard with a pen attached to the clip by a piece of string. I signed next to Ms M Langham. Mine was one of only three names on the visitor list; the other two had "Dr" instead of "Ms" before their surnames.

I buckled the leather belt Gale handed me around my waist, running my fingers over the alarm button, the key fob and the benzo gun.

I've never had to use the gun myself. but in an orientation many years ago I was told that it delivers the precise dose of a drug that would render a man unconscious within a few minutes and weaken him almost immediately. It's not like the guns from before the change, as you have to be close enough to actually push it onto his skin. Also, it's no longer any of the benzodiazepines delivered by the tiny needle – they've synthesized more advanced drugs over the past few decades – but the name stuck.

Gale gave me the usual list of dos and don'ts and I listened patiently, although I could've repeated it back verbatim if required. They were all young, these women – the sanatorium training programme is only open to those born well after the infestation. The men here, and others like them in sanatoriums across the country, are studied, monitored and cared for by eager, fresh-faced twenty-somethings on work placements, often hoping that their posting here will lead to a coveted place in a medical degree programme. April, I knew, had been planning to do research into the effects of new ketamine derivatives on depression in SANS patients after she'd finished her four-year placement.

Gale guided me towards his room rather than to the visitor centre, which wasn't a good sign.

"What's his week been like?" I asked as we walked down the dingy corridor. There were bars on all the doors and

windows. A pane of glass in the fire door at the end of the
corridor had been smashed and was boarded up with wooden
planks, stopping more light from filtering in. There was also a
strong chemical smell, one that took me back to a place I didn't
want to remember. That choking acrid smell of the infected.

"Good," she replied, leading me up a narrow staircase and
slowing her pace to allow me to keep up. "He had a good day
yesterday. He was lucid for about thirty minutes, so you might
be lucky."

"Today?"

She sighed. "He's already had two episodes. The last was for
nearly an hour. I haven't upped his dose, as I knew you were
coming, but we might have to, I'm afraid."

I didn't answer, our echoing footsteps on the stone stairs
was the only sound. Gale guided me through another door, the
kind with a thick glass panel halfway up that was embedded
with mesh. This opened out into another long, gloomy corridor
with low strip lighting and cream wallpaper, dry and peeling
at the corners and flocked with a swirling pattern. The smell of
damp hung in the air and patches of black mould spread from
under the old cornicing.

From a nearby door came a sharp cry and a crashing sound.
Gale stopped. "Would you mind waiting over there for a
moment?" It wasn't really a request and I stood well away
from the door, as per her indication.

Gary Pole – No.: 78921 was penned onto a little plastic plaque
at about head height, just above the small glass window into
which Gale now peered. She frowned and flicked a button on
her lapel. "Azi? Where are you? I'm here with Mr Pole."

More chaotic noises came from the room, a low yell and
the thump of something heavy being thrown against the door.
Gale didn't even flinch as she stared in through the window.

Then a voice called from down the corridor, "I'm here!
Sorry, Gale."

A pale, blonde girl came scurrying towards us, panting.

"Mr Pole wanted some extra art supplies. I'm sorry, there was no one else available to fetch them and I thought, well, I left him secured."

Gale jutted her chin at the window. "Secured, Azi?"

I caught a glimpse through the thick glass. There was a man fastened to a chair by what looked like leg callipers. However, his upper half was free.

"I didn't think he needed a full lockdown. I was only gone for a second." The blonde woman scrambled for the benzo on her belt, flicking the tiny hood so the needle tip was unsheathed and ready.

Gale turned to me, "Sorry, Mary. I just need to help Azi and then I'll be right with you."

"I'm fine," I said, although my heart was pounding. I stood further back as Gale and Azi entered the room, both of them dodging hurled paintbrushes and a plastic pallet.

The man was rocking in his chair as if he wanted to topple himself over. Suddenly, he caught sight of me through the door and began to shout, his eyes fixed on mine, "I don't belong here! Tell these bitches not to touch me!" He was spitting as he shouted, every crease on his face pulled deep into a mask of bitter rage. It had been a long time since I'd seen the effects of the infection, and his snarling face caused some of my own memories to try to break free. I put my hand on the benzo at my waist and rubbed my thumb over the hood catch. It was there for me, just in case.

Gale grabbed the seated man's arms, firmly, deftly, as Azi pushed the needle into his neck. He bucked in his chair a few more times, but his head was already drooping as the women backed away towards the door.

Gale turned to the other girl. "Give it a couple of minutes, then check him for any injuries. I don't see anything obvious, but when the doctor arrives, get her to also check him over just to be safe. If you wait a bit, I'll give you a hand with that mess." She jerked her head towards the ransacked room.

"I'm so sorry. Please don't tell the Warden." The girl was near tears, doubly embarrassed, I expect, as I was there to witness her mistake. "I need this placement for university."

"It's okay. It happens," said Gale, placing her hand on the girl's arm. "But you need to follow protocol every time." She held the girl's eyes, and her voice grew firmer. "*Every* time. He could have hurt himself."

The consideration in Gale's tone had me rethinking my initial impression.

Azi nodded with vigour, "I will. I swear I will. I'm really sorry."

We left her checking the man over for injuries and continued our journey. We passed by what might have once been a conference suite, now some sort of activity room, where half a dozen or so men were sitting in a circle, their eyes glazed. A Debussy CD was playing and next to the men stood another carer, benzo in hand. Gale gave a curt nod to the carer as we passed and she nodded back. I thought of all the men in the country in places like this – the sons, the husbands, the fathers, the friends – and of all those who didn't make it. Were these the lucky ones? What had happened to all the men I'd known? I always tried to look in each door I passed, just in case.

Then Gale stopped, having arrived at the door bearing a familiar little ticket. The one for the man I'd come here to see.

Nicholas Chester – No: 4457

CHAPTER 9

Gale peered through the window and, apparently satisfied, unlocked the door.

"A visitor, Mr Chester," she said brightly.

The room was small but sunny, longer than it was wide, with a window at the end looking out onto the poorly maintained road. Along the left wall stood a thin desk with a chair tucked underneath and upon the desk, ready for battle, stood an army of model soldiers, all painted in bright blues and clear reds. But no paints. They were only handed out when a carer was present. There were some books on a shelf above the desk, many I'd brought myself over the years: *Alice Through the Looking Glass*, *Charlotte's Web*, *The Chronicles of Narnia*. April had once told me that he sometimes got them down and flicked through them, but she wasn't sure if he'd actually read them. One or two had been torn up in a fit of rage over the years, but these had survived. Next to the desk was a door to the latrine, slightly open and emitting a faint whiff of bleach. On my left, and a little further into the room, sat a fat, flowery armchair which had seen better days, the demented pattern not quite able to hide an assortment of scuffs and stains.

Nicky was lying on a single bed along the opposite wall, facing away from us. He was dressed in dark jogging pants and a hoodie, and he turned over as we entered. A soft cord, about two metres long, was fixed to his left ankle and connected to a metal screw at the foot of the bed.

He sat up, his face sleep creased and pale, but said nothing.

"Hey, Nicky," I said, and then looked at Gale.

She nodded, and I went over and gave him a swift hug. He hugged me back tentatively. Later, my clothes would smell of him and I would sit on my own bed, back at the facility, and bury my face in my sweater.

Despite this, it was I that broke off first, stepping back from the bed, dropping my arms to my side. Gale took the chair from under the desk and placed it by the window so it was half facing into the room. Then she took a book from the shelf, sat down and started flicking through the yellowing pages. April had been well practised at pretending not to be there, and I was often surprised when I looked over and saw her sitting in the same spot as Gale was now, quietly and unobtrusively monitoring any changes in Nicky's tone, his movements. But Gale was a new entity, and I couldn't help but feel self-conscious in her presence. I sat in the armchair, strategically placed about three metres from the bed.

In his fifties, Nicky looked old, perhaps even older than me. The infection ages you – few make it to sixty. His wispy hair was a yellowish off-white and his scalp showed through it in pink patches. From his bloated face, his eyes regarded me with a watery indifference, the skin beneath them puffed up into bluish pouches. He constantly squinted, which made his eyes even smaller and piggish. An old scar ran down his right forearm – a farrow just visible below the cuff of his sweater. I remember when I first saw that scar, in a field hospital near Oxford, back before all this quiet, gentrified organisation. I closed my eyes and tried to put it out of my mind.

Nicky lifted his hand to his stubbly face and rubbed his palm on his cheek, then ran his left hand over his scar as if he, too, was remembering its origin. He shifted on the bed.

"Mum?" he said, and his voice was phlegmy and thick.

"No." I replied, smiling. "It's me, Mary, from the facility. Remember?"

He stared at me for a moment, then dropped his gaze. He shrugged. "Okay. Sure."

He was calm, lucid. These were the days I prayed for, the ones I lived for. I've had whole visits during which he did nothing but lie on his bed and stare at the wall, or ones during which he was so agitated that I had to leave in case I made him worse. Sometimes he just sat and wept, not knowing why he was crying, or why a strange woman was sitting in his room and watching him do it.

He half-smiled, showing a jagged line of greying teeth. "Is my dad here?" He looked hopefully towards the door and I felt my smile sag.

"Your dad's not here, no. But tell me what you've been doing? I haven't seen you in three weeks." I put three fingers up as I said "three".

He looked at me, unsure, and I could see that he was trying to remember, trying to collate his thoughts as they spiralled away from each other like fireworks. He looked like he was concentrating as hard as he could when he said finally, "April's gone."

"I know," I said. "Gale is going to look after you now."

He glanced at Gale, who looked up from a battered copy of *Charlie and the Chocolate Factory*. "That's right, Nicky," she said. "You and I are going to get along fine."

Nicky frowned. "I miss April," he said, slumping back on his bed and leaning up against the wall.

"Did you paint some more models?" I asked, changing the subject, tiptoeing through the minefield of his emotions.

He looked longingly at the desk and the painted plastic soldiers. "I'm only allowed to play with them after dinner," he said.

"Yes," I replied. "But did you paint any new ones?"

He shrugged and rubbed his hand over his face, hard, as if he were trying to rub something off. The rubs got more insistent until he was slapping his face. Gale darted over and held his wrists, pulling his arms away from his face. "Come on now. Don't be silly," she said, in a soft voice. "Otherwise, you'll have to have extra medicine."

After another few moments, Nicky stopped struggling and sighed. "Okay," he replied, and when Gale returned to her station, he sat on the edge of the bed with his head bowed.

I prattled on for a while, asking about the food, and whether Nicky's pumpkin was doing well. Usually, Nicky loves talking about his pumpkin, but he just sat silently, covering his face with his pudgy, furrowed hands and occasionally sneaking glances at Gale through his fingers. Gale didn't look up from the book she was reading.

I talked about the men at the facility, how the play was going. I mentioned Olivia, but only briefly. Just to say that I'd made a new friend. I didn't mention anything about the trip she'd suggested.

Later, after I'd run out of things to say and Nicky had laid down on his bed and stared at the ceiling for a while, a girl who looked too young to be away from school came round with a trolley and poured warm chamomile tea into colourful plastic cups. Then she handed out plates of dry fruitcake to me, to Gale and to Nicky. Before he ate any, he spent ages picking out all the dried fruit and piling it up by type – raisins, cherries, peel. He consumed the plain dry cake whilst staring at the three small piles on his plate. Then he left them there and put the plate down on the bed for Gale to collect.

The sun continued to edge across the carpeted floor and dust danced in its amber shafts. I could see a few threads too, in the filtered light. It didn't make any difference to Nicky, of course. He was already infected. The conversation lapsed into a soothing silence.

Nicky lay down, then rolled to face me. "Mary," he said, and then looked very pleased with himself. "Maaaarrrrryyyy."

"Yes?" I answered and smiled.

"What was it like before, Maaaarrrryyyyy? Before..." he

frowned as if trying to find the words. "Before I came... here?"

I felt a coolness creep into the room, despite the sunlight. I didn't look round, but I felt Gale stop reading and turn a fraction towards us.

"We've talked about it before, Nicky." I tried to keep my voice from catching, but it's one of those things. If you think about it – you make it happen. It was a lie, anyway. I'd never spoken about it. He'd never asked. I said nothing else.

His smile slipped, and he turned over to face the wall.

After a few minutes" silence, I closed my eyes against the afternoon sun.

Mary – then

We decided that it would be better if I tied them to radiators – separately, on opposite sides of the room. Actually, it was Adrian who decided, gripping one of the radiators and pulling on it as hard as he could. We'd looked up online how to bind Ryan's hands with rope so that he had some flexibility. He was able to lie down flat with his bound hands out in front of him. We didn't tie his legs. For Adrian though, it was more difficult. He got me to cable tie his hands together behind him with another tie looped through the first, attaching it to the radiator. He also made me cable tie his ankles together – just in case I had to run away from him, he said. He was smiling as he spoke, as if joking.

The whole thing was absurd, tying them up like that. But the gnawing knot of anxiety in my stomach eased slightly as I slipped those plastic bands on my husband's wrists. My fear competed with a deeply held optimism. *It's a precaution. It won't happen to us.*

I checked the windows and doors again and started washing our clothes and bedding, like the BBC news expert had suggested.

I flicked through Facebook and Twitter on my iPad.

Confused posts, conspiracy theories, friends posting about those who hadn't come home. One long post from my hairdresser about how scared he was to go to sleep in case he didn't wake up.

I tried to call my father's care home, but it just kept ringing and ringing.

I stood in the kitchen for an age, debating whether to make Ryan's favourite meal and use up some valuable dried pasta or prepare something that might go off soon, like cauliflower cheese, maybe. I looked over at Ryan, face pale, slouched against the radiator, and I reached for the macaroni.

Ryan navigated his pasta with his hands tied in front of him and ate with enthusiasm. I felt the stirrings of that old, familiar nausea, so could only manage a few bites.

"Not hungry?" asked Adrian.

Tell him. Claire's words came back to me and I nearly did. But as I looked at his shackled hands and feet, the words caught in my throat. "Just the stress of it all," I replied.

I had to feed Adrian with a spoon. Ryan looked over at us and rolled his eyes when Adrian asked me to make the "choo-choo" sounds he liked and refused to eat until I'd played along. I was pleased to see Ryan smile when he turned back to his food. I loved Adrian for that, for trying to make light of it and not giving in to the fear.

At about eight o'clock Claire called. I took the call in the kitchen.

"They're rounding us up," was the first thing she said.

"What? Are you okay?"

"Yes, I'm fine. But they're coming for us."

"Who are?"

"I don't know – the army, the government. Me and dad got a text. We were told to be ready, but we aren't allowed to bring anything."

Her tone was calm, but her breath was heavy on the line. Of course, they would collect her, and she would be herded into a truck with all the men, with all the "other" men. I didn't know what to say. "What can I do?"

"It's just, they need a contact number of a next of kin, a woman, a *biological* female, I wondered if..."

"Of course, put me down."

"Okay. Thanks."

"Shit, Claire, this is all so fucked up," I said.

She paused. "I survived Harrow. I guess I can survive this. Is everyone okay at your end?"

I heard a couple of successive sneezes from the other room. I didn't know if it was Ryan or Adrian, and I savagely crushed the rising tide of panic in my chest. "I think so. For now," I replied. "How's your dad?"

"Same self-righteous prick as usual. He thinks that this is a punishment from God."

"What for?"

"Oh, you know, everything – me and my kind, working mothers, snowflake liberals, the fall of the Empire. Listen, keep yourself safe, angel. I'd better go; they'll be here in a minute."

"Okay, love you."

"You too."

I ended the call and went into the sitting room to try to make Ryan and Adrian more comfortable. Ryan had fallen asleep curled up on the floor with his roped hands in front of him. Doc was laid out next to him, head on paws. I shucked off Ryan's trainers, trying not to think of the girl with the milk, trying not to think about anything other than getting through the next few hours. I leaned down and covered him with a blanket, then I kissed his warm, damp forehead.

"Who was on the phone?" asked Adrian.

"Claire."

He was sitting at an awkward angle up against the radiator with his hands behind his back. "How's she doing?"

"Not... great."

Adrian grimaced and tried to get himself into a more

comfortable position. "Yeah. None of this is great. I woke up this morning worrying about a presentation. I'm going to sleep on the floor tied to a radiator."

"He's warm, Adrian." My voice was low and urgent. "And he's been sneezing, I mean, what do we do if…? They said on the news that half just die in their sleep. What if…" I looked over at our boy, curled up on the floor.

"Look, somebody right now is coming up with a cure. The TV said that they had the best people working on it. We've been careful since we got in earlier. It's his allergies." He paused and shuffled around so he could look at me properly. He lowered his voice, "We'll be fine."

Should I have told him then? About the possible collection of cells that were still the size of a kidney bean, about the terrible, but wonderful thing inside of me? But then it would be fully real, and given the circumstances, it was going to be complicated. What did I say instead? Something about that we'd do this together, that this was what it meant to be married. I also decided against mentioning what was happening to Claire, about the people in suits rounding up men and presumably boys. Why worry him more? *We'll think about it tomorrow*, I thought. Although there was also another thought lurking in the recesses of my mind, a much more selfish thought hovered on the periphery – what if he didn't want to go? What if he suggested he and Ryan hide? And that's when I realised that I wanted him to go with the people in the suits. I wanted to follow the rules, to let the government sort it out. I wanted to give my husband and my teenage son to the protection of whoever was best placed to sort it out. And I didn't know if Adrian would agree.

I tucked some cushions around him to try to get him more comfortable. Then I gave him some wine in a tumbler with a straw, sitting with him on the floor. The TV was on low in the background, with its constant round of breaking news, updated reports, and interviews from expert's home offices and kitchen tables. None of which seemed to know what was going on. But we weren't watching the TV, my husband and I, that first night of the infestation. We were both watching the slow, even breathing of our sleeping son. Out, then in. Out, then in. Out.

"Mary. MARY!"

I was so relaxed, what with the sun just reaching my feet and Nicky's steady breathing, as he lay dozing on the bed, that the shout made me jump. He would have reached me if Gale had not grabbed my arm and pulled me away.

Nicky lunged at us both, his face a sudden snarl. "YOU KILLED HIM!" he screamed. I scrambled back, but Gale was still close enough for Nicky to reach her. The rope stretched taut between him and the bed. He grabbed her around the waist, and they both fell to the floor in a struggle.

"Mary! Benzo!" cried Gale, but not before Nicky landed a full-fisted punch on the side of her head. I jerked the benzo free with shaking hands. I'd never had to use it before. How did the cap detach? Did I thrust, then pinch or pinch then thrust? Nicky was curling his fingers around Gale's neck. The woman was fighting back, but she'd given up her advantage by grabbing me and pushing me out of the way. And now Nicky was on top of her. I finally flicked off the cap and hovered over him. I'd forgotten everything April had told me, every safety briefing I'd ever had. As I stood there dithering, someone brushed past me and plunged a needle into the man's neck.

Nicky sagged and then rolled off, his head bumping on the floor as he fell. Gale pulled in a long gasping breath, then scrambled to her feet, holding the side of her face where the flesh was beginning to swell.

She was still gasping as she backed away and she was overcome by a coughing fit. I did nothing. The woman from earlier, Azi, rolled Nicky onto his side and began checking his head.

"How's his breathing?" asked Gale, still coughing a bit but trying to suppress it.

"It's okay. I'm checking for trauma," replied Azi.

Gale straightened up fully and addressed me, "I think it's time to go now, Mary."

I hesitated. "I just need to know that Nicky is…"

"Now, Mary. Let Azi work. I'll update you tomorrow evening by phone."

I nodded mutely and followed as she led me to the door. She called over her shoulder as she left, "Stay with him until I return."

I turned and glimpsed his eyes, half-open, staring blankly from the floor. "I'm really sorry," I said.

But whether I was addressing Nicky or Gale, I wasn't sure.

CHAPTER 10

I nearly told Olivia that night, when we were sitting in the darkened gloom of the corridor, the thing I buried deep all those years ago. Why I was visiting a stranger named Nicky. My dirty little secret. Perhaps she'd tell me I did the right thing. I balanced on the precipice of confession. Pride and shame pulled me back from the edge – one on each arm.

After I'd gone through the decontamination process – painstakingly scouring every inch of myself, combing my short hair, checking the creases behind my ears, under my breasts, scrubbing under my nails – I found Olivia at the nurse's station filling out paperwork. Her attitude was tense. Gone was the easy-going manner, the friendly nudges and pats on the hand. She hardly spoke for the first hour. I'd resigned myself to a long and awkward shift, feeling the hours shuffle past.

Then she said, out of the blue, "Do you think it's better now?"

I didn't know what she meant. I thought for a moment that she was talking about the new facility. I was about to answer *of course it's better!*

But then I saw her face, and I knew.

It was something I tried not to think about. It made me feel ancient. Life without men. It wasn't like I was some ardent feminist before it all changed. I sighed. "I don't think it's a fair comparison," I said. "I wish it hadn't happened, if that's what you mean."

She nodded and offered a half smile. A sad smile. "Do you

want to know what happened with Emily – how I met Jen Harting?"

I nodded.

"Everyone from back then remembers the moment they knew that nothing would be the same again, you know?"

My mind flicked back to the birds, to the girl with the milk. But it was Olivia's turn to speak.

"I realised the world had changed about a minute after entering that emergency department."

Olivia – then

There were many bodies lying on gurneys in the corridor. Some were covered in sheets – tented and still – but some were uncovered. Those I could see all had the same blue veins snaking out from their darkened lips and down over their cheeks, necks and shoulders. They all seem to have died with their eyes shut and their mouths open in a silent blue scream. There were shrieks and gasping cries from further within the hospital, but these men before me were silent. Just the occasional beep or ping from an unseen phone could be heard. There was the smell too, not death, not yet, but a chemical smell above the usual hospital disinfectant. Like old-fashioned hairspray, the type my mother used when she went out, acetone catching in the back of the throat making your eyes water.

That smell we all got used to in the weeks and months afterwards.

There was no one in the corridor by then, although I could hear plenty of cries for help coming from the wards that branched off to the left every twenty metres or so. I texted Emily and got no reply. I was scared and I was edging along the corridor. I had the creepy feeling that one of the men on the beds might grab my arm or sit up and cry out. Too many zombie films, I guess. I also feared that a man, not one of the blue-mouthed ones, but one of the crazed ones, would come round the corner and run at me.

I crept down the corridor, following the signs to "C Unit", looking out for places to hide, just in case. I ignored the cries from the doors to my left. *Help! We need help in here... is anyone there...? What's going on?* I kept on moving. At one point, I passed a makeshift operating theatre. I stopped by the half-open door. There were two surgeons operating on a woman. For a moment it gave me hope – that here were men, unaffected, trying to save this woman's life, that perhaps not all men were infected. But then one of the men laughed and began gently patting the woman on her cheek, "Wakey, wakey, rise and shiny," he said in a childish singsong voice.

The other man was studying the scalpel in his hand, as if he'd never seen one before, watching the light catch the blade in little flashes. As I watched on in horror, he drew it slowly and carefully over his own gowned wrist. A plume of blood arched over the woman on the table – the woman whose eyes, I could now see, were open and lifelessly blank.

I ducked out of view and kept going, fighting down a wave of sickening fear.

The corridors and staircases were endless and confusing. Suddenly, a man burst out of one of the wards. He was right in front of me. I had no time to hide, so I just stood there, frozen. I waited for him to pounce, but he didn't.

"I need to find my daughter," he said, putting his palm up to me as if to say "stop". It was a strange gesture, mechanical almost. He carried on speaking, but his eyes were focused to the right, above my head. "She's seven. We were at home and my wife was at work. I was feeling ill, and then... and then... I was here." He raised the other hand and absently gestured to his surroundings. He was middle-aged and slim, wearing a checked shirt, navy chinos and pale moleskin slippers. Two blotches of something dark and rusty coloured, one bigger than the other, stained his right slipper. "I need to find Melody. Do you think she's at home?" he asked.

I nodded slowly but didn't speak.

"I live on West Street," he said. "Do you know it?" His tone was warm and friendly, as if we'd met at the bus stop and were just passing the time.

I did know it. "Yes," I said, relieved that I could still speak. "It's near the park, behind the tennis courts."

"That's right!" he said. "Is it far?"

I shrugged, "A couple of miles, maybe a bit more."

"I'd better go. Melody shouldn't be left on her own. She'll get scared." He started up the corridor, back the way I came, but his gait was stiff and strange, lurching from step to step.

I headed deeper into the building, trying really hard not to think about Melody and those two blotches of blood.

Then I saw the sign:

C WING, Intensive Treatment Unit – Follow the Yellow Line

I sped around a corner, guided by the yellow stripe on the floor, straight into a gridlock of gurneys. I actually bashed my knee on the first one I came to, unable to slow down and prevent the collision. Its occupant – a young man in a green hoodie – stared up at me with glassy eyes, his pale face covered with blue spidery veins. It was the first time I'd seen a blue's eyes, how those indigo veins had crawled up his face and bled out over the whole of the whites of his eyes. Eerie and alien.

Bodies lay on the beds and on the floor, blue-mouthed men mostly. One female doctor sat up by the wall, her head resting on her shoulder, eyes closed. Blood covered her chest – her blood or someone else's? I couldn't tell, but she wasn't moving.

I was picking my way through the maze of trollies, pushing them gingerly out of my way, terrified my arms would brush one of the cold, bluish bodies, when my phone buzzed. A message from Emily:

Im outside in trucks where r u?

A spike of anger surged through me, whether it was because

she hadn't texted sooner, or that she hadn't needed my help, or that she hadn't bothered to come and find *me*, I don't know. I felt like screaming, *I'm starring in some George Romero horror show because of you!*

Instead, I texted: *I'm coming. Stay where you are.*

She replied almost instantly: *Quick leaving soon!*

I turned back the way I'd come and came face to face with one of the surgeons I'd passed minutes ago. He was dark and heavyset, in his thirties maybe, and still wearing his surgeon's mask.

He leered at me over a sea of dead bodies. "You don't look well," he said. "Can I help?" His eyes were wide and bloodshot, and his hands were clenched before him in an unnatural pose, as if he were holding an invisible steering wheel. "I am a doctor."

"I'm fine," I said, inching back from him slowly.

"I should operate," he replied, as if he hadn't registered me speaking at all. He was holding some sort of small hacksaw in his right hand. It had tiny teeth, and a crookedly looped handle. He waved it at me. "It's what I do, you see." He squinted his eyes at me, his mouth drooping in a parody of sympathy. "Don't worry. I'll put you under first."

I turned then, tried to fight my way through the maze of gurneys and dead bodies littering the corridor. The man was just behind me, leaning over, reaching and clawing at my shirt. I tried to keep at least two gurneys between me and him as I waded deeper into the crush, but it was getting harder, the trollies seemingly fused together as if refusing me passage. I considered crawling under them, but the confusion of wires and metal struts made it impossible to get through. He was making his way towards me, muttering nonsense in a singsong tone, "*Oh, in extremis, cannibals eat people's globus...*"

I wasn't going to make it. He was going to catch me and kill me, just as he had that other woman.

"*... pallidi instead of their HEARTS!*" He grabbed me from behind and pushed me down onto the edge of the nearest bed, crushing my face into the hard black polythene. "I must make you better," he said into my ear as he pushed his body onto mine.

I cried out and managed to flip over to face him. "I'm not sick. Please," I begged. "Please."

His eyes above his mask and inches away, focused on mine mournfully. "We're all sick now," he whispered. "Didn't you know?"

I struggled and kicked, but he was heavy and stronger than me. A white-hot surge of fear and frustration burned through me. But it didn't matter. No matter how hard I struggled, I could do nothing to free myself.

The sound of a gunshot smashed into the air, its echo ricocheting off the sterile walls.

"Stand up and put your hands in the air. I have the legal right to use extreme force." The voice came from behind us, and the body on top of me froze. My arms were suddenly free and I pushed hard at the blood-covered maniac who was pinning me to the bed.

The armed woman was dressed in body armour, light hair scraped back, face set and grim.

"Hands up!" she shouted at the man. He was unarmed and he seemed to be fighting some internal struggle, frightened and looking for an escape but trapped by gurneys.

"Put. Your. Fucking. Hands. Up!" she shouted again.

The surgeon's face twisted and he snarled. He pushed me out of the way and ran towards the woman, hands up and clenched like claws.

But she didn't shoot. Instead, she switched the gun to her left hand and punched him hard in the face. As he bent over, clutching his nose, she took what looked like an epi-pen from her pocket and stabbed him in the shoulder. He tried to get up, but then he just sat down again and held his face in his hands.

"We need to wait for a few minutes until the full effect kicks in. Then we can put him in the truck." She was alone but it was a moment before I registered that she was actually talking to me. She gestured out of the window. I could make out two army trucks with a group of women holding automatic weapons standing guard.

"What's going on?" I asked. It sounded stupid, but it was all I could think of to say.

The woman paused, and then pointed to one of the men on the beds, the one with the blue veins over his face. "With these guys, you mean? Some die and some turn. We don't know why."

I shook my head to try and make sense of it all. "The ones that turn, do they get better?" I asked. This was the first person I'd spoken to who had even the slightest notion of what was going on. I was thinking of the man in the checked shirt, the one on his way back to his daughter. What would happen when he got home? Assuming the blood on his slipper was not his daughter's, of course.

"We don't know yet. Some regain their sanity for a bit, but then they turn again. That's why we are having to keep them tranqued. We're calling them manics," she added and nodded to my attacker, who was now lying on the hospital floor.

There were so many things I wanted to know right then. Was it everywhere? Have any women been infected? Is it a virus? "Why didn't you kill him?" I asked instead, nodding at the drugged man, who a few minutes earlier had wanted to chop me up with a small saw.

"It was a split-second judgement. I thought I was probably stronger than him, that I could get the tranq in before he hurt me."

"Oh. Well, thank you."

"I'm Jen."

"Olivia."

"There's no reasoning with them when they're like that," said Jen. "You've just got to make the call."

I nodded and thought about the woman on the operating table, of the man laughing as if this whole thing was just one ridiculous joke, of the two dots of blood on a moleskin slipper.

Gunfire sounded in the distance and the woman moved back to the window, scanning the road. "Come on, help me," said Jen, taking the man under the shoulders. I grabbed his feet and we bundled him onto a free gurney.

"What should we do about all these bodies?" I said as we manoeuvred our package towards the nearest exit.

"We'll have to leave them for now. We'll deal with the blues later." She gestured to the beds.

Blues, I thought to myself, SANS, tranqs, manics: every new order has its own glossary. Later there would be sire houses, Contributions, preps and visitations to add to the list.

When we reached the truck, a couple of women wearing similar armoured jackets to Jen helped hoist the man up. I could see the truck was full of unconscious men, many of them teenagers, a few over sixty, lying in lines on the truck bed. Two women sat on a side bench, looming over the men. Armed and with their rifles raised.

"Where are you taking them?" I asked.

"They're going to a secure hangar – until we find a cure." As we spoke, another two women were dragging an unconscious man towards the truck. Jen and I moved out of their way, then walked around to the next truck. As I moved, I heard gunshots. Closer this time. There was an assortment of women and girls in the trucks of all ages, some in PJs and dressing gowns, many with cuts and bruises on their faces. A woman dressed in army fatigues came to meet us and helped me up into the truck.

"Liv!"

It was Emily. She leapt up from the bed of the truck and wrapped her arms around me. I returned her embrace. I wanted to ask her what happened and how come she hadn't texted again. I wanted to hold her and bury myself in her neck, draw in the scent of her hair, but there were about thirty women watching us, so I just patted her awkwardly on the back. "It's fine, I'm fine," I said, sitting down and pulling Emily in next to me.

Jen spoke to the woman in army fatigues, "Go back to base, Dena, drop off the women."

"Yes, Ma'am," replied the soldier. "How are we doing for benzos?"

"Not good," replied Jen. "We managed to grab more from the hospital, but not enough. I'm going back to the field hospital with the manics in case there's any trouble."

The other woman, Dena, nodded and held a walkie talkie, "Call me. I'll come and find you, if necessary."

Emily started frantically tapping her phone. "It's not working. I can't get a signal. Fuck!"

She looked at Jen and Dena, pale with panic.

Jen replied as she got down from the truck, "The networks keep going down. They're not expected to last much longer."

Emily sagged down next to me and began to cry.

CHAPTER 11

Friday – I was reminded that it was visitation day by Daisy. Olivia and I were just finishing up our shift. Nothing Olivia had told me the night before had shocked me – the surgeon, the carnage in the hospital – it was all part of the shared trauma of that time. There were schools that hadn't sent their pupils home when the infections hit – that was the most horrifying to me, how they must have had to separate the kids, how they dealt with the deaths and the violence in classrooms, in playgrounds and in nurseries. I've only met one teacher from before, a deputy head from a secondary school in Leicester – she point-blank refused to talk about it.

I was wiping down the carers' station and clearing away the mugs when Daisy swept around the corner of the corridor, smiling. "Morning, girls!" she called as she approached. "Visitation day – so much to do!"

Olivia, facing away from her, rolled her eyes, and I had to stop myself from doing the same. She reached us and we paused our work.

"Did you see the noticeboard? I'm going to need all those not booked in for a visit on duty from four pm."

I nodded, although I felt, as I always did on visitation days, a little hard done by. Just because I hadn't chosen to spend this evening with one of the residents, I was automatically placed on the rota.

"Will you be on a visit, Daisy?" asked Olivia, although I suspected she'd heard the rumours and knew the answer already.

"Well, actually, yes, I will be. Luca accepted my petition for this evening. I can't lie, I am very much looking forward to it. This will be the first time I've tried him. I've heard good things about him from some of the other girls." Daisy's voice was high and breathy; it lacked her usual condescension.

"Me too," replied Olivia. "I mean, I've also heard good things about Luca. Will your wife be joining you?"

Daisy's smile dropped a fraction and a small pink blush stained her lower jaw. "Alas, no. Suzanne has to work late at school – maths club. Graduation projects are coming up and whatnot. She's sad to miss out."

Olivia nodded. "That is a pity. I hope you have a good time, anyway."

"Thanks." Daisy gave that small smile I've seen before, the one where her lips barely stretched over her even, white teeth, and turned to me. "Mary, don't forget to pop in and see me soon. To talk about rotas."

"Yes," I replied, aware that Olivia's gaze was fixed on me.

"Not tomorrow morning, of course!" she said with a girlish giggle. "I may be tired."

I forced myself to smile back. "Sure."

"Great. Let's say Monday morning, after breakfast." Then she flounced off down the corridor without waiting for my reply.

Olivia was silent for a moment and then spoke, her eyebrows raised. "Rotas?"

I hesitated. I felt torn between the warm feeling of complicity I'd had with this woman and my traitorous pact with Daisy. Then again, all Olivia's talk about husbands, the way she'd encouraged the men's questions in the viewing room, made me wonder whether we were sharing a bit of harmless dissent or skirting something much more serious. Despite my misgivings, it'd been a long time since I'd felt connected to someone, and I wasn't ready to let that feeling go. I found myself confessing.

"She asked me to keep an eye on you."

Olivia nodded in her usual reassuring way. "And you agreed?"

"Kind of, I mean, it's Daisy, so I was never really on board, but…"

"What?"

"She threatened Tony, said she would ban him from the play. I just thought I could…" I shrugged my shoulders and squeezed my hands together in my lap.

"That you could give her something to get her off Tony's back?"

I nodded. I didn't mention what she'd said about my visits to Nicky. That would have meant going into the whole painful story.

She didn't seem angry. It was as if she'd been waiting for something like this, that this was confirming a suspicion she already held. She stared off down the corridor, seemingly lost in thought. The pause stretched out for so long that I thought the conversation was over. I was about to pick up my cloth and carry on wiping down the surfaces when Olivia's voice broke the silence, forcing me to face her once more.

"Listen to me," she said as she caught my arm. Her expression was serious, more serious than I had ever seen her. "We will give Daisy something, I promise. But you must swear to me, whatever you find out tomorrow, you will not tell Daisy about it."

I nodded.

"Say it."

"I swear. You can trust me." As I spoke, Olivia's grip on my arm slackened and she turned back to finish her work. But the grimness in her tone and the harsh grip on my arm worried me. The intrigue of our little adventure drained away, leaving behind a muddy bed of doubt.

An hour later, the men were shouting and jostling over breakfast. All the men had been petitioned, a few had declined, politely, of course, citing fatigue or other issues, but most had agreed, and the air was shrill with anticipation and excitement. Their medication is adjusted a few days before the visitations. The removal of some of the testosterone blockers enables the men to participate better in the evening; however, it does mean that they can be harder to handle in the days leading up to the event. They are chattier, more physical. It's been known for fights to break out, so it pays to be vigilant and hang around a bit, even after you have finished eating.

I sat with Tony and Luca and a few others. I was the only carer at the table, as Olivia had bowed out to get some extra sleep. If I were being honest, I'd say I was glad she'd left. The memory of her fingers gripping my arm and the fierce look in her eyes kept drawing my thoughts back to the weekend and our mystery trip. I pushed it to the back of my mind and chatted to Tony as a way to divert my thoughts.

Tony was one of the few men not booked into an evening with company. When I asked why, he made me laugh by saying, "Ah, Mary, women are all a bit soft and squelchy for me. And they smell a bit strange – not unpleasant!" he was quick to assure me, "but different. I've always felt a bit lost *down there*, so now I cry off. Unlike Luca here, who is a big fan of visitations."

Luca would not be drawn on his upcoming evening, except to say that he had no problem with the squishiness of women. Tony pretended not to care, even going as far as giving Luca a few wholly misguided anatomic pointers, but I sensed that underneath his forced bravado skulked misery.

The men's ebullience continued after breakfast and I was glad to escape to bed at about 10am. However, as I lay in my clean, bare room, the spectre of Saturday loomed above me and I had terrible trouble getting to sleep.

When I did, finally, nod off, I had the dream.

The one in which I am strapped into stirrups and the nurses are wearing plastic. The one in which the antiseptic burns my

skin, its smell clawing my throat mid-scream. The heavy dream
in which I cannot speak because the pain is too great and my
tears are too many, but I feel that if I could just find the right
combination of words, these women would understand – that
they would stop.

An incubator on wheels is looming to my left as the pain in
my abdomen detonates once again.

"It's nearly over." It's so cold in the dream that the whisper
arrives on a puff of chill white breath.

"Please," I croak, but I want so many things that the word is
all sign, no signifier.

"Pant, Mary. Now!"

I don't want to. But I do it. And then with a last aching
push, my links are broken and I fall slack to the bed.

"The mother's rhesus negative, give her anti-D."

"First birth?" They talk over me as I gape.

"It says here second. Both male."

"*Fuck*, that's rough."

"Do we name him, or do they do that at the prep house?"

"Just a first name and a number. Check the list. I think
we're up to *N*."

I lie there for a moment and tremble. A thin cry rises in the
freezing room and I hold out my arms but meet only empty
space. Someone pricks my arm. Rubber wheels squeak on a
sterile floor. The room fades to black.

It was almost time for the visitations and I was standing in
the foyer of the visitors' wing, awaiting the visitors' arrival.
I was in charge of about ninety of the four hundred or so
women assigned to our facility that evening; capacity had
increased over the last few years. They'd already completed the
sanitisation process and now they padded down the corridors,
hair still damp, to the V-wings, which are in a different part of
the building to the men's usual dorms.

Each visitor wore a long, cream, silk robe provided by the facility, under which they were naked. They were one-size-fits-all, so some of the shorter women were bunching up the fabric with one hand, raising the hem to avoid tripping. Nothing from the outside is permitted inside, but many of them held a complimentary glass of locally produced wine.

They filed through – tall, lean, stocky, fleshy but everyone with their hair chin length or shorter, as per visit regulations. There was a chatty buzz amongst these women as they stood in the large, unfurnished foyer space, awaiting instructions. The conversation flowed, the crowd mingled, friendly and relaxed. It reminded me of a spa day I went to once, in the time before – some voucher Adrian had won in a raffle at work. Ryan was a baby, and I'd not left him before, not for longer than an hour, so I spent the whole day being pampered and petted and fretting over whether Adrian was coping. *Would he remember where the spare wet wipes were kept or, more importantly, to test the temperature of the formula on his wrist? Would he stick to the routine, or would I get home to screaming chaos?* I think I left the spa early, raced home, slick and scented, only to find father and baby fed, happy and curled up on the sofa watching Pingu.

I looked around at the mingling women and noted some familiar faces from the staff. But not Daisy. Maybe she'd found Luca's room already. I was glad she wasn't there. Olivia was late for her shift, and I was worried that Daisy would have taken her to task for it.

I finished the dregs of my tea, put the mug down and made my way to the front of the group, holding the laminated list of visitation guidelines, even though, by now, I knew them by heart. I cleared my throat and was gratified when the room became silent – a flock of eager, smiling faces awaiting my address.

"Dear visitors," I projected my voice so that those at the back could hear too. "Welcome to our facility. For those who have not attended before, please listen carefully to the following

visitation guidelines. For those who have been here before,"
I looked around with an apologetic grin, "well, just bear with
me." There were a few good-natured groans and one or two
nervous giggles.

"Firstly," I continued in a more serious tone, "and most
importantly, please be mindful that the men you have
petitioned live in very different circumstances to you. Always
remember that they are not able to enjoy the same freedoms
and advantages, and that this lack of sophistication means that
it is up to *you* to manage the visitation. It is *you* who must
ensure that both parties feel respected and free of coercion." I
punctuated my words with some direct and matronly glances.
"The following guidelines have been drawn up by the Men's
Welfare Authority to ensure that this visitation is a pleasant
experience for all those concerned."

My voice became louder, "Any transgression of the following
guidelines may result in termination of visitation rights and, in
some serious instances, prosecution."

I looked around at the women gathered before me to check
they were paying attention before continuing. They were
receptive, politely hiding their boredom.

"Number one, both parties have the right to terminate the
visitation at any point and for any reason, or no reason, before
or during the visitation. If a resident indicates any form of
discomfort, whether verbal or non-verbal, explicit or implied,
any sexual activity must cease *immediately* and advice sought
from one of the duty carers. A duty carer can be found at the
carers' station located at the end of each corridor," I gestured
with my hand to the nearest station, "or, in an emergency,
called for via the red button that is positioned to the left of
the headboard in each room." I smiled at the stricken face
of an obviously new visitor at the front of the crowd, then
lowered my voice, "It rarely happens. If you're unsure about
something, just explain to your resident that you need a few
moments and come and find one of us."

I continued from where I left off on the guidelines, "Number two, to avoid attachments, infatuations or the emotional manipulation of residents, all of which are illegal under the Men's Welfare Anti-Grooming Act of 2049, visitations with the same partner are permitted no more frequently than once every six months."

Some of the women were getting impatient now, their wine glasses drained. They were fidgeting and looking in the direction of the individual rooms. I picked up the pace.

"Number three, incendiary topics of conversation including politics, ethics, philosophy and current affairs should be avoided, as these can lead to high levels of anxiety in the residents and, in extreme instances, can cause disturbances to the smooth running of the facilities..."

"I wasn't planning on doing much talking!" interrupted a woman who looked to have taken more than her allocation of complimentary wine. Her comment garnered a slightly more raucous response than I thought it merited.

"Thank you, yes, thank you, if you'd just bear with me for a few more–" But I'd lost their attention and individual conversations started bubbling up from the ranks. I'd pretty much finished the guidelines anyway, so I let it slide. I asked, loudly over the rising clamour, if there were any questions and, when no one paid me any mind, I pointed the women in the direction of the line of individual suites and bade them enjoy their evening.

In the month of confinement, these suites of rooms, known as the V-wings, contain the men when the risk of infection is so high that the best way to keep them safe is to keep them in one place.

But outside the month of confinement, they are used for the visitations. Each room has a bed, a shower cubicle, sanitiser wipes and, on visiting days, scented candles to try to cover the acrid whiff of disinfectant. Music is piped through the tannoy system. Unfortunately, CDs are rare and on a strict library rotation, so one always has to make do with what is available. On this occasion, we had *Wagner's Orchestral Favourites* – not exactly sexy, but not completely terrible. The time before it'd been *Whale Song for Childbirth*, which hadn't gone down well at all.

Some nitwit working the day shift had forgotten to put the numbers on the doors, so there were a few minutes of scurrying and nudging as everyone checked the little nameplates. It became a cheery game of Pelmanism.

Aren't you looking for Owen, Melody?

Yes!

He's over here, this one…

Has anyone seen Byron?

I think he was further along.

Thank you!

For goodness" sake, where's Pericles?

Followed by the slap-slapping of doors, petering out into silence.

I was still waiting for Olivia at the carers' station when a young carer named Isla turned up, a girl I recognised from the dining hall, but not someone with whom I'd spent much time.

"Hi," she said, offering a smile that reached right up to her pretty, almond-shaped eyes. "Let's hope it's a quiet night."

"Hi," I said, looking up and down the corridor for any sign of my friend. "Are you swapping with Olivia this evening?"

She shrugged and her eyes widened a little. She looked nervous. "I'm not sure. I found myself allocated this shift earlier today. I don't know whose shift I'm covering."

"Oh," I replied.

Isla gave me some fresh report forms. "When things have calmed down here, one of us should go back to the dorm station and check on the men that don't have visitors. I've just looked on the dossier and there are only two men there but someone needs to be around, I guess."

I nearly asked if she'd seen Olivia on her way over but

stopped myself. I had a tight feeling in my gut – a fear that events were shifting and that now shapes moved in shadows.

I picked up my mug and hurried off to the dorm wing, as the swelling chords of the *Ride of the Valkyries* crashed around me.

CHAPTER 12

Olivia wasn't by the dorms, so I spent a long night at the carers' station with Isla, wondering what had happened.

Maybe we weren't as close as I'd thought. After all, we'd only known each other for six days. It felt longer, but no, that first night, wrapped up in our stories, when she told me about the man in the Warden's quarters, that was less than a week ago. And what about this trip tomorrow – were we still even going? A part of me hoped we weren't. The prospect was gnawing on my nerves. But then again, I felt like Olivia had chosen me, had nudged me along that cosy road of friendship, and I didn't want to let her down. Also, I wanted to know what this big secret was and why she wanted me in particular to be part of it.

Time passed, as it does on night shifts, pensive and slow. To stretch my legs, I wandered down the corridor. I poked my head round the door of dorm B to find Tony, the only occupant, sobbing softly into his pillow. When he saw me at the door, he turned over so he was facing the back wall.

I shuffled over in the half-light from the doorway and sat on his bed. "Oh, petal," I whispered as I patted his shoulder, "is it Luca?"

There was a phlegmy pause before he replied, "I'm sorry. I know that I'm supposed to, you know, respect his right to the visits and I know we aren't even really a couple, that he's not into... that... but..." He started sobbing again and I felt the vibrations through the mattress.

I stroked his damp hair and let him cry for a while.

"So why Luca?" I asked when he'd quietened down a little. "Why not turn your attention to one of the other boys? You're very popular, Tony."

He turned over in bed to face me, his cheeks blotchy and puffed. "I think it's cos he reminds me of Logan." He sniffed, wetly.

I nodded. I suspected as much, as I'd felt the same way at times. Logan had been louder and more earnest, more passionate than Luca, but there was a similar charisma.

"I miss Logan so much," said Tony, sniffing and wiping the back of his hand over his cheeks. "I just wish I could see him or visit him. Just speak to him for a few minutes and know that he's okay. Do you remember his voice, Mary? So deep and serious."

I thought about my visit to Nicky the previous day. Logan was at a similar facility somewhere in the country – they hadn't told me where, but I could probably find out. But what then? Tony would never be able to visit. Logan would be, like Nicky, drugged most of the time, and even if he weren't, he probably wouldn't recognise anyone.

But as I stared down into Tony's puffy eyes, I heard myself saying, "I know the sanatorium he's in. It's a really nice place."

The words just fell out of me. I wanted to snatch them back. It was such a stupid thing to say.

Tony's eyes grew wide. "Where is it? Is it close by? I mean, I know I can't go, but I'd like to think that he's nearby. Have you seen him?"

"I haven't seen him, no." I regretted my words bitterly, aware that this conversation was breaking about a hundred rules, but Tony was so full of hope that I kept on talking. "I hear he is doing fine, that the sanatorium has a gardening programme and a cookery programme, and that he's generally quite happy."

Tony was smiling now. "He'd love gardening, Mary. I mean,

he used to talk about it a lot, when he wasn't banging on and on about men's rights. He loved the idea of being outside in the sunshine. I bet he's got his own small patch of garden all to himself and that he plants all sorts of things. I bet he plants vegetables as well as flowers." Tony had a distant look now, his eyes glazed and soft. He was in a garden somewhere with Logan.

"It's time to get some sleep now," I said briskly.

As I got up, Tony caught my hand and kissed it. "Thank you, Mary. You are the only one who understands."

I patted him on the cheek as he wriggled back under his sheet. "Tony," I whispered.

He looked up at me.

"Best not mention that we discussed Logan's location. I might get into trouble."

"No problem," he whispered back from the darkness, "*tigers couldn't drag it from me.*"

Logan and Tony didn't get on at first. Logan acted like Tony was an attention-seeking flirt – which, of course, he is – and Tony resented Logan's popularity, jealous, no doubt of his confidence, and the respect the other men gave him. Tony used the attention he gained as the new guy to point out Logan's defects at every opportunity – "But he's so serious", I'd hear Tony whispering to the other men. "And preachy – all that stuff about men's rights. And he talks to you like you're stupid… *Tony, if you have to chatter on and on, try and think of something interesting to say.*" Tony could do an excellent imitation of Logan's grave voice. Then there would be a smattering of chuckles from the other men, as Logan from the other side of the room rolled his eyes.

Another boy came to the facility at the same time as Tony – Roberto. Unlike Tony, who settled in immediately and went about cultivating a small gang of acolytes, Roberto was shy. Tall and painfully thin with dark stubble and pasty skin – he kept his head angled to the right, eyes downcast, therefore he always seemed to be in the process of turning away. I took it upon myself to try and get him involved in some of the activities on offer, gardening, cookery, art classes. He'd answer me with a mute shrug, but I could never get him to speak. I'd often find him roaming the halls instead, having drifted from the rec room when no one was looking.

It wasn't just me who noticed Roberto's isolation. Logan watched him too, and although I had little success in getting the young man to open up, Logan had patience with the shy ones. Soon Roberto could be found on Logan's periphery. Not close, by any means, but Roberto would raise his eyes to Logan when the older man spoke, and I even caught the ghost of a smile when Logan made a rare joke.

Tony continued to bait Logan but could get no rise from him. Life continued like this for a while, until one horrible event which reminded everyone who the real enemy was.

I was on duty in the rec room with a carer named Delilah. I didn't know her well. She was young, she did her job adequately if not enthusiastically, generally treated the men with respect. We sat in the corner and watched as the men played rummy or did large jigsaw puzzles, an old Abba CD playing on the tinny speakers.

Tony sidled up behind Logan and flicked his ear. Logan brushed his ear in an unconcerned manner, as if swatting at a fly, and continued reading a laminated pamphlet. Tony upped his game and turned to Roberto, "You should dump this old guy and come sit with us," he said. "We won't bore you with complaints about visitations and education."

No answer.

"Fine, perhaps you two deserve each other. At least you've got a willing audience, Logan."

Logan smiled, not even raising his head from his reading. "It's funny, Tony. For someone who claims to be annoyed by me, you spend much of your time hanging around."

Tony bristled. "I'm not the one hanging round – he is!" Tony jabbed a finger at Roberto. "Your ghostly shadow, when he's not haunting the corridors around B block."

This got a few sniggers from the men now crowding around. Roberto blushed.

I stood up to intervene. I'd been beginning to like our new boy, Tony, his energy, his sass, but he was being mean. Perhaps he hadn't had his hormone medicine calibrated yet. Delilah put a hand on my arm to stop me. "Wait. Let them sort it out between them."

Logan looked at Tony with a disappointed frown. I thought he might say something – call out Tony for being cruel. But to everyone's amazement, it was Roberto who spoke. "It's okay, Tony. I know you like Logan. We're just friends. I'm no threat."

The room fell silent. Tony's face went pink. "Just… just… bugger off," he muttered. "No one wants you here." Then he shuffled off to the other side of the rec room. I lost track of Roberto after that. I suspect he snuck out and went off wandering the corridors alone.

Maybe the cleaning detail hadn't been quite on it that day. Or the decontamination system had a fault. Maybe a worker – a carer? a cook? – was late that day and didn't shower for the full ten minutes. Or perhaps a participant in the visitation programme hadn't followed all the protocols.

The men at the facility are taught from birth to be mindful of their surroundings. To watch for any evidence of a thread. They wear light-coloured silken robes, and groom each other every night, checking for anything suspicious. The world beyond the walls of the facility is both dazzling and terrifying for them – But it always contains death.

During showers the next morning, Delilah and I were preparing to hand over our shift, cleaning down the surfaces of the carer's station. I was looking forward to a long hot bath, my limbs and eyes heavy with lack of sleep.

Logan came towards us, pale and wide-eyed. "It's Roberto," he said. "Come see."

I could smell the young man before I saw him. The weird old fashioned hairspray smell of the infected. I held my baton in case I'd have to defend myself, but he was a blue, the tell-tale indigo blotches lining his lips and chin, his eyes bulging but lifeless.

The other men began waking up.

"What's going on? What's wrong with Roberto?"

Delilah tried to keep the others calm, usher them from the dorm. "Come on now, off to the showers, quickly!"

But it was too late. The men initially crowded round but when they realised what had happened, they recoiled in horror.

"Is it the air conditioning?"

"Are we all infected?"

"What should we do? Should we shower?"

"Is it too late?"

The men backed off and rubbed at their arms, their shaved heads. Some began to cry and whimper.

"M… M… Mary, what's going to happen to us?"

And in the middle of this lay Roberto, staring at the ceiling. Gone.

I tried not to remember all the faces I'd seen like this, ink-stained and blank-eyed. Faces of men I'd known and loved. Delilah and I fell back on our training, using firm voices, herding the men from the room and towards the showers, locking the doors of the other dorms as we went.

The facility went into a lockdown for two weeks – all the men in isolation. Visitations were cancelled and the whole building was submitted to a deep clean.

Tony took the news of Roberto's death the hardest, harder than Logan even. "I was horrible to him," he sobbed to me from his small room. "I told him… I told him nobody wanted him here." Tony looked at me, his face puffy with tears. "Do you think it was my fault, Mary?"

"No Tony, of course not. He was infected. There was nothing anyone could have done."

But Tony wouldn't be reassured – not by me anyway.

After lockdown, the men needed to be coaxed out into the rest of the facility. Most were still afraid of infection, spending long stretches of time studying surfaces and checking under beds and in corners. From then on, everyone gave Tony a wide berth, all his previous popularity gone after his spat with Roberto. He became persona non grata, shunned by all, as if he'd killed the young man with his ill-chosen words.

All except Logan.

Logan helped Tony forgive himself, checking on him in the mornings, sitting with him at mealtimes when no one else would. They developed one of the strongest bonds I'd ever seen. Monogamous and committed, they were together for years.

Right up until Logan's infection.

I found Olivia at breakfast the next morning. She was pushing her scrambled eggs around her plate whilst staring down at the bench.

"Where were you last night?" I was aiming for nonchalance, but even to my own ears, I sounded like I was whinging. "I thought we had a shift together."

"I was needed elsewhere… I had to drive a transfer."

I looked at her in surprise. "Who? And why are men being transferred in the middle of the night?" Transfers were usually planned weeks in advance. The men had to be sedated and wheeled out in specially designed pods, which were then secured in the back of ambulances. The whole process was laborious and risky.

She shrugged. "It was not 'men', it was just one man. The paperwork came through late, and my name was on it. Daisy called the MWA to check, and she spent an age trying to stop the transfer."

"Daisy? But I thought she was on a visit?"

She didn't say anything for a bit, so I pushed it. "Why did Daisy care so much that a man was being transferred? Who was it, anyway?"

Olivia sighed. She looked exhausted. "Let's talk about it later, after our trip, yeah? You're still coming?"

I'd been toying with the idea of backing out, probably because I was feeling sore at Olivia's cloak-and-dagger act. But now I really wanted to know what was going on – people being transported in the middle of the night wasn't normal. None of this was making sense.

"Okay," I replied, after swallowing. "In about an hour, at the car depot?"

"Yeah."

"I'll be there."

"Good." And then, as if it were an afterthought, she added, "Oh, and bring your phone and the charger."

I was about to ask Olivia what on earth she wanted with an old mobile phone but before I could, she pushed away her half-eaten breakfast, stood up and strode away towards the dorms.

Oh, the joy of being in a car!

Just two people with the freedom to choose their own destiny. Admittedly, in the time before, you didn't need army-grade reinforced tyres or Land Rover suspension to transverse the now-dilapidated minor road network. In the old days, there were far more cars on the road and far fewer animals. At one point, we startled a family of deer grazing on the A287 just past what was once Haslemere. Olivia had to swerve hard to avoid hitting a startled young buck, and we nearly careered into a pothole bigger than the car itself.

After a while, we began driving through the smaller lanes. This required a slower pace.

Olivia was very quiet. I tried to start a few conversations, but I was met with shrugs or a dismissive *hmm*, so I gave up. She would not be drawn on our destination or any details regarding what to expect when we got there.

The landscape became more wooded and more like the shires of Tolkien. We wound our way down tracks flanked by oaks and sweeping birches, where early summer evening light filtered through the leaves, causing a kind of red and gold strobe effect when I closed my eyes. When I opened them, there was something wrong with the light. I was confused. Surely I hadn't dozed the day away? But the sun was dimmer, muted. I looked over and Olivia was holding the wheel so tightly her knuckles were blanched white.

"What's going on?" I asked, my voice husky and thick.

She jutted her chin forward. "It's nearly the Eclipse."

I looked up. The sky was swarming with moths. They danced and swirled like large brown snowflakes, like ashes on the wind. I hadn't seen a surge like this for many years. Some clung to the car windscreen, forcing Olivia to set off the wipers.

"I've never seen so many," I said, squinting at the leaden sky. "Not before the Eclipse."

"It's early this year," replied Olivia. "We need to start getting the men into isolation." For most of the year, the moths were not dangerous to women. The worst you might get, if you spent a long time near the moths, was a headache. A massive dose of the toxin, like if you were to wander around in a swarm, would give you exposure sickness – hallucinations, fatigue, a kind of waking dream. Some women actually went out into smaller swarms in days leading up to the Eclipse. It was like a religious experience, they said. They'd dance and meditate amongst the moths. Or they let the fat caterpillars crawl over them. I hear that the dreams can be quite lucid, mind expanding even. It's dangerous, though – if you stay out too long you could pass out, slip into a coma. And repeated high doses can damage your heart. So, on the actual day of the Eclipse, when the sky grows black with moths, only a lunatic would go out. I thought at first that that was why it was called the Eclipse, because of the darkness, but one of the women at the car repurposing plant told me it was from the time before. It's the group noun – an eclipse of moths – like a pride of lions or a murder of crows.

As they passed over us, the sky went from mottled grey to a soft blue.

"I hope the facility's filter system can cope," said Olivia.

"I'm sure it'll be fine," I said. "It's relatively new."

She didn't reply. We passed a dilapidated pub by the side of the road with its mouldering sign still partly visible: *The Hatch – Fine Ales and Good Food. Families Welcome!* The sort of place you'd break your journey on your way to the coast – fish pie, steak and chips, somewhere with a garden for the kids.

"Mary, you mustn't tell anyone about where we are going."

"I know, you've said that three times already." My nervousness shifted into irritation. "I've said I won't say anything, despite the fact that you won't tell me where we're going and why." The swarm had not helped my mood. Looking up and seeing those fluttering creatures suddenly felt like a terrible portent, that I had made a horrible mistake. I wanted to go back to the facility. I was about to say as much when Olivia said, "Do you remember me telling you that I knew Jen Harting from years ago?"

I nodded. "Yeah," I said. "You were telling me about the hospital, about Emily."

It was clear that Olivia was building up to something, so I stayed quiet. But there was a long pause and I thought that perhaps the moment had passed.

Then she sighed. "Things got really bad," she said finally, "after the hospital."

Olivia – then

Emily and I were taken to Merville barracks in Colchester where Jen Harting was our commanding officer. For the first few

days, we just rounded up all the men we could find. Emily and
I were paired together. Two days after we arrived, I remember
Jen leading about thirty of us to the armoury and handing out
flak jackets and weapons. A gun was shoved towards me, the
first gun I'd ever held. It was lighter than I expected. As I took
the jacket, I couldn't believe how heavy it was.

"Put it on," said Jen.

It was a bit too big, so I rolled up the sleeves and used a strap
to winch it in round the middle. We spent a few hours learning
how to use the weapons, how to strip them and clean them,
basically how to avoid accidentally shooting each other.

Then Jen called us all together. "I'll be with you for the
first mission." She gave each of us a steely look. "Remember
– keep the safety on your weapon unless I say otherwise.
When I tell you to, and not before, release the safety. If I
give the command – *shoot*. DO NOT HESITATE. Am I clear?"
Then she knelt down and gave us a quick overview of what
we should expect when we went out. Emily looked on edge.
Her hair was scraped back behind a thick black band and
she looked like she'd lost weight. There were dark shadows
under her eyes. I knew Emily's mum lived in France with her
little brother, and that she hadn't been in contact with them
since we'd arrived.

I felt I was doing okay. I'd managed to catch a few hours'
sleep, and I'd started to get used to the adrenaline, the feeling
of being detached from the real world. I didn't think about my
parents, not then. Not until much later.

"We move in pairs," said Jen. "If the men come at you and
there are too many of them – shoot. That's the first thing you
need to know. Just do it. If it's you or them, make sure it's them.
Tell them to kneel down with their hands over their heads. If
they comply, approach with extreme caution. Even if they seem
sane, keep your guard up. They could be pretending. Cuff them
and tranq them. Try to get details if you can – from any men who
can still hold a conversation or, even better, any female relatives."

"What if they run away?" asked Emily. "The infected ones, I mean."

"They won't," replied Jen. "I don't know why. It's like they're amped up on coke or meth. And, also, they sometimes work in packs. You can be concentrating on one of them, and another two can be sneaking up on you from behind. Always keep looking around." She handed out a bunch of injector pens. Emily took four and shoved them in her rucksack, along with a bunch of cable ties.

"If you find a kid, younger than, say, ten or eleven, don't use the benzos. They might kill him. Just cuff him and drag him to the truck. But be careful – check their hands. A ten year-old can cause serious injury with a box cutter. Ask Eva."

We all turned to look at the girl to which Jen was pointing. She was about my age and she held up her heavily bandaged arm. "He was nine," she said, grimly.

Then Jen picked up a walkie-talkie from her belt. "S-eleven requiring more benzos, over?"

In a tinny, crackly tone came the reply, *"Copy, S-eleven, limited supply. Work with what you have. Over."*

"Copy. Out." Her face was like carved stone. "Don't waste the tranqs. Only use them if you are sure you can get the man into the truck. Otherwise, shoot. Rescue as many women as you can and get them in the trucks marked *W*."

We rolled out of the barracks in convoy, about six army trucks. I was sitting next to Emily. After no more than a few miles, she shouted and pointed out of the back of the truck. "Over there!" A woman was tied to a nearby lamppost, naked, sagging into the rope. Jen shouted for the driver to stop the truck. She scanned the street and then jumped out, running over to the woman. As she reached her, four men emerged from a nearby hedge running full pelt. Jen could barely get her gun up in time but when she did, she floored the men without wasting a shot. When she reached the naked woman, she just turned and jogged back, scanning the area for any more men.

As she caught my eye climbing back into the truck, she shook her head once. She called for the truck to drive on.

I found out later that Jen hadn't even been in the army, not really. She'd been a reservist, called up a few days prior to the first few cases of SANS in the UK. As an officer, she'd found herself in charge when those above her got infected, were killed by their male comrades or went AWOL to find their families.

It was rumoured that she'd forced every man left at the base in Pirbright, infected or not, into a bunker at gunpoint, and then shut the door. She'd ordered the women not to open the door until it fell quiet inside.

On that first day out, we rescued eighty-seven women and rounded up twenty-three men. I didn't have to shoot anyone.

I can't remember thinking about my old life at all. It was as if home, family and friends had suddenly stopped existing and instead there was just me and Emily. And I wasn't the only one. Nobody asked about family in the barracks – it was an unspoken rule. I was adapting to this new situation, enjoying it, even. You have to remember: I was nineteen.

On day four, everything changed.

Emily was becoming more and more withdrawn. She barely looked at me as she climbed into the back of the truck, holding her gun under one arm with its strap trailing on the floor.

"Carry your gun properly!" barked Jen, looking at Emily. I caught the roll of Emily's eyes as she picked up the gun and took her seat on the hard bench of the truck.

It was becoming more difficult to find surviving women, in houses at least. The women who'd made it came looking for us, rather than the other way round.

Some mothers were keeping their sons at home if they were young enough to restrain. But they were struggling to keep them hydrated. We had a number of mothers bring us younger boys that day – small, pink, warm little bundles, clawing at us with weakened, scrawny limbs. Every time, I promised the mother that her son would receive proper care back at the hospital. I looked her in the eyes whilst making that promise. I thought I was telling the truth.

All the men we found were infected. Some we subdued with a benzo, two or more of us working together, others we just left – drove past, especially the packs of them. There were a lot of blues lying on the verges at the sides of roads or slouched in shop doorways. Blue crew, that's a detail I'm glad I was never on. Occasionally, moths fluttered around the dead or settled near the eyes – always the eyes.

After driving for about two hours, we pulled up into an estate. Ten or so big houses with long, well-cut lawns sat in a crescent, overlooking an oval-shaped green, with a fancy car, sometimes two, parked on each drive. There were no women hovering by the front doors, no signs up, like we'd seen in other roads – posters or bed sheets with things like *baby needs formula. Please help*! Or *John, we've gone to my mother's – we love you*. And the air didn't smell right. Some faint mustardy tang was drifting from behind the houses, like the smell of cigarette smoke in clothes. But what was putting me most on edge was the feeling of being watched.

"I think we should move on," I said. We stood in a group, about twelve of us, on the silent road. "Something feels off."

"We need to check out at least a few houses," said Jen. "There might be some women trapped."

I could tell from the way her eyes flicked from house to house that she felt it too, that feeling of being watched by some hidden squatting thing.

"In pairs, go knock on the doors. Keep your guns high." She glanced at Emily when she said this, before picking four women to stay behind with the truck, including the driver.

Emily and I took a house to the right of the truck, one with a thick, grey, modern door and a new, black Jag on the drive. I felt exposed walking up the driveway. I looked over and Emily was looking down at her feet, her hair falling over her face in stringy clumps. "Shall I knock?" I said.

She looked up at the door and shrugged. "Try the bell."

It was one of those doorbells with a camera eye. A loud peal of tinkling notes played inside as I pressed the button.

Nothing. The tiniest movement caught my eye from the front lower window on our left. I jolted back and raised my gun, sighting it as I'd been shown.

"What is it?" whispered Emily, also with her rifle up.

The sight was wobbling all over the place as my hands shook. But nothing else moved. "I thought I saw… there's nothing there. Forget it."

We lowered the guns and as I looked around I could see that the other pairs hadn't found anyone either. Jen signalled to us from a few doors down to check round the back. The gate to the back garden was locked.

"I can climb it, if you give me a leg up," said Emily.

I knelt down and she stood on my shoulder. For a moment she just stood on me. "What are you waiting for? You're not light," I hissed.

"Sorry. I was checking it out."

Then I felt her boot press down hard on my back as she got the momentum to jump.

"Fuck! Ouch!"

A scrambling noise had come from above my head before the thud of boots hit the floor on the other side. Emily drew the bolt and appeared from behind the now-open gate. "It seems clear, but the garden's huge. I can't see what's round the back of the house."

As we moved, I raised my rifle, sliding the safety bolt to the left. The mustardy smoky smell was getting stronger.

When we rounded the corner, I noticed that the garden was extensive. A path navigated around a number of trees and bushes before disappearing into a distant hedge. The lawn had been meticulously clipped into semi-circular shapes, the borders lined by crowds of flowers.

I couldn't see any people, so I slid the safety catch back on.

"They've probably gone to a holiday home in Wales," I said, turning to Emily.

Emily wasn't listening. The colour had drained from her face, and her eyes were wide. I followed her stare to the left of where we stood, about a hundred yards away. Someone had been having a bonfire.

The fire was long dead. All that was left was a dark clump of charred wood and ash that drifted up on gusts of breeze. Although it was a way off, it was definitely the source of the smell. A tall structure rose from its centre, about six feet high and curved over at the top. But I couldn't quite make out what it was. I started towards it, but Emily held my arm. "Let's just go back."

"I'll be two secs," I said. "Wait here, if you want."

As I got closer, I realised that the fire must have been made around a garden pagoda, one of those ornate metal ones for flowers to climb up. Half of it still pointed upwards from the centre of the ash pit, before bending slightly, and the metal was twisted and charred with bits peeling off it in weird angles. It was only when I got closer that I realised it wasn't just the metal that was twisted. There was something fixed to the structure, tied to the metalwork and part of the tangled mess.

When I got really close, I could make out the shape – the remains of two figures fixed to the pagoda, one larger, although still much shorter than the pagoda, with its arms around a much shorter one. A small arm, burned and sinewy, reached for me from the black mass. Above it, part of a face looked out from the carnage – an eye socket and a blackened cheek, half a jaw and, above that, just the shape of a head and shoulders, like an old-fashioned wooden clothes peg. It was difficult to separate the two figures. They'd fused with the structure, and with each other.

My eyes absorbed the scene, but my mind refused to. I looked down at my feet and, at the edge of the scorched area there was a plastic Barbie looking up at me. I reached for it, noticing how its hair was singed off, its face melted like a cartoony Halloween mask. The sparkly lime-green dress was untouched and obscenely bright against the black earth. Before I could pick up the doll, bile rushed to the back of my throat. I bent over and vomited on the lawn. As I heaved, bent double, aching with the effort of throwing up, Emily screamed.

Then the shooting started.

A mob of men ran at me, streaming forwards from the direction of the hedge. I was caught between turning around and running full speed back to the truck, and opening fire. I chose the worst: a combination of both options. I started running backwards whilst trying to aim and pull the trigger. I couldn't work out why the gun wouldn't fire until I realised I still had the catch on. And it was whilst I was fumbling with the catch that I fell backwards and landed sitting on the grass. They were nearly on me, ten yards away. I could smell the smoke on their clothes and something else – the sharp stench of petrol.

I fired, for real this time, spraying at the mob in a panic. I got some in the arm, some in the leg. They jerked like puppets when I found my mark. I was filled with a wanton hatred, a heady sickness that I'd never felt before. *Bastards! Monsters!* I wanted to keep on firing. Those loud cracks were like short screams, signifying how I felt.

Then a hand reached and grabbed my shoulder from behind. I swung my rifle around and nearly fired, only freezing my trigger finger at the very last second. I was panting. "Emily."

"They're dead. They're dead, Liv. It's okay."

But I wasn't okay. I struggled to get my breath. "They… burned… girls."

Emily held my shoulder and gave it a squeeze. "I saw this kind of stuff online before the networks went down. Try not to think about it."

The truck horn started to beep – three loud honks: the signal to get back. I heard some sporadic shots from another garden as Emily helped me to my feet and we jogged back to the gate, our rifles raised. A man came at us from the direction of the road, just as we went through the gate. I shot him in the chest without hesitating. He fell forwards so that Emily and I had to step over him to get out of the garden.

As we got to the front of the house, the door opened and a man dressed in a pressed suit and a purple tie appeared in the doorway. He had his arms up. "Help me," he sobbed. "I don't know what to do."

"Kneel down," shouted Emily. I kept my gun trained on him.

He complied immediately, the expensive material of his suit pulling taut on his thighs and rising at his ankles to reveal a pair of bright green socks.

Emily was head down, searching for a cable tie and a benzo in her rucksack, when I shot him. I pulled the trigger and watched him crumble to the side onto the doorstep. Emily whipped her head up and jumped to her feet.

"What did you do?" she asked. Her voice was quiet and shaking.

"He was about to jump us. He was faking."

She looked at me, frowning, "I didn't see him move, Liv."

"You weren't looking," I replied. "Let's go."

CHAPTER 13

"We're here," said Olivia in a clipped tone, slowing the car to a crawl.

I realised I'd been holding my breath. She'd told me she'd killed a guy in cold blood and now it was hard to tell what she was thinking. As she'd been speaking, her voice had become monotone. The only concession to the horrors that she'd been reliving was the way she wasn't looking at me, even though I was staring at her. Instead, she kept her gaze fixed straight ahead.

She turned off the road and onto a narrow, overgrown track that led up and to the left. The car lurched and bumped its way for another two hundred yards or so, then came to a stop in front of a grey farmhouse, weighed down by an extensive blooming wisteria and a tangle of ivy. A woman, in her early sixties, at a guess, slender and tall with long, grey, curly hair, was hovering outside the door to the house, obviously waiting for us to arrive. She had her arms crossed tightly over her cardigan.

"Stay here a minute," said Olivia, still not looking at me. She got out of the car and went over to the waiting woman. They shared an awkward-looking hug and spoke for a few moments. The grey-haired woman looked in my direction at various points in their conversation. I smiled, but she didn't smile back. Finally, she shook her head and went inside. Olivia came back to the car.

"Okay," she said. "Come in. But try to keep calm. Remember, it's all fine."

Nothing is guaranteed to set your nerves jangling more than somebody telling you to stay calm. I really didn't want to get out of the car. "Your friend. She didn't seem to think everything's fine. She looked like she didn't want me here when you were talking."

"Emily's just on edge. We both are. Let's go inside and talk." She looked around at that, as if worried that there was someone hiding behind a tree, which didn't help my mood.

Emily. "The same Emily as..." I allowed my voice to trail off.

In reply she offered an impatient nod.

I unfolded myself from the passenger side, then slammed the door. The noise was sharp in the silence and a few birds flew from a nearby tree, startled. The farmhouse was surrounded by woodland. At this time of year the trees formed a lush canopy. Blades of light filtered to the ground, but most of the sun's light was blocked so that the ground was shrouded and gloomy. Olivia moved quickly towards the farmhouse. My legs hadn't quite woken up from sitting so long in the car, so I was forced to hobble after her. It was cool under the trees and it smelt of damp earth. It was the sort of place the moths like to settle, and I looked around to see if there were any lurking in the trees. I couldn't spot any but they're hard to pick out. I was still unsettled by our earlier encounter with the swarm.

I caught up with Olivia when she stopped beneath an ancient oak tree, its thick arms straining under the weight of its summer harvest. The trunk split into two, one stout shaft rising skywards and a second – slimmer but still the thickness of a man's thigh – arched off to the left at about head height. She patted the rough bark of the smaller limb. "Check it out," she said, pointing to a deep hollow in the branch, about the size of a letterbox. I stood on tiptoe and looked inside. It was full of silvery webbing, millions of pale strands, crisscrossing over each other, lining the inside of the branch, which seemed to have been hollowed out. It smelt rank and sweet, like rotting fruit. Then I saw movement from within the webbing, an undulating of the fibres, like little fingers, probing, trying to find their way out. A lone caterpillar crawled across the surface of the sac, pale and maggoty, haloed by a mane of long bushy hairs. The sight of those hairs made me shudder, and I stepped back. "Should we report it?" I asked. It was against the law to leave nests like these. The habitation authority had teams that would come and burn them out, although these days people cared less than they used to.

"No," said Olivia. "I just wanted to show you." Then she moved off towards the farmhouse.

I took a last look at the tree and thought I spotted the mottled brown of a moth's wing fluttering in the canopy above.

We entered the old building through a heavy front door that led straight into a large, dim kitchen. The smell of the woods seemed to follow us inside, added to the note of damp coming from the thick stone walls. Despite the mildewy smell, I couldn't shake the putrid, sweet stench of the caterpillar nest. The woman from outside was placing something heavy onto a lit stove – a kettle, maybe – so she had her back to me. I looked to my right to a huge pine table, covered in papers and books and a collection of unlabelled tins.

The room had one other occupant.

Instinct sent a jolt through every nerve, and I backed up across the room, flattening myself against a dresser, already scanning the kitchen for a makeshift weapon.

"*Luca!*"

He was standing next to the table holding his hands in the air, in a "don't shoot!" pose. He was wearing an old flannel shirt and a pair of tracksuit bottoms, both of which were too small for him. His young face was creased into an expression of uncertainty and his eyes flicked from Olivia to me and then back to Olivia, as if not sure who he should talk to.

"*Luca!*" I turned to Olivia, keeping him in my peripheral

vision and edging closer to the door. "What have you done? He's been exposed. He'll become– But *why?* Do you even have any benzo?"

"Mary," said Olivia. "Mary, stop for a moment and listen. He's not going to become infected, I promise. Please, come and sit down." She gestured to the table in the centre of the kitchen.

My mind went through a number of possibilities in quick succession. Maybe he hadn't been out long enough; maybe he had just got lucky for a while. Perhaps the moths were less entrenched here. But then the image of the earlier swarm passed through my mind. And the nest. There was a nest of caterpillars right outside the door! This place, more than most, was completely infested, and yet here sat Luca, sentient, coherent and placid. "So," I said. "He isn't showing symptoms yet. He will. Give it another four hours, six at the most."

"He's had some medicine, Mary, a type of vaccine," replied Olivia. "It protects men from the toxin, for a while, at least."

I looked at Luca as he sat at the table, his eyes wide. When he spoke, his voice was trembling, "They said it's going to be okay, Mary. I'm sorry to scare you like this."

"How can you be sure? Where did you get it?" I addressed Olivia, not going towards the table, as she seemed to be suggesting, but not moving further towards the door, either.

Olivia inclined her head towards the woman with the curly, grey hair and the serious expression, who had turned to face us holding a tray with a teapot and some mugs. "Emily, she's been working for the MWA. It's a long story, and we'll explain later, but for now, sit down and have some tea."

I took a seat at the kitchen table opposite Luca, not taking my eyes off him for a moment. He was as handsome as ever, but his face was puffy, as if he'd been crying.

Olivia sat down on my right, and the other woman placed the tray on the table before taking the seat to my left. So, this was Emily. Olivia's story of her feckless, phone-obsessed friend came back to me, but I couldn't quite square the image with this careworn, serious-looking woman. Olivia reached over, poured some steaming cups of tea and placed them in front of us. The room was quiet for a few moments, the steam rising from our tea in vaporous coils the only movement.

Emily moved over to the dresser. Opening a drawer, she took out a test tube of pinkish pills, each the size of a pea. She placed the test tube on the table in front of me. It was then I started working through the magnitude in my mind. I grabbed Olivia's arm on the table and gripped it tightly. "The infected? Does it work on them?" I held my breath for the answer.

"No," she replied, her voice puzzled. "It's a vaccine, not a cure. Why?"

I took my hand from hers, shrugged and exhaled, allowing my heartbeat to slow. "No reason. I just... It's a lot to take in, that's all."

I gripped my hot mug to stop myself shaking and took a few sips of the tea while Emily explained.

"The male immune system is not weaker, exactly, but less vigilant than the female one. This is true for any sort of contagion: men's bodies tend to notice a pathogen less quickly, so their immune response is mobilised at a slightly later stage. As this toxin is so fast acting, this small difference in response time proved disastrous for men. By the time their immune systems notice the toxin, it is already in the brain, and the inflammation their own bodies cause in response to the foreign invader is actually what kills them, as it occurs in such a vital organ." She replaced her tea on the table and I noticed her hands were shaking. "It's the men's own physiology that kills them or renders them insane, and whether they die almost instantly or turn psychotic depends on what part of the brain the toxin has reached when their inflammatory response is activated. Women are spared because our bodies notice and react to the toxin before it has a chance to reach the brain in any significant quantities."

I looked at Olivia, then back at Emily. "Olivia didn't tell me you were a doctor."

"Lab assistant," replied Emily.

"Emily was part of the team that worked on it, two years ago," said Olivia. "I think it's time we filled you in."

Emily tucked her hair behind her ears and told me the whole story. She spoke of how she'd worked with a doctor by the name of Desai. How they took a leaf out of the book of the scientists working on the Covid vaccine years ago. How, recently, they were able to isolate a protein from the toxin that they could use to teach men's immune systems to recognise and attack the intruder before it has a chance to harm them, only to have the MWA close the project down and order them to hand over their notes. She explained how Desai had refused, withholding her notes and the prototype serum, threatening to go public.

"They made it look like a suicide," said Emily. "They even planted a note, but I knew it wasn't her writing and – anyway – she didn't want to kill herself, she wanted to get the vaccine out there: it was what she'd dedicated decades of her life to." Then, after a pause, "They followed me for a while, but when they realised I wasn't going to cause any trouble, they transferred me to another department. I'm sure her death was a message to me too, though, warning me to keep quiet. Bastards. She just wanted to help the men," she finished bitterly.

I was no fan of the Men's Welfare Authority, but murder? That was pushing it. "So, how come Luca's sitting here drinking tea, not turning blue or trying to kill us, if you handed over the prototype?"

Luca hadn't said anything since I'd arrived. He'd sat hunched over with his elbows on the table, staring quietly into his tea. He looked up when I said this. "Don't say such horrible things, Mary," he said. His eyes were damp with tears.

"I'm sorry, Luca. I didn't mean to… I'm sorry." I went to pat his hand but then stopped myself. A man outside the facility was a danger – I couldn't brush away forty years of caution in an instant.

Emily looked over to Olivia, who nodded, encouraging her to go on.

"About six months ago, a package arrived at my house out of nowhere. I've no idea who delivered it. I can only assume that Sanga – that is, Dr Desai, gave it to someone she trusted until things died down. I guess I was the backup plan. But… I didn't know what to do with it. I was worried I was still on the MWA's radar."

"So she came to me," said Olivia.

Emily put her mug down. "I knew I could count on you." She reached over and took Olivia's hand from across the table. Her voice was suddenly thick with tears. "I'm sorry, Liv. Your girls, and Lucie, I've put you all in danger."

Olivia squeezed Emily's hand. "You let me worry about them. If we're careful, we'll be fine."

It was a lot to take in. I was never a believer in conspiracy theories, even in the days before the infestation, when the Internet spat them out twenty-four seven. "So, why are the MWA against this? I mean, why aren't they shouting about it from the rooftops? This has got to be good for them, right?"

Olivia let go of Emily's hand and turned to me. "Maybe they're scared that it'll disrupt everything and it might go back to being like it used to be. Men in charge."

A small but imperious voice in the back of my mind suggested that if this was true, then *they* might actually have a point.

"But I don't think that's the only reason," cut in Emily. "It's about keeping control. If the vaccine is made public, the government will own it. The MWA is the best-funded and most powerful authority in The Union. They run the facilities, the Insemination Department and now the visitations. Without the toxin, those things become much less important."

My mind was drawn back five years, to the face of an MWA advisor – Skylar. Her eyes gleaming as she looked around the small green room. *I bet loads of women would love to try it, at least once. The MWA could really make this work.*

I frowned. "So, why don't you take Luca and show him to the Council? Drive to the Citadel right now and march him up to the gates of their offices."

Olivia looked at Luca, sitting with his shaved head in his hands, staring down into his empty mug. She gave a deep sigh. "That's exactly what we would like to do, but I'm not keen on taking Luca into the centre of the Citadel, or even sneaking him in, for that matter. A man at the gates of the Council would cause panic for a start, he might get injured in the confusion. Also, the MWA will be on the lookout. I don't know how far their reach stretches, but they've already murdered to keep this quiet. We don't know if they suspect Emily or me, but we have to assume that they might."

"Daisy asking me to keep an eye on you...? Does that mean..."

"Possibly," replied Olivia. "At least, we have to assume they have their suspicions."

Whilst Olivia, Emily and I were talking, Luca had taken our cups over to the sink. He'd rinsed them out and refilled the kettle and put it on to boil. Now he turned to Olivia. "Please – am I allowed to go outside? Just for a minute?"

Olivia smiled. "Of course. But stay near the house. Oh, and don't touch any plants or insects. You might get stung."

Luca's eyes widened. "Would I die?" He regarded the woods beyond the window with apprehension.

"Go on, Luca," said Olivia. "You'll be fine." It was coming up to nine in the evening, but it was still light outside. "Go get a jumper," she said. "It's chilly now. And if you hear a car, come straight back. Okay?"

"He'll be fine," said Emily, seeing the look of concern on my face. "When we tested the vaccine, the men could actually put a caterpillar on their bare skin and not be affected. It's even stronger protection than women's natural immunity." There was a note of pride in her voice.

Olivia gave a small smile. "He could probably put his hand in that nest out front, Mary, and not experience any adverse effects at all."

I shuddered at the thought. "Where are those men – the ones you tested it on? Why not use one of those as proof?"

Emily lowered her head. "They were staying offsite, on a farm about a mile from the lab. When Dr Desai died – when she was murdered – I went there but the test subjects were gone. There was no sign of them. I guess the MWA rounded them up. Hid them away... or worse."

Luca came back to the table holding a chunky, yellow jumper. "I'll stay round the back. Don't worry." He put on the jumper and opened the door. He stood on the threshold as the dying light of the day filtered through the trees and bathed him in amber shafts. Then, taking a deep breath, he stepped outside, shutting the door quietly behind him.

Olivia, Emily and I sat in silence and I allowed what I'd learned to sink in. This was much bigger than I'd imagined. Tony, Logan and every man who'd ever begged me to describe the smell of grass or the taste of snow could be free to experience it for themselves. I rose from the table, ignoring the glance between Emily and Olivia, and went over to the window. Luca stood still amongst the canopy of trees, face raised to the sky, his eyes wide in rapture. How unfathomably big the sky must seem to him. He stretched out his arms as if wanting to fly, then he began to spin in place, still staring upwards. I smiled, remembering a small version of Ryan doing the same thing, afterwards staggering towards me on unsteady legs, laughing, begging to be picked up. I remembered doing the same thing, myself, as a little girl; such a long time since I'd felt that kind of uncomplicated joy. Luca stopped spinning and began to jump, his arms outstretched, hands open and grasping as if trying to catch the sky, a grin plastered over his young face.

Sky.

Everyone deserves sky.

It occurred to me that, in the old world, had Ryan been father to a son, that son could have been Luca's age. A boy Luca's age would have been more interested in music and Xboxes than running about in the woods. But even so, what would it have been like? Roast dinners on a Sunday? Family holidays? Weddings? Babysitting? I thought I'd come to terms with the loss, but I felt it engulf me, a choking nostalgia for the things lost. Perhaps it didn't have to be like this.

But the risks were considerable.

I dragged myself away from the window, returning to the table. Sitting down, I faced the other two women. "How did you get Luca away from the facility?"

It was Emily who replied. "A friend of mine in the MWA, one we can trust, sent over Luca's transfer request. It wasn't hard, actually. Luca was already set for a transfer."

"Where to?" I asked. "I haven't heard anything about it."

"Well, that's the odd thing," said Emily. "His destination was classified. My friend took advantage and moved up the date. In fact, that's why we chose Luca in the first place. It gives us time until his actual transfer is due. When someone realises that he didn't make it to his destination, wherever that might be, they will be able to track it back. We've got a few days before he's missed." She looked around at the door and I followed her gaze, as if a bunch of Law Abidance officers were poised on the other side, waiting to storm the room.

Then Olivia spoke. "The MWA are only one member of the voting Council. There are six others. Some of them, we suspect, are in the pocket of the MWA, but not all. If we can get Luca to the Citadel, or proof of the vaccine, then we can force the Council to acknowledge the vaccine. It'll come out then – all of it. The MWA, the murder, the missing men. We can pull down their operation. Without the toxin, we won't need the facilities."

We. I noted the shift in pronoun and its implications. A small part of me hotly resented Olivia for getting me involved.

What about Nicky? What would happen to him if something happened to me? The MWA ran the sanatoriums and there were places far worse than Elmwood.

The door burst open, and I jumped about a foot into the air, but it was just a very excited Luca who ran into the kitchen. "You'll never guess! There are small furry animals climbing all over the trees. They have these enormous tails and they move so fast! Are they tigers, Mary? Come look!"

I forced myself to smile and said brightly, "I'll look in a minute, Luca, I promise." Then I turned back to Olivia and Emily sitting at the table, and the smile dropped from my face. "How do I fit into this?"

CHAPTER 14

Later on, when Luca had come back in from exploring the woods, he wanted me to go upstairs to show me his room, but I told him I'd see it next time. Olivia gave an annoyed sniff when I said "next time" and Emily wouldn't look at me. He was crestfallen, but then he saw the mobile phone on the table. "Can I hold it?" he asked, then, as he cradled it in the palm of his hand, "What does it *do*?"

"Not much these days, Luca," I replied. "You used to be able to call people all over the world with one of these – see them too."

Luca looked dubious as he turned it over in his hand and inspected it from every angle. "How?"

As I left with Olivia, Emily and Luca were sitting close together at the kitchen table, leaning over my old mobile phone, their faces bathed in the screen's reflection. Emily held it and flicked through the pictures. I saw a flash of Adrian standing at a fairground, Southsea perhaps, with Ryan as a podgy toddler sitting on his shoulders. I wanted to run over and prise it from her hand, save my last link to a time that held a place for me. But I left them to it. I left Luca at the table, his eyes wide with wonder as he scanned the visual echoes of a world long dead. "Remember to delete all of Mary's stuff before you start recording," said Olivia as we left, "and when you're done, hide it where I showed you."

It was getting dark, the black silhouettes of the trees only just contrasting with the darkening sky. Olivia slammed her door as she got in beside me and fumbled angrily with the key. I looked out of the passenger window and we started off.

The silence stretched on for a few miles. Olivia stared forwards, using the illumination of the headlights to pick a path through the potholes. The air in the car was heavy with things unsaid.

"I gave you the phone. That's enough, isn't it?"

No answer.

"I'm too old, and I'm tired. You shouldn't even have asked."

Again, nothing. I couldn't see her clearly in the shadowy light cast back from the headlights. "Contact Jade Philips yourself and explain, or any of the other Heads of Council. You don't need me."

More silence.

My voice was becoming whiny now, and I hated myself for it. "I only met her one time, years ago. She won't even remember me. That story I told you... I made more of it than there was." I felt my face grow hot, and I was glad of the dark to hide it. "You have the phone. The recording, it'll be enough."

"Forget it, Mary. I'll try and contact her," she spoke quietly and calmly, which didn't make me feel any better. Then she turned to me, her face drawn and tight. "But she's more likely to take your call, Mary, and you know it." She turned back to the road. "Sure, I might get through to the secretary and leave a message. But who might read that message? Who might intercept it? The MWA doesn't leave things to chance. Someone warned Daisy about me, so they probably know about my connection to Emily." Her voice became higher and more insistent, pleading even. "If you could just speak to her, convince her, tell her that we're going to have recorded proof. If you could just call her–" She broke off and her voice grew sharp, "Oh, forget it!"

Recording Luca on the phone outside was a good idea, so was photographing the notes. I'd given them that phone, handed it over even though it contained the only pictures I had of my husband, my son. All those memories, wasn't that a big enough sacrifice? If I became more involved, I might end up risking more than my own life. I might end up risking Nicky's, and that I could not do.

We both sat in mutinous silence for a while. The weight of Olivia's disappointment heavy in the confines of the small car. "What if they're right?" I asked into the darkness ahead.

"What do you mean?" she asked.

I stared down into my lap. "You were there, in the time before. What if – do you want it to return to how it was?"

What followed was the longest silence so far. Then, eventually, "It wouldn't."

"Really?" I folded my arms tightly over my chest. "What about all that stuff no one has to worry about anymore – walking around at night constantly looking over your shoulder, strangers online calling women fat pigs?" I began to warm to the subject. "Remember the slut-shaming, the double standards, the glossy magazines with pouty women in pointy shoes… What about…"

"What about Luca!" Her cry shot through the car like a cracking boulder. "What about all the men at the facility, and the facilities around the country, all of them with their faces pressed against the glass, gasping for just one breath of fresh air? What about Tony, sitting alone back at the facility, unable to leave or move or start again, stuck in a sterile box, with nothing but laminated bird books and am-dram for the rest of his life? You can't do this one thing – just for him!"

Tony. I closed my eyes in the dark. He was going to take Luca's departure hard. First Logan, and now this. I sighed and massaged my temples to try to ease a nascent headache. "You don't know everything about me, Olivia. Okay?"

She changed the car into fourth gear and sped up as the road became clearer. "What? What don't I know, Mary?"

I could have told her then about Nicky. Maybe she would have understood. Perhaps she could have helped me protect him. But I'd been hiding the truth for so many years, even from myself, that when it came to it, I turned towards the passenger window and looked out into the passing darkness. "You don't know what I've got to lose," I whispered.

I thought she hadn't heard me over the rumble of the road, but then she replied, "I know Luca hasn't got much to lose, or Tony. I know I did some bad things back then, things I'm ashamed of. And I know that I've been given a chance to do something right."

Olivia – then

After the bonfire, I smelt the smoke on every man I met. I adopted a *point-shoot-move* approach. Jen Harting must have approved of my attitude, as a few days later she promoted me to group leader – but now we were on hunting expeditions rather than rescues. We still found a few women hiding in attics or barricaded into shops. But the men we found were no longer to be collected. All the benzos went to the hospitals. We were left with bullets.

We worked non-stop for days. Jen was coordinating the whole men's hospital operation. There were facilities spread from Dorset right up to Leeds and no phones, only a military radio system. At the barracks, more refugees were arriving every day, supplies had to be salvaged; food, drugs and bodies had to be dealt with, beds found, vehicles fuelled and maintained. The men needed to be looked after in the hospitals, sedated, fed. Then the power started to cut out. Jen told me that there weren't enough women engineers to keep the grid up and running and that what was left of the government didn't know what to do about it, because they were, in her words, *a bunch of fucking idiots.*

It was hard on everyone. A few weeks before, we'd been mothers, managers, students, solicitors. Now we were shovelling, fighting and, most of us, grieving. It began to sink

in that I might not see my family again. There was an ache –
part fear, part loss – that caught you unaware and forced you
to freeze, to gaze into nothing. You would occasionally pass
someone and see them like this, blank eyed and still. If you
touched them on the arm, they would flinch and turn, a cold
half-life returning to their eyes. But the thing I remembered
most about that time was the smell of smoke and the sharp
crack of a rifle.

I started volunteering to go out on more and more rescue
missions, or patrols, or trips to local towns to salvage supplies.
I'd come back to the dorm and fall into bed exhausted after
twenty, sometimes thirty, hours without a break. I didn't want
to give myself time to think. Unlike Emily, who spent most of
her time crying – or sleeping. She could sleep for twenty hours
straight.

I remember about a week after we arrived at the base, Jen
called me into her office, a tiny box room with a low ceiling
and thin partitioned walls. I could see from her face that things
were grim. She'd been up all night sorting out a problem with
a group of women. They didn't like the rules, and wanted to
leave and take their chances, find their men. Jen was fine with
this, of course – this wasn't a prison – but they wanted to take
food and supplies, and we couldn't spare them. Tensions had
become febrile, and scuffles had broken out. Jen had ordered
that the group be escorted to a nearby town, one that had yet
to be cleared and salvaged. All this whilst trying to ensure there
was enough food for the barracks and organising the men's
hospital programme.

I knew from working with her so closely that she hadn't
slept in days. We'd both been filling in on cremation duty, as
few were willing to do it, even despite pointing out that if we
didn't get rid of the bodies, it was going to get a lot worse.

I sat across from her in the cramped space and noted the
dark circles under her eyes.

"This is from the medics at John Radcliff Research Lab."

She waved a sheet of hand-written notes at me. "It says that the manics won't eat or drink unless they're heavily doped. We can use benzos mixed with a few kinds of antipsychotics – none of which I can pronounce – but we don't have the stock. The report says that the men are not going to get better. The damage to their brains is permanent. There's no time to find a cure."

"That's bad," I said, but we knew it already. When I now said, *we're working on a cure*, the words came out hollow. It had taken six months to find a vaccine for the previous pandemic to ravage the globe, six months with all the finest minds in immunology working on it. We were only weeks into this, and men were dying in their thousands. It didn't take a scientist to tell me that we hadn't a chance of saving them. When Jen didn't say anything else, I asked, "What are you going to do?"

She looked at me long and hard. "What do you think we should do, Olivia? I'm running out of ideas." Her usual briskness had faded, and her voice was weary with an edge of irritation, as if I were being intentionally slow-witted.

I leaned my head back and thought, my sleep-deprived mind trying to conjure ideas from the mist. "We could draft more women into the hospitals. If they can get the men to drink when they're lucid, then..." I trailed off and half shrugged.

"They're not lucid for that long, twenty minutes maybe. And the time gets shorter and shorter the sicker they become." Her voice still had that sharpness to it, as if I were failing her. "You'd have to have one woman between two or three men for it to work. It would mean over half of the women left going into the hospitals. And what would they find there? Husbands, brothers, and sons tied to beds, delirious, screaming and violent. You'd have women begging for more drugs, drugs we haven't got. And what about the other jobs that need doing? Maintenance, salvaging, security? We need to find the moths, burn their nests, clear the roads, keep the peace." She sighed and sat back in her chair.

Despite her tone, I felt a swell of pride to be included like this – to be sought out by Jen, involved in the discussion.

She gave me another hard look from across the desk. "We have to think about what we want this world to look like in the future. We have to start planning for *after*."

My mind fixed on the image of a Barbie doll in a lime-green dress, with a melted face. I thought I could smell the diesel from the generators outside. "We could separate the men. Save those we can." I wasn't sure how the words would sound when they came out of me, but my voice was calm, almost casual.

There was another pause before Jen finally spoke. "And the ones we can't save?" Her face was all hard angles for a moment as she put her palms flat on the desk between us, as though she was stretching her will towards me, flexing.

A small hand reaching out from the charcoal. I looked her straight in the eye as I said, "We say that there was nothing more we could have done."

Did Jen know that this would happen? Did she wait for me to say the words for her – thought if she created a void, I'd rush to fill it, partly absolving her? I think so.

Jen looked back down at the medical report she held in her hand and her voice was quieter than I'd ever heard it. "Those with injuries, those that are too far gone – the weakest?"

I stared at her, offering silent tacit agreement.

"I'll give it some more thought," she said, although we both knew that the decision had just been made.

I got up to leave. The room and the smell of the generators were giving me a headache. We were going out again that evening on patrol and I was looking forward to it. *Point-shoot-move.*

As I was leaving, Jen spoke, "I've suggested to your friend Emily that she go and work with the team at John Radcliff. We need the bright ones researching this thing and I don't think here is the right place for her."

It was true. Emily had become more and more withdrawn over the last few days. She barely looked at me and anything

I asked her was met with a shrug or a non-committal word: *sure, okay, maybe*. I had an hour before patrol and I found her in the dorm, packing the few items she'd collected whilst here – a couple of man-sized t-shirts, some men's boxer shorts, a hairbrush – chucking them haphazardly into her rucksack whilst staring blankly at the bed. I nodded at a small pile of benzos and cable ties on her bedside table. "I don't think you'll need them where you're going."

She turned to me and half smiled but said nothing. At least she looked at me.

I didn't want her to go. I'd spent nearly two years in love with this girl, even though I knew that she didn't feel the same way. She was the last hold I had on my life before. But I was also glad she was going. I had to keep moving. Go forward. Jen was depending on me, and Emily was part of the past. At least that was how I saw it then.

She came over to me and put her arms around me. She was shorter than me and I tried not to think about the figures from the dead bonfire, one taller than the other.

"I'll miss you, Liv," she whispered.

"You too," I managed.

She looked up into my face – she was so close and I could smell the sandalwood shampoo she'd found a few nights ago in one of the soldier's drawers. "Don't... don't lose yourself in all this," she said.

"Trust me, Em," I replied. "It's going to be okay."

And then she stood on tiptoe and kissed me softly on the lips. "I'll see you again."

I went out on patrol that night and part of me was relieved. I wanted to prove to Jen that I was strong, and now that I didn't have to worry about Emily, I could be.

A fortnight later, Jen sent me down to a field hospital in Exeter to run the clean-up operation. I was the first in and I wasn't prepared for it, seeing them all stretched out like rotting starfish in their cots, the angry living blanket of flies protecting their decaying hoard. Despite the mask, I could taste the vile funk of death.

We burned the bodies in the car park. That mustardy smoke stayed with me for days, no matter how much I washed myself. It clung to my hair, my skin. I could even smell it in my bedding.

Everyone knows what happened over those next few months and years, that is, everyone of a certain age. They don't teach all of it in schools, of course. They teach the forming of the Union, how the remnants of the government and the army divided control of the country into seven separate authorities. Jennifer Harting is held up as a hero, a woman who made the hard choices when it mattered. I suspect that if public opinion had swung the other way, towards retribution and outrage, that Jen would have pointed at me. I was her insurance policy, her sacrificial lamb.

Later, Jen offered me a position with her, running the MWA. I declined. I went to work in the sanatoriums and, later, the facilities. I spent years thinking over what happened, wondering if there were other less final things we could have done.

I've never spoken about what I did back then, not to my wife Lucie, not to anyone. Lucie was eighteen during the change and had holed up in her university digs for the first few weeks, blocking the doors and living on watery porridge and cup-a-soups. She said she spent most of the time reading Jane Austen novels, before venturing out when the worst was over and being sent to work in a vehicle repurposing plant.

The next time I saw Emily was in an abandoned playground on the outskirts of Coventry about eighteen months ago. It was October and the sky was milky white, the colour of cataracts. She was gaunt, grey and exhausted but still beautiful. She was sitting on an old metal bench, partly hidden by the scrubby bushes that had somehow sprouted from the crumbling concrete.

She was clutching a large, brown envelope on her lap. "Thanks for meeting me," she said. "I knew I could count on you."

CHAPTER 15

Christmas. An old church hall smelling of damp paper and dust and polish and vanilla. Adrian next to me, filming on his phone as a four year-old Ryan solemnly strides down towards a manger clutching a stuffed toy lamb. Dressed in an old pillowcase with holes cut for arms and head, a cord wrapped around his waist, a tea towel fixed upon his small crown with an old sweatband, he joins twenty or so infants singing *Away in a Manger* in varying keys and tempos. It is the sort of memory that catches you when you're working or walking or dreaming or when you're sitting in a sunny canteen on a warm summer's day and the cooks have found some vanilla and added it to the porridge. Or when you're hunched over, rubbing your temples on a plastic sofa in the viewing room and someone has lit a vanilla-scented candle.

Nobody celebrates Christmas anymore. A kind of spiritual agnosticism seems to have taken root – *all-kind* is what it's referred to in schools and preps. No gods, no doctrine – a respect for the natural world, perhaps, but no actual worshipping. Some celebrate the solstices, but that's more to do with agriculture than faith.

Everyone celebrates the Day of Commemoration. Everyone, that is, except uninfected men. The 22nd of July usually falls within the period of confinement, the time of the Eclipse. It means that the facility needs less staff and those who have families can take leave.

I sat in the viewing room and tried not to think about

everything that had happened over the last twenty-four hours. After Olivia had finished her story, she'd beseeched me again to call Jade Philips. And I'd repeated my firm belief that Jade Philips would almost certainly ignore a call from me, and that I'd given them my phone, so my part was done. Then Olivia had gone quiet, and nothing I could do would get her to talk. I didn't tell her about Nicky. I think the whole story would have made her even more adamant that I get involved. But I wasn't about to risk my visits to Elmwood. Not for her, not for Luca, not even for Tony.

News of Luca's transfer swept through the facility. When I visited the men in the viewing hall after breakfast, I expected them to be deep into their rehearsals for the talent show later that day. This had always been one of my favourite days of the year – singers warming up their voices, groups of dancers practising intricate choreography, laughter, horsing around – but today the festive mood was muted. The men sat in small huddles, mostly silent, with just an occasional whisper. On the tables, the snacks and wine that were usually snaffled up with relish lay untouched. The carer on duty was trying her best to rally the performers but was being met with indifferent sighs, truculent looks and silence.

Tony was nowhere to be seen.

"I'm supposed to take over the part of Julian to his Romeo," Sylvan said, eyes downcast. "I told him I'd learn the lines, no problem, but he just went off on his own. Without Romeo, it's hard to practise."

There weren't many places he could have gone. I went to the dorm room and found him seated on his bunk, a small pallet of eye shadow and a hand mirror at his side. His face was a glory of mauve, yellow and blue, expertly done, immaculate apart from the tear streaks down each cheek.

"Oh Mary, sorry, I was just making up. So much to do, so much to do." His voice was soft, and it was as if only part of him was speaking to me. The other half was dazed and lost behind the elegant contouring of his face. He was looking past me into nothing. "The thing is, every time I make up, I– start to c– cry and I have to start all over again." There were little hiccups in his voice as he spoke, and he held out a pink makeup sponge as if demonstrating the problem.

I sat down on his cot, taking the sponge from him, placing it on the bedside cabinet and clasping his clammy hand in mine. As he stared ahead quietly, his profile looked haggard, his eyes hooded and the makeup reflected in every crease, making him appear much older than late twenties. We didn't say anything for a long time. After Logan was infected, we'd sat in this very spot. But that time Tony had been full of fury and vigour. *How could Logan have left me like that! What was he thinking? It was just like him, Mary… selfish!*

There was no fight in Tony now. "Did they tell you where he's been transferred to Mary?"

"Sorry, they don't tell us anything." I hated lying to him.

"But did they say why?" He looked at me and his kohled eyes fixed mine with such a sad intensity that I felt the lies die on my tongue. Instead, I said, "He told me to tell you goodbye."

"When did you see him!"

"Just… just before he left. He wanted to say goodbye himself but there wasn't time."

Tony closed his eyes and bowed his head. He stayed quiet for so long that I thought he'd forgotten I was there. "I'm so tired of it, Mary."

He leaned into me and I held him then, for a long time. I allowed him to snake his arms around my waist and cling to me. I felt him sob twice, and then he was still.

Suddenly he drew back from me, brought up his head and took a deep, shaking breath. "The show must go on!" His voice had a brittle edge, but his small smile seemed genuine enough. "We cannot disappoint our adoring fans, now, can we?" With that, he picked up his face paint and mirror and began to dab his face with his little finger, touching up the damage his tears had wrought. "Let them all know I'll be along in a moment. And Mary…"

I'd started for the door, and now I turned back towards the man on the bunk. "… tell the chorus dancers that their *Bravura* is out of sync, that it needs a lot of work before it's even halfway good enough and that they are not to expect even ten minutes' rest if they want to avoid embarrassment this evening."

"Tell them yourself, Tony, they won't listen to me," I said over my shoulder as I left the dorm, feeling like perhaps it was going to be okay.

The viewing room was full to bursting, and I sensed the pre-show buzz building. Earlier, Tony had rallied the troops with a *Churchillian* speech, espousing how the men were to perform in honour of Luca, wherever he was, and that they were to make their friend proud. He stood in front of the men, fully made up and draped in a silk robe, and spoke of how they'd all miss Luca – but now they must play their part and no man could, in good conscience, let the facility down. He won them round and his final words were met with a resounding cheer.

It was nearly time. The beige and insipid hall was decked in the men's artwork. The lights were dimmed by a canopy of scraps of silk, and the room smelled of herbal oils that had been sent up by the kitchen staff. The whole effect, backed by the crimson evening sun, was magical.

Many of the kitchen staff were in attendance, as were the carers and ward sisters. Most of them would be off tomorrow, back to their families and lovers, and making ready for this year's Commemoration in a few weeks' time. I would stay, as I always did, having nowhere else to go, and try to make the men's confinement a little more bearable. On Commemoration Day itself, assuming moths were not swarming, Nicky's carer would sometimes let me take him out around the gardens. As I settled myself into one of the few remaining seats at the far edge of the room, I found myself wondering if Nicky's new carer, Gale, would be as flexible.

Tony had commandeered a nearby storeroom as "backstage" and even though the players were hidden, I could hear excited cries and whispers as they readied themselves for the show. Some of the men, those who were not involved in the actual performance, sat at the front on the floor; a lack of chairs also meant that the women who came in last had to stand at the back.

Olivia entered and her eyes scanned the room. I avoided her gaze. Unable to locate a seat, she stood with a small group near the door.

Then a lot of shushing and one of the older residents, Matthew, took to the stage, resplendent in an indigo silk gown. His face was chalked and pale with a beautiful dove inked on one cheek. "Ladies and fellow residents, welcome to..." He raised his arms to display a clever arrangement of folded silk between his waist and his underarm, creating wings that made him look twice as big as usual. There was a gasp from the audience at the effect. "...an evening of *enchantment!*" The audience cheered and clapped, and Matthew ushered in the first act.

There was comedy, some truly subversive impressions of the staff, myself included. I was unaware that my use of arm gestures was quite so pronounced, nor that my voice was so shrill, nor that I shuffled around in quite such a decrepit manner. But there were plenty of laughs, so I guess the impression struck a chord. The entire audience was moved to tears at a choral rendition of *The Sprig of Thyme,* and the dancers produced lifts and tumbles that drew *oohs* and *ahhs* from those seated. I remember thinking, as the candles in coloured glass jars flickered around the stage, casting jumping lights onto the men's happy faces, that this was just what I needed to take my mind off things. Tomorrow, as the men settled into their month-long confinement, I would consider the momentous events of the last few days. Maybe it was time for a move anyway: a new facility or retirement, even – it was about time. If Olivia and Emily succeeded and the facilities were closed down, I'd be out of a job anyway. But I could think about that later – and here was the star of the show.

Tony rose onto the dais with the dignity and presence of an actor who had trained all his life at the Royal Shakespeare Company. The lighting complimented the shading of his makeup to give him an unearthly magical appearance, yet youthful with expressive darkened eyes and a softly contoured blush smile. He began to speak. A smooth baritone reverberated around the room, and we all held our breath.

"But soft…"

It was perfect.

Sylvan appeared at the side of the stage in a cream silk dress, nipped in at the waist with a length of ribbon. Tony wore embroidered trousers, something the head of costume had worked on for months and which was allowed as a small dispensation for the night of the performance.

The speech was truncated from the original but both actors created such a believable love story that the omissions didn't matter. Sylvan stumbled over his words a few times, and Tony gave him a quick prompt. But the overall effect was magnificent. As Tony's words of *"Sleep dwell upon thine eyes, peace in thy breast!"* echoed around the room, I was in rapture.

We then watched Julian take his own life. Not the false suicide of the original. Sylvan instead mimed stabbing himself and threw a plume of red silk out onto the stage, falling to his knees as it slithered in a pool to the floor.

Then Romeo gave his final lament to Julian. The speech that I had, in my former career, inflicted upon many a year-ten student, but never to such effect:

O my love! my lover!
Death, that hath suck'd the honey of thy breath,
Hath had no power yet upon thy beauty…

Each word dripped with such hurt and such love that I felt a hard knot of feeling weighing on my chest until he finally released us all with the line: *Thus with a kiss, I die.*

He knelt before the now prone body of Sylvan and kissed him gently on both cheeks before collapsing slowly to the floor in a tableau of doomed lovers.

There was a moment of profound silence, and then a momentous cheer swept through the viewing hall. Tony and Sylvan scrambled up as the room got to their feet and cheered in wild abandon. The men on the stage bowed and the noise level rose higher still. Tears streamed down my face as I clapped and whooped with everyone else, but I felt something more than joy. A vast pride swelled in my chest. I knew how hard it must have been for Tony to do this without Luca. I wanted to tell him how proud I was of him. I tried to approach the stage, but the men seated at the front had surged forward and were now lifting Tony and Sylvan aloft, chanting their names as they carried them around the room.

A few minutes later, when the initial hubbub had calmed down, a number of trollies carrying plates of sandwiches, cakes and jellies were wheeled in and an old Queen CD started playing on the PA system. The men embraced their last night of freedom before the start of their confinement. There was even some very raw-tasting nettle wine, although the men were only permitted one glass each.

Some paired off and went and found a quiet place. Some stayed in the hall and clowned around or played games. Some went to double-check the list of belongings they planned to take into the single rooms tomorrow. This evening, the carers and ward sisters took a more relaxed approach to the rules and to the whereabouts of the men, as long as the gates and doors to the outside were locked.

I'd managed to catch up with Tony, who seemed quiet but content. "Luca would have loved it," said a young man who came up to slap him on the back and congratulate him.

Tony turned away, but not before I saw the flash of anguish on his face. I had a sudden urge to tell Tony about the vaccine, but instead I forced a smile. "Try to enjoy yourself, Tony. You've earned it."

Tony nodded. He didn't smile back.

We finally got them all calmed down into their bunks by about 1am.

I was exhausted. The viewing hall needed clearing up – but there was plenty of time for that. The men would be transferred to the single rooms tomorrow, and then my job would become a lot quieter. I crawled into bed without even undressing and slid into a profound and fitful sleep.

Mary – then

The morning after the infestation, Doc woke me, although I don't even remember being asleep. I remember watching Ryan's breathing. I remember Adrian waking in the night – asking for paracetamol and blaming his headache on the wine. But then there was a time unaccounted for, a space of indeterminate blankness so that when Doc growled and I opened my eyes, I felt I'd skipped some hours and it was getting light.

The TV had stopped broadcasting. There was just a message, white text on a black screen: *Sorry. There was a problem connecting to Virgin Media Services. No signal – Please try again later.*

Ryan was awake, sitting up and staring at me. Doc was pressing himself against the door. He was growling – a low, frightened sound – and he was looking directly at Ryan.

"Untie me, Mum."

I nudged Adrian with my foot, but he didn't stir.

"How are you feeling, Ry?"

"I feel okay, but I really need to go to the bathroom."

Had it not been for the dog, I wouldn't have hesitated. I'd have unshackled my son and helped him up the stairs. But I'd never heard Doc growl at Ryan, not once, not even as a puppy. This was the first thing that set off an alarm in my overtired mind. The second was how calm Ryan was. His eyes held mine with fixed intent, void of doubt, as if an adult, one I'd never met, were crouching behind that curly hank of hair, peeking out.

I leaned down and shook Adrian hard. He was breathing, but it was shallow and fast. His face was hot, like sun-baked stone. I slapped him lightly, then a little harder. "Baby, wake up." Nothing. He just lay still, eyes closed, panting with an odd wheeze. And there was something else, unless I was imagining it – a blue tinge to his lips. I leaned over him and I could detect a weird chemical smell coming from his breath.

"I don't think he's waking up, Mum, and I really need to go, like now. Please."

"You need to hold on, Ryan, until I wake your father." I ran into the kitchen and soaked a tea towel with cold water. I squeezed it over Adrian's face and wiped it. No change.

"Just untie me, Mum, just for a minute, so I can go to the loo. Why are you being like this?"

"Just wait!"

"I can't wait. Please, Mum, get these ties off me, *please*."

And I wanted to – because when your kid wants to go to the loo, you feel their urgency as if it is your own. Also, if I could let him go, then maybe this was just me being overanxious – maybe I was making too much of it and Ryan was fine and then Adrian would wake up and be fine, and everything would be okay. If I acted like everything was okay, it would be. But there was a small lizard-like part of my mind that knew that this wasn't fine, that I was in danger.

"You'll just have to do it there, Ry. I'm sorry. It's only until your dad wakes up." I stood and backed a few steps away from my son.

"I'm not doing it here! I don't *believe* you won't trust me. I'm fine." He was whinging now, a familiar sound. It was Ryan. I knew him, I loved him. Nevertheless, that cold-blooded instinct made me take one more step back.

"No, Ryan, I can't, I just…"

"LET ME GO YOU FUCKING BITCH!" He lurched towards me and was yanked back by his bindings. "YOU STUCK-UP PIG! HOW DARE YOU TIE ME UP, HOW DARE YOU!" Ryan was struggling with his bonds; he kicked out at me whilst twisting his hands. It was then I noticed that the cord fixing him to the radiator was fraying, as if he'd been working on it for some time. How long had he been awake? A cold, hard fear took root in my gut. None of this was going to be okay.

As Ryan continued to shout at me – terrible things, words I didn't even know he knew – Doc was barking sharply, adding to the confusion, and Adrian lay still by my feet. His breathing slow, shallow, completely unresponsive.

"Please, Ryan, just take a deep breath and try to calm down, please don't–" A long, high-pitched scream came from outside the house. I froze. I moved to the window and flicked the corner of the curtain to look out. My son continued to rant. The dog's barks had slowed to a low snarl, punctuated with occasional yips. It was still early in the morning, but daylight was bleeding into the shadows. As I watched, three hunched figures jogged past the window. I dropped the curtain back into place and stood to the side, my heart thudding.

Ryan screamed, "YOU SLUT! YOU FUCKING SKANKWHORE!"

"Stop it, Ryan. Please stop. Baby, be quiet."

He turned to me and spoke through gritted teeth, "I'm going to rip you apart for bossing me around, for acting like a dyke cunt. I'm going to string you up and cut you to pieces." Then he spat at me. The face of my beautiful boy was red and contorted. He bared his teeth, dribbling from one side of his mouth. "Be ready, Mum. When I get these ties off, I'm coming for you, and I am going to get a knife and then it'll be just like Josh's sister…"

"Stop it, Ryan, for Christ's sake, just stop!"

Turning, I ran upstairs, taking them two at a time, and shut the door to the bedroom, leaning against it. I could still hear Ryan's voice from downstairs, listing all the gory things that awaited me when he got free. I held my hands over my ears so hard that all I could hear was the laboured throb of my beating heart. On one level I knew he had this thing, this disease, but it was *his* voice coming from *his* lips. The words were coming from *his* mind. I sat by the door and tried to think. I stared at the laundry basket overflowing from earlier and concentrated on calming my breathing.

Scratching at the door made my heart leap in my chest, but I recognised it as Doc. I opened the door, and I couldn't hear Ryan shouting. Doc jumped on the bed and I sat next to him and buried my face in his fur. I lay there for a few minutes working things through in my head – sometimes the men get better; on TV, it had said that they get better. Ryan was young and strong, so he would be one of the ones that recovered. I just had to wait it out.

"Mum, you've got a text message," Ryan's voice came from downstairs. It sounded matter of fact, as if he hadn't been threatening to carve me up five minutes earlier. "You'd better look at it."

Was this how it worked? Did someone just snap out of it in a second, untouched by what had just happened? But then I heard two loud metallic clunks coming from downstairs, like Ryan was trying to hit the radiator with something. No, he wasn't okay.

I rose and looked out of the bedroom window. There was a man in his twenties maybe, stout and bearded, in the middle of the road. He wore jeans, and a black t-shirt with a band's name on it – one I'd never heard of. I think I recognised him from around the close. It was lighter now, the clear beginning of a hot day, and his shadow stretched out before him on the ground. He was staring at the house, our house, and in his hand he was holding a hammer.

He approached the house and the downstairs window. I

couldn't see him properly after that as the upstairs sill got in the way.

There was a great thumping noise on the window downstairs, then a sharp crack. Doc began to bark, a desperate bark, quick and high. I clutched the duvet in my hands and held it to my chest. The window was too high for me to climb from. There were no weapons to hand. My phone was downstairs. The bathroom lock wouldn't hold out against a hammer. And then I heard Ryan scream, "Mum! Mum! He's gonna kill me."

An image of the old man at the store beating the teenager charged through my mind. I got up and ran. If I could just make it to the kitchen and grab something, a knife or anything, I could fight him off. I could keep Ryan safe. As I stormed down the stairs, I came face to face with the man and Ryan standing next to each other in the living room. They were smiling.

"*Help me! Help me, Mama!*" said Ryan in a mocking girlish tone, rubbing his freed wrists. I could still hear Doc barking upstairs.

Glass surrounded the bearded man and he was bathed in a shaft of bright sunlight. The hammer lay on the floor and he now held a chef's knife. This close, I could see that his t-shirt had darker wet patches and his neck and cheek were smeared with blood. "Hey bitch, nice tits." This drew more laughter from both of them.

I backed away.

"Where're you going, Mum? I was hoping we'd spend some quality time together," said Ryan, taking a step towards me. I turned and bolted towards the kitchen, but I was too slow. One of them caught me from behind and bundled me to the floor. I hit my face on the doorframe as I fell and felt the weight of a body press down on me.

They squashed my face to one side. As the horror unfolded above me, I stopped fighting and found my attention drawn to the layer of dust under the fridge. There was a penny sinking in the furry sea and a dead spider on its back, legs folded into its chest like the bones of a flower. I lay there, overpowered, and waited for it all to be over.

This is how the story ended for so many. That day and the following days and weeks were full of stories like these – rape and violence, murder and torture – committed by strangers, friends, sons, fathers, husbands and brothers. The world devoured itself and the cries were manifold. I think about the women who didn't make it through the first wave. What happened to my students? Later, I would sit in the library and look up the names of those I could remember on the public database. "Found dead, stab wounds to the face and neck", "burned and found in a river," "disembowelled", "sodomised with an iron rod and strangled with a belt." Many cases were left unrecorded, the bodies too decomposed to identify or already buried in a mass grave.

This is how the story finished for many women and girls. I would love to tell you that I pulled myself together, fought them off – the stranger with the knife and the stranger my son had become. I would love to say that Ryan's love for me was able to transcend the toxins attacking his brain, and that we fought off the other man together. But like millions, perhaps billions, of other women that day, as I lay there running out of fight, I was reminded – I'm physically weaker than two men. It's just a fact.

They held me face down. A man's weight pressed on my shoulders and thighs with a boy's hands holding my arms behind my back. My face, still thumping from the knock, was squished into the doorjamb and I could feel the serrated edge of the knife nudging my cheek.

"This is going to hurt," said the man with the knife, lying heavy on my back.

"Ryan, *please!*" My voice was muffled, and I was probably crying by this point. I couldn't hear the dog and I wondered where he'd gone – if he was hiding. And then a foot kicked me hard in the side. I cried out – no words, just a guttural expression of pain.

"SHUT UP, PIG!" screamed a man's voice from above me.

I started to rise. I wanted to look at my son one last time but as I lifted my head, fingers – fleshy and cold – coiled around my throat, cutting off my air. I tried to gasp but I couldn't get purchase, just empty retches.

I hovered between harsh light and merciful darkness, waiting for the final strike.

But it didn't come.

Instead, the pressure on my throat fell away.

"What's wrong, Mum?" said Ryan, sounding uncertain.

There was another pause and the weight on my back eased enough for me to flip over and push myself into the corner, facing my two attackers. Ryan stood over us. He looked at me, confused. "What's going on? What is this?" He took a handful of his hair and began pulling at it. "Where's Dad?"

The other man, the man with the knife, was staring past my shoulder at the wall, completely transfixed. I looked to where he was looking; it was just empty wall next to the fridge. His pupils were black and dilated, and his eyes moved as if tracking some invisible action. "Hannah?" he asked the empty space. Looking down at his t-shirt, at the patches of blood, an expression of horror spread over his face. "Oh god," he said, in a half whine, half sob, his fat lips lank and wet. He raised the knife and I flinched, turning my face to the side and bringing up my hand to protect myself. But he just knelt there, staring at the edge of the blade. "I'm sorry," he said, but he wasn't looking at me. The movement, when it came, was swift. Raising his chin and exposing the pale flesh below his beard, he pulled the skin taut with his left hand and then yanked the blade in a grim line across his neck.

CHAPTER 16

"Mary! Mary!"

I woke up like a deep-sea diver ascending too quickly, disorientated and flailing around in a panic. Still lying down, I peered at my watch. It was twenty past three in the morning. The young carer from the day before, Isla, was hovering half in my doorway, shooting looks of distress down the corridor and then turning back to me, her eyes wide. "I'm so sorry to wake you, Mary. I didn't know what else to do."

I thought for a moment that they'd found out about Luca, that they'd found out about it all – Olivia, the house, everything – and at any moment someone from Law Abidance would be coming along to take me in for an interview.

"What is it?" I asked, mustering my senses.

"There's been an incident. I couldn't find anyone, and Olivia was supposed to be with me but–" Isla looked over her shoulder and dropped her voice to a whisper, "but she didn't stay for her shift."

"What incident?" I was already sitting on the edge of the bed and slipping on my shoes, forcing my complaining back to bend down so I could straighten up the backs. "Calm down, girl, what's going on. Where did Olivia go?"

"I don't know. A carer came and handed her a message and Olivia just left. Told me to cover for her. I've been here on my own since then."

She was backing along the corridor in the direction of the

viewing hall, trying to lead me towards the south side of the building, towards the men's dorms and the viewing room.

I followed her, struggling to keep pace. She spoke over her shoulder as she hurried along. "I think he's trying to break the window, and he's blocked the door. I was going to get Daisy, but I didn't want to get Olivia in trouble."

"Who?" I said. "Who's breaking a window?" But then suddenly, I knew who – and I knew why. There was a lurching sensation in my stomach, and I pushed past Isla, setting off at a hobbling half run. I reached the entrance to the viewing room and hammered on the door.

"Tony, open up!"

The only reply was the repeated *THUD* of something heavy striking a window.

Isla turned to me. "He's gone crazy," she whispered. "Do you think he's infected?"

"Tony!" I shouted into the door crack, trying to sound both authoritative and sympathetic at the same time. "Tony. It's Mary. I need to talk to you, right now."

The banging paused for a moment, and hope flared, but then it started up again, louder than before. How could I have been so stupid! Of course Tony wasn't okay. *None of this was okay!* "How did he get out of the dorm?" I asked sharply.

"When I checked the dorm at three, the lock had something wedged in it, hang on…" She fumbled about in her uniform pocket and produced something small and pink. I took it from her outstretched palm and squeezed it between my fingers. A fragment of a makeup sponge. "Tony was the only one missing. So, I went looking for him. After the show and all, I thought he might come back here. But I couldn't open the door. And then the banging started… Why is he doing this?" she said, eyes wide, wringing her hands. "Doesn't he know what might happen?"

"Can we break down the door?" I looked around for anything that I could use to lever open the door, but there was nothing, just an empty corridor. I wondered if I should run down to the kitchen. I might find something there. Guilt prickled over my skin like a rash. I should have seen this coming. I should have done something. Then a monstrous crash came from inside the room, followed by the tinkling of broken glass.

"TONY!" I started hammering persistently on the door with my clenched fist, so hard that I thought the thin bones in my hand might shatter. "I have to speak to you Tony – *I have to tell you something!*"

There was a pause. Then, through the door, I heard him speaking from the other side of the room. "I can feel the breeze, Mary. I've never felt anything like it. It smells like when you rub the stem of a tomato between your fingers and then hold your finger up to your nose. It smells *warm.*" He made a sound, which I took to be a sob, and his voice softened. "I don't want to be here anymore, Mary."

I imagined Tony peering out through the broken window, into the summer night, the breeze beckoning him to freedom. "Tony, please let me in. You'll get infected; it's nearly the eclipse. I saw a swarm last night, near here. You don't have much time. Please."

"What difference does it make to anyone? I don't care if I'm infected. I just want to make bread and garden… and be with Logan again, even if I'm a dribbling idiot."

Isla whispered behind me. "Why does he think that the sanatoriums are so… nice?"

I didn't answer, but I knew why, of course I knew, and I had the decency to blush.

Isla carried on, "Shall I get Daisy?"

"No!" I rounded on the young carer. "Go and find some towels, wet them, and bring them straight back here." Even if Tony wasn't infected, Daisy might use a suicide attempt, a *second* suicide attempt, as an excuse to transfer him. She never liked him. I waited until Isla left before turning back to the door and keeping my voice low, "Tony, listen to me. I lied. I

lied about Logan, about the sanatoriums. I lied about it all."
There was a silence from the door, so I carried on talking. "I
wanted you to think that Logan was happy, but the fact is...
The fact is..." I struggled to speak. "It's a terrible place. The
men are not very happy. They are drugged most of the time,
and when they're clear-headed, they're miserable. Even if you
found Logan, he wouldn't know you, and you wouldn't know
him. Please, Tony, before it's too late. Open up." I leant my
forehead against the door and placed my palms flat on the
smooth, cool wood. "Tony, I'm begging you."

There was a long pause and then Tony's voice came from the
other side of the door, an inch from where I'd laid my head. "I
don't care, Mary. If this is all there is, this... this prison, then I
would rather be drugged and mad and be done with all of it."

I felt bloated with shame. I looked up and down the corridor
to see if there was anyone there, and I pressed my face to the
door, keeping my voice soft but urgent, "There is another way
Tony, but you will have to trust me."

There was a pause. Then Tony replied and his words, spoken
in a small voice, broke my heart, "But I don't trust you, Mary.
Not now. You lied."

I looked behind me to check if Isla was in earshot. I couldn't
see her. "They have a vaccine, Tony. Luca has it and I can make
sure you get it too." Although I couldn't see into the hall, I
could feel Tony listening.

Then he said quietly, "What is a vaccine, Mary?"

"It's like a type of prevention – it means that you could go
outside without getting infected – just like women can. Do you
understand?"

There was a pause and then, "Yes... maybe."

I sensed a note of desperate hope in his voice, despite his
misery. I pushed my advantage. "It will take a little while, and
some bad people are trying to stop us, so we have to keep it a
secret, but I will get you the vaccine, I swear. Open the door,
Tony, right now. You're running out of time." My voice broke

at this and I laid my cheek on the door. "If you get infected, I can't help you." I waited and offered up a silent prayer to whoever claimed sainthood in this godless world.

"You've already lied to me. Why should I believe you?" His voice was just above a whisper.

"I'm telling the truth, every word. Just give me a chance and I'll prove it to you."

No reply, just silence, as the seconds dripped by. I pictured all those tiny toxic hairs floating along on the evening breeze, whirling towards Tony in a deadly rush. I smacked my palm on the door, hard, and it rang out down the corridor like the crack of a whip. "For Christ's sake, Tony! Don't leave it too late. I swear to you there is a vaccine. Olivia and I, we're going to help all the men here, I promise. We're going to close places like this down, and then you can go out, Tony. You can see Logan *and* Luca. But, Tony, *you have to open this door, now!*"

Another pause stretched out into the silence and I thought I'd lost him. But then scraping came from the other side of the door, the movement of something heavy, and Tony's red puffy face appeared around the frame. "If you're lying, Mary..."

"I'm not."

"I couldn't bear it if you lied to me again, Mary."

"I won't."

He looked over my shoulder, and I turned to see Isla standing behind me, clutching some damp towels.

She'd heard. I could see it on her face, in the wideness of her eyes. *Shit.*

But I'd have to worry about that later. For now, there were more pressing matters. "Tony, you need to strip right now." I barked out orders. "Isla, start rubbing him all over – *everywhere* – do you understand?"

She stared at me for a moment, still shocked.

"Quickly! Do you want him to get infected?"

Whatever surprise she was feeling, that snapped her out of it and she got to work.

We rubbed him down there in the hallway. I saw no fibres, but that was not to say he hadn't breathed any in. I did find some scratches and a nasty gash on his arm, which I wrapped up in a towel. "We'll keep an eye on him for the next few days," I said to Isla, as we worked. "You'll need to watch for any symptoms. Perhaps, if we're lucky, no one else needs to know." Then to Tony. "You're all in confinement because of the eclipse as of today, anyway, so it could have been worse, I mean, if–"

"*What foolishness is this?*"

Daisy marched towards our little trio, flanked by two carers, her face aglow with fury.

I darted a quick look at Isla; she was frozen, towel in hand.

I stood up straight. "Daisy, thank goodness! I wanted to send Isla to tell you, but there wasn't time."

"Tell me what, Mary? What's going on?" She pointed to Tony, who was sitting naked on the floor, surrounded by wet towels.

I frantically tried to think of a way to explain Tony's situation. If Daisy thought he'd done all this on purpose, that he was a danger to the other men, she'd transfer him, and not to a better place. I drew a blank. "I…er…we–" I stammered.

"He's drunk!" Isla's voice came out as a squeak. "Mary and I found him in the viewing room, singing. He's finished off all the leftover wine, and he's broken one of the windows."

Daisy's face turned a deeper shade of red. "You mean there are threads swirling around in there *as we speak?*" She jabbed her thumb to the door to the viewing room. "How dare he endanger the facility!" She glowered down at him, her breath coming in small puffs. "Why, Tony? What possible explanation do you have for this lunacy?"

"Arr didn't mean to, Darcy," said Tony, his head flopping back and fixing Daisy with an affected drunken leer. "I was standing on a table to see out and I just *fell…*" Then he grinned.

"And the window went *ka-boom*!" He held up his arm and showed her the cut.

Daisy pursed her lips, wrinkled up her nose and turned to one of the carers by her side. Her voice was low. "Get him to confinement and update his notes. He is to be checked for infection every three hours." Then, turning to the other carer, "Call maintenance to block up this door. We'll sort it out when everyone is safely in confinement – Mary!" her face was still flushed, and her tone was cold. "Where's Olivia – isn't she supposed to be on duty tonight?"

"She told me she had a personal matter to attend to. I agreed to cover," I replied, not looking at Isla.

"In that case, you were the senior carer on duty. This mess is on you."

I nodded and looked down at the floor. "I'm sorry."

One of the carers helped Tony to his feet and led him back towards the confinement wing. He weaved from side to side as he walked and, on turning the far corner, I heard him sing, "*Darcy, Darcy, give me your answer, do. I'm half… sourcy, all for the love of youuuu!*" in an unsteady falsetto. The other carer hurried off to wake up maintenance.

Daisy took in a deep breath and then released it, long and hard, as if she were in a Lamaze birthing class. "I will need a full report, Mary – everything that happened. I'm going to have to send it off to the MWA…" She paused, and I detected something in her tone that suggested that she was warming to the idea of speaking to the MWA. "… along with my recommendations for Tony, and for you."

"I really am sorry," I replied.

She shook her head and gave me the look of weary disappointment one might give an errant child, but it was an act, and we both knew it. She was enjoying what she perceived as my fuck-up. "I told you we should have removed Tony for his own good and for the safety of the other men."

I didn't answer.

She leaned in and whispered to me, although Isla was standing right next to us, "What sort of example does it set to new staff, allowing men to wander around drunk, damaging property and endangering the other residents, hmm?" Then she frowned. "When Olivia returns, tell her to come to my office."

I remained expressionless. "When I find her," I said, "I'll let her know."

I was desperate to tell Olivia that I'd changed my mind. I wanted to tell her that I would take the phone recording to the Citadel if I had to, call Jade and beg her to listen – whatever it took. I needed to apologise, tell her that I thought she was right, and things couldn't go on like this, not if there was another way. I wanted to do this for Tony, even if it meant taking risks. If we succeeded – *when* we succeeded – the MWA would be under investigation. Nicky was in a secure compound, he'd be safe. It occurred to me that Olivia might have already left without me, that the reason she'd vanished last night was to take Luca and the phone to the Citadel. If that were the case, I would catch her up.

"Did she tell you anything about where she might be going?" I asked Isla. We were carrying the pile of wet towels and walking back to the carers' station.

She shook her head. It looked like the night's events had taken its toll on her. Her eyes had dark shadows underneath, and her skin was pale. "Mary, were you just saying those things to Tony, about the vaccine, to make him open the door?"

I thought about telling her that it was a lie, but I was tired of lying. It was time people knew.

"Yes," I said. "It's all true."

"Even the part about the MWA not wanting the men to have the vaccine?"

"Yes."

"That's awful. I mean, that's so wrong."

I felt a twinge of guilt at how obvious the wrongness of it was to Isla, after all the hand wringing I'd done. This woman, a girl raised without knowing any men, understood it straight away.

"What about when they get the vaccine, Isla, do you think things will change?"

"What things?" She frowned.

"If men start taking part in society, having a say about the way things are run. How do you think that will affect you?"

She started to laugh. "Oh, Mary, don't be ridiculous. Their brains aren't wired for complex ideas. They're too..." she paused searching for the word, "blinkered."

"And what happens if we take those blinkers off?"

She looked away for a moment, turning the idea over in her head, before turning back to me with a puzzled frown. "Will it make much of a difference? Essentially, they're just men – emotional and fragile."

I nearly laughed then.

She was quiet for a moment and moistened her lips. I felt that she was deciding whether to say what she was thinking.

"Go on," I said.

She took a deep breath. "It's the older generation, your generation, Mary, who are wary of them, of what they once were. The rest of us hardly think about them at all. I mean, before I worked here, I knew nothing about them, apart from what I was taught in history. The first wave, that sort of thing. I doubt vaccinating them will change anything. Places like this will stop having to be sterilised, but they'll need somewhere to live, won't they? Somewhere to eat and paint and play music."

We carried on walking. Was she right? Was I just shoehorning my own outdated views into a place they didn't fit? Or was she the naive one – woefully unprepared for what the future held? They had a chance, those in charge. A one-time opportunity to build a truly equal society. Then I thought about the MWA and the murder of Dr Desai. No, Isla was wrong to think this wouldn't make a difference to most women. The vaccine was going to change everything.

When we reached the nearest carers' station, we put the towels down the laundry chute, then carried on to our own station. "Go have a shower," I said to Isla.

"Are you going to find Olivia?" she asked. "Do you know where she's gone?"

I nodded. "I have a pretty good idea. I'll need you to cover for me if Daisy comes back – tell her I went to check on Tony. It's only a couple of hours until shift change." It was true. It was coming up to half three. It would be getting light soon.

"No problem," replied Isla. "And if there is anything I can do to help, ask me. I think it's the right thing to do. I don't know why the MWA are against it but don't let them stop you."

I patted her on the arm. "Thanks. You just keep Daisy off my back for a bit."

I hurried towards the depot, trying to remember the route we'd taken to the farmhouse. I dropped into my room on the way and felt around in my top drawer. It was at the back, behind a candle, and one old, dusty mitten – a fat wad of travel tokens and accommodation slips squashed together with an old rubber band. Working in an institution had its perks. My living expenses were covered and I hadn't taken a trip in years, not since finding Nicky. I grabbed my coat and slipped the stack into my pocket. Then I thrust the torch into my other pocket.

I walked as fast as my old legs could go, despite the fact that I was beginning to feel bone tired. I hadn't slept well for at least a week. I thought about what I would say to Olivia. I was looking forward to telling her that I was in. We could deal with the MWA – we'd both dealt with far more in the past.

I reached the travel depot. The open-sided warehouse had a number of cars parked in neat rows. I walked to the far-left corner, across the dark concrete floor, and on to the silent, unlit office area where the keys were kept. No one was about, hardly surprising at 3am. What was surprising was that the key drawer in the desk, which is usually locked, sat a little open. I checked it and the side had a splintered ridge gouged out, as if something long and metal had prised it open. It must have been forced earlier. Olivia?

I pulled the drawer out fully and stared at the keys lying in their grid-lined sections in the drawer. One square was missing a key, there was just a note with a number plate reference in green marker pen.

I could wait here. I mean, she was going to have to return the car – but what if she didn't come back? What if she and Emily had brought the plan forward and were right now taking Luca to the Citadel, ready to show him to the Council? Maybe they'd got through already, and I could just forget the whole thing, wait for news of the vaccine to reach the facility through the official channels, the weekly radio broadcasts of *Union News*.

But there was something about the way Olivia had left Isla on her own that didn't sit quite right with me. The farmhouse had a landline. If I'd known the number, I could've called and found out what was going on. I looked around the depot, still deserted. I fished out one of the sets of keys. The note under it read BC74 JHY. After walking up and down the line of cars on the warehouse floor, I found the corresponding reclaimed hatchback and got in.

I'd always hated driving at night, even before when we had proper roads and working streetlights. I wasn't entirely sure I could remember the way. I imagined turning the key and the engine roaring into the night's silence. It would mark the end of what was and the beginning of what was to come. I realised that, up to this point, I'd learned to fit myself into the world instead of changing the world to fit me, and change was laden with risk.

But I'd made a promise. It was the right thing to do.

I squeezed the key between my thumb and forefinger and flipped it forwards. I was met with no sound, so I assumed that there was something wrong with the engine. I clicked it on and off a few more times before remembering the silence of EVs – no roar, nor clutch, nor gears – just start and stop.

Idiot, I thought as I pulled away.

It was a slog. After about an hour of crawling along, avoiding fallen branches, potholes and the rusting corpses of abandoned cars, I was regretting my earlier bravery. My hands ached with the force of my grip and my shoulders had fused into a permanent hunch. I was very aware that I'd managed only a few hours of sleep in the past two days. I peered out into the two meagre pools of headlight before me and yawned.

After an hour of navigating dark, uneven terrain, I came to a clearer stretch of road and I was able to relax a little. The scenery wasn't exactly speeding along, but I was able to reach the dizzying heights of forty miles an hour. I recognised the pub from before as it swept past on my left – *The Hatch* – I was on the right road and it wasn't far now. Another few miles and I'd be turning off the main road. I felt stirrings of hope, of movement rather than paralysis. My mind returned to the vaccine. What could be achieved with a whole new generation of men – free and strong, and ready to work? With the facilities closed down, would the world start to look a little more like how I remembered it? I allowed myself a few moments of nostalgia. Men jogging through streets or working in shops, boys playing football in peaty autumn mud. Is this what I wanted? Isla may have been unfazed by the prospect of the return of an entire gender, but she'd never experienced the other side. I remembered my A-level lessons, a quote by Alan Bennett – *history is women following behind with the bucket.*

An image of Adrian floated up before me – crisp suit, white shirt, aftershave, dark cotton socks, shiny tan shoes. He was opening a bottle of wine after work. I could hear the soft pop of the cork leaving the neck. But what was he saying to me? *I'm sorry, Mary, I wanted to wake up, but I couldn't.*

Wake up when, Adrian? When did you wake up?

Somehow, I'm lying down and he's above me. Reaching down, he grabs the front of my jumper and lowers his face to mine. I think he's going to kiss me, so I try to touch his cheek with my hand, but I can't move my hand, I can't move anything. He hasn't aged, and I suddenly think he must be repulsed by me, this aged decrepit thing beneath him. His eyes don't seem to mind. He still looks at me with desire and he does kiss me. It's as soft and sweet as the ripest peach.

I pull back and I see that it is not Adrian at all. It's a boy with white hair and pale skin. His eyes are just dark spaces rimmed with fine white lashes, like tiny worms. *They came for my eyes, Mary*! He hisses, his voice is raw and low. *After you left. And I couldn't move. I couldn't make them stop. I hope it was worth it, what you did to me?*

I still can't move, although I know I must. The boy grabs me tighter and begins to shake me up and down like a rag doll. *It wasn't supposed to be me.* He pounds the breath from my chest and then strikes me hard on the side of my head.

I'm jolted awake as I am flung from side to side. I try to wrestle back control of the car, but it's already left the road and branches beat a tattoo on the windshield. I skid and turn hard left, just in time, so that it is only my back right panel that collides with the tree.

I sit for a moment, bewildered, my fingers fluttering like panicked birds over the steering wheel.

Break? Clutch? Key?

CHAPTER 17

It took a few minutes for me to calm down enough to move. I rubbed at a dull ache in my right arm, courtesy of a heavy bump on the door, and gingerly slid out of the driver's seat. I stretched my legs, which were, thankfully, no stiffer than usual. Relieved to have the torch, I passed the beam over the back of the car. The damage looked bad; the back right wheel arch was crumpled in over the tyre. The car wasn't going anywhere. What had I been thinking, at my age, storming off into the night all pumped up and ready to take on the world?

I shuffled off into the dark, keeping to the edge of the road and looking out for the turning. After a while I started thinking that I must have missed it, that I'd passed it whilst dozing on the drive and overshot it. I walked for what felt like hours, although, when I checked my watch, it had only been forty minutes. I was about to give up and start walking back towards the smashed car when I flicked the torch to the right and just caught the red gate and the sign – *Roundhurst Farm*. Turning up the drive, it was less than a minute before I found the entrance to the farmhouse.

A facility-issue reclaimed saloon was parked on the gravel drive. It was the same green Ford that Olivia had been issued with the first time she'd brought me here a couple of evenings ago, so she was here. I felt relieved. I hadn't wanted her to have left yet. I was ready to go with her, speak to Jade Philips – be part of the solution.

The house sat dark and silent. It was well past 3am and it

was therefore possible that everyone was asleep. But Olivia? Would she have gone to sleep here after rushing out? It seemed an odd thing for her to do. I shivered in the cool morning air, making my way as quietly as I could over the gravel. A breeze worried the trees, and I could hear the eerie creak of an old tree limb as the wind pushed at its laden branches. I felt as if something alien and shadowy was watching me from those trees, and I pictured a line of moths, perched high up and looking down at me. I shuddered and quickened my pace as I made for the door.

I tried the handle and felt no resistance.

"Hello?" I called out into the dark kitchen, "Olivia?"

No answer. I fumbled for the light switch and the room came into sharp relief. It was deserted, quite chilly. I noticed that the fire was dying in the grate. Everything looked normal.

I moved over to the staircase and called again. "Hello? Olivia?" I called louder this time. "Luca?" Perhaps this was the wrong thing to do. Perhaps I should have crept up the stairs and tried to surprise any stranger I found there. But I really wanted Emily or Olivia or Luca to come padding down the stairs half asleep and tell me off for making such a noise. That didn't happen.

I climbed the stairs, still hoping to meet Emily on the landing, confused and clutching a robe about her. But the silence was heavy all about me and I found myself tensing at every sound I made, as if I were trying to avoid waking a sleeping dragon.

The landing at the top of the stairs was dark and narrow and I moved towards a door that had been left ajar. I opened it and poked my head inside to find a large bedroom. The ceiling was high, with a thick beam running the length of the room. A watery light filtered from a window and showed an empty, but slept in, double bed. The blankets were folded back, and there was a dip in the groundsheet. I moved over to the sheet and ran my hand over it. Cold.

The second room I came to was much smaller, with a heavy

wooden single bed along one wall. This bed was neatly made, a brocade coverlet tucked in at the edges. Along the far wall was a line of large storage cupboards, built into the eves, and on the dresser stood a comb, some lip balm and a selection of children's books: Enid Blyton, Roald Dahl, the whole *Harry Potter* series. *Harry Potter and the Chamber of Secrets* was lying on the bedside table, face down and open.

I came next to a bathroom, clean, tidy, well-stocked with paper and toiletries. Hanging up over the bathtub were a number of socks draped over a line and a large, dark t-shirt. I backed out of the room and a sickening ache formed in my stomach. I told myself not to be silly. Luca had probably got scared; it was, after all, his second night away from everything he knew. He must have gone to find Emily or Olivia. I would walk in to find them asleep and safe. I clung to this idea as I moved towards the door at the end of the corridor.

I pushed down the handle and opened it, lingering on the threshold, and peered around. This was the biggest room I'd come to, and it was dominated by a large double bed. I nearly called out, alerting the bed's occupant to my presence, but the call died on my lips. It was all too still.

I couldn't bring myself to flick on the light. Instead, I went over to the curtains and pulled them back. There was a fair amount of light in the early dawn, enough to see what was in the room.

Luca, his torso naked, was half sitting up in bed. His skin was pale, even against the white of the sheet, and his head was turned to the side, his eyes fixed, it seemed, on my face, expressionless and void. My heart was pounding so hard I thought I could hear it in the silence of the room. Stepping back, I balled my shaking hands into fists. On the bedside table, next to Luca, stood an empty pill bottle and a half-empty glass of water.

Luca's left hand was cuffed to a railing in the headboard, and his arm hung at an odd angle, his elbow obscuring his mouth. With his head turned to the side, it was as if he were staring past me to the far corner of the room. I followed his gaze, looking behind the door I'd just opened and lurched backwards to the wall, leaning on it to keep myself up. My breathing came in small shallow gasps, like sobs.

Olivia was sitting, head bowed, with her back against the wall, legs straight out. She was still wearing her facility uniform. Her arms rested on the floor, out to her sides, palms up. Each wrist was neatly scored lengthwise up her forearm, rather than across, forming matching alien-like eyes gaping up at me from her flesh. She gazed down at her lap like a penitent child might, chin to chest. In the thin light of the room, her blood-covered thighs drank in the light, black as tar. By her leg something glinted in the dawn light – a Stanley knife covered in blood.

I looked again at Luca in the bed, his handsome face slack and vacant, and then back to my lifeless friend. There would be no cure, no new dawn. There would instead be a scandal. That was what this scene was suggesting. A woman kidnaps a young man, uses him for sex and then, when the guilt gets too much, ends it for both of them.

But there had been a vaccine; I'd seen it. I forced myself to look closer. The cuts were too neat, the tableaux too fixed. I went over to Luca and eased his torso forward, supporting his chest with one hand. His skin felt as cool as glass. On his shoulder, just underneath a small patch of freckles, was the tell-tale mark of a benzo gun, still with a small, indented ring around the puncture wound. No – this was staging, done by someone who took pride in their work. I wanted to move them both, to destroy this narrative.

But then I heard the long drag of wheels crawling over the shingle drive cut to silence.

I edged to the window. The car was marked with the Law Abidance logo, two hands cupping a blooming rose. I caught a glimpse of two women as they got out, one in her fifties or sixties, and the other I couldn't see very well, a little younger, maybe. I considered for a moment the possibility of running downstairs and out of the back door, hiding in the woods, and waiting for them to go. But who was I kidding? I'm not James Bond. Instead, I crept into the room next door, Luca's room. I clambered into a storage cupboard, forcing my complaining limbs to curl up so I could fit. After a few minutes, the sounds of footsteps echoed on the stairs.

I could just hear mumbling from the room next door, but no words. They were both there for quite a while before coming onto the landing, and I could hear a little better. I could make out two distinct voices.

"Pretty grim. It's been a while since I've seen something like this," said a dry, rasping voice, one that might have smoked a pack a day, if cigarettes still existed.

"Is it a resident from the facility?" A nasal tone, higher and younger sounding.

"She's also from the facility, by the look of her uniform," said the rasping voice. "It's disgusting, look. She cuffed him, drugged him too, I bet. That's why I don't trust those women at the facilities. I mean, why choose to work there, eh?"

"Was it a sex thing, do you think?"

"I expect so. You won't remember, but this kind of thing used to happen a lot just after the change." The rasping voice coughed, a throaty, wet-sounding heave. "Even with the sire houses."

"Was there a note?"

"No," said the older voice, clearing her chest. "I checked any obvious places. The clean-up team might find something. I didn't see a blade either. But I'm sure it's there somewhere."

I could hear them walking around, then a rattle, perhaps of the pill bottle.

"And do we know any more about where the tip-off came from?" This from the younger voice.

"Nope."

So, someone wanted this found, and soon.

The speakers paused for a moment, then the younger voice asked, "Has this place got a phone?"

"I think so, in the kitchen. You go call it in. Let the facility know. They'll have to inform the MWA. I'll have one more check round."

One set of receding footsteps on the stairs. I held my breath as the owner of the raspy cough walked into Luca's room, stopping by Luca's bed, as I had – perhaps to look at the books and consider the bed's unruffled state. She came towards the cupboard and began opening some of the doors. I clenched my teeth and dug my fingers into my thighs, desperate not to move.

I could have come out, I supposed, hands raised, and explained that this had been a mistake, but what reasonable explanation would I give as to why I was hiding in a cupboard in the middle of nowhere in a house with two corpses? I turned over the bloody Stanley knife in my hand and considered launching myself at her like some beast from the Serengeti, pushing her over and making a run for it, but I doubted my muscles were as keen as my will. I tensed my legs, feeling the sore ache of confinement. The light under the cupboard flickered as she came close. As I raised the knife, I could feel my hands shaking.

Something, I don't know what, saved us both from the awkward spectacle of my heroic last stand. I thought I heard the other officer calling her from downstairs. Whatever it was, the woman left and I clung to myself, trembling with fear and unused adrenaline.

I waited until I hadn't heard a sound for many long minutes. Part of me wanted to stay in the cupboard longer, but I was beyond uncomfortable, and I was aware that I might have a slim window of escape before the "clean-up" team arrived.

I slunk from my hiding place, ears cocked for the slightest sound, and moved to the room next door. It was lighter now;

dawn had well and truly broken, and the curtains were open. I tried not to look at Olivia's pale face or catch Luca's lifeless stare. I kept my eyes down noting how the blood on the carpet beside Olivia had dried a deep brown – the colour of uncooked liver. At the window, I checked the drive: no Law Abidance car, just Olivia's green Ford. I tiptoed from the room downstairs, still not daring to make a noise, despite the fact I was obviously alone, and made my way over to the dresser. I opened the drawer and found no tube of pills. I looked around and I couldn't see any sign of my phone – surely Olivia or Emily would have hidden it. I ran about the house checking under the chairs and in beds but there was nothing. They had to – they must have forced Olivia to tell them where it was. Without Luca, the pills or the phone, it was hopeless. There was nothing else to do. Anger welled up in me, a white fury that I hadn't felt in decades. If I had to scream it from the spires of the Citadel, if I had to kidnap Jade Philips and make her listen to me, I would. Those responsible for this would pay. I grabbed Olivia's coat from the back of one of the chairs, searching the pockets. I found the keys and also a note.

I have to go back. Come and watch L. Love, E.

It was written in black pen, the letters spindly and rushed. Had Emily lured Olivia here for this? Had the MWA got to her somehow? It was a horrible thought, but not one on which I had time to dwell. I had to get to the Citadel.

I stuck the note in my pocket and left the house.

As I was making for Olivia's car, I saw the tree that Olivia had shown me, the one with the V-shaped bough and the silken nest. I caught a whiff of that sweet, rotten smell as I passed it and a hopeful – yet also horrible – thought occurred to me. Had she shown me the nest to prove to me that the vaccine worked or was there another reason? *He could probably put his hand in that nest out front, Mary, and not experience any adverse effects at all.* If you were going to hide something, putting it somewhere where nobody *wanted* to look would be a good idea. I approached the tree. The hollow looked moist in the watery morning light, rimmed by silvery trails, like slug-spittle. The smell was much stronger now, and I covered my nose with the lapel of my jacket as I approached. I peered in to find the entire cavity rippling with movement. Gone were the silky strands. Only a few frayed ribbons clung to the edge of the hole. In their place was an orgy of caterpillars, hairy and burrowing. The greyish-white creatures carpeted the sides of the hollow, crawling over each other in a frenzied awakening. Right at the back of the hole, thrust in as deep as it could go, was a glistening black edge partially submerged amongst all that grey – the glassy lip of an old mobile phone.

I was tempted to go back into the farmhouse and get something I could use to fish it out – anything, a tea towel or, better still, some long fire tongs. But I was really pushing it on time. I wrapped my right sleeve around my hand and started fishing about amongst the caterpillars. I knew that this much fresh toxin might well affect me, if not immediately, then soon. Each time my fingers brushed up against those furry little bodies, I yanked out my hand. I couldn't help it. It took every ounce of mind-over-instinct not to cut and run. The smell alone made me gag, and the feel of those wormy, toxic bugs plucked at some innate revulsion buried deep in the back of my mind.

I was sweating despite the chill in the air. I had to slip my bare fingers from my sleeve to grasp the edge of the phone. As I did so, I could feel the tickle of soft fibres brushing on my fingertips, delivering their poisons into my flesh. They stung too, like tiny, hot needles. The appearance of my arm had agitated them and they clung to it, marching up it as an army climbs a hill, so it was like I had a thick, furred sleeve on top of my own. My fingers finally touched something hard and cold, and I pulled the phone free, backing up so quickly that I fell over a root, and landed hard on my behind. I struggled to my feet and shucked off my jacket, patting myself and flicking off one determined caterpillar who'd made it all the way up to my neck.

I felt the area where it had been and found a line of tiny, raised bumps, ditto on my fingers. I didn't know how far I'd get, before it all kicked in – the drowsiness, the hallucinations, the nausea.

I was about to move down the path towards Olivia's green Ford when I heard a car coming from that direction.

Caught between making a run for it deeper into the woods and racing for the car, my mind fogged. There was itching inside of my ears and at the back of my throat, and my stomach tensed ominously. I turned, half stumbling, half running into the woods, passing the house as fast as I could without looking back. Brambles struck at my face and tree roots tried to hook me off balance. I got as far as I could, away from the driveway – so far, in fact, that I couldn't even see the farmhouse when I turned back. There was nothing but me and the dawn chorus, screeching and chattering louder than I ever thought possible. I looked up into the swaying canopy and I felt the ground move beneath me. I bent over and retched hard into the mossy earth. Nothing came up except a few spits of bile. I retched again and held on to the trunk of a tree, rough and sharp in my palm, trying to support myself. But it was no use.

My legs gave out, and I slumped down onto the hard-packed dirt.

CHAPTER 18
Mary – then

I was sitting in the corner of my kitchen, covered in a stranger's blood.

Ryan was pacing around, pulling at his short hair and repeating, "Oh God, I'm sorry." But not speaking to anyone in particular. The bearded man in the black t-shirt was slumped over my feet, a pool of cooling blood stretching out over the linoleum. The knife lay a few metres away, discarded when its wielder had no more use for it.

"Mum…" It was Ryan's voice.

"Ryan!" Struggling upright, the pain in my head made me gasp, and the room lurched. I tried to focus, but there were small white flashes in the corners of my vision, blinding me.

"Ryan, sweetheart." I tried to get up, but my legs felt oddly weak and it took a few attempts to stand. Also, I had to be careful not to slip in the blood. I reached up to my neck. It was tender, and I winced as my fingers tentatively explored under my chin. I moved them back and found a swollen lump on the side of my head.

"I don't know what happened to me, Mum." Ryan sat down on the floor. He bowed his head, allowing his curly hair to flop down and cover his face. "I was angry and then, then… I blacked out." There was shame in his tone in those last few words, a hesitancy that suggested he might not have completely blacked out. I managed to get to my feet and hobbled over to him as fast as I could but hesitated when I reached him. Did he still have it? Would he start again? He was shaking, and his eyes were bloodshot and half-closed. "I'm sorry, Mum." He gave one big heart-wrenching sob, and I fell to my knees before him, gathering my son into a resolute hug. He cried like a small boy – great gulping sobs without shame or restraint.

"It's okay," I repeated over and over again. "It wasn't you. It wasn't you."

When his tears finally calmed down and he was able to speak, he raised his head. "What about Dad?"

I wiped my son's wet face with the flat palm of my hand. "In the living room," I said.

Adrian lay on his back. His face was covered in blue marks, which now looked darker than before. His eyes were closed and he was still. Doc was lying in the corner and now and then he whined softly.

"What's wrong with him?" Ryan asked.

I went over and checked his pulse

"Is he breathing?" he asked, his voice becoming high and thin.

I didn't say anything, caught between saving Ryan from more hurt and telling the truth.

We stood there for a moment. I didn't really know what to do. I wanted to say something to Ryan, to take away the pain, but felt that if I made a noise, it would make this whole unbelievable nightmare a reality. Adrian was always so animated, so funny, so... alive. I couldn't look at this parody of the man I'd spent the last sixteen years with. I turned away and back to Ryan.

"I'm going to need to tie you up again." It was all I could manage to say.

Ryan nodded, eagerly, almost. He tore his gaze away from his dad and moved over to the bottom of the stairs and sat quietly, waiting. I went into the kitchen, avoiding the blood as best I could, and took some scissors from the drawer. I then went into the garden and cut down a length of washing line.

It would dig in less than a cable tie. I took it inside and bound up Ryan's hands, fixing them to the banister. I did it gently and carefully but made sure it was tight.

I was just readying myself to drag Adrian's body into the kitchen, away from Ryan, when there was a thumping knock at the door. In a panic, I ran back to the kitchen. The knife was still lying on the floor, covered in drying blood, but I couldn't bring myself to touch it. Instead, I picked a rolling pin and a meat fork from the nearest drawer and took them to the front door.

A woman's voice shouted from the other side. "This is the British Army. We need you to open the door."

I stood in the hallway, holding my odd Dalek-arm weapons, and breathed deeply, giving no reply.

"You should have received a text message outlining the government's response to the SANS pandemic. Ma'am, please open the door or we will be required to break it down."

A memory drifted to the surface, Ryan's voice calling up the stairs as I cowered in the bedroom. *Mum, you've got a message.* I shuddered and flicked up the latch.

Three women stood on the doorstep, all in flak jackets and face masks. They were armed.

"Are there any infected men on the premises?" The soldier nearest to me barked this into my face through her mask.

"What's happening?" I asked, my voice shaking.

Two of the others pushed past me and into the house. I heard one shout back after a few moments. "One alive, two dead."

"My son is better," I tried to say to the two women who were now heading for Ryan. "He had it but he's okay now." I started to follow, but the first soldier grabbed my sleeve. "All women need to report to the truck with the W painted on the side. It's for your own safety."

"No," I said. "I'm going with Ryan. In the other truck."

"You can't," was the soldier's brisk reply.

"Why can't I?" My voice was rising in pitch and the stress

of the day was coursing through me, tipping me into hysteria. "He's my son. He's only fourteen."

The stocky dark-haired soldier on the doorstep looked as though she was trying hard not to lose patience with me, like this wasn't the first conversation of this type she'd had today. "We're taking him to hospital so that we can monitor him, just until we can find a cure."

"Which hospital?"

The soldier sighed and peered into the house impatiently. "I can't tell you. It's at a secure location. That's all I know."

The other two soldiers, now leading Ryan, pushed past me and out of the house. He was stumbling, hardly able to walk, and his eyes were half-closed. I tried to grab him as they dragged him from the house, but they yanked him out of reach.

"Mum," he mumbled, as they yanked him away.

"I'm coming, Ryan," I shouted after him and then turned to the woman still clutching my arm. "You can't stop me. I'm his mother and I'll stay with him." I was shaking, and I hated how the quiver in my voice was making me sound crazy.

"Look," said the woman in the flak jacket, her voice cold and firm. "If you insist on staying with your son, then I will unload him from this truck into your care. You can take him back inside and wait for the drugs we've just given him to wear off and for the toxin to eat further into his brain. He will become more and more aggressive and far less lucid over the next few hours. I assume he's had an episode already?"

I thought about lying, but she was staring at the marks on my neck. I nodded and looked away.

"You can try to look after him and take your chances. But know this: if he escapes or is deemed to be a threat in any way, he will be shot." She leaned in. "Coming with us is his best chance for a cure. I'd grab it with both hands if I were you."

Every part of me hurt. My head, my side, my stomach, my heart. I tensed and the woman before me tensed, too.

I wanted to talk it over with Adrian.

The eyes of the women opposite me slid to the truck. "Well?" she said.

"Okay," I replied, trying to hold back my tears.

The woman let out a breath. "Write your details down here, your name, your mobile number, along with a physical description of Ryan. Then go and pack a few essentials, and don't forget to bring your phone. It's how we'll keep you updated on his condition."

I filled in the form, then went and changed out of my blood-soaked tracksuit bottoms and sweater into a clean pair of jeans and a hoodie. I grabbed a few more clothes, some underwear, as much cash as I could find, my phone, charger, passport and a thick eiderdown coat, which belonged – *had belonged* to Adrian.

I wondered whether I should bring any food, but I couldn't face going into the kitchen. I didn't want to see the blood or the blank face of my would-be killer. I emptied my gym bag onto the floor and then stuffed it full of everything I'd collected, squeezing the air out of the coat to make it as small as it would go. By the time I got outside, the truck containing Ryan was just leaving. I fought the rising panic as I watched it trundle down the road and turn the corner. *Just until they find a cure. Keep it together.*

I was helped into the second truck, the one with W painted on the side, by a woman, fifty or so, with shoulder-length bleached hair tied back, and wearing a lilac t-shirt. She looked vaguely familiar to me as I took the seat next to her.

"I'm Shona," she said, "and this is Wynne."

"Mary," I replied, still looking in the direction they'd taken Ryan.

As the truck rolled out, heading for the next street, I sat peering out of the back, watching the house I'd lived in for eleven years, the house in which Adrian and I had raised our son, retreat into the distance. Then I heard sharp and urgent barking. Doc came bounding along the road, chasing the truck.

"That's my dog!" I said to the weary, frightened faces around me. "Stop the truck. That's my dog!" As much as he tried, Doc couldn't keep pace with the truck as it hit third gear. The truck rounded the corner, and I lost sight of him, but I could still hear his desperate barks even over the engine.

"You can come back and get him later," said the woman in the flak jacket, the same one who'd said that they were working on a cure.

She lied on both counts.

Doc's barking finally receded. The army truck rumbled its way through the suburban streets. As I looked out of the back of the truck, there seemed to be no one about. Occasionally, small gangs of men and boys – the infected – ran alongside the truck, arms outstretched. Sometimes they shouted things: lurid suggestions, sexual slurs, the sort of thing you might have heard if you were to walk past a certain type of pub on a Saturday night alone.

The woman in fatigues, the one who'd persuaded me to let them take Ryan away in a different truck, introduced herself to us all as "Sarge".

Sarge told us to keep away from the open back of the truck and then began barking statements into an old-fashioned walkie-talkie, "We're heading north on Chertsey Street, advise, over."

Hostiles reported on North Street, reroute via Leapale Road, came a crackling voice from the other end.

About thirteen of us were inside the truck. We were quiet, sitting around the edge on hard benches. Occasionally, someone tried to start a conversation, but the atmosphere was muted, and these deliberate acts of noise seemed intrusive. Also, what could we say? *Hi, I'm Shelly, my husband and my uncle just pushed my mother out of a third-storey window. Nice to meet you...*

The truck lurched forward.

The woman who'd helped me into the truck, Shona, gazed silently, a vacant look in her eyes. Her daughter, Wynne, was very still and had tears running down her freckled cheeks.

"You okay?" I asked quietly. The question seemed inadequate, insensitive even. None of this was in any way okay, and only a sociopath was going to be fine with it. But overnight, the question had taken on a different meaning – *are you keeping it together?*

"Yeah," she whispered back, sniffing hard. "You?"

I nodded. "Where do you think they're taking us?"

Wynne shrugged. "Me and Mum were watching it on TV last night. Dad came downstairs and said he was leaving. He had a suitcase in his hand. He said that he'd seen the reports on the internet and that he didn't want to risk hurting us, so he just up and left, got in the car and drove off into the night. I thought that, if he got it, he might get picked up by the same people sending the texts, that he might be taken somewhere safe." She looked at Sarge, rifle strung casually across her arm. "Now I don't know what to think. What if this is all some big mistake and the men just need time to calm down?" She turned her head to her mother, who still seemed deeply lost in thought, then looked back at me and leaned in close. Her voice was as quiet as the truck engine would allow. "What if my dad gets it and someone hurts him? What if he hurts someone else? He'd never forgive himself."

My neighbours. Of course. That's where I'd seen them before.

The woman talking to me couldn't have been more than twenty-five. I remembered her dad as the man from across the street who had an electric car. It was a bright red saloon, really fancy. Ryan and Adrian were in love with it and would wander past it sometimes when walking Doc, shuffling past his drive to get a better look. One day, about a year ago, Adrian and Ryan came into the kitchen to find me, faces flushed, eyes wide and bright, talking over each other:

Mary, he gave us a ride in it–

It went so fast, Mum, so fast–
We could get one–
Mum, I could feel the Gs in my face–
We could look at re-mortgaging…

Then I thought of Ryan and the bearded man, how they looked at me and laughed, and the weight on my back, pushing me into the kitchen floor. I reached out and took Wynne's hand. "I think your dad did a really good thing by leaving. I think it was the best thing he could have done." I gave her hand a squeeze. "When we get where we're going, we'll find out where they're taking care of the men. We'll find your dad and my son. Okay?"

She took her hand back and wiped her face. She didn't look convinced. "Okay," she replied with another sniff.

It was hot in the truck, and it smelt of sweat and fear. I was starting to feel really sick. "How far is it?" I asked Sarge, but she ignored me and I didn't want to make a scene. I spent the next hour and a half trying not to throw up as the truck lurched and swerved along the hard shoulder of the M25.

We eventually turned off near Oxford, into what looked like a military compound, all high fences topped with savage-looking ringlets of barbed wire. Four armed and uniformed women stood at the entrance as the truck pulled in. One of them poked her head in the back. "What's it like out there, Sarge?" she asked.

"It's getting pretty bad. What's it been like here?"

"Women have been coming in all day. Some in the trucks, some in cars. The message seems to be getting out."

"And the men?"

"I haven't seen any. Not outside the fence."

"Inside?"

"Restrained and doped, most are on their way to the hospital. No more casualties."

"Good. Now let us in. I've been doing this all night and I'm dead on my feet."

The soldier waved the truck onward.

I caught the word *hospital*. I had visions of well-tended patients in neat, clean wards, food on trollies and effective medicine. It was the first tiny glimmer of hope I'd felt for days.

The truck was ushered into a space in a busy hangar by a plump woman in her mid-fifties holding a clipboard and dressed in a dark skirt suit. She stood, waiting for us. "You're all in Buller Barracks," she said loudly as we clambered down from the truck. "Follow me."

She led us over a bustling parade yard to a set of squat, grey buildings. Sarge stalked off in the opposite direction without saying anything. Everywhere I looked, there were women moving around with purpose – some carrying armfuls of clothes and blankets, others laden with boxes. Some were in uniforms, but most were in jeans, t-shirts, tracksuits, nightwear or bathrobes. The absence of men was jarring, especially in a place like this. As we left the hangar, another two trucks were pulling in, filled with more scared-looking pyjama-clad refugees.

The grey building to which I was allocated turned out to be an apartment with six bedrooms and a small kitchen area. Each bedroom was supposed to sleep two, but we were told by the dark-suited lady to arrange the rooms to fit four. The rooms still contained the belongings of the soldiers who'd lived here before: photos of parents, smiling women and young children; calendars featuring pouting underwear models; aftershave and trainers. We were told to use what we could and box the rest up, then to come to the kitchen for a briefing. I picked up a baseball hat with "Make Britain Great Again!" emblazoned on the front and tossed it into a box along with a car magazine, an electric shaver and a couple of postcards.

About twenty of us squashed inside the tiny kitchen area. Up until that point, we'd been pretty subdued as a group, shocked and afraid and not knowing what to do. But being together in the tight confines of the kitchen was reassuring. I could feel a lurking anger amongst my fellow refugees, as if being here was the cause of everything, rather than the solution. Here was an enemy that could be seen.

The middle-aged woman who had led us from the truck stood in the doorway when we'd all filtered in and spoke at length in a flat tone, a speech she'd obviously repeated a few times that day, "I am Doctor Phillipa Blake. I am a medic in the British Army. I'm sure you have questions. Please allow me to explain what we know so far, and then I will try to answer you as best I can."

The group fell silent. Wynne and Shona, a few faces along, exchanged a glance.

"Four days ago, we began getting international reports of a possible pandemic – Severe Acute Neurological Syndrome or *SANS*. It only seems to affect males and, as far as we know, only human males, although reports suggest that the moths may also be highly toxic to other animals, especially birds."

I thought about the birds in the field. How long ago was that? Yesterday morning? It felt like a year.

"Roughly half of those infected stop breathing in their sleep." Her voice softened a little. "I'm so sorry if you've lost someone in this way. Please know that there is nothing you could have done."

A short, quiet sob came from someone behind me. I stared resolutely ahead, only focussing on the information, refusing to consider the implications. If I was going to help Ryan, I couldn't afford to think about anything else.

Dr Blake carried on. "The rest of those infected develop a neurological condition. They display violence, especially towards women, become impulse driven and show a profound lack of empathy. They retain some memories and their linguistic faculties remain intact. But they experience periods of mania, psychopathy and lucidity, and these episodes are unpredictable. In fact," she paused, "it affects different men in different ways. Some become violent, some disorientated, some suicidal. We don't know why. We don't know if there is something already in their psyche that triggers this behaviour or whether it's exposure to differing amounts of the toxin. There's so much we don't know yet."

I tried to block the vision of the bearded man's face as he opened up his throat, and the sheet of blood, viscous and dark, cascading down his chest before he slumped to the floor.

"Why only men? Why not women?" asked Shona. A murmur went through the room.

Dr Blake looked annoyed at having to deviate from her script. "We don't know that yet, either. Our immunity might be genetic, our lack of a Y chromosome, for example, but we haven't had time to investigate it. Please let me give you the information I have before you ask questions."

A second wave of mumbling rippled through the group, but no one asked anything else.

"You are here under the protection of the British Army. Due to a few precious days of forewarning, we were able to set up these compounds for your protection. You are free to leave at any time, but the army cannot guarantee your safety outside these gates. You will be given a few hours to acclimate yourself, but then you will be expected to assume some responsibilities. You will be expected to uphold the rules of this base, to defend this base by force, if necessary, and you will be asked to partake in activities that will ensure that this base continues to function as a place of safety. As of 2pm yesterday, the UK was placed under martial law. Due to the ratio of men to women in the forces, this has proved difficult; however, the more civilian recruits we have, female recruits, obviously, the more chance we have of surviving until we find a cure."

Then her attitude changed, her voice dropped and became less monotone, more strained. "There are many out there who still need our help." Dark circles of exhaustion ringed her eyes as she looked up at us. "Any questions?"

All the women stared at each other. "How many facilities are there, like this?" one of the women asked.

Dr Blake cleared her throat. "Across the country, we are in contact with approximately thirty bases that are running a similar operation to this one." There was a pause.

"Is it all the men, or are some immune?" Another voice, this time from the back of the crowd.

"We haven't found any man immune so far. Some seem to recover but only for short periods. That said, if an intersex individual presents as male but has no Y chromosome, in theory, they could be immune."

"Where's my husband?" called out a woman behind me. "He was in the other truck."

Dr Blake breathed in deeply and nodded. "The men have been taken to separate facilities and are being sedated." There was a surge in nervous chatter at this.

"When can we see them?" It was the same woman speaking as before, but now her voice was joined by others, clamouring to know what had happened to their men. *Are they okay? Do you have a cure? He's only eleven – he needs me with him!* I stayed quiet, kept my eyes fixed on the doctor.

"Soon," she said. "We have to make sure it's safe."

Soon is a vague term. A temporal marker – as I used to tell my English students – a shift in narrative time. Kids see it for what it is, a deflection, along with *we'll see* and *maybe later*.

We were herded into a canteen, which was packed with women. The atmosphere was subdued. I allowed my plate to be filled with baked beans, bacon and toast and sat down near the end of a long table. I nibbled on the toast, but I couldn't face the beans or the bacon. Murmured conversations washed over me. Stilted and quiet, those around me introduced themselves. I mumbled my name when asked but kept my eyes on my plate. *I'm Sarah; Freya; Hi everyone – Leanne; My name's Claire.*

Claire! I took my phone from my pocket and turned it on – no signal.

"The networks went down a few hours ago." I looked up, and Wynne was just taking a seat to my right.

"That can't be right," I said. "They told me they would contact me about Ryan on my phone."

Wynne gave me a hard, long look and then turned back to her breakfast. "I'm going to find my dad tomorrow," she said, shovelling beans into her mouth like she hadn't eaten in weeks.

"How?" I asked. "Where?"

"I hung back and spoke to Dr Blake after orientation. I volunteered for medical service in the men's hospital. Dr Blake's taking me and some others over."

"Can I come?" There was an edge of desperation in my voice at the thought of finding my son. Why didn't I think of hanging around and talking to Dr Blake?

"I'll take you to see her after lunch, but if she asks if you're looking for somebody, tell her no, or she won't let you go. I heard her say it to the girl before me."

I nodded. "Understood," I said, before forcing myself to eat some bacon.

CHAPTER 19

Putting my hand in that moth's nest must have resulted in a massive dose of the toxin, even for a woman. I was lucky to be alive. I woke curled up at the foot of a tree, like a dryad. As I sat up, a tumble of twigs and dirt fell from my short hair. What a state – my mind was still tainted by images of the past. I checked my jacket pocket – I still had the phone, and then checked my watch – 6.30am. I'd been out about an hour and a half.

I heaved myself to my feet, using the trunk behind me for support. The forest spun around me and it took a few moments for me to be able to stand up on my own. I had no idea if the Law Abidance crew were still at the farmhouse. I tried not to think about any "clean-up" operation. I didn't want to imagine them picking Olivia up and laying her out on a stretcher, uncuffing Luca and covering him in a body bag, before carrying both out to a waiting ambulance. How long would it all take?

Reluctantly, I started to move away from what I suspected was the direction of the farmhouse and towards where I thought I might come out on the main road. It was hard going, especially as I wasn't yet over the toxin and my limbs shook as I walked. I hadn't slept properly in days, and I was feeling it. Feelings and memories long stuffed down had started to bubble up to the surface.

Shameful ones.

I ploughed on, just concentrating on placing one weary foot in front of another, until I eventually found myself squeezing through a gap in a hedge. I rested by the main road for a few minutes; then I stuck out my thumb. If Law Abidance came along, I could always say that I was on my way into town to run errands when I'd had a car accident. I could point them to my bashed-up car as evidence. I was so tired by this time, so desperate to get back to the facility, that I was willing to chance a raised eyebrow of circumstantial suspicion. And, in any case, I doubted they were actively looking for anyone in connection with the deaths of Olivia and Luca. To an outsider, it seemed like a clear-cut case of murder-suicide.

I had to wait by the road for a while, but it's illegal to pass a hitchhiker without stopping, so after about half an hour, a beaten-up minibus pulled up alongside me, the passenger side door sliding open.

The woman driving looked to be in her thirties, smiling, with a ruddy freckled face. A couple of younger women sat in the back, both sun-baked and muscular. Farmworkers, I surmised from their build and blackened nails.

"Where you goin'?" said the driver, her teeth bright against her tanned skin.

"The South Downs facility," I replied.

She gave a short nod, perhaps relieved that she didn't have to drive into town. "Hop in." She had a slight West Country twang to her accent.

I smiled gratefully, and then climbed into the grubby van, moving some old pamphlets and papers into the footwell so I could sit.

She pulled off without bothering to look behind her. I kept quiet, hoping to process the horror of the past few hours, but my driver had other plans, "So, whatcha doing out here all by yourself?"

I was prepared for the question. I'd practised my answer in my head on the walk. I decided brevity was the key to deceit. "I was on my way back from a friend's house, when I skidded off the road on a patch of mud."

"Mmm," she said, "was you driving one of them new kind, them grey ones? I hear they slip 'n' slide all the time. Problem with the torque. Not like a good ol'fashioned *re*-claim." She patted the dash of the minivan and a small puff of dust rose from the plastic.

"Yes, I was," I said, hoping that was the end of the conversation.

But after another few moments, one of the young women in the back asked, "That facility you work in, is it one that does visits?"

I buried a sigh. "Yes, it is."

The third girl spoke. "Well, I don't think it's okay, those women who *partition* the men. I mean, it's not like the olden days. There are better ways to get pregnant now. I think it's wrong."

"I dunno," said the driver over her shoulder. "I think the men enjoy it. Don't they?" She was addressing me. "Do the men enjoy it?" She gave me a meaty wink.

The other voice from the back cut in. "They might *say* they want to do it, but you never know, Jules. They're men, after all. Who knows what goes on in those weird little heads of theirs?"

"Wait, wait," said the driver. "Let's see what this lady says. She should know best." There was a pause and all eyes, it seemed, were on me.

I was so weary that I could hardly find the words to answer. "I... yes... most of them like it. I think." I just wanted sleep, some time to get my head straight, let the last vestiges of toxin work its way out of my system.

"Hmm, well, the whole thing gives me the heebies," one of the girls mumbled from the back. "It just ain't, you know, *natural*."

The driver laughed, "Oh, Cresta, you'd give it a go if you could afford it, don't say you wouldn't."

"No. Yuck. *I wouldn't!*"

The other two ganged up on Cresta, making it a game. "You would, you'd love it, all that in-an-out-ing..."

"*Ooo, what a big pickle,* you'd say. *Sire me! Sire me! Mr Big Pickle!*"

"You can drop me here," I said, over Cresta's protestations at the notion of sleeping with a man and the raucous laughter of the other two women.

"Nah, it's fine," said the driver, struggling with her hysterics. "I'll get you to the gates." She pulled up outside the facility. I left the car, desperately hoping no one in the facility was noticing what was going on in the driveway. As I turned to quickly thank the driver, she said, "Do ya think ya can hook Cresta up, then, with a visit?"

Cresta started to squeal from the back of the van. "No! Stop it! I ain't joking. Stop it."

"I, err, there's lots of paperwork involved," I replied weakly.

That made the driver laugh even more. They sped off, and I could still hear Cresta's squeals of indignation from the open window.

"Where've you been, Mary?" It was one of the cleaners, Lark, coming on her first shift and leaving the showers at the same time as me. I cursed the fact that I hadn't timed it slightly better. "Just a quick walk after my shift. Clear the head, you know. How's the new baby?"

"She's grand, slept six hours last night. Trisha's really happy."

"Great," I said. "Make the most of it."

"Have you heard," she said. "About that new carer out in the woods?"

So, the news had reached here before I did. "What did you hear?" I asked, trying to keep the emotion from my voice.

"Apparently, it was a case of grooming. I heard that the carer took the man and held him in a deserted house. They found handcuffs and whips and all kinds of kinky stuff."

"Is that so?"

"Yeah, they think that there were others involved, like a gang. I met her a couple of times and thought she was really nice."

I could already see how the MWA might spin this. I had to be really careful. "You never really know someone," I said over my shoulder as I walked away.

I managed to get back to my room without meeting anyone else. I was immeasurably glad of this. I didn't know if I could hold one more conversation without crumpling into a sobbing mess. I entered my room and lay down on my bed, feeling a hard lump at my side. I felt around, took the phone from my pocket and rubbed off the last of the caterpillar residue. From its blank screen, my haggard reflection peered back at me in ghostly shades of grey. I flicked it on, but there was no picture of chubby, three year-old Ryan sitting on Adrian's shoulders staring back at me. Emily, good as her word, had wiped the photos, and I felt a stab of regret that I hadn't tried harder to memorise those final images of that ghosted life. I flicked to the video icon and pressed play. The video was Luca, heartbreakingly happy, running around outside and exploring the forest. I could see that there were hours of saved footage. I scrolled through and watched as Emily turned the phone on herself and explained how the vaccine worked. The phone also had at least sixty photos of notes and schematics, everything one would need, I assumed, to recreate the vaccine. I had no charger, and the phone was on forty per cent. Hopefully, it would all be enough.

Then the tears began to roll down my face. The fear, the shock and the adrenaline all drained away, and what I was left with was oppressive, heavy grief. I stuffed the phone in the drawer in my bedside table and muffled my sobs with my pillow, weeping into its feathery bosom.

Sitting in the Warden's shared office, I could hear my stomach rumbling. I'd only just woken up, and it was past lunchtime.

There were twelve of us carers, all squashed in amongst the piles of paper, the cluttered desks and the stuffed filing cabinets. Daisy was sitting at her desk, her eyes red-rimmed. Danika, one of the other ward sisters, stood by the far wall. She was tall and kept her head shaved. She'd once told me, when we'd shared a shift, that she kept it this short so it was easier to shower and quickly dry off.

Danika stood up and offered me her chair. I took it to avoid offending her, although, after the events of the previous night, I felt like a fraud pretending to be frail. I didn't feel frail this morning, despite just five hours of sleep. I felt numb.

There was tension in the air. The carers were muttering. We were just waiting for a couple more to arrive. Isla slipped into the crowded room. She blushed as people looked around at the latecomer. "I'm sorry, I was finishing off the breakfast round."

"Okay," said Daisy, facing the group. Her voice was thick and quiet, not the officious griping of the evening before. "I thank you all for coming. The men are, of course, in confinement now, which is actually very good timing, because something awful has happened." She looked down at the floor for a moment, and she looked genuinely upset. She continued, "Luca was found this morning, outside the protection of a facility."

My colleagues, I'm sure, assumed that he'd been infected. He'd either have been in a coma, his internal organs shutting down one by one, or hysterical, raving and confused. I sat and listened to Daisy speak about Olivia and the terrible crime she had committed, about how she must have taken him, tied him to a bed so that she could subject him to her desire and, when the guilt got too much, she'd ended it for them both in the most cowardly way possible. She spoke about how we must all be vigilant and report anything that might be suspicious – and all the while I dug my nails into the underside of the chair and stared straight ahead, concentrating on the rota that was pinned to the opposite wall, still showing Olivia's name and mine marked together for three upcoming shifts.

There was one point at which I thought I would break down. It was when Daisy said that Olivia's wife and daughters had been informed and that they were being counselled by professionals at the Law Abidance Department. I'd forgotten those conversations we'd shared not long ago about her wife, her daughters: *agriculture management, marine conservation.* I felt a rising tide of nausea rush through me when I thought of all three being called into a room at the local Law Abidance Office, sat down, treated with gentle voices, explaining, probing. *Were there any signs? Last year in Coventry, had she talked about this sort of thing? Sorry to be vulgar, but… was it something you fantasied about together? None of this is your fault, of course, anything you remember at all, Ms Goodfell? Anything?*

I wanted to stand up and address everyone in the room, to tell them what was really happening, that they worked for monsters who put their own ambitions and ideologies over the freedom of the very men they were supposed to be protecting. But I didn't. These women couldn't do much to help, even if I showed them the footage on the phone. And I had to be careful. Someone knew that Olivia and Emily had taken Luca to that farmhouse. Maybe someone here. Everything would come out soon enough. On that, I was resolved.

Suddenly I realised that everyone was staring at me. I thought, for one terrifying moment, that I'd been mumbling my thoughts out loud.

"Mary, I just said, I'd like you to stay behind. We need to have a quick chat," said Daisy.

My stomach did a small flip, and it had nothing to do with my hunger. *Shit, she knows everything. Law Abidance are on their way. Maybe they are waiting outside the door.*

"One last thing," continued Daisy. "There has been an incident in the viewing room." She gave me a quick look of annoyance. "Maintenance is on it but we need to be extra aware of stray threads until the area has been fully decontaminated." I looked away and tried not to fidget.

"Other than that," she continued, "thanks, everyone for your work this year, and those who are off home on holiday – enjoy the Commemoration."

As the women filtered out of the room, I caught some of the muttered comments: *I should have known, after all that business in Coventry. I always thought there was something odd about her and just think, she was doing it here – under our very noses! I heard the men say that she talked about before the change, about men working and educating themselves.* Isla was the last to leave. As she did so, she turned and gave me a peculiar look and a half nod.

Then there was quiet. Just me, Daisy and Danika. The room, which had seemed cramped a few moments ago, now felt much bigger, and I felt exposed. I wished I'd refused the chair and stood at the back, as I'd wanted to.

Danika spoke first, and I got the impression that this *little chat* had been planned that way. The ward sister smiled as she spoke, and her voice was conciliatory. "Mary, I heard you had an interesting evening last night."

My heart sped up. This was it! But if Danika knew about the farmhouse, why was she smiling? Why wasn't the LAD standing there right now, ready to take me in for questioning? I just sat and stared at her, as the cool fingers of fear stroked up and down my spine.

Daisy interjected sharply, "Tony and the whole viewing room debacle, Mary. You didn't think that we would be able to let it go, did you?"

Danika gave Daisy a quick *I'm handling it* look and Daisy scowled.

I felt myself sag in my seat. That was what they wanted to talk about. Not my late-night expedition and my plans to topple one of the seven Prime Authorities in the Union. I found my voice. "I am so sorry. It won't happen again, I swear it." I tried to arrange my features into a suitably abashed expression.

Another look shared between the two ward sisters. This time Danika looked a little embarrassed and Daisy frowned.

"There's something else," said Danika.

I felt my heart rate increase again, and I clutched the arms of the chair. "What is it?" I was surprised at how even my voice sounded.

"Well, we've had a meeting this morning, Mary," said Danika. "The ward sisters and the Warden and, well…" She took a breath. "We think it's best, that is to say, we think it's time for you to retire."

I nearly laughed out loud. In less than twenty-four hours I was hoping to show the Citadel Council proof that the MWA was involved in a clandestine conspiracy and effectively shut down these facilities forever. Everyone was going to be out of a job. I let out a long, shaking breath. "That's… understandable." I looked at them and they were both frowning. I realised that they had been expecting me to put up more of a fight, and my acquiescence might look suspicious. "I mean," I said, trying to look offended, "it's extremely disappointing. Devastating, in fact."

"You will, of course, be eligible for state aid, and the MWA will contribute to your state welfare as a thank you for so many years of service."

I nodded and bowed my head. "That's kind of them."

Daisy, however, it seemed, could not contain herself. "I asked you to keep an eye on Olivia! Didn't I, Mary?"

"Daisy!" exclaimed Danika.

"Well! This whole mess could have been avoided if we'd been able to find out what was going on. The MWA specifically told us they suspected Olivia of sedition when she arrived, didn't they? And Mary here was the one who was regularly on duty with her." She turned to me. "You couldn't even do that one thing! You don't deserve the MWA's welfare."

"Daisy, enough, that's not fair," said Danika, but the woman would not be interrupted.

"And now, and now, Luca is dead! After having to endure goodness knows what at the hands of that… that *monster*." She was nearly in tears.

I wondered if I'd misjudged Daisy. I hadn't realised she cared this much about the men. Then I remembered her dismissal of Tony's suicide attempt and it became apparent to me – it was only Luca she'd cared about.

"That's enough!" Danika rounded on Daisy, who sat back down under the other ward-sister's stare. Danika turned back to me. "Mary, I hope you understand that this was a difficult decision and one we thought about long and hard."

I got stiffly to my feet. "I do understand, and Daisy–"

She looked at me, and I could see great resentment nesting behind her eyes.

"I really am sorry about Luca."

She sniffed and half nodded, half shrugged. I could tell I wasn't forgiven.

"You can take a few days, Mary," said Danika. "Stay here and plan your next move."

I shook my head. "No, it's fine. I've got some travel tokens saved up, and I've been planning a trip for a while now. I'll be out by this evening, if that's okay."

Danika came over and patted me on the arm. "If you're sure."

I left the room, my mind whirling. This was happening; there was no going back. Outside, I was surprised to find Isla lurking in the corridor.

"What happened?" she asked, her warm brown eyes flicking about nervously.

"I'm retiring. As of now."

"What are you going to do?" she said, again glancing up and down the corridor.

"I'm going to the Citadel. To see some friends."

She leaned in, grabbing my arm. Her hold was surprisingly strong. "Is it about the vaccine? It's real, isn't it? I… I want to help." She let go of my arm. "If this is real, I want to… we owe it to the men."

I considered her then. She was so young, twenty maybe,

pretty, softly spoken. She probably had a great life ahead of her. Did I really want to drag her into something like this? "I need you to keep an eye on Tony for me. Sit with him in isolation. Can you do that for me?"

She looked a little crestfallen. "I'll do what I can," she said.

"Are you on duty tonight, in the isolation wing?"

She nodded.

"I'll call for an update on him." I patted her arm. "I've got to go."

CHAPTER 20

I wanted to visit Nicky once more before I left, but I knew I didn't have the time. Instead, I used the phone on the carers' station to call Gale at Elmwood. I think Gale was surprised to hear from me, but she hid it well. "Is everything okay, Mary?"

I wanted to ask her to keep a close eye on Nicky, to fight his corner, if I couldn't be there, but I couldn't think of a way to say it without sounding suspicious or crazy. "Is Nicky all right?" I asked, eventually. "I... had a bad feeling, and I thought I'd just call."

Her voice changed slightly. It took on a calm patience, the tone I used to use as a teacher with any overly worried parents. "He's fine, doing well, playing with Lego all morning. He had a good breakfast."

"Has anyone been there?" I asked, trying and failing to sound offhand. "To visit him, I mean."

"No," she replied, "I mean, not apart from you and two doctors." She paused. "Are you sure everything's okay?"

A group of cleaners passed by the station chatting and laughing. I turned away, cupping the phone for a little more privacy. I felt my throat contract. "Tell him I am thinking of him," I replied with effort.

"I will, and Mary? Don't worry. He'll be fine."

She hung up, and I reluctantly put down the phone.

It didn't take me long to pack. Everything I owned fitted into an old backpack. I squashed the big wad of travel and accommodation dockets into the side pocket. It was enough

to get me to the Citadel and to find somewhere nice to stay –
somewhere public. I didn't know what the MWA knew, but I
had to assume that if they'd got to Emily, they knew about me.
And the phone.

One of the other carers was driving into town that evening
to collect a package and I caught a lift with her to the bus
station. She wanted to talk about the scandal with Olivia
and Luca. Did I know her well? Did I suspect? Had she said
anything – anything *at all*? But, met with my muted responses,
she lapsed into a disappointed silence.

As we drove, I wondered how we would have fared if
the whole thing was reversed, if men hadn't been the ones
infected. Would they have kept the trains going? The power
on? How long would it have been before the internet was
up and running? I tried not to think about what a facility for
women might be like.

She dropped me off at the entrance of the sanatorium with a
curt, "bye, then," before driving off almost before I'd unloaded
my stuff.

I made for the derelict train station: one of my favourite
places. The bus stop, only a few hundred metres away, had
been renovated, offering at least three busses into the Citadel
per day. But the train station had hardly been touched. A few
seats remained, hard plastic and steel, but comfortable. Much
of the track lay buried beneath long tufts of grass. Where
visible, the metal lines were a dark rusted brown, and the
stony ground of the old platform was pitted and rough.

It was a convenient place to wait for the next bus, being
close to the bus stop. I would hear the announcement when it
came, so I settled myself, my bag at my feet. The sun reflected
off the gravelly stone, and the air had been heating up all day.
I was glad of the shade, but I was still sweating through my
dress.

I thought about the men back at the facility. The air
conditioning wouldn't quite be keeping up with the hot

summer weather, and their rooms would be stifling. I'd visited Tony before I left. He was showing no signs of infection. It had been over twenty-four hours, so he was probably in the clear. But his mood was low, as low as just after he'd lost Logan. He'd sat in his room staring at the wall, not acknowledging me, ignoring the double helping of contraband honey cake I'd managed to smuggle him in from the canteen. It wasn't until I was leaving that he finally spoke, and his voice held such a note of desperation that I got a hard lump in my chest just listening to him.

"Mary," he said, "I don't want to keep on doing this." He gestured to the room that would be his home for the next month. "If you don't come back with the vaccine… I'll find a way out." His guitar leaned against the wall. He had a pile of laminated scrolls by his bed, a canvas, some pens, some paints and a new deck of cards still sealed in its cellophane wrapper.

I might have reminded him how lucky he was, that at other facilities the men were doped for the whole of their confinement, but the words lodged in my throat. Instead, the ghost of another conversation drifted into my mind, an echo from a nightmarish time just after the infestation. *I don't want to live like this, Mary.* I pushed it back down, to the circle reserved for the worst memories, the ones written in regret. To Tony, I'd replied, "I'm going to make it better. I swear. I'm going to come back and get you, and I'm going to take you somewhere safe. I'm going to help you."

There was anger in his eyes. "It didn't help Luca, did it, your vaccine?"

I sat on the edge of his bed, not surprised by his anger. Tony had refused to talk to me about it since he found out about Luca's death.

"You tell me one thing, Mary, but Daisy tells me something else. She said that Olivia kidnapped Luca, that she hurt him. She warned me that if anyone tries to take me somewhere *safe*, that I should scream and find a ward sister."

"I know – but Daisy's wrong. That's not what happened, Tony. I can't tell you everything now. I'll find out the truth, and I'm going to get you the medicine, I promise."

I could see it in his eyes, other promises I'd made and broken, but in the end, he nodded his head once and said, "Will you come and see me as soon as you are back?"

"Yes," I said, "of course."

As I sat by the track at the crumbling station, I gazed upon the dilapidated platform on its other side, and I tried not to wonder whether I would come back. Whether, in fact, Tony might get a message handed down via gossip. Maybe Daisy would take him to one side. *I know you and she were close... just died in her sleep. Quiet, painless. She was old, Tony. It was hardly unexpected.*

Across from me was what had once been a kiosk, shuttered now. I assume that at some point it had been searched, its resources gathered and catalogued, before being boxed up and sent to Woking, the nearest distribution centre. The ghost of some graffiti still clung to the bottom corner of the shutters. Once upon a time, *Jordan* had felt compelled to tell the world that he loved *Lauren* in red indelible marker. The heart that accompanied the message was now a faded, watery pink.

Beyond the kiosk, in the middle of what once must have been the platform, stood two large, rectangular marketing boards, smashed and empty. Void of adverts for meal deals or the latest blockbuster movies or bestselling books, there weren't even any messages encouraging me to run a marathon to beat breast cancer. Just blank obelisks, like doorways. I wondered if I crossed the tracks and leaned into those blank spaces, whether I'd find myself back there, amongst commuters and shoppers and groups of high-spirited teenagers. I could duck through and find myself in another life, one in which I was standing on a platform, on my way home from London or Guildford after a day out. Maybe I would find Jordan, one hand draped over the thigh of Lauren, the other fiddling with the red marker in his pocket, weighing up whether he could get away with his vandalous plan. So strong was the vision, that I could hear echoes from the other side, the high whine of an incoming train and the flat echoing tone of an announcer calling out times, and smell the aroma of freshly ground coffee.

I dozed off, so I nearly missed the call from the bus station. *Next bus to the Citadel leaving in three minutes.* I grabbed my battered pack and shifted it onto my back. I had to walk fast and when I arrived, the last person was just getting onto the bus.

The girl in front of me, a teenager, smiled at me. "Just in time," she said, before holding out her hands for my bag. "Let me help you with that." She heaved it into the hold, and I winced at the thought of the phone buried within. I thanked her and followed her up the steps, handing a travel docket to the driver as I passed.

There weren't many seats left, so I sat at the front, the places reserved for those with disabilities or small children. The young girl who helped me with my bag stood next to me, holding onto the top rail as the driver spoke over the tannoy, "Please belt yourselves in. Some roads between here and Maidenhead are going through a period of restoration, which can result in a bumpy ride."

The standing girl, dressed in a red jumpsuit with colourful braids in her long, dark hair, looked around for somewhere to sit. I flipped down a seat next to me and patted it.

"But it's for, you know, disabled people," she whispered.

"No one will mind," I replied, "and if anyone says anything, I'll say you're my travel assistant."

She smiled. "Okay." And sat down next to me. "I'm Cody," she said.

I hesitated, "Faye," I replied. "Nice to meet you."

I found my belt and slotted it home, as did Cody, and off we went.

About a mile out of town the landscape turned to crops and

homesteads. Occasionally we went through a bigger village, more of them inhabited than I remember when I last came this way. We made good time, but then the road became more troublesome, and the driver had to slow to a crawl. We passed a crew of road maintenance workers, tanned and toned, some shirtless in the warm July sunshine, clearing rocks and vegetation and pouring buckets of gravel into holes. One worker, rangy and lean with a mane of thick dark curls, turned her head and winked at Cody as the bus edged around the worksite. My eyes lingered on the pinkish scars where her breasts used to be. For some, they just got in the way. The young girl smiled back through the window, then caught me watching her and blushed a little.

It turned out that she was a little older than I thought, twenty, and in her second year of university. I asked her if she was going home for the holidays.

"No," she replied. "I've been too busy with university. I want to be a carer and I've been doing a tour of some of the facilities and sanatoriums, so that when I start, I'm used to being around men."

I wanted to ask if she'd been to Elmwood. If she'd met a man called Nicky, but I said, "I hear it's tough. That the carer-to-warden programme is a hot ticket." The MWA had done a lot to raise the profile of the facilities in the past decade, raising the pay and adding in benefits, my pension being one of them.

"Mmmm. There was a lot of competition. I came in the top eight per cent in my year at Winchester, but I was still placed on the reserve list for the internship."

"Why did you want to go into caring?" I asked, secretly pleased that my job... my *ex-job*, was so sought after.

Cody hesitated and looked out of the window, out at the countryside that was passing us by a little faster now that we were on a clearer stretch of road. "Well, I like to help people, to care for them. I think the men are interesting and I believe that keeping them safe and uninfected is the right thing to do, despite the, you know, resource issues."

I nodded and let her go on facing forwards, not looking at her.

She paused. "I nearly opted for male paediatrics, but I was told it was a lot harder at the preps. Some women get very attached to their wards and then have to watch them leave." She turned to me. "I wouldn't want to do that."

I shifted uncomfortably in my seat.

"My parents wanted me to go into caring, to work my way up to Warden, even onto the Council one day." She was talking more to the window than to me. "There are eight of us, and my parents could only afford to send two of us to college. The rations we have don't stretch that far. If we had more land, then we could expand our holding, but it's expensive. The thing is, none of us wants to, you know…"

She let the sentence hang there, and I finished it for her, "Contribute?"

She nodded. "My mother did, at the start, before the Assisted Insemination Programme was up and running and before you could choose. But then, she did it for the Union. Back then they really believed in all that duty stuff."

She looked at me, unsure, as if worried that she may have said something that might offend me.

I smiled. "It's okay. Contribution is a very personal choice."

She turned back to the window. "I hate the idea of one of my sisters having to go through it, but the incentives just keep getting bigger and the rations get smaller. I mean, how are we supposed to manage without Contributing?"

I didn't answer. I don't think she expected me to. My mind flicked back to the mother at the bus stop, my suspicion that she'd recently Contributed. Was I angry at her? The government's nudging policy was not perfect, but it's better than forcing women to have male children, as they did before, justifying being forced to give him up by calling it a moral duty. I thought about what would happen if… no, *when* the vaccine became available. I wondered if the government would let men choose with whom they had children. What kind of world would that be?

We were passing the edges of a larger town now, one of the southern London districts. Richmond, possibly? The landscape was unrecognisable but strangely beautiful. What were once engineered lines of urban living were now smutched with flora and grass. Saplings had sprouted up unexpectedly, defiantly, in doorways and out of pavements. The shops and houses, long stripped of resources, crumbled in on themselves as the wild reclaimed the land upon which they stood. What did it look like further into the city, I wondered, in places like Croydon and Brixton, would they be recognisable as what they once were?

"I heard that people have started living there again." Cody nodded towards the passing ruins. "The Habitation Authority sends in troops sometimes, to round them up, but even the troops can't search everywhere."

I shrugged. "What harm can they really do, anyway? Rambling around on their own?"

She nodded and then turned to face me. "Have you visited the Citadel before, Faye?"

"Mmm," I said, in a non-committal tone.

"What is it like?"

"I don't know. Everything was different back then."

"Do you mean at the beginning?"

"Yes, and before."

Cody was not put off by my vague responses. "In history, we're taught that those first facilities were terrible places. But if those first carers hadn't looked after the men, we would have died out, like the Americans." She was staring at me, the back of her head bouncing slightly on the headrest as we lurched our way past the outskirts of Hounslow. "I bet it was tough at the start – before the facilities."

All of a sudden, I hated her, this young confident woman, who knew her place in the world and had never been encouraged to doubt herself. This woman who wouldn't have to fight to survive and could enjoy her opportunities without reservation. I knew I had no right to, that she was everything the Union stood for – but I couldn't help thinking of Tony in his small, hot room. "Actually, Cody, I might have a quick snooze if you don't mind. I'm a bit tired."

"Of course," replied Cody quickly. "Shall I wake you just before we reach Maidenhead?"

"Yes, thank you." I balled up my cardigan into a pillow, stuffing it between my neck and shoulder. Turning away from the young woman beside me, I closed my eyes and tried to forget just how tough it was – before the facilities.

Mary – then

She didn't believe me, of course, Dr Blake, when I told her that volunteering had nothing to do with locating a family member, whilst resolutely meeting her gaze.

"The women running the field hospital will kick you out, Mary, unless you do what you're told. They won't give you a stern telling off or put you in prison. They will send you out – and there are infected men out there. Do you understand?"

"Yes," I replied, still looking her directly in the eye.

"Fine. We need everyone we can get, I guess. But it's rough there, really bad. Don't say I didn't warn you."

"I'm ready."

But I wasn't ready, not even close.

The next morning, after a sleepless night in an uncomfortable cot, Dr Blake drove me and Wynne and one other woman the thirty or so miles to our destination in a Lexus. My eyes were itching with tiredness. More trucks had arrived at the barracks in the early hours of the morning, and women had fumbled their way into our quarters, making themselves beds on any patch of floor they could find. I picked my way over them when it got light, those women with the cut arms, the bruised necks and the black eyes.

We took back roads and there seemed to be fewer abandoned cars. The only person we saw was a man sitting with his back to a lamppost, head in hands. "They're not doing well," said Dr Blake, as we passed him.

"What do you mean?" asked Wynne, who was sitting in the front passenger seat.

"The infected men. They don't eat or drink. I suspect it's an issue in the hypothalamus. The men, when they come in, are very dehydrated."

"Well, isn't that good news?" asked the young girl sitting next to me in the back. "They can't try to kill us if they're dying of thirst."

That may be the first time I noticed it, that plural pronoun – *them, they*, that group noun of the othered that was to become part of the language for men.

I'd pictured lots of tents in a field, the way the doctor had said "field hospital" had brought this to mind, I guess, so I was surprised when we drew up to an enormous conference centre just south of Sunningwell. All steel industrial pipes and sheet glass, it was the sort of place that would hold expos, motor exhibitions and grand conferences. Adrian's work used to have their Christmas parties at a place like this, one of a hundred small companies all doing it together with food and entertainment included – dry turkey and drunken dancing to Abba's *Money, Money, Money* with a bunch of people I didn't know. Every year, I had to force myself to go and every year, Adrian and I would get into an argument about who was driving and the extortionate cost of a babysitter at Christmas time.

Outside, in the vast car park, women in pairs were carrying men on stretchers towards the building. Some of the men walked, their hands tied and their heads flopping forwards, slowly led through the large, glass entrance. We followed Dr

Blake as she weaved her way through the clustered doorway
and into the building.

Dr Blake paused at the doors into the main arena and
looked back at us. "Be wary of the men. They may be tied up,
but they will hurt you given half a chance." She looked right
at me. "Do what you're told and *do not* untie the men under
any circumstances, even if they beg you, even if you recognise
them."

I dropped my eyes to the ground and gave a shrugging nod.

"Okay," she said. "Good luck." Then she opened the doors.

The sound was crushing. A thousand moaning, wailing
voices amplified by an industrial, uncladded roof. I'd never felt
a stab of fear so sharp and so visceral. I forced myself forwards
into the chaos.

"My God," said Wynne, as our small group shuffled inside.
"What the fuck is that *smell*?"

It was humid in the arena, despite the high ceiling. The
briny stench of urine swallowed us in a fetid cloud, but there
was something underneath that reminded me of nail polish
remover or petrol – the smell of the infected. It clung to our
clothes and our hair and our skin, impossible to escape. I
concentrated hard on keeping hold of the cereal I'd had for
breakfast.

"I... I can't," said the young woman we'd arrived with. She
turned and bolted out of the door. Every molecule in my body
was screaming for me to do the same – *run*.

I could barely see the end of the auditorium, so vast was the
space. Before me, arranged in a way that made it look like they
merged somewhere in the distance, lay seemingly endless lines
of hospital beds. Each bed held a man, spread-eagled, with his
wrists and ankles secured to rails on either side. Most of them
were screaming.

I tried to get the attention of a woman dressed in scrubs
and a mask, to ask her where we should go, but she brushed
past me as if I hadn't spoken. I followed her, repeating *excuse*

me in an increasingly louder voice, but nothing. It wasn't until Wynne patted her on the arm that she turned to face us. She looked surprised to see us there. Then she wiggled a pair of rubbery earplugs from her ears. "Sorry," she said, "but without these, I can't hear myself think. Did you just get here?"

Wynne and I nodded dumbly. Wynne seemed to be as bewildered by the place as I was.

"Right," said the woman in scrubs. "You need to report to the volunteer station. Over there, near the children's section." She pointed. My eyes must have lit up when she said "children's section" because, after looking up and down to see if there was anyone close, she leaned in, speaking as quietly as the surrounding bedlam would allow. "Look, I'm a civilian. I don't really care if you're here searching for someone, but don't make it obvious. They don't like it and they might just kick you out onto the street." She sighed and looked at the beds in their interminable lines. "You might not be able to do much for him anyway, even if you do find him."

Wynne and I moved through the sections of beds and towards the volunteer section. In some of the beds we passed, the men were asleep or sedated. But most were awake, barking commands or leering, threatening, spitting. *Whore... suck my cock... untie me, bitchface... you're gonna get it when I get hold of you!* Wynne grabbed my hand and held on to me as we made our way onwards.

My eyes flicked everywhere at once. *Curly hair? Hazel eyes? Black hoodie?* But I couldn't see him. What I did see will stay with me until the day I die. Boys, some as young as three or four, so tiny that the bindings on their arms and legs had to be connected by a long chain of cable ties to the sides of the hospital bed, were writhing and crying out into the strip-lit cavern. One boy, about seven years old, called out as I went past. *Mum! Is that my mum?* I paused for a moment. When his eyes met mine, they were sane and very scared.

"She's coming," I said, "soon." The boy began to sob, his

little bottom lip curling under wetly, like a small red slug, and his eyes narrowing to nothing. Wynne took me by the arm and led me away.

The woman at the volunteer station introduced herself to us as one of the resource coordinators and handed us some scrubs, which we were to put on over our clothes there and then. I'd thought there'd be an induction talk or training of some kind, but our three-minute talk with the coordinator was all the training available.

"How are you with needles?" said the woman over the din.

I felt the blood drain from my face. "Not very good." I couldn't even watch them being given. I had to get Adrian to take Ryan in for his vaccinations whilst I cowered in the doctor's waiting room.

"I'm okay with them," said Wynne. "My nan's a diabetic."

"Good. You go to the pharmacy," she said, pointing Wynne to a partitioned area on the left wall of the arena. "They'll give you meds and tell you what to do. We're running low on everything, so only dope them if they're manic."

Wynne started towards the pharmacy, scanning the beds as she went, before turning back to me. "Good luck."

I nodded. "You too."

The coordinator went and picked up a large bottle of liquid that was light pink, like barley squash, some straws and some stacked plastic cups from a nearby bench and handed them to me. "Okay. You're on H2O patrol. Try to get as many men as you can to drink this."

"What is it?"

"Water, vitamins, salts... mixed with some Ambien. Only give it to the ones that are already doped or, even better, the ones that are lucid, if you can find any. And for God's sake, don't untie anyone. Start in the Red section, then work your way back here to Yellow." She pointed to the coloured signs on the wall, which I hadn't noticed before: Red, Blue, Green, Yellow, Purple. There were probably more at the far end. Red was about twenty rows back and on the left-hand side of the hall. I wanted to stay in the Yellow section, the children's section, to look for Ryan, but the coordinator was staring at me, so I waded out into the fray.

It was exhausting work.

Most of the men were hostile, howling obscenities or thrashing against their bindings. Some had dislocated a wrist or an ankle in their struggle and were whimpering in pain, only to start thrashing about again when I moved into their eye-line. Those who'd been doped were easier – if I could wake them. They'd come round and stare at me, dazed and unfocused, drink weakly from the straw in my fingers, before closing their eyes and retreating to whatever sanctuary the drugs were providing them.

Then there were the few that were confused but lucid. The hardest to deal with. They would strain desperately at the straw, their cheeks concave with the effort. Then came the questions, the ones I couldn't answer. *My wife? My son? His name's Connor... Have you seen my wife, Debbie... Deborah West? Jayden... he's four... My daughter, Louise? Do you know what happened? Can you help? Can you let me up, just for a minute? Just to look?*

I gave the same reply over and over again, "Somebody will be along to explain soon. Just try to get some rest."

Finally, there were those that I knew wouldn't wake due to the tell-tale blue veins around their lips.

Hours passed. I'd gone back to the volunteer station and refilled my bottle many times, each time scanning the sea of beds around me to see if I could catch a glimpse of Ryan. The volunteer coordinator had her head on her arms at the counter, obviously exhausted. She jerked up as I reached her. "There's a sandwich and a couple of bottles of Coke for lunch." She gestured to the food on the counter.

I washed my hands in the nearest bathroom and caught sight of myself in the mirror. The bright lights cast a greenish shadow on my face, illuminating every crevice and shadow and making me look ghoulish. The walls of the bathroom tempered the noise, and I stood for a few moments, relishing the relative peace. Then I went back into Bedlam to eat my lunch.

As I was standing at the counter, trying to ignore the smell of the arena, I chewed on my soggy tuna sandwich. Wynne came back, and I raised my eyebrows at her. She shook her head slightly. Using the same code, I gave my head a slight shake in return.

"They're moving some of the men to another facility," she said, "a bigger one, up near Birmingham." She gave me a meaningful look.

I understood. I needed to find Ryan, and soon. I threw the half-finished sandwich in the bin and readied myself to go back out.

"There was a man back there," said Wynne, as I was about to leave, "who looked like a woman, I mean, I really thought she, I mean *he*, was a woman. Makeup, boobs, everything."

I froze mid-step. There's loads of trans women. It wasn't necessarily her.

"She even said she was a woman, but then I saw the Adam's apple, and I realised she was one of those trans people."

"Show me," I said.

I found Claire in the Blue section. Tethered to her bed, her eyes were closed, and she had mascara tear tracks running down the side of her face. She was wearing the same culottes and gypsy shirt that she'd been wearing at work two days ago, a gold necklace bearing her name, *Claire*, in a swirling font at her throat.

"Do you know him… her… him… sorry, I don't really…" said Wynne.

"Yes. She's my best friend." I leaned down over her and brushed my hand over her forehead. "Sweetheart," I whispered, leaning further down.

Wynne hovered indecisively. "Do you want me to stay?"

"No. Look for your dad," I said, not looking away from Claire. "I'll be fine."

Claire opened her eyes. I didn't know what to expect – anger, fear, violent screaming. But it was her usual soft, low, lovely voice. "Mary? *Oh, Mary!*"

"Yes, yes, it's me." I took her bound hand, noting how the cable tie had bitten into her wrist, creating an angry red welt. I entwined my fingers with hers.

She looked up at me, her eyes wet with tears. "Is my hair a mess?" she asked.

I gave a half-laugh, half-sob. "You look beautiful," I said, smoothing her hair and tucking it behind her ear. "Your eye makeup needs a touch-up though."

She sniffed, "I bet," and then, after a pause, "this is madness, Mary."

"I know."

"Ryan? Adrian?"

"I'm trying to find Ryan. Adrian…" I shook my head.

She squeezed my hand. "I'm so sorry."

We stayed there for a few moments like that, me standing, her lying staring up at me, our hands entwined. I had to keep glancing around to check that no one was paying us any attention.

"I don't know how long before it starts again," said Claire. "The rage, Mary, the *rage*. It's all I can remember. I thought terrible things. I felt hate and outrage and I wanted to…" She looked up at me from the bed and fat tears began to fall, sliding horizontally past her ears and dripping onto the sheet by her neck.

"Don't think about that now." I gently rubbed the red welt on her wrist with my fingertips.

"What if they don't find a cure?" She pulled at the binds on her wrists, still tied to the rails of the bed. "And I'm stuck like this forever? I don't have my meds. I don't want that. I wish I'd caught the type that just killed you."

"Don't say that Claire. I'll speak to them. I'll ask them for your meds."

"They won't care, Mary. Not with all of this going on."

"They'll find a cure. Soon. You can start your meds again."

She lowered her voice even further. "I don't want to live like this, Mary. Not after everything. You have to promise me that if they don't find a cure..."

"It's time to go." It was Wynne. "The transport to the women's camp is leaving in ten minutes."

I turned to her. "But I haven't found Ryan."

"It's the end of the shift. If we don't go back, they'll know something's up."

"You go," said Claire. "I'll be fine."

"I can get you a drink before I go."

"Dom Pérignon? Chilled?"

"They only have Moet."

"Fuck that. *Pass.*"

I laughed. She could always make me laugh. "I'll be back tomorrow. I promise."

Then I leaned in to give her a kiss and as I did so, she whispered to me, "If there's no cure, you have to help me end it."

I drew back and stood there looking at her for a long time, my beautiful friend. "Okay," I said, finally. "I promise."

I asked about Claire's hormones at the pharmacy on my way out. The woman behind the counter gave me a look of exasperation. "Are you insane?" she said. "It's the end of the world and your friend is worried about some extra body hair? You're not even supposed to be looking for your friends here. I should report you."

I left quickly, intending to try again the next day. At the time, I was convinced that a cure was just weeks away. We all were. We just had to cling on for a short while and it would all go back to something like normal. I could get Claire her meds, find Ryan, look after them, and then we could start to rebuild.

For those first few days, trucks would arrive frequently, delivering women and girls to the barracks. The night after I found Claire, I was woken by a young girl and her mother entering our, already crowded room. The mother was desperate to keep the girl quiet, "Shhh, Stacy, please don't cry."

"Why was Daddy so angry?" the little girl sobbed in a high, small voice.

"He didn't know what he was saying, baby. He didn't mean it. Shhh."

"Where is he now?"

"Let's just get some lovely sleep and talk about it in the morning. You're so tired, baby."

I got up and offered the bed to the mother. "It's still warm," I said in a weak attempt at humour.

Then the woman burst out crying, made worse by the fact that she was desperately trying not to let her daughter see how upset she was. "Thanks," she managed through clenched teeth and streaming tears.

I left them to it. It was getting light anyway, so I headed to the canteen. As I ate my scrambled eggs on toast – smaller portions, I noted, than when I'd arrived a few days ago and no sausages this time – I thought about what I could do when I went back in. I could ask Dr Blake about the hormones; she might be sympathetic. I could sneak into the pharmacy – but I didn't know what I was looking for. Then there was Ryan, I needed to find him, look after him.

I sounded Dr Blake out in the car later that morning, on the way back to the hospital. I phrased it hypothetically, if a trans woman could be given the right drugs, would she consider it?

"Mary, I have so many other things to worry about," came her reply.

"But we could help her, a little. And it's not like we can help the others at the moment."

Dr Blake didn't say anything then for a long while as she drove. The pause was so long that I thought I might have offended her and she was giving me the silent treatment, but when she finally spoke, it was with a sigh of resignation. "You're right. We can't help most of them. If you were to *hypothetically* take me to her, then I might *hypothetically* have a look at her, see if there is anything I can prescribe."

I was ecstatic. It was something. The place was just as noisy and fetid as yesterday, but I hardly noticed as I raced around to Blue section as soon as I arrived, desperate to tell Claire the good news. I knew she might be manic, might be screaming and ranting, but if I could wait, I could catch her when her mind returned, and I could go and get Doctor Blake.

She wasn't there. Half the beds were empty.

Claire, along with hundreds of others had been transferred in the night, to other hospitals, better-resourced hospitals they said, across the country. I couldn't even look for her, later, when things had settled down. I didn't know her father's surname. I knew her as Claire Magdalene, but that wouldn't have been what was on her file.

I couldn't even look.

CHAPTER 21

Cody woke me at Maidenhead, as she promised. When she tapped me on the shoulder and called me Faye, I opened my eyes and frowned at her in confusion for a moment, before remembering my thin subterfuge.

It had been many years since I'd last visited the Citadel. Even back then, it had changed beyond recognition from the military stronghold of just after the infestation. I remembered it last as a busy and colourful commune, a place where the newly formed Council had held large outdoor debates long into the night, in Merton and Saint Clement field. Back then, I also attended a midsummer festival at Christ Church, with drums and dancing and overflowing mugs of moonshine.

It was still as busy, busier even. The street teemed with rickshaws, a few horse-drawn carts plodded by, electric bicycles swept past and couples and families wandered down the pavements. The reclaim depots were crowded and there were a few shops offering goods for tokens. However, there was something less anarchic about it than I remembered, more muted. In my mind, the lines of Victorian terraces had been painted in wild colours, curtained with bright, non-matching fabrics. I remembered front courtyards littered with outdoor benches made from old leather car seats. But the houses I looked at now were painted white, the front gardens neatly trimmed and chairless. Perhaps I'd imagined it. Perhaps this was a different part of the Citadel, although I was sure I recognised the white stone of the art deco bus station.

My young friend Cody bobbed around me, marvelling at the hustle and bustle. I noticed a few other women wearing versions of her fitted cotton jumpsuit in cheerful colours, and realised it must be the height of fashion. It seemed that people were wearing fewer reclaimed clothes these days, although where the cotton was coming from, I couldn't say. Australia, perhaps? The new-looking outfits of those around me matched. Despite berating myself for being too old for such nonsense, I self-consciously smoothed down my rather provincial-looking tea dress, which hadn't been in fashion, I suspected, since about two-thousand-and-twelve, and left my polka-dot cardigan in my bag despite the evening chill.

"It was nice to meet you," I said to Cody. "I hope it all works out in the carer internship programme."

"Thanks," she said, but she wasn't really listening to me. She was asking directions to a hostel from a tall woman in a brightly coloured strappy vest and a tight pair of cut-off jeans. The woman smiled and laid her tanned arm around Cody's shoulder as she spoke into her ear, pointing down the road. The tall woman must have said something really funny, because Cody burst out laughing and then took a mock swipe at her new friend's shoulder.

I wandered off to find a public booth, feeling for the precious phone in my backpack and experiencing a great sense of relief when I felt the smooth screen. I exchanged an allocation slip for a roll of old twenty pence pieces from a woman stationed near the line of booths. There was no privacy booth on any of the reclaimed phones, just a line of six bolted onto a wall. Three were in use, so I moved to the one right at the end. I took a coin from the papered roll and ran the pad of my thumb over the picture of the Queen. Around the edge was written 2020 ELIZABETH II and then some Latin phrases. It hadn't taken long for these little disks and their wealthier paper relations to become worthless. In a recession, cash is king; in an apocalypse, it's clean water and canned stew.

I pressed the coin into the slot of the phone and dialled the facility, calling the direct line to the wing in which Tony was isolated.

"Isla, is that you?"

"Yes. Mary?" She was whispering, and I thought I detected fear in her voice.

"Is everything all right? With Tony."

"Yes, he's fine. No infection. It seems he got away with it."

"Are you okay?" I asked, frowning.

"Two women from the MWA were here earlier. Asking questions about you."

"What kind of questions?" I clutched the handset a little tighter as a gentle breath of fear brushed the hairs on my neck.

"Your whereabouts last night, how close you were with Olivia. Where you planned on going today."

"Did they ask about a place called Elmwood?" I felt cold despite the warmth in the air.

"No, I don't think so. But they did say that they were looking for you in connection with Luca's abduction."

How did they know I was at the farmhouse? "What did they look like, Isla, the women? Did they give you their names?"

A number of short noises sounded on the line, suggesting my time was running out.

"No names. One was skinny with short black hair, about fifty, maybe, the other was a little older, short and plump, with glasses."

"Okay, Isla. And be caref–" My money ran out before I could finish.

My mind turned to the farmhouse. It was Emily who called Olivia and got her to go there. Emily was the only one, other than Olivia and me, who knew about the vaccine, and Luca, of course. Could she have betrayed us? But why bring the vaccine to us in the first place? Perhaps the MWA got to her in some way, threatened her. But I couldn't quite reconcile the person sitting at the farmhouse table, talking about her murdered friend, with someone who would betray us.

I went back to the street and found a cab. "The River Hotel," I said to the driver, "if it's still open." I'd stayed there about ten years ago on my quest to find Nicky.

"It is," she said, and moved off.

The driver drove us around the Citadel with ease. No potholes or cracked brickwork to slow us down. The whole place had a freshly painted smooth feel, a far cry from the mismatch of the villages around the facility. We passed a crocodile of small children holding hands, two by two, all in dungarees and t-shirts, twirling their canvas bags and jostling into one another. One teacher led from the front and one herded from the back. The kids didn't even give us a passing glance. Back in the villages around the facility, the arrival of a car like this would be an event, one to savour and to talk about for weeks.

"It's *Romeo and Juliet* tonight."

"What?" I said, turning away from the children.

"The performance – it's *Romeo and Juliet*." The driver nodded to a theatre we were passing. "Are you a Shakespeare fan?"

"Yes," I replied. "I love Shakespeare." It was, of course, the same play that I'd watched only a few nights ago. The memory of Tony's artful and subtle delivery flashed back to me, his mournful expression, the tears, and the cheers of the audience. That was before his suicide attempt, before Luca's dead blank stare and Olivia's supplicant bow.

"These days, historians think that it wasn't actually William Shakespeare who wrote those plays, not on his own anyway. I've read that there's a lot of evidence suggesting it was his wife, Anne Shakespeare." The driver, a woman of about thirty with a ruddy complexion and short, coppery hair, turned to where I was in the back seat and lowered her voice in a conspiratorial manner, "I mean, there were so many stories and such emotional intelligence. One can't imagine that a man did all of that." She turned fully forward again and sighed. "To be honest, I don't really enjoy the classics. All that man stuff... It's just so obsolete, so... *queer*. But there are some new hypno-dramatists that I do really enjoy. How long are you staying? Perhaps you can catch a show. Honestly, it's life-changing."

"I'm not sure…" I replied, still trying to navigate her use of the term "queer" in my mind. "Not long, probably."

"I went to a hypno-dram last week," she continued. "It was a dramatisation of a conversation between a therapist and her patient. Halfway through the play, the actors broke character and asked the audience to contribute experiences, traumas, whatever they felt that the performance had thrown up for them. Anything they wanted to say, they could just stand up and say it. It was all so liberating and every time someone spoke, the whole auditorium clapped and cheered. I spoke about a horrible breakup that I've never really recovered from. Talking about it in front of all those people – it was, what's the word? Cathartic – that's it! Then actors carried on with the performance, but they used the audience's words and wove them into the story, like the play was evolving in front of our eyes to encompass everyone. My breakup was played out in front of me. I felt that old pain just drain away. I swear, it was the best five hours of my life."

"That sounds… fascinating," I said, making a mental note to avoid hypno-drams at all costs.

My room was palatial after the pokiness and sterility of my dorm at the facility. Spongy cushions sat like fat cats on a huge bed, and the linen was so fresh it actually shone in the late afternoon sunlight.

But I felt sick to my stomach. I took a deep breath and wished I'd stopped by the bar on the way up. A stiff drink would have been exactly the thing that might have made the call I had to make easier. But it had to be done. I summoned up the image of Luca tied to the bed and Olivia's penitent bow and I picked up the phone by my bed. When I spoke to the receptionist, I was pleased that my voice sounded normal, confident even.

"Could you put me through to the office of Jade Philips?"

There was a pause then, "Er, do you mean Jade Philips, the Council Member?"

"Yes, please." I was clipped, efficient.

"Hold the line, please, madam."

There was a long pause before the gentle clicks of a call being placed. Then it rang.

"Hello, this is Jade Philips' office."

This was it. "Put me through to Jade. We're... friends. She told me to call. I have some extremely important news for her." I used as firm a tone as I could muster.

There was some rustling on the other end and then, "Can I take your name, please?"

"It's Mary, Mary Langham."

"Please wait a moment."

A longer pause this time. And then the same woman came back on the line. "Ms Philips is very busy. She's asked me to take a message." This was it – the very thing I was afraid of. Jade Philips was not about to take a call from some carer she met briefly five years ago. I pressed on anyway, doubling down on the sharpness in my tone. "I *insist* that I speak to Jade. Please impress upon her that she specifically asked me to speak to her if I needed to, and the information I hold is of national importance."

"Er, hold on."

Another pause – the longest of all. And then a blank tone. I thought for a moment I'd been cut off, but then another voice came on the line. "Hello? Mary?" It was Jade Philips. The woman couldn't keep the note of wariness from her voice as she spoke, but it was definitely her.

"Hi," I said, suddenly unsure how to start.

"Mary, I'm very busy right now. I appreciate the call, but Caroline will make you an appointment for a few weeks' time..."

I cut her off mid-sentence and told her everything, all in one breathless stream. It came out upside-down and backwards but it was all there: Luca, the vaccine, the phone. Everything.

When I'd finished, there was silence.

"Hello? Jade, are you still there?"

Eventually she spoke, "Well, that's an extraordinary story, er, Mary. I'm finding it hard to... do you have this phone, this recording device? I mean, do you have it with you?" There was still a note of hesitancy in her voice, a tinge of disbelief.

"Yes. I have it."

"Okay. I'm tied up with an Australian delegation this evening, but can you come to the Council Offices first thing tomorrow morning?"

"Yes," I replied, relief spreading like a warm wave through my body. "First thing."

The line went dead. Did she believe me – probably not. It sounded outlandish as I was saying it. But she wouldn't be able to deny her own eyes when, tomorrow morning, I arrived at the offices and showed her the footage.

I replaced the handset and crawled into the smooth sheets, spreading myself out like a starfish. I dug my fingers under the pillows to reach their cool, soft underbellies. Had I not snoozed on the bus, I would have slept right then. But I was not at all sleepy, so I turned over and lay there for a moment, looking at the amber shafts of light streaming in through the sash window. The light illuminated motes of dust, and a few eyelash-shaped fibres, those spindly specks of woe, which, at the facility, we'd learned to dread. I tried to pluck one from the air but as I moved my arm, I disturbed the air, and the fibres shimmered before me in an impossible whirling dance. The Eclipse was coming.

I wandered over to the window and prised it open a few inches. Below, the river eased past. Ferns waved in the current, as if longing to follow the flow. I watched a slender boat, a punt, in which a couple larked around; one woman, dressed in shorts and a checked shirt knotted at her slender waist, was trying to balance on the end of the little boat, pole in hand, while the other woman, in a broad-brimmed hat, rocked it from side to side, laughing as her companion staggered about.

A chair and a small desk stood by the window. Some paper – real paper, not the pulpy tissue that we had to make do with back at the facility, envelopes, a fountain pen with ink, and a silver letter opener lay in the early evening light. I sat at the desk and looked out onto the sparkling water of the river, thinking about what I would say to Council Member Jade Philips in the morning. I wondered what would happen if the MWA got to me first, made it look like suicide, or worse, if Jade Philips was part of the plan. I couldn't imagine it, thinking about the smiling, idealistic young woman from five years ago, but it was possible. And if that was the case, well, I was running out of options.

As I sat there, dark clouds rolled in, giving the light a feeling of premature nightfall and the room began to feel muggy and oppressive. I needed some food. I needed some fresh air.

I had a quick wash, changed into a pale blue wraparound skirt, sandals, and a navy shirt. I shrugged on my jacket. In my right pocket I could feel the phone and a wad of tokens, much depleted after I'd paid for the room up front. As I was walking to the door, something caught my eye in the light from the window. I picked up the small silver letter opener with the pale handle. As weapons go, it was pretty pathetic. I put it in my pocket anyway.

I left the hotel and walked for a while, enjoying the novelty of the Citadel, with its business and its colour. I stopped at a pizza stand, surprised to find meat on the menu, and ordered a large slice of BBQ chicken. The sweet meaty cheesiness was divine. I ate whilst walking down the street and when I'd finished, I paused, considering going back for another slice. As I stopped, some small part of me decided I was being followed. I had no evidence to support this. I didn't see anyone. But I knew. Millennia of instincts means that we all have, buried deep, a tiny patch of neurons that reacts to the predator's eye. Mine were firing up like Christmas lights.

I turned down a few streets and started to walk quickly. I stopped and checked in the reflection of a shop window to see if anyone was watching. It had begun to rain, not hard, but persistent. People were hurrying now, and no one was loitering. *You're imagining it – get a grip!* And then I saw her, a figure over the side of the street. She was tall and thin and had her hood up on a dark green woollen coat, a heavy choice for summer. She was too far away for me to see her face. When she saw me look at her, she cast her eyes down at the floor. But she stayed there.

I felt for the miniature knife in my pocket. Would I really use it if the time came? As I looked back, I saw her follow me, deliberately keeping her distance. If this was the MWA, and it probably was, I needed to be somewhere public. Unfortunately, the rain had made the crowd on the streets thin out. I put up the hood on my jacket and turned down another road. The sign was high up at the end of the street: *Romeo and Juliet – playing tonight.*

CHAPTER 22

I walked through the rain without looking to see if the woman was still following me and entered the theatre. The bell girl asked if she could check my jacket, giving me a quick and brutal up-and-down glance. I declined and paid for my ticket.

She rolled her eyes when I handed her my tokens. "We don't take these anymore. They were replaced a few years ago."

I looked back to the doorway, terrified the woman following me would be lurking outside. But I couldn't see anyone. I turned back to the girl. "Please, I haven't been in the Citadel for a few years. If you could…"

The woman behind her, older, probably her manager, took pity on me. "It's fine," she said, and ushered me into the lobby.

I must have looked a state. I was wet through and, as I looked around, conspicuously underdressed. I consoled myself with the fact that I was old, and the aged get to wear what they like. I remember being a teenager and looking at my mother's heavy woollen skirt and blocky brown shoes and thinking, *shoot me if I ever think that's a stylish combination*. Well, here I was, dressed for a picnic when everyone else seemed to be auditioning for *Vogue* – if *Vogue* still existed, which it did not. Never mind, I was in public, surrounded by several of the Citadel's dignitaries: eager, confident young women in beautifully cut dresses. If the MWA wanted to take me away, they'd have to do it in front of all these people, and I would make a very loud scene.

I wandered between groups of women holding champagne glasses and chatting in low voices. I was half smiled at, as you might smile at a rich, eccentric aunt, but nobody spoke directly to me. I looked back and couldn't see my mystery companion. After about fifteen minutes, I was ushered to my seat; the lights dimmed, and the show began:

Two households, both alike in dignity.

The actors were very good. Believable. Professional. I amused myself by considering that I was the only woman there who'd seen the play performed with all the parts played by men and then, in a different performance, all the parts played by women. Although, what does it actually matter? Gender, these days, is not based on chromosomes - the moths had taken care of that decades ago when they'd banished everyone with a Y chromosome from society.

Some actions of the male parts were, I'm sure, alien to the audience, or *queer* as my driver had put it – It's rare now, for example, that someone gets stabbed to death in a street fight – not unknown, but rare. On the other hand, I'm sure that young girls still fall in love with other young girls of whom their mothers are not enamoured. They disobey, they run away, whilst parents wring their hands and despair and blame each other. The men in the facility are considered able to consent to sexual activity at eighteen. I realised that I had no idea as to what the legal age of consent was for women. Not that the information would be particularly useful to me, but I was curious. I made a mental note to find out.

Someone was shuffling past everyone in the row on their way towards the aisle, apologising and stepping over coats and bags. I looked up as I scrunched my legs sideways to allow her to pass and stared into the face of my follower from earlier, same green coat, same build.

It was Emily, looking down at me.

I felt like a balloon had suddenly inflated in my stomach.

She slowed her shuffling as she reached me, and even in the darkness I perceived an unmistakable nod in the direction of the bathroom. I left it for a few minutes, then stood, apologising to my neighbour as I climbed over her. "Old age," I said and rolled my eyes.

"Oh yes, of course," she said and squeezed in to let me pass, as did everyone else on the row, mostly with good-natured grace.

The play continued: *Alas, poor Romeo! He is already dead, stabbed with a white wench's black eye, shot through the ear with a love song.*

I clambered over the last couple of people, offering quiet apologies as I went.

The bathroom, when I reached it, was large and seemed newly decorated, all clean, white surfaces that reflected the glow of a row of tasteful up-lighters. It was empty, except for the last stall, which had a locked door. I didn't know what to do. What if I spoke, and it wasn't Emily? What if I'd misconstrued the nod? I held the letter opener in my hand.

Thankfully, the door opened, and out came Emily. She walked over to the glimmering sinks and began to wash her hands before even looking in my direction.

"Oh, thank goodness," she said, quickly drying her hands on a small towel. "I was leaving the Citadel when I saw you at the station. Are you okay?"

"Yes, I mean, other than, you know, everything with Olivia and Luca."

A flash of misery crossed her face, although it could also have been guilt. She stood back from me and sniffed. "You know what they're saying, don't you? That it was grooming."

"I know. I know. I was there when it happened."

"*What?* When they were murdered?" Every muscle in her long frame tensed up, her hands curled into fists. "*Who…?*"

"No, not when they were murdered, just after. I found them. It was obviously a setup."

I told her then about the hidden benzo marks, the way the bodies had been staged, the missing vaccine. I watched her the whole time to see if I could sense how much she already knew.

She was trembling. I thought she'd cry. I could hear the performance from the auditorium: *The clock struck nine when I did send the nurse; In half an hour she promised to return.* That meant that we were nearing the end of Act Two. And that meant the interval.

"Emily. Did you call Olivia that night at the facility, ask her to come to the farmhouse?"

Emily nodded, her face a mask of guilt. "I had to leave Luca. One of my contacts at the MWA had some information for me, but she didn't want to give it to me over the phone. Later, she told me that the MWA has been tapping and tracing the phones. I should have left him there alone, but I was worried about somebody coming. I thought with one of us there, then he'd be safe. Oh God, if I hadn't called the facility and left that message, Olivia might still be alive." She placed her hands over her face.

I couldn't be completely sure, of course, but my gut told me she was telling the truth. I placed my hand on Emily's shoulder. "Whoever killed Olivia and Luca knew what they were doing. If you'd been there instead of Olivia, they would have killed you."

"Maybe," she said with a small sob. "I can't believe she's gone. After everything."

"All we can do now is get the phone to Jade Philips. I have an appointment with her for tomorrow morning."

"You have it here, with you?"

"I've hidden it," I replied.

"Where – *Wait!* Don't tell me. If they catch me, it's best I don't know." Emily stood still for a moment, her hands balled into tight little fists, so tight that her knuckles were blanched pale against the rest of her skin. "The MWA are onto me. I have a friend there still and she says they issued a search request to Law Abidance last night."

"You need to find somewhere safe to lie low. Just until I've spoken to Jade. Once this evidence gets put before the Council, the MWA are finished. They won't be able to touch you."

Emily nodded. "I've got a friend in Merton who'll put me up. But what about you?"

"I'll be fine," I said, wishing I felt as confident as I sounded.

She nodded and wiped her face with the back of her hand. I thought she was going to say something else, but at that moment a stream of women began filing into the bathroom. Emily and I spun away from each other, her to the basins, me into a stall.

When I came out a few minutes later, she'd gone.

The play finished predictably: lifeless, star-crossed lovers in a heap on the stage. Accomplished as the actors were, they couldn't hold a candle to Tony's heartfelt monologue.

The walk back to the hotel was long and punctuated by my glances over my shoulder every few seconds to see if anyone was following. Every doorstep and shadowy corner seemed to harbour an unseen assassin ready to cut me down. It was about 11pm and I was feeling tired – a hard, bone-deep weariness.

I stumbled into the hotel, desperate for this night to end. Then I made my way up the curving, carpeted staircase to my door, fumbling on the wall just inside the room for the light. I was thinking about those sheets and that glorious, deep-filled mattress.

I finally found the switch and flipped it, illuminating a roomful of aftermath. The small desk had been dragged to the middle of the room, its drawers open, the paper and envelopes strewn across the carpet. The chair was on its side with its padded seat ripped open and white billows of stuffing erupting out of the seat cushion. The bed was stripped, those lovely silken sheets and soft covers were lying in puddles by the frame, and the mattress was lounging half on, half off the bedframe, with a long gash down one side. Part of its foamy guts lay in ribbons on the floor. My backpack was empty, lying underneath the chair, and my meagre possessions, my socks, my underwear, had been tossed around the room. I crept into the bathroom to find that the shower had been dismantled. Sections were lying in the tub like an appliance autopsy.

I turned and jumped at my own reflection in the bathroom mirror, a surge of adrenaline making my blood pump loudly in my ears. I thought it was someone else standing there, someone ready to pounce. I steadied myself by leaning over and holding on to the sink.

As I looked up again, I found a note taped to the mirror: *Bring us the proof. We have your son.* And an address.

I turned on the taps and splashed water on my face.

This evening wasn't over – not by a long shot. They'd found the one thing in the world that would guarantee I'd play ball.

The landline in the room had been smashed. I checked my jacket pocket, made sure I had my tokens and the note with the address and hurried down to the lobby. The hotel phone was at the reception. As I dialled Elmwood, I asked the girl on the hotel counter if she'd seen anyone go up to my floor, anyone she didn't recognise. She shook her head, "I'm sorry, no." Then she paused. "Is everything all right, madam? You seem upset."

No one was picking up at Elmwood House, not even a disgruntled nightshift worker. "No. Everything's fine," I said, unable to keep the curtness from my voice. I didn't have time for questions, and the state of my room would cause a few of those. "Can you call me a cab, please?" She looked a little hurt by my tone but proceeded to place the call.

When my cab arrived, an upmarket reclaim, I gave the driver the address. She frowned. "Are you sure? This is a two-hour drive."

"Yes, is that okay?" I said, pulling out my store of tokens and showing them to her.

"We'll have to recharge on the way, and I can't wait for you when we get there," she said. "My wife's expecting any day, and I don't want to be that far away all night." I could see the concern on her face, and the question – what was this woman of advanced years wanting in the middle of nowhere in the darkest hours of the night?

"That's fine. I don't need a lift back." If it was the MWA who left the note, I probably wasn't coming back.

This driver was nowhere near as chatty as the one I'd had earlier, and for that I was thankful. She had a CD playing, and I began to doze, slipping in and out of awareness as the lyrics to *The Dark Side of the Moon* forced their way into my nightmare.

CHAPTER 23
Mary – then

With Claire transferred, I feared the worst – that Ryan had gone too, somewhere far away. I went back to the huge expo in Oxford for the next few days, becoming more and more desperate. Each day, Wynne and I forced ourselves into the madness of the men's hospital. Her to try to sedate as many men as she could without getting bitten, and I to offer the water solution to those capable of drinking. Wynne found her father on day three. He was what they were calling "a blue": *Death by asphyxiation due to the inability of the brain to control breathing.*

I held her in the bathroom as she sobbed into my chest, both of us listening out for anyone who might come in. More and more women were coming to the facility now – looking for relatives. The lists of names the soldiers had were on paper and kept getting lost or taken to different compounds and facilities. No one knew anything. At the door of the hospital, women turned up with photos and names. They begged us to look for their sons, their husbands, their fathers, their brothers.

I turned to Dr Blake on the fifth day and asked, "Why don't we just let them in? They can look after the ones they love. We can do the rest. What harm could it do?"

The doctor looked at me long and hard. "Who are you looking for, Mary?"

I was taken aback by the question, and my eyes flicked from side to side. "No one. I told you."

"Well, what if I told you that soon we – you and I – are going to have to start making some really hard decisions, that those in charge have already started to make some difficult choices?"

I looked at her blankly. I really had no idea, and I was still in the mindset of just getting through these weeks and that things would be okay – they were looking for a cure, after all.

"We're down to our last few boxes of benzos and barbs, and we can't get them to eat or drink without them. They won't let us clean them or dress their wounds. We're having to dilute the drugs we give them – stretch the supply further every day." She leaned in. "How long do you think before we can't help them anymore?"

The horror must have shown on my face because the doctor's own face softened and she spoke more gently. "Is he here?" she whispered. "The man you're looking for? Don't pretend you don't know what I'm talking about."

I shook my head, close to tears. "No, I don't think so. I've looked everywhere."

"What's his name?"

"Ryan Langham. My son."

"Date of birth?"

"03/09/2007"

She left and walked quickly over to the pharmacy. From where I was, I saw her unlock a file with a key from her white coat. She scanned a few pages and then replaced the file, locked it, and put the key back in her pocket.

When she returned, her voice was low and urgent, "He's not too far away – in an air hangar in Chalgrove."

"How… how do I get there? And what do I do when I find him?"

She paused and at the time I didn't think I'd ever seen someone quite as tired or as sad. "Take my car. It's got about half a tank. I'll grab a ride back on one of the trucks. But, Mary, you haven't got much time. They're saving some of the men but not others – do you understand?"

I nodded slowly. "Thank you," I said, taking the key from her. She turned away and moved on to the next bed.

I strode out of the hall and into the warm air. Men were still being brought into the hospital – dehydrated, weak with hunger, tied to a stretcher or dragged by two or more women. Few were able to walk unaided. I found Dr Blake's Lexus and tried the inbuilt sat-nav, which mercifully lit up. Satellites are still working, I thought, as I pulled out of the car park – for now.

It was late afternoon when I drove up to the hangar. Even with a sat-nav, I still took a wrong turn and had to double back. There were more soldiers about than at the hospital I'd just left. Most of the women were dressed in ill-fitting uniforms, unsure, encumbered by the rifles slung over their shoulders.

I walked towards the hangar, trying to look confident, purposeful.

"Where are you supposed to be?" barked one young soldier, sweating in her thick jacket and combat boots. "I don't recognise you."

I stood up straight and spoke clearly, staring her directly in the eye. "I was sent from Oxford. I'm a carer and they said you needed help." Then I smiled and rolled my eyes, in what I hoped was an I-don't-want-to-be-here-either kind of way. "Nobody else wanted to come. I guess I drew the short straw."

She smirked. "You certainly did." She jerked her head towards the hangar. "There's not much help you can give that lot. The drugs have run out, and the IVs are being saved for the tags." She wiped her beading forehead on the back of her sleeve.

"Tags?"

The woman paused, and her eyes narrowed in suspicion. "Who sent you, again?"

"Oh, Dr Blake. She wants to know how it's going over here. With the, the *tags* and everything."

"Oh, she does, does she? Fucking doctors. Always sending others to do the hard work." The soldier's face was flushed and there was a raw bitterness to her voice. She walked away muttering about *damn orders*.

Dr Blake's words came back to me from earlier: *How long do you think before we can't help them anymore?* Dread bedded down in my gut.

I could hear the men's cries from outside the hangar, but they were nowhere near as loud as the hospital. When I entered, I realised it was because the men weren't able to make much sound. They'd screamed themselves raw over the past week or so, and now they lay on their beds or sat on the floor tethered to struts, their mouths opening and shutting in breathy, rasping gasps. They smelled rank, despite the hangar being open at both ends. The salty urine smell was still there, but only as an undertone to the smell of rot.

I picked up a bottle of water and a straw and began striding through the ward, trying to look like I was exactly where I was supposed to be. There weren't many women caring for the men here. I could only see a couple of others, and they were on the other side of the building. Walking through the large open space, I noticed that some of the beds had a small yellow plastic loop fixed on the frame, the sort of bracelet you might be given on your way into a festival or theme park. I stopped by one and held it in my fingers, rotating it so I could see what it had written on its side. SANATORIUM printed in bold letters, and on the other, a number and a year, *3792 – 1998*. The man lying in the corresponding bed was about thirty. Silent and still, but for the rhythmic rising and falling of his chest, his face was unshaven and slack.

I raised my head towards the sound of voices coming from the far end of the hangar. Four women, dressed in army fatigues, were wheeling two of the beds out of the hangar towards some trucks waiting outside. Both of the beds they were pushing were marked with the same yellow tags.

Yellow tag – good, no tag – bad. Was this what she'd meant by difficult choices?

I turned and started to hunt for Ryan, trying not to look like I was searching, but frantic nonetheless. The hangar was smaller than the hospital in Oxford, but it still contained hundreds of men. There were six long lines of beds and a few poor, bedless souls bound on the floor or tied to chairs. Moving along the avenues between the beds, I couldn't help but notice that only about half had the yellow tags attached to their bedframes.

The faces of the men began to blur as I passed and I kept thinking, *what if I've missed him? Should I go back and recheck this line?* A few times, I stopped by a bed. *Hazel eyes! Curly hair! Slight build!* But none were him, and I was getting dangerously close to the end where the soldiers were milling about, loading up the men and taking them away. The first soldier's words came back to me: *The IVs are reserved for the tags.* Whatever this SANATORIUM was like, it had to be better than here. Without drugs and IVs, this place was going to become a morgue.

"Mum." The rasping voice came from a few beds away.

I looked over and into the hazel eyes of my boy, my sweet boy.

"Oh, Ryan." I scooted over to his bed, checking the end of the hangar as I went. No one was watching, so I bent down and gave him the briefest of kisses. "I'm sorry," I said. "I'm so sorry."

He was groggy, and the skin on his lips was chapped and broken, peeling off in little white flakes. He was soiled; I could smell it and the bindings had chafed his wrists raw. He was so weak that he was barely able to raise his head as I put the straw to his lips. But once he began, he drank it down quickly. I had to pull it back. "Small sips."

He spoke to me between sips. "Is it you? The… real you?" His voice didn't sound like his. It was hardly above a whisper, and he paused between words as if he was thinking really hard. "When I wake up... remembering stuff... I don't know. And then I'm angry, and I'm always thirsty."

"I know, baby. It's going to be okay." I ran my hand lightly over his forehead, trying somehow to magic away the furrows in his brow, then checked his bed. I couldn't find a tag.

Ryan's eyes were wide and unfocussed. "Are we going home, Mum?"

There was a hard pain in my chest. "Soon," I said, and hated myself for the lie. "We're going somewhere else first."

"Where?" His lip trembled as he spoke. "I want to go home. I'll be good. I won't argue."

"Somewhere much better." I tried to keep the tears from my voice. I looked up, and the same four soldiers were looking at the tags, pointing at different men and checking a clipboard one was carrying. They were closer this time. One of the soldiers gave me a puzzled look and spoke to the woman next to her, the one with the clipboard. They both looked at me and frowned.

I gave Ryan the straw again and pretended to be absorbed in helping him drink. They both turned their attention back to the job at hand. Their subject was thrashing about and trying to break free of his ties.

My gaze fell on the surrounding beds – an old man, overweight, and wheezing as he fought to keep his eyes open, a boy of about six with bandages on his skinny arms, sleeping fitfully. A young man was deeply asleep on my right. He was slightly older than Ryan and he looked in better condition, better cared for. His lips were not dry, and his face was not drawn and gaunt like Ryan's. He had long, blonde hair, almost white, tied back in a ponytail. Clumps of hair had escaped and clung to his face and chin. His skin was naturally pale, so much so that you could see the blue of his veins in the side of his neck as he lay with his cheek to the mattress. His eyelashes were fair, short and stubby, and there was a rash of light freckles on his nose. He looked peaceful, sedated and calm.

Unlike the older man and the little boy, he had a little yellow tag on his bed.

Yellow tag – good. No tag – bad.

My feet felt heavy and unresponsive, but I forced myself to walk to the foot of the bed and roll the tag around so I could read it, all the time sending darting looks over to the end of the hangar.

4457 – Nicholas Chester, 2006.

2006. A year before Ryan was born.

The boy sighed and his head flopped to the other side on his pillow. I stood back sharply, worried that I'd woken him. He remained still, death-like in sleep.

I glanced again at the end of the hangar. The women were chatting together, heads bowed. They looked serious. I thought I saw one slide a look at me, but it could have been my imagination. Quickly, silently, I unclipped the plastic tag from the young man's bed, crushing it into my sweating palm as I casually made my way back to Ryan.

I didn't look up. I stood close to the bedframe and fumbled with it, finally looping it over the metal bar along the side, just as it had been placed on the other boy's bed – on Nicholas Chester's bed. Fastening the popper, I squeezed it so tightly that it left a small tear-shaped indent on the pad of my thumb.

I heard a low whine, and I jerked my head up, terrified I'd been discovered. Ryan was watching me, his red-rimmed eyes blank and unfocused. "It's okay," I said, looking from my son, back at the boy in the bed. "Ryan, it's going to be okay."

Then, despite his weakened state, he started to scream.

"Shush, baby." As I tried to put my hand over Ryan's mouth, he tried to bite me, his jaws snapping like the sound of a cracking nut. I whipped my hand away just in time.

The soldiers were looking at me now, all four of them. I didn't know if they'd seen what I'd done with the tag, but they were moving towards me through the beds. My son was working himself up into a frenzy, spitting and listing all the terrible things he was going to do to me when he got himself free.

"Everything all right?" asked one of the women, noting my name tag. "Mary, is it? Mary Langham?"

"Yes," I replied.

"Do you know this boy?" They pointed at Ryan, who had now directed his anger at them and was calling them fat pigs and whores.

I shook my head. "No, I don't."

One of the other women moved closer and checked the tag. She ran her finger down the list. "This one is... *Nicholas Chester*."

All the women relaxed slightly, and Ryan kept on ranting. About how he was going to teach us a lesson, and that we'd be sorry, and we'd bleed, and our blood would be coming out of wherever. The woman nearest to him turned to me. She looked exhausted. "Why do they come out with this crap?"

The one next to her said, "He should have had his dose by now. Don't worry, we've got loads of morphine in the truck, enough to calm him down until he gets to where he's going."

"And where's that?" I asked casually.

"Classified." The woman shook her head. "Somewhere these boys can be looked after properly."

The first woman spoke again, "It's the rest of these poor bastards I feel sorry for. Seventeen dead already today. Can't get the liquids into them. Still, that will be the problem of the shift after us. Hopefully, they'll get new supplies by then. Let's load this one now. He's giving me a headache."

I looked at the woman who had just spoken and wondered if she didn't know. Perhaps she thought that they were just sorting the men for transport and had no idea that they were leaving the rest to die. Or maybe she did know, and this was just her way of dealing with it.

I watched dumbly as they took *4457* away, into a system that would keep him from me for a decade – a slow, bureaucratic paper trail that I had to navigate, write begging letters, chase up lost records, until I finally tracked down Nicholas Chester in a repurposed Travelodge by the name of Elmwood House, just outside Frimley in Surrey. Had he been listed under the name Ryan Langham, they wouldn't have allowed me within a mile of him. They would have blocked my request. It had happened to so many other women.

I turned and walked towards the door, not thinking about the implications of my actions. Any mother would have done the same, right? That's what I kept telling myself. From then on, I had to keep moving, for Ryan's sake. I tried not to look at Nicholas Chester, the *real* Nicholas Chester, as I walked towards the exit. I was terrified that he'd be watching me. But I couldn't help myself; my gaze fell on him as I passed. His eyes were open, pale grey, like mist. He wasn't looking at me. He was looking upwards, to the highest point of the hangar, up towards the pitched metalwork, the struts and bars that supported the ceiling. I followed his gaze, and there, lined up along the struts, perched in the shadows as if waiting, were thousands upon thousands of large, brown moths.

CHAPTER 24

"The turning's about a mile up here on the right," said the taxi driver, bringing me out of my half sleep.

I sat up, noting a crumpled A to Z map that must have appeared some time into our journey lying on the passenger seat. I checked the clock on the dash – just after 2am.

We turned into a long, sweeping driveway, the kind for which the heroine in a Jane Austen novel might yearn. It was dark still, but that didn't hide the lines of oak trees flanking the wide road that led up to the house, nor the size of the manor house as it loomed into view.

"Are you sure this is the place?" asked the cab driver doubtfully. The cab stopped on the gravel drive. Two other cars were parked up, both grey, both plugged into a bank of chargers.

"Yes," I said, handing over a pile of tokens, "I'm sure."

The car rolled away and I stood on the drive, gazing up at the two-storey building. In the moonlight, the brick was pale, almost yellow, except for some darker patches where water had dripped down the walls over the years. The roof was slate and the gardens, what I could see of them in the dark, anyway, were well maintained. The whole manor was pristine, as if newly renovated. My eye was caught by one sash window on the upper left of the front of the building. It was half open, unlike the others, which were all closed. As I craned my neck, looking up, the curtain twitched by the open window, and I thought for a moment I saw a figure. The light behind the figure was dim, a candle maybe, so it was hard to make out, but it seemed like someone tall wearing a dark shirt, face obscured by the reflection of the top part of the window.

"Welcome, Mrs Langham." I tore my eyes away from the window. Before me stood a man, dressed in a dark, well-fitting suit and, in an incongruous nod to what was already a bewildering situation, white gloves. He looked like a butler from an Agatha Christie novel. That he was a man, outside, and greeting me so pleasantly, led me to the assumption that he'd been vaccinated.

"Hello," I said.

"My name is Kami. I have been sent to look after you." Early twenties, tall and athletic, he moved with the grace of youth as he beckoned me into the house. Following behind him through the grand stone entrance, I noted that the floors were clean and scrubbed, the walls and pictures dust-free. It must take an army of staff to clean a place like this. He stopped and turned as I reached the inner doors to the main building and indicated I should go into a small antechamber to my left. "I'm extremely sorry, Mrs Langham, but I must submit you to a search before you enter the main house. I hope you understand."

"I... I guess so," I mumbled. The idea that I would be touched by a man, a stranger, caught me off guard. On the way over, I'd anticipated that my visit might begin with a search. But I was expecting a woman. I would have closed my eyes and let her get on with it, like I had so many times before on the way into Nicky's sanatorium. But a *man*. And a young man at that.

I raised my arms like I did in the sanatorium searches.

He was detached, gentlemanly, I guess you could say. He didn't look me in the eye, and he kept the same polite expression throughout. I wanted him to go quicker. I wanted to find Ryan.

Finally, he rifled through my pockets, feeling for the proof, I guess. He ignored my wad of tokens but pulled out another item, the paper knife I'd taken from the hotel room. "I'll keep hold of this," he said. "The woman you are meeting is in the salon having a nightcap." He spoke in the clipped, received pronunciation of a nineteen-forties newsreader. "Please follow me."

He said it mildly and graciously, as if he'd just taken my coat at a party.

I followed him through a massive hallway, across a gleaming mosaic floor with a geometric pattern of blue and gold, and I scanned the rooms we passed for other people. We moved through a series of smaller rooms until he opened a large oak door to what I assumed was the salon.

The dark panels and viridian wallpaper gave off a middle eastern air, as did the many potted yuccas and ferns. A recording of soft jazz, crystal clear, came from the corner of the room, from an iPod in a speaker docking station.

"Mary! Welcome." A wiry woman, about my age, with neatly combed grey hair and wearing a pair of round glasses, got up from a low sofa and padded across the Moroccan rug. She wore black tailored trousers and an expensive-looking ivory shirt, open at the collar, and she clutched my hand before I could pull away. She held it prisoner in her own cool palms. "So glad to finally meet you. I'm Jen. Oh, my dear, you're trembling. I apologise about the search. I hope that Kami wasn't too rough."

So, this was Jen. The woman who gave the order for the deaths of thousands of men, who worked with Olivia, who may well have had Olivia killed. I expected her to be taller, sterner from Olivia's description. But she was diminutive, owlish almost, with her round glasses and cropped hair.

Jen turned to Kami and raised her eyebrows questioningly.

Kami shook his head. "Just this." He held up the letter opener.

Jen sighed. "Oh, Mary. You don't seem to have brought the proof with you? This complicates things. And what were you hoping to do with that thing?" She nodded to the paper knife in Kami's hand. "Scratch us to death?"

I took my hand back. "Where's my son?"

She gave a small smile. "In a little while, Mary. First, let's go and have a chat."

I didn't want to go anywhere with this woman and her weird butler, but I followed as she led me through a foyer and another large central space. A chandelier on the high ceiling illuminated a wide, richly carpeted staircase directing the eye up to the second floor. A balcony bordered the space above. I followed, looking everywhere for where they could have stashed Ryan. Jen led me up a short staircase and, as she moved, her pocket stretched and for a second something pale and plastic poked out of the edge. A benzo gun. Did that mean that she didn't trust Kami completely? Or perhaps it was meant for me, later, once she had what she wanted. I saw no one else in the oak clad corridors and adjoining rooms. I couldn't hear any other people, but that was hardly surprising. It was well past midnight.

"This used to be a sanatorium," she said as she led me through a labyrinth of passages. "Before the aging infected started to die of old age."

"And what is it now?" I asked, keeping my gaze on the back of her head as she walked.

She laughed. "Now, it's a retreat. A place for us girls to come and unwind."

"The MWA?"

She turned her head round to me as we walked and gave a small smile. "Yes, and others. Friends from over the years."

"Like Olivia?" I replied.

Jen stopped walking and turned to me, her smile replaced with a cool glare. "Tell me, Mary. What difficult choices did you make, to protect the thing you love most?"

I blushed fiercely at the image of a boy with pale hair and pale blue eyes. I couldn't meet her stare.

"I thought so," she said as she led me into a vast dining hall. At its centre stood a long table, the kind that can easily seat forty people. It was covered with the remains of a large formal dinner. Empty bottles of wine, glasses and napkins lay abandoned amongst candles, still burning but low now, with lava-like tendrils of hardening wax congealing around the holders. The plates and dirty cutlery had been cleared. Kami pulled out a chair and ushered me to sit down.

I sat and stared at Jennifer Harting, the Council Member responsible for the Men's Welfare Association and the woman who organised the Assisted Insemination Programme – the woman who was responsible for the sire houses. At some point, she, or one of her underlings, must have also signed off on my permission to visit Elmwood.

"Please, I just want to see my son?"

She peered at me myopically from behind her round steel-rimmed glasses. "Have some wine, Mary. Relax," she said, taking the seat opposite me. After Kami had poured pale wine into a couple of cut-glass flutes, Jen turned to him. "If you could tell our friend that Mary has arrived, Kami."

He bowed, "Ma'am," and left the room.

I'd been mulling over a desperate plan that involved overpowering Jen, stealing her benzo gun, using it on Kami, and then searching the whole building for Ryan. The fact that there was at least one more actor in this odd farce would have put that idea into doubt if it wasn't already laughable.

"Honestly, try the wine. We make it on the estate. The grapes are from a vineyard in Surrey. If you were here longer, I could show it to you. But I suspect we won't have the time."

"And the vaccine? Do you make that on the estate too?" I asked in a tight voice.

She shot me a hard look over her glasses and I felt for a moment the cold force of the woman before me. "Nearby," she said.

I left the wine on the table. "I won't tell you anything until I see Nicky."

Jen, seemingly unmoved, took a large swig of the wine and replaced the glass on the table. "Don't you mean Ryan?"

I couldn't help it. My face sagged in shock.

"You don't think I haven't got access to all the files from back then, do you, Mary? Numbers, dates, next of kin, locations."

I couldn't breathe.

"All in good time. Drink up. It's not poisoned."

I took a sip from the glass of wine, annoyed at how much my hand shook as I lifted the flute to my mouth. The wine was bitter.

"Ryan is still at the sanatorium. We have someone there keeping an eye on him."

I forced down my mouthful of wine and felt anger brewing inside me. "What do you mean, keeping an eye on him? Who? Why? If you ever want to see that proof, then you need to start explaining to me what's going–"

Jen stood. "Ah, Skylar."

I turned to the door, to the direction Jen was facing as the woman entered.

"I think you've met Skylar before."

She was the same as I remembered – chic, thin and this time dressed in a well-tailored navy suit and a crimson tie. Her expression was wry and bored.

Skylar sat, sliding easily into the chair next to me.

Kami came in with a tray. He placed a platter of delicate sandwiches and tiny crab tartlets on the table. I sat and looked at them. Another bizarre prop in this little performance. "I put them by, earlier," he said, before retreating to the side of the room.

"Great, I'm starving," said Skylar. "I've been driving all day. Have you apprised Mary of her options?"

"No, I thought I'd wait until you'd got here," replied Jen, picking up a tartlet and taking a small bite. "Mmm, good."

"Have you had a look through the phone?" asked Skylar

"Mary didn't bring it," said Jen through a mouthful of pastry.

"Oh, Mary," Skylar shook her head in a parody of despair. "I should have known you'd pull something like this." Her patronising tone made me want to stab her in the eye.

"How did you know about the phone?" I asked, not really expecting them to answer. I wanted to know if they'd picked up Emily. If she was the one who had told them.

Skylar looked at Jen and then back at me. "We tap the phones at the facility, at Jade Philip's office, even at Elmwood. It's easy to do on this type of landline." She sounded smug, boasting almost.

"Has Jade called anyone – about the phone?" asked Jen.

"No. I've had someone on her line all day."

I kept quiet, looked at the table.

"We even had an agent listening in earlier, Mary, when you checked in at the Facility to see if one of your pet men had been infected. Toby, was it? I remember that you have an unhealthy fixation with the men," said Skylar. "Didn't I say, Jen, that she was quite attached to the men?"

"You did. And here we are. But I suspect that we can convince her of what's in everyone's best interests."

"Enough," I said quietly, pleased that my voice didn't tremble. The other two women stopped chattering and turned to me. "The phone is with a friend. But if I do not get back to the hotel safely by 9am, the phone will be taken straight to Jade Philips. Now tell me where my son is."

Skylar sighed. "Fine. We thought you might pull something like this. We also have a *friend*, who currently works in the sanatorium where your... *son*," she grimaced slightly as she said the word, "is currently living. If you call that living. Our friend will ensure that Ryan, Nicky, whatever you're calling him these days, has a mishap if you do not give us the location of that phone."

He wasn't here after all. I didn't know whether to feel disappointed or relieved. "The same kind of mishap that happened to Luca and Olivia?" I asked with bitterness.

Skylar looked at Jen again, who gave a what-difference-does-it-make kind of shrug. "Yes, just so you are in no doubt as to how seriously we take this, our agent also dealt with the situation at the farmhouse," said Skylar. "Philips, like you, it seems, has always been a hand-wringing liberal when it comes to the men's rights movement. If she gets proof of the vaccine, if she presents it to the Council, it would force us to change our plans."

"A change that we don't think is for the better, not for us nor for society," replied Jen.

I gave a snort. "This is not about men's rights. This is about keeping the visitations going. It's about power."

"Partly," replied Skylar, flatly. "But there are other players too who want the vaccine. People with power and resources. We have a lot invested in keeping control over the vaccine, Mary." She grabbed my wrist, hard. "If you don't tell us where the phone is, you'll lose Ryan. Our agent is waiting on our word."

I sat and stared at them.

After a long pause, Jen sighed. "I think I understand. You traded poor little Nicky's life once, Mary, didn't you? For Ryan's. You left Nicholas Chester to die alone, crying out, no doubt, for his own mother. Do you think this will absolve you? Do you think that all you've done for the men in the facilities and the prospect of a vaccine will stop you from thinking about Nicholas Chester's death?"

I said nothing. The three of us sat for a few moments in silence and let the seconds tick by. It was an impasse that none of us wanted.

Jen broke the silence, "Mary, listen. Let me sweeten the pot, so they say. We have a little surprise for you."

I'd had more than enough surprises over the last few weeks. And if Ryan was still at Elmwood, what could they possibly want to show me?

"Come on," said Jen, and both women got up from the table. "You're really going to want to see this."

CHAPTER 25

I was taken back through the old house. It was dark and from the windows it was hard to see how far the gardens extended, but in the soft glow of the moonlight I could see a bank of tall trees in the distance. Between us and them, there were a few shadowy clumps of bushes and sentinel trees dotted about. I could hear music, the sound of someone singing, drifting from deeper within the house and I was being led towards the sound.

Skylar and Jen strode onwards and I followed because I was expected to.

Something brushed passed the window, the flutter of paper-like wings, and then again, a soft *ping, ping, ping* as if something was trying to fly through the glass.

"The Eclipse is pretty much here, I'd say," said Skylar, nodding towards the darkness. "It's a bit early this year."

I thought of the swarm I'd seen a few days ago with Olivia, driving to the farmhouse for the first time. It felt like a decade had passed since then.

"We'll have to keep everyone inside," replied Jen. "The vaccine should protect the men, but you know how they get when they see one, even at a distance."

I could imagine. After a lifetime of being told that their survival rested on keeping away from them, that one touch would cause immediate, irreversible catastrophe, men would understandably be nervous, even, it seemed, after their vaccine.

"And the guest will need to stay," continued Jen. "Unless

they've got their own protective gear. We don't want anyone going down with exposure sickness."

As we reached what felt like the deepest part of the old house, I could hear the murmuring of voices and the occasional muted laugh. The chink of a bottleneck touching the rim of a glass. Mixed into the general hum, I recognised baritones, tenors. We entered the room through a double door of heavy oak. As Skylar closed the door behind me with a loud clunk, I could still hear the gentle tap tapping of the moths' wings beating against the window, attracted by the light, no doubt. We walked through a small lobby, modern, unlike the rest of the house, with wood panelling, a quirky, colourful armchair and a three-legged side table that gave the space a Scandinavian feel.

Jen spoke over her shoulder to me as she moved towards one of the doors off of the lobby. "Don't go upsetting the men, Mary. It wouldn't do you or your son any good if you started droning on about rights and freedoms and whatever. Leave well enough alone."

I offered no reply. I realised that she thought I was some kind of revolutionary, a rampant... what would be the word? Masculinist?

We went through the door and the room opened out. It was an expansive room, hexagon shaped, with the struts meeting in the middle of a gently pitched roof. Large windows spread around the walls, although they were draped with heavy curtains. On the other side, two closed glass-panelled doors looked out into the dark grounds. As we stood, the three of us, just inside the door, there was a lull in the conversation. Thirty or so curious pairs of eyes looked towards me from an assortment of colourful chairs, pouffes and sofas. Some stood in little knots of twos and threes. About half were men in their twenties and thirties, dressed in short-sleeved shirts and chinos or dark jeans; one wore a pale blue crew neck sweater. It was the first thing I noticed, their clothes. Smart casual we used to call it, styles from just before the change, the linens and cottons crisp and new. They reminded me of the mannequins at a mid-range department store – all handsome, lean, well groomed, but a little staged and stiff looking.

The women were in their forties and fifties; a few were wearing heavy makeup, put on without much skill, a little heavy handed on the blusher. Others wore no makeup. There was one younger woman, sitting alone at the back of the room, pen in hand, her nose buried in a document. She was the only one who hadn't looked up when we came in.

Jen ushered me further into the room.

There were some smiles and the raising of champagne flutes before most of the room's occupants turned back to their conversations. A young man in his twenties strode over and handed me a flute full of pale gold liquid. "Welcome," he said. He smiled, high cheek bones and white teeth against his smooth, dark skin. His arms were smooth too, hairless.

I didn't want the wine, but he looked at me with such dazzling politeness I found myself reaching for the glass. "Thanks," I mumbled.

A shrill voice sounded from a sofa to my left, "Skylar! Sweetheart! I heard you were at the Citadel earlier. Any news on the Australian delegation?" A middle-aged woman, blonde and large, dressed in a flowery silk blouse and silky red culottes, spoke from a nearby sofa. Next to her sat a man, older than the others, with a face framed by carefully tended stubble. He was wearing a gleaming white shirt and had his arm draped casually over the speaker's shoulder. The woman stroked his forearm, ran her fingers slowly, almost absentmindedly, over the coarse, dark hair.

Logan.

My breath caught in my chest. I was about to say his name, but he caught my wide-eyed stare and gave the slightest shake of his head.

Skylar went to join the woman who had spoken on her sofa,

sitting on the woman's side of the lounging couple. As she sat, the woman leaned away from Logan, who retrieved his arm in one fluid motion and stood up. "I'll leave you two to talk," he said, although neither woman was listening to him.

"Arianna," said Skylar, and gave the woman a quick kiss on her scarlet cheek. "I was able to get a quick debrief from one of Jade Philips's aides and…" she lowered her voice as the two leaned into each other and the conversation was lost in the swell of the others speaking.

"Logan," said Jen, smiling, "Are the others in the recreation suites?"

He nodded. "Marcus, Titania and the new guy are in there at the moment. They've been in there a while." His voice was as low and deep as I remembered, like a note from a cello.

"Good. I'll be back soon. Could you take care of Mary for a moment?"

Logan smiled, a look that didn't quite reach his eyes, and nodded. "My pleasure." He beckoned for me to follow him to a couch a little further away.

"Go on, Mary, he doesn't bite," said Jen.

There was a smell mixed with the earthy sandalwood scent of the timber walls. It was sickly, a flowery perfume gone bad, and it felt like it was inside my mouth. I did what I was told and went over to Logan, placing my wine on the coffee table and sitting next to him. I shuffled up to one end of the chaise longue and Logan shuffled himself over next to me, close – so we could talk without being overheard.

Logan leaned towards me, and I could tell that he was shocked to see me. His smile stayed in place, but his voice trembled. "Tony?" he whispered. He was staring at me, but his eyes kept flicking around the room. "Is he alright?"

I thought about Tony, alone and depressed back at the facility, about his attempt to escape and how badly the news of Luca had affected him. "He misses you – but he's fine." I answered. "You know Tony," I finished, lamely.

Logan offered, a sad smile. "Sure. You can't keep that man down for long." His eyes shone, wet with tears. A couple of women sauntered over, and Logan blinked and gave his face a quick wipe with his palm.

"Logan, I was telling Gina here all about you. I hope we could spend some time in the recreation suits later," said one, placing her hand on his shoulder.

Logan cleared his throat and when he spoke his voice was light, playful even. "Sorry ladies, but Mary here has me booked all evening."

"Oh, that's disappointing. Well, enjoy!" The woman addressed the last word to me with a grin.

I blushed every shade of red.

When they'd gone, he turned back to me. "Sorry, Mary. I didn't mean to embarrass you. She's a good client, and I didn't want to offend her." His calm mask-like smile was back in place.

If I'd been in any doubt as to what this place was before then, the term *clients* put those doubts to bed. The men here were all of a similar type, clean cut and smooth – no muscled barbarians or long-haired highlanders or sharp-suited lotharios. They were all handsome, of course, but in an understated way – an unthreatening way.

"How did you get here?" I asked.

His smile dropped a touch, and he looked away for a moment, as if unsure as to what to say. "I... I don't really know. After the riot at the facility, they told me I was infected – that I was being moved to a sanatorium. But I think they just drugged me. Instead, they sent me to be part of a trial. Me and some men from other facilities were given tablets to protect us from the moths. We were staying at a farmhouse. But one night I woke up and there was a woman standing over me, a stranger. She injected me with something, and I woke up here."

Emily's trial with Dr Desai. This is what happened to the men. "What about the rest of the men here? Are they from the trial, too?"

He paused and frowned. "No, there's no one else here from the trial. The rest of the men here came straight from facilities, transferred at night in ambulances."

I thought of Luca and his dimples and his classified transfer. Was this where he'd been headed, handpicked by someone from the MWA, a woman on a visitation day, maybe?

Logan leaned over and picked up my hand from my lap. My initial impulse was to take it back, but Logan held on. "Act like it's okay, Mary."

I let him hold it in his palm, so soft against mine, let him move his other hand so he could run the tips of his fingers down the back of mine, in light trails. He was putting on a good show. "Why are you here, Mary? What do they want from you? These women, they're dangerous. How have you got yourself mixed up with them?"

I didn't know what to say. I looked around us. Men and women mingled. Music played. You could be fooled into thinking it was like a normal party from before. Except I noticed that the women were doing most of the talking, whilst the men listened, laughed and refilled drinks. As I watched, it seemed that the men only spoke when directly addressed, and even their responses were brief and confirmatory. Some men and women had paired off and were sitting together quietly sipping wine, whispering to each other. The young woman with brown hair sat at the far end and as I looked round, I caught her staring right at us. She dropped her head to the papers in her lap as if she hadn't been watching.

"Who's that?" I asked, flicking my eyes towards the girl.

"That's Sophia," he replied quietly in my ear. "She's not here for, you know, for us, she works with Jen and Skylar."

"What does she do?"

"I don't know. But she's always working. We're good friends, though. She's really nice; we talk sometimes, you know, when there are no clients. She even asked one of the women to leave when I said she'd been too rough." Then, after an awkward pause, "There's no red button on the wall here." His voice was soft and full of shame. A flash of misery crossed his features before being replaced by another plastic smile. I couldn't believe this was the same man who spoke out so passionately to the men at the facility on education, on rights. He seemed small, broken. "You do what you have to, what you're told to, or they threaten you, say they won't keep giving you the vaccine."

"It's okay," I said. "I understand." I squeezed his hand and he squeezed back. I considered why the men hadn't rebelled, fought their way out of this place. But of course, these men had been raised to do what women told them and raised to be terrified of the outside. Even with the vaccine that conditioning would be nearly impossible to overcome.

"I want to get out of here, Mary. I want to go back to the facility – to Tony."

There was a long pause before I could answer. "I don't think I can do that, Logan. I'm so sorry."

"I know you can't. They won't let me leave. But if you get back to the facility, can you tell Tony… tell him…that I love him, so much." He moved towards me, and I threaded my arms around him. To anyone there we might have looked like lovers sharing an embrace, but I could feel the sobs he was so desperately trying to hide.

Over his shoulder I caught Sophia's eye and she was looking at us. Again, she dropped her gaze. There was something in that look, a flash of anger, maybe – or jealousy.

When Jen returned, she was not alone. She had a man in tow in his early forties, with curly sandy hair, dressed in a dark shirt, dark jeans and trainers. They came over to where Logan and I sat.

"Ah, Mary. I'm glad you're settling in. Logan is one of our most popular residents. I've brought someone else to see you."

I knew the man with her at once. I'd always wondered how I would feel, meeting him. Would I feel anything at all, or everything at once – a lifetime's joy and misery all mixed into one overwhelming emotion? Would I even know it was him?

The reality was feeling like I'd been kicked in the chest by a horse. He looked a little like Adrian, older and with lighter hair. There was a leanness to his face, a longer slant of the nose. His mouth, unsmiling and pensive, was smaller than Adrian's.

"This is Nathan," said Jen. She could tell by my face that I knew who he was – that is, who he was to me.

"Hi!" he said, smiling and looking straight at me. It was Adrian's goofy smile, but those blue eyes were all mine.

I couldn't speak or move. I just stared up at him.

He looked to Logan, uncertain. "Did I... did I do something wrong?" The uncertainty in his voice was heart-breaking.

"No, you're fine, Nathan. This is Mary," said Logan.

There was a long pause before Nathan replied. "Can I get you anything, Mary? A drink?" Then he saw my full glass of champagne on the coffee table. "Or something else? Some chocolate, maybe?" He seemed to be struggling, flailing around in a new role.

"I...I... No. Thank you." I smiled at Nathan. I wanted to reach up and stroke his face, to touch him. "Thank you," I said again. I was still holding Logan's hand and my desperate grip must have alerted him that something was wrong because he placed his other hand on my wrist.

Nathan looked at Jen, worry etched into his face, and I wanted to slap her for putting him through this. I didn't know what she'd asked him to do when he came in, back there in the other room, but watching him so anxious was more than I could bear.

Jen turned to me. "Where's the phone, Mary? You and *both* of your sons are running out of time."

I wanted to take her by the throat. Anger was expanding in my chest, crushing out all the air. I took my hand from where Logan was still holding it and balled it into a fist. "Why?" I said so loudly that the few stragglers left in the room stopped talking and turned to look. "Why are you doing this?"

Jen answered, "I don't need to convince you that it's the right thing to do, Mary. I just have to show you that it is the right thing to do for Ryan *and* Nathan."

I sighed then. A heavy cloak of defeat descended upon my shoulders. I stood and my joints ached more than I ever remember them aching. I led Jen away from Logan and my son. "If I tell you where it is...?"

Jen leaned in to speak. "Then you can take Nathan with you, tonight. He can return with you to the farmhouse. I'll supply you with vaccine every few months, as long as you don't tell anyone. You will have the full support of the MWA. Ryan will continue to live at Elmwood. You can visit him whenever you like. All happy ever after, Mary."

I closed my eyes. "And if I don't? If I give the phone to Jade Philips, to the Council?"

"Well," her voice became even lower, "we'd have to make sure there was no evidence of this place. Get rid of all those loose ends, including your sons."

And Logan. So that was the deal. My sons in return for all sons.

"Tell us where the phone is and Nathan can go with you, right now."

I opened my mouth to speak and saw the gleam in Jen's eye. She leaned in further towards me and rubbed her lower lip on her teeth. She was so close, almost pressed into my side, her breath in my face. I stepped back.

"I need the bathroom. Could you point me in the right direction?" I asked, wearily.

She hissed in annoyance. "Don't play with me, Mary. I'm deadly serious."

I just stared. Said nothing.

She sighed. "It's through the door we came through and off the lobby where we came in. Don't be long. My patience is wearing thin."

CHAPTER 26

The bathroom was clean and brightly lit. I entered a cubicle and locked the door, sitting on the closed loo seat to think. If I gave them the vaccine, what proof did I have that they would hold up their end of the bargain, and how could I betray Tony and all the other men around the country? It was like the field hospital all over again, saving my own sons by condemning others. I closed my eyes and sat in the quietness of the bathroom. My head hurt, as a profound tiredness beat at my temples. There were no good choices here. After a few moments, I noticed a light tapping on the window behind me, like raindrops. I turned to see an orgy of flapping shadows outside the frosted glass.

Moths – lots of them.

If I didn't act soon, then it wouldn't be safe to leave. If the Eclipse became too thick, then even a short trek over the grass to a waiting car would be risky. Like the caterpillars in the nest, in these numbers, the threads would be potent. I didn't want to end up passing out under a tree again.

I was trapped in every sense. Even if I could get Nathan out, tell Law Abidance about Elmwood, I'd still need to find a car to get us far away from here. I couldn't wander round in the Eclipse and anyway, there's no way Nathan would come out into the dark with me, into a plague of moths. He'd be terrified.

I wanted to sleep for a thousand years. Never had I felt my age as such a suffocating presence.

I dragged myself to my feet and padded out of the cubicle

without looking at the frail woman reflected back at me from the mirror. I would tell them where the phone was and lay myself down upon their mercy. Save Ryan, save Nathan, live out my remaining few years at the farmhouse, or in jail, or wherever the fates abandoned me. My old bones felt hollow and brittle, my muscles thin and slippery, like raw oysters. I was done with this.

My head was bowed when I exited the bathroom into the lobby.

"Mary," said a voice quietly, "you need to leave. You need to get the phone to Jade Philips." The mousy-haired girl, Sophia, sat on the armchair. She'd been waiting for me. She looked at the door to the main room. "We don't have much time." She stood up and gave me a set of car keys and a bottle of pills. "It's the one on the farthest end, number 732. It's fully charged. There's enough vaccine for a couple of weeks. Logan will know when to take it. You have to take him too."

I stared at the key fob and the pills in suspicion. "Why help me? What do you want?"

The young woman looked towards the door to the main room, in the direction of the music and the low drone of conversation. Her voice was low and urgent. "Put them in your pocket," she said, "quickly." And then, when I'd done what she said, "You get Nathan. I want Logan out of here as well. You need to get far away."

"How?" I struggled to keep the incredulity out of my voice. "And what about Ryan? They'll kill him."

She stared at me in silence.

"Why Logan?" I asked.

She smoothed down her light tan trousers and didn't meet my eye. I noticed that her hands trembled as they moved over the fabric. "He shouldn't be here. None of them should, but Logan is... well he's..." She didn't finish. She didn't have to. I could tell by the red flush climbing her neck and the self-conscious way she hooked a lock of fine straight hair behind her ear as she talked about him. "I don't want him here. I want him safe. I don't know what they'll do when this place is discovered. I'll try to protect the others when that happens."

She finally looked into my eyes, and I could see confusion and fear.

"You're in love with him?"

She looked away. "He shouldn't have to go with those women. I know he doesn't want to."

I leaned in close and whispered in her ear, "It's hidden in the lining of a seat in the second to last row of a theatre on St George Street." I remembered sitting in the dark of the auditorium. The cool handle of the letter opener in my palm, as I pretended to watch Act Four whilst gently slicing through the thick cloth:

Romeo, Romeo! Here's drink. I drink to thee!

Sophia's eyes widened for a moment as the information sunk in. Then she fixed her expression into one of grim resolution. "I'll make sure it gets into the right hands. Where are you going to go?"

But before I could answer, the door to the main room opened and out came Jen, a cool expression on her small, neat features. "Ah, Sophia, well done. You have located our guest. I was beginning to worry."

I followed Jen back into the main room. "Have you decided yet, Mary? The lives of Ryan and Nathan or a doomed attempt at reinstating the patriarchy? What's it to be?" Her tone was light, jovial, but beneath it I detected the tiniest note of fear. "Here," she said, "perhaps Nathan can talk some sense into you."

She led me through the chattering couples to Nathan sitting on a sofa. He jumped up when he saw us approach. "Mary... I mean... *mother*." He checked back at Jen, who nodded in encouragement. "I wanted to speak to you about something very important." He was flustered and afraid, and I hated Jen for making him do this. "I want to leave here – with you. I don't like the… the way things are here, and I want to go, with you. And Jen says that the only way that this is possible is if you give her the phone." He took a deep breath, and I noticed how tired looking he was, how his skin seemed grey with tiny red veins in his irises. "Jen said," he continued, "that if I explained to you that I really didn't like it here, that you would want to help me. Because that's what mothers do. That you would want to take me away with you." It was painful hearing him talk like this. It reminded me of Tony when he was in the recreation room after the play. *I don't want to do it anymore, Mary.* Just before he broke the window.

"I want to take you with me," I said in a whisper. "I want us to leave here together." I reached over and held his hand for a moment and as I did, I felt a sudden sickening feeling, like somewhere I was letting go of another hand, like I was slipping a little yellow band from one bed and fixing it to another. I stuffed the feeling down, ignored it. Nathan smiled – Adrian's lopsided grin.

"Well, that's great news," said Jen, hovering over us. "So, where is it, Mary?"

I got up and wandered casually towards the double doors opposite, ornately old-fashioned with thick glass and two curved metal handles meeting in the middle. A fat iron key poked from the lock.

Jen followed. "Tell me, Mary, and you can leave with your son. I'll call off our woman on Ryan. All of this will be over." Her voice was rising, tinged with anxiety. I liked that. I liked that she was scared. I pretended to gaze out of the doors, to the darkness beyond. The moths fluttered around and hit the glass, trying to find the source of the light. Why did they do that, I wondered? Was it something to do with moonlight? Navigating? At the top of glass doors, moths clung to the outside corners of the frame, meshed together and still, resting perhaps, after mating and before finding a sanctuary in which to lay their eggs.

"Mary!" The other woman took my arm, and her voice lost its condescension. Her face twisted with irritation. "Enough. It's time to stop playing games."

I brushed her off and placed my palms onto the cool glass and then onto the handles. In one smooth movement I twisted the key and pushed the windows open with all my strength. I felt the large frames move under my hands, the cool night air stream past me carrying with it a thousand moths.

The effect on the room was immediate and profound. Confusion first, then screams from the men and the women, but mostly from the men. People running, batting at the air as the moths swarmed into the light and filled the space with the beating of their wings. The creatures danced and dived as everyone tried to slap them away, stepping over each other to reach the exit. Even Jen was taken by surprise and I was able to push past her as she was set upon by a horde of excited moths.

I tried to see through the fluttering swarm, to find Nathan and Logan but in every direction I just saw flapping wings and people running. The moths were not leaving me alone either, and I could feel the beginnings of exposure sickness, a raw itching of the inside of my throat, a slight dulling of my reactions. I was running out of time.

"Mary!" It was a man's voice, Logan's. He stood with his arms around Nathan, protecting him from the swarm.

"Follow me," I said. "I need to take you away from here." The moths continued to swarm, and the room was almost empty of people. "We have to go."

Logan, his face grim, tried to drag Nathen forward but my son stood, rooted to the spot, shaking.

"I can't. We can't go outside," said Nathan, squeezing tighter to Logan's arm. "There'll be more out there. It's not safe."

Jen staggered over to us. "It's not safe for you, Mary. You'll die if you go out there." Her voice was slurring, and she was rubbing her palm over her bloodshot eyes.

I too could feel the familiar heaviness in my limbs, the toxins working their way through me. I shook my head to try to clear it. Had to get the boys to move – outside to the car.

"Our woman at Elmwood will kill Ryan, Mary. You're killing Ryan right now." Jen's voice was hoarse.

I looked over to her, but she was shifting and changing before my eyes. Nicholas Chester was staring at me – the real Nicholas Chester with his pale blue eyes. *You're killing me!*

Logan and Nathan stood before me, Nathan sobbing like a child.

I was weakening, and I had to get him to move.

I only had my voice.

I dug deep and pulled out the voice of every parent who has ever seen their child in danger – the tone reserved for when a toddler darts onto a road to collect a dropped ball or reaches their hand toward a hot surface. My teacher's voice, the voice of my own mother. The sound of pure and irresistible command:

"Nathan! – You follow me RIGHT NOW!"

For a moment I thought it hadn't worked, but then he came. Tentatively clutching Logan.

I grabbed them and stumbled out of the doors and into the moth-infested night, dragging them with me. *Farthest end, number 732.* I pressed the car fob, and it felt strange, like I was pressing my thumb all the way through the plastic. A car's lights flashed on and off a few times in the distance and we raced for it, all the while moths caught in our hair, in our clothes.

"Where are we going?" said Logan, as he and Nathan batted away the moths from their faces.

My strength was at an end. I didn't even have the energy to swipe the moths away. I let them land where they pleased and just concentrated on getting to the car. I was clinging to both men, allowing them to support me as we reached the vehicle.

"You drive," I said to Logan, throwing myself onto the back seat.

"I can't drive," he replied.

Everything was spinning. "It's electric, just put the key in, press the button and steer."

There was fumbling, and then the car lurched forwards.

"Where should I head for? Mary, where are we going?"

"Anywhere – as far away from here as you can get."

Suppose I had one last dream. I am curled up in the back of a car, in the arms of a man who looks like Adrian. Dawn has broken, and the sky is a canvas, clear of clouds, home to a newly born sun.

He tells me to keep talking, so I tell my story. I leave out many details. But it still takes a while to tell it all. I talk about his brother, Ryan, how his favourite subject was computing and how he liked playing online with his friends. I stop and draw in a breath, but it's hard and the pain in my chest is coming in waves. I keep talking – about his father, Adrian, and how he would hide behind doors and jump out on me, or spend ages setting up photos and then get annoyed when Ryan and I got bored and wandered off. I talk about how much I've missed Claire. I talk about Tony and Logan, Luca and Olivia. I tell him about Nicholas Chester.

And then I am silent, as I feel like I have no more words.

Without my story keeping me together, I break up.

Join the Eclipse – something whispers in my ear – *Come!*

At first, I am a thousand slips of paper, fluttering in the breeze, swirling around the car. Nobody notices. Why would they? It's my dream, after all. I float upwards, and in different directions, dancing on the eddies of a breeze.

What is written on us? I wonder, and I try to twist around and look upon the tiny backs of every scrap.

But on our backs are not words, but wings.

We understand. We must make for the gaping, needful sky. The window opens and we stream out into the bright morning and join our brown and kindred legion. Out we fly, out, out, into the world we remade. Everything – from the temperature of the air to the feel of the light, the smell of pollen and the soft beating of a million gauzy wings – everything is all perfectly suited to us. We feel a throbbing in the air as we dart and turn. We are the wind now and we choose our course. We eat and mate and fight and play, for no one can stop us.

Way down below me a young woman is talking, "The vaccine," she says, "will it change anything?"

But her words are drowned out by the vibration of our song.

Now, we sing.

The time is *now*.

EPILOGUE

Elmwood burned to the ground.

It wasn't only Ryan who died that night. Thirteen other residents perished, and two staff members were badly burned in an attempt to free them. Gale was one of those injured. The Law Abidance Department are looking for an employee by the name of Azi Metcalf, last seen leaving the area shortly after the blaze took hold.

Jen denied everything, of course. But they say that it will all come out in the trial. Sophia has agreed to testify, as has Emily – abuse of power, coercion, the ordering of violence, the grooming of men. It was suggested that some of the men testify, but this was dismissed as unnecessary. Their testimony may be seen as unreliable. I don't have to testify, they say, on account of my age and my poor health. That last bout of exposure sickness weakened my heart. I mostly just sleep these days.

I can't really eat very much. I sometimes manage a little soup or a cup of tea, maybe a biscuit, but that's about it. For the most part, I lie in this hospice bed and listen to the nurses gossiping and try not to think about those last few moments of Ryan's life, about whether he thought of me, cried out for me as the smoke and flames came to claim him. Was he scared? Did he understand what was happening?

I had a visit from Jade Philips a few days ago. That was how I knew about the trial. She looked the same, except she'd cut her hair shorter. She was kind, told me she remembered me from the facility tour and said how impressed she was at my part in uncovering the truth. She said she was sorry about Ryan – but she was hesitant when she said it – unsure of the protocol. No one from after really understands what it's like to lose a son.

Nathan and Logan are being looked after in a secure location. The news of the vaccine and the idea of men moving around freely outdoors has caused some tension in the wider population. The hospital at which the men were originally looked after became a rallying point for men's rights activists across the Union. A large group, hundreds apparently, turned up to demand that all uninfected men be offered the vaccine immediately. Many others turned up to demand that the vaccine be withheld until laws could be put in place to protect the Union's core values and protect the rights of women.

What happens next with the vaccine is to be decided by the Council – minus Jen Harting, of course. Skylar was not found during the raid on the manor house in Surrey. The current theory is that she and Harting were in the process of selling the vaccine to New Australia and that she has claimed asylum there. The New Australian government have yet to comment.

Jade told me that she suspects there will be a limited roll-out here, a modified vaccine that needs to be taken monthly. The men will be permitted to live with a mentor in the community and will be monitored. However, none of this will happen for a while, not until the process can be organised properly.

I like to think that I could have been a good mentor. But it's unlikely I'm going to make it to next month, let alone next year.

I hope Tony understands that I couldn't come back for him. I wish I could be here to watch him walk free. Will he find Logan? I like to think so. What will the world look like ten or twenty years from now? Will the men integrate, or will they dominate – try to return to the old economies, the old designs? Who will raise the sons of the Union?

Without Ryan, the threads holding me here weaken every day.

It's a curious thing. When I close my eyes, I can still hear the humming of the wings and the drumming of the air from the car that night. I can feel the whispers of mothers and daughters and sisters. But our thorax is thrumming with a new rhythm, now, something more complex. I feel them – the sons and fathers, husbands and brothers, and all those who defy the narrowness of these terms. They're unfurling their wings and finding their voices – soprano, alto, tenor and bass combining into one song.

It's time. They sing each time I drift. It's time to wake the new world.

AFTERWORD

Thank you so much for reading *Moths*. I really hope you enjoyed it. If you did, *please* review or rate me on Amazon and Goodreads – these reviews are my lifeline amongst a crowded market of wonderful dystopian books. If you would like background information or additional content regarding the dystopian world of Moths visit me at www.janehennigan.com where you can sign up to my newsletter and be at the front of the queue for news and giveaways.

ACKNOWLEDGMENTS

I began writing Moths on the 9th of July 2019. Why do I recall the date with such precision? On that date the BBC published an article, "Toxic processionary caterpillar plague spreads across Europe". That evening I sat down and wrote the opening pages of what was to become *Moths*.

It's been a difficult journey since then, not least because – at almost the moment I wrote those two hallowed words "the end" on my first draft and did a little dance round the kitchen – there was a report buried at the end of the news cycle about a mystery virus emerging in China.

I would like to offer a huge thank you to all those who have made this book possible.

Firstly, an enormous thank you to my brilliant agent, Liza, who's vision, support and tenacity have been the stuff of every writer's dream. I will be forever grateful that you decided to take a chance on me. Also, a big thank you to the team at Angry Robot, for seeing the potential in *Moths* and patiently guiding me through the publishing process. Gemma, Eleanor and the whole team, thank you for your hard work - you are all superstars.

To those there at the beginning – the original writing group – Emma, Hannah, Kari, Julie, Evan, Seth and Manuel, whose enthusiasm pushed me on and whose discussions on what women would and would not do for a bunch of imprisoned men, greatly influenced Mary's eventual journey. To Celina – your enthusiasm for this project knew no bounds – thank you for your fabulous editing insights and for telling every human being you met about this story.

Thanks too, to those who read the manuscript and gave me such wonderful feedback especially Lucy, Helena, Issy, Tamara and Caitlyn.

Finally, the biggest thanks goes to my husband James who supported me and didn't take it personally when I wrote a book in which all the men go mad or die. And Flo who kept me sane on the crazy, emotional, terrifying, wonderful, exhausting journey of writing a novel.

Sane-*ish*.

ABOUT THE AUTHOR

Jane is a forty-something mother of two living in Hampshire in the UK. She finally made it to university at the age of thirty-four, studying philosophy and English literature. After graduating, Jane began teaching English and philosophy, squeezing her passion for writing into any spare time she could find.

COMING SOON
FROM JANE HENNIGAN

Toxxic
Book 2 of *Moths*

Forty-four years ago, as any schoolgirl can tell you, the moth's eggs hatched and an army of caterpillars spread their tiny toxic threads on every breath of wind. Since then, men have been cloistered, protected from birth against the deadly poison.

But now there's a vaccine - a way that men can leave the facility without dying or suffering from psychosis. Emerging, into their new world, eyes wide with wonder at every new experience, the truth soon becomes clear.

This world was not made for men. And they are not safe.

Toxxic explores the post-apocalyptic world introduced by Hennigan's smash-hit debut novel, *Moths*.

ANGRY ROBOT

We are Angry Robot

angryrobotbooks.com

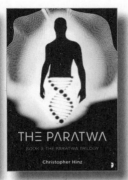

We are Angry Robot

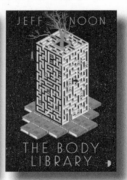

angryrobotbooks.com

  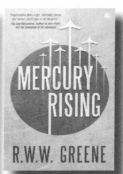

We are Angry Robot

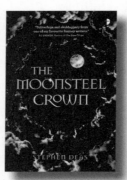  

angryrobotbooks.com